Praise for *These Granite Islands*

❧

"One of the joys of reading is coming across a book in which
language is perfectly wedded to story. *These Granite Islands*
is a marvellous first novel…"
Colum McCann

"*These Granite Islands* is the kind of book that instils a
hunger for more; like a well-paced feast, it continually
stimulates the appetite and puts off satiety
until the very last course."
Los Angeles Times Book Review

"Stonich's rich debut is a romance in the best sense
of the word: it's a tale of love and
adventure set in a remote time…"
Publisher's Weekly

"Reminiscent of Anita Shreve's works in its lyrical blend
of past and present… Stonich perfectly captures the essence of a
woman facing her death…A wonderful read;
recommended for public libraries."
Library Journal

THE ICE CHORUS

SARAH STONICH

ALMA BOOKS

ALMA BOOKS LTD
London House
243–253 Lower Mortlake Road
Richmond
Surrey TW9 2LL
United Kingdom
www.almabooks.com

The Ice Chorus first published in the US by Little, Brown & Co. in 2005
This revised paperback edition first published by Alma Books Ltd in 2009
Copyright © Sarah Stonich, 2005, 2009

Reprinted July 2009

Sarah Stonich asserts her moral right to be identified as the author of this
work in accordance with the Copyright, Designs and Patents Act 1988

Printed in Great Britain by CPI Antony Rowe

ISBN: 978-1-84688-082-7

For Sam

The Ice Chorus

Chapter One

Sea Iris, brittle flower,
one petal like a shell
is broken,
and you print a shadow
like a thin twig.

H.D.

An ocean-hued piece of silk rests over her hand like a landed butterfly. As she moves through the unheated rooms her footfalls disturb air thick with odors of previous dwellers, an old woman's perfume and the acid tinge of cat. Her eyes water and the stripes of silk blur, seaweed bleeding over the slate of swells, blue slate smudging the white-green of sea glass. The cloth is cut from a dress she no longer wears but once cherished, a vivid scrap of her past.

Along the hallway her suitcases and crates are stacked under dust-white rays from the one grimy window set deep in the plaster wall. Trying the door, and finding it warped snugly into its frame, she pushes against it, backs up, then pushes again. One determined shoulder frees it, and the door gives too quickly, caught by an Atlantic gust, so she is pulled suddenly over the threshold and into the late winter day.

She blinks in the brightness and takes several strides down the path before turning back to better view the isolated cottage.

The outer walls are pocked by years of sea spray and in need of whitewashing. Loose mortar dulls the grass and ragged hedges shivering along the foundation. Paint is battered from the window sashes, so only a few flakes of red curl from weathered wood. The entire building seems to lean away from the sea, even its chimneys.

In spite of the neglect – or perhaps because of it – the place draws her. That the cottage still stands after three hundred years is an assurance. The place has survived generations; it can endure the history of one more woman.

She looks down at the cloth, now wrapped around her finger like a wedding band, and thinks of dim rooms within, imagining the walls painted in these soft hues, so that walking through the cottage will be like moving through moods of the sea, like wading through one of Charlie's paintings.

Yes, she thinks. *I could live here.*

So much is old in this new place. In the driveway of crushed shells, her 1960 Morris Minor sits like a forgotten toy. Her second day in Ireland she'd found it parked outside the café where she'd been having tea, *For Sale* lettered neatly over its windscreen. Circling the car in the cobbled lane, she'd noted that its robin's-egg finish still shone, the fenders had only a few shallow dents, and the upholstery had been mended but was clean.

Touching the paneled door, she'd inhaled the odor of wood wax – a smell of the past. The gloss at her fingertips was the same sheen as the walnut of her father's desk.

How often she'd crawled into the shelter of its kneehole, to read or daydream, sometimes falling asleep. Her father's dark serge knees would eventually invade her nook, jostling the book in her hand or nudging her awake. Her father never seemed surprised to find her there, would only whisper, "Out you come, Roo," and press his legs aside.

Roo. One of the many nicknames he'd given her – there was Mitten, of course, and Gertrude, which she hated, but he'd only called her that when she was being awful. Most names are lost to her now, but one comes in a whisper. As first drops of rain splatter down the windscreen of the little car, she remembers weeping over some silly thing, and her father blotting tears with the heel of his palm, tempting her into his lap with "C'mon, Drizzle".

A lorry sped past. She peeled her hand from the car as rain began in earnest. Crossing the street to a phone booth, she squinted through the glass and dialed the number on the Morris's windscreen.

She chooses to believe driving a car her own age is providence. As she walks toward the car, the keys jangle a tune from her fingers. The drive is little more than two ruts carved in sea grass. As the Morris bumps up the rough incline, the house and sheep barn are reflected in the rearview, solid grey blocks behind the cartons stacked on the backseat, the household goods she's purchased: cleaning solutions, light bulbs, towels, a broom, an electric kettle. Things to start with. She'll buy paint in the village.

Puddles in the ruts are lidded with ice – long mirrors of Irish sky that shatter under the weight of the tires. The glint of ice and the sound of cracking echo a game she'd often played on her solitary walks to school. Finding a frozen puddle, she would count the number of jumps, knees pumping and book bag pounding at her back, until the ice broke and the sudden squelch of dirty water would darken the leather of her loafers. These deeper memories slip more easily into frame now that she's so far from them. Since coming to Ireland she has wondered whether it isn't the silvery coastal light – surely a stop or two brighter – that has endowed these days with a clearer view to the past. Or perhaps she's simply ready to remember.

The Morris's shock absorbers are loose with age, and with the next jarring break through ice she bites her tongue. The car is quaint with faults; the heater fan labors and the indicator lights barely wink. It is too sluggish to drive safely on the N5 when it's busy. But the car has one modern feature – the new CD player she'd had installed down in Galway. Turning onto the main road, she slips in a favorite disk and begins her terrible singing.

It is a song she's heard dozens of times, but since her affair with Charlie the lyrics can affect her breath. *You are in my blood like holy wine*. When she first began to think of it as "their song", she'd blanched at the sentimentality of pairing songs to lovers. It was more interesting, really, to consider the idea from the songwriter's perspective – how wonderful it would be to witness the dramas, the dances and heartbreaks your own lyrics might serenade. Syncopated voyeurism – lovers tangled in hotel sheets, leaning close in smoky bars, murmurs and cries a muted beat behind the tune. *You taste so bitter and so sweet.*

Charlie had asked once which songs she wanted played at her funeral. It was just after they'd both nearly drowned. They'd been lovers only a few days then but already knew they would like to grow old together, die together.

"Which songs?"

"That's easy." Her answer was half-serious. "Samuel Barber's *Agnus Dei* sung by a full choir, and 'Muskrat Love'."

If asked now, she would add this old Joni Mitchell tune. As she sings, an ache for Charlie catches under her ribs and she can imagine herself becoming ill again. During the weeks after they'd parted, Charlie had written his most melodramatic letters, claiming what they'd had together was no mirage, comparing their separation to being lost in a desert, overcome by thirst.

I could drink a case of you...

But now, after all this time?

...and I would still be on my feet.

Dark exhaust trails the car and she makes a note to check the oil. She's taken her eyes from the road too long and must swerve to avoid a cat. The tires rock into the chippings of the ditch, the rasp of it startling her just as Joni Mitchell's cigarette voice gives out, singing, *I'd still be on my feet.*

Usually she enjoys driving, but here, on the wrong side of everything, she must concentrate, and finds being left-handed is no help at all. The roads are narrow, making the smallness of her odd car an advantage, but even so, the fenders swipe the gorse with each oncoming vehicle. In Ontario the roads barge through the countryside, but here they only meander as the land allows. The coast road is a brown shelf dividing hillside and beach. It's an effort not to be distracted by the scenery. Far up the checkered hillside, sheep graze like slow chess pieces, and to her right the surf chimes. She makes another note to order film stock from Dublin and to drive this route again with her eight-millimeter camera, when the light is the same, wide and benevolent.

She feels blindly for her sunglasses, not daring to take her gaze from the road again.

The village lies at the narrow end of a V-shaped bay. There are two sleepy streets and a few lanes of row houses slanting toward a pier. Scum-bottomed boats tilt, and three boys she imagines should be in school are draped over the seawall, fishing and punching one another. They stop long enough to aim ice chunks at a gull pecking near their bait bucket. Obscene shouts trail the bird until it lands precisely out of range on a leaning mast.

A sexual smell from the sea mingles with diesel fumes and smoke rising from a trash barrel. Parking near the town center, she need only turn a half circle to take in the entire main street. Strung between two churches are a post office, a petrol station, six pubs, a laundry, a grocery, a combined fishmonger-butcher, an ugly modern community center, and a dozen houses with tiny gardens. The once graceful façade of the Arches Hotel has been covered over in pebble-dash, with a modern glass door as added insult. Litter swirls in eddies at either side of the hotel's broad stoop.

This is not postcard Ireland, just a small town at low tide.

It's easy enough to find the hardware store, Conner's, its door flanked by two rabbit hutches carpeted with scattered droppings and candy wrappers stuffed through the mesh. Several lop-eared whites cower in far corners. On a card atop the hutches, £5 has been crossed out and *Free* scrawled over it. Inside, the shop is dark and crowded. A man in coveralls ruminates over a row of hammers. A housewife brushes past her with a shopping bag sprouting a duster and sponges.

Approaching the counter, she suddenly feels silly about her request. She haltingly explains the piece of colored cloth, and the young clerk raises her freshly pierced eyebrow and takes the scrap by a corner. After a beat the girl loudly calls for someone named Remy and, while they wait, the clerk stares at her until a clomping on the boards grows near and an elderly man with a high lift in his shoe appears. The girl hands him the cloth and shrugs.

"She wants paint."

He squints at the cloth and sniffs the air near the girl's ear. "I can smell the fags on you, Siobhan."

The girl rolls her eyes, shutting the register drawer with one hip.

He turns away. "C'mon then." With his neck craned the old man limps ahead, leading her through the shop and out a low door to a small courtyard – a sunlit chaos of metal shelves and bins of brown nails. Glass is stacked in jagged piles, and three chrome kitchen chairs surround a cable spool turned on its side to fashion a table. The man raises his head, blocking her sun. In the eclipse, she notices his profile makes a familiar shape, the sloping brow and protruding upper lip reminding her of a tortoise. He holds the silk high in the air and, when he squints, his eyes nearly disappear in pools of wrinkled flesh. Sun on his chin catches a spot missed by the razor, a shimmer of silver-and-gold stubble. There is enough curl left in his hair to suggest he once had a ginger-colored mop of it.

He grunts and hands back the cloth. "I've no such colors in my formulas."

Sighing, she opens her purse to put the cloth away, but suddenly the old man plucks it back with a grin.

"Ah, now, that doesn't mean I cannot do it. It'll take a bit though, so sit yourself, missus. I'll get her started."

He hitches away, favoring his right leg. Had he meant for her to wait here? As she turns, her elbow catches a shelf of discarded hardware and buckets of scrap metal. She pulls her arms close, trying to recall the date of her last tetanus shot.

After brushing soot from one of the chairs, she sits, and one of the chrome legs immediately buckles. Cursing, she catches herself and shifts into the next seat. The old man pops his head out, warning, "Watch that bandy-legged one, missus. It's as steady as I am." He stomps his special shoe on the threshold.

He's been watching her. She wonders for how long. Of course she is a curiosity here – surely there will be speculation. She idly muses over what the people of this tiny place will think, or, more likely, what they will surmise.

After a few minutes the girl with the raw eyebrow appears, scowling against the sun and balancing a metal teapot and yellow teacups on a tray.

"For me?"

"It's only tea." The girl jerks her head toward the door. "*He's* eaten the biscuits."

"Thank you… Siobhan, right?"

"Uh, yah."

When she offers her own name, the girl shrugs. "That's pretty, but what do people call you?"

"You mean like a nickname? Well, my friends call me Lise."

"*Leez-eh*? Weird." The line of the girl's mouth softens a fraction and she brushes aside her bangs, revealing green eyes fringed in black lashes. Her skin is flawless eggshell, save the yellow swell around the piercing. Siobhan catches Lise's glance and nods. "It feckin' aches, yeah, but nothing like when I had my nipple done. Jesus, that."

They both laugh, Lise rather nervously, and as the paint-shaker shifts into full rattle she wonders if Siobhan's revelation was meant to shock her. Why would the girl pierce herself in such painful manners – why would anyone? Had she altered her body for a boyfriend, or in a simple fit of vanity? *What women suffer for love.* She begins to ask, "How could you..." but flounders, rephrasing to finish weakly, "I mean, how could *I* find the library here?"

Under Lise's inquisitive gaze, the girl's face is open; there is no malice on her. How old could she be? Anywhere between seventeen and twenty-seven. The girl looks younger when she smiles.

Siobhan tells her where to find the library, such as it is, next to the community center, which doubles as the theater on weekend nights. She lists the two outdated American films currently playing. "*My Best Friend's Wedding* and *Erin Brockovich*, as if Julia Roberts is the only thing on legs," she groans. "Why not something with Clive Owen or Colin Farrell? Even fat old Russell Crowe, but no, it's a man who runs the place and orders the films, so there you are." As she frowns, the ring through her eyebrow glints. "Last week it was *Notting Hill.* Could you puke?"

"You like films? My son is—" Lise is interrupted when the man shopping for a hammer pokes his head out the door. He stares at them a full measure before holding up his choice like a baton.

Siobhan mumbles through a clenched grin. "Needs more than a hammer, that one." She takes her time meandering back into the shop, running a finger along one of the outdoor shelves, looking back once at Lise and feigning shock at the grime.

The girl's easy charm reminds her of Adam, though these days it's difficult to remember her son being easy. She thinks of the last silent weeks in Toronto and his terse farewell. As she presses a sudden sting from her eye, there is nowhere to look except her lap.

"Too bright?"

She straightens to see Mr Conner has appeared and is shifting toward her. He shores the broken chair with a crate and sits heavily. Once settled, he commences cleaning his stained nails with a match end, stealing the odd glance. "Are you not cold?" He thrusts his chin at her unbuttoned coat.

"Not at all."

While the tea cools she feels compelled to tell the old man things he already seems to know: that she has rented old Mrs Kleege's place and has come from Canada. She fumbles for adjectives to describe how beautiful she finds the coast. When she can think of nothing else, they sit in silence.

He pours tea, apologizing for the absence of biscuits. Scowling mildly toward the shop, he says, "The girl's eaten them all."

Lise smiles and cradles the cup of tea, which is too hot to drink. Mr Conner gulps his and makes a trip inside to check the paint, re-emerging with small rectangles of glass dipped in color. These are lined up on an overturned barrel, their shades deepening as they dry.

"Have you relations here?"

She shakes her head.

Mr Conner's brow arcs. "You've rented that trap of a house, so you must be staying on with us for a while?"

She shrugs. "I guess."

It's obvious he's after her reasons for choosing his village, or perhaps why she's chosen to arrive in the unlikely month of February. But he won't ask directly, she realizes. She can play his game just as well.

He blows over a wedge of glass in his palm. "You've come for the excitement and high drama then?"

"Like watching paint dry?"

He nearly laughs, at least smiles enough to show the wide gap between his front teeth. As he places the bit of glass with the others, a cloud passes overhead. "Surely you've not come for the weather?"

"And why not? It's never dull." Her real reason simply sounds too ridiculous: *I saw this coast in a painting.* She doesn't want to be considered mad before she's even unpacked. "It's the loveliest bit of the country, isn't it?" she adds.

His eyes slit as if he knows all she's really seen of Ireland is the back end of a lorry while driving the N4 from Dublin. "So" – he sighs – "you've come for the ocean, for there's nothing else."

He's right, in a way. She brightens, remembering the view on the old coast road. "Yes, I may even gather some footage – there's an amazing place out past the caravan park."

"Footage?"

"*Film* footage."

Mr Conner slaps the table. "Right, so! Kevin from the FedEx said he'd brought some of those metal equipment cases out your way." He grins broadly, pleased to have solved her mystery. "So you're here to make a film, then?" He pronounces the word "fil-um".

"Oh, no, I hadn't planned, I only might."

"What'll it be then, a love story, a crime caper?"

"Nothing like that. I only make documentaries."

The phone jangles near the back door, and the old man scowls before tilting from his chair. She's been saved further explanation, but while he's inside, Lise realizes she needn't really explain herself. She can let Mr Conner and the other villagers assume what they want. The old hardware man might simply assume she's an eccentric visitor with a movie camera, and that she is choosy about her paint to the point of weirdness. Or perhaps he'll imagine something more dramatic – that she carries a shameful secret, or has escaped a difficult life. That she's come to the sea to grieve.

There *was* truth, however small, in each possibility. People prefer intrigue to loss, she knows.

When Mr Conner comes back, he asks before even sitting, "Documentaries – like those how-to films?" He settles down as if he has all day, making her wonder if the pierced girl, Siobhan, is running the shop.

"More like stories. *People's* stories."

"What kinds of people?"

"All kinds." Cocking her head at Mr Conner, she decides to turn his curiosity back on him. She's already noticed the worn gold band on his finger and leans in, daring to be personal. "Are you married then, Mr Conner?"

"I am, about a hundred years now."

"And how did you meet your bride?"

His eyes narrow, as if she's being cheeky – the same look he'd given Siobhan earlier. "Now why would you want that rag of history?" He tops off her cup with steaming tea and peers at her.

"Well, I suppose I'm just curious." She grins. "Like you."

"I see you are. You'll fit in here just fine then." He begins in a very matter-of-fact monotone: "Well, it's a plain enough story. Her name is Margaret, and she was a gorgeous girl – still is, mind you. But back then... well." He shakes his head and offers empty palms, as if there aren't words to describe his wife. "Our Siobhan's nearly the spit image of her, so you can imagine."

Lise nods toward the shop. "*Your* Siobhan?"

"Our granddaughter." He sets down his tea. "When Margaret was Siobhan's age she took no notice of me, a course. But then she wasn't cruel like some, either." He pushes his lame foot forward. "I went to every healing well between here and the North, hoping to get cured so that I might catch her eye. Girl like her, what other chance'd I have, save a miracle?" Mr Conner shakes his head. "But in the end, only after I'd given up, the charm happened, but not the way I'd thought."

"What was the charm?"

"Just a song. I only just sang her a song once – to cheer her, while she was ailing." His smile seems weighted. "She took notice of me after that."

"That must've been some song. Would I know it?"

"Maybe." Without the slightest hesitation he stands, clears his throat, and breaks into a ballad with words so thickly accented she can barely make them out. Mr Conner's voice rings pleasantly in the courtyard and, after a few bars, a calm spreads over his features, as if singing is his natural voice. And in singing, the melody transforms him to near handsomeness; his face opens and he stands straighter, less anchored by his leg. His tune recalls the Cape Breton sea ballads that Lise had learned in school – tragic stories of lovers wrenched apart by the ocean's appetite for sailors, or by the dangerous sirens who entice men into icy depths. But this song, at least what she can make of it, suggests the beloved might make it ashore, might claim his girl after all.

As soon as he finishes, Mr Conner sits quickly, a flush blooming over his already pink cheeks. "Ah, you're thinking, *These Irish, they'll sing to a mad dog if he has one ear.*"

"Not at all. I'm thinking it's no wonder Margaret took to you. That was marvelous." She leans in, feeling bolder. "You must have had quite a courtship."

He looks at her with straight suspicion. "'Twas well enough. Certainly brief, so. We knew what we were meant to do." His focus founders before landing on the teapot. "Here, another cup, before it's stone cold." After pouring, he leans back, bands his stocky arms around his chest, and clamps his mouth shut.

After a few dumb moments she nearly gets up to sing herself. That might break the ice, she thinks, for surely Mr Conner's never heard a voice like hers. Instead she taps a nail over the glass wedges of dried paint. After a dozen counted breaths, the silence becomes unbearable to Lise, so she breaks it with a blurted apology. "I'm sorry, Mr Conner, I didn't mean to pry."

He considers her briefly before shaking his head. "Jays, don't be calling me Mr Conner. I'm only Remy." He presses a broad thumb over his chin. "Now, where were we? Margaret, right, so. As I said – she liked my singing well enough and later even got used to my face. Course those days there weren't many lads to choose from, so many left to fight the war, and later even more gone off to London after the Blitz to rebuild." He drums a rhythm over the leg that would have prevented his doing either. "Maybe Margaret took me on, thinking if I had a notion to leave I wouldn't get very far, at least not very fast." His laughter, deep as his singing voice, fades quickly. "But courtship isn't the thing, is it?" He looks sternly at her. "It's the afterwards that matters. Sure, isn't that it?"

By the time the paint is mixed and the glass samples are dried and approved, she's learned the Conners have one son, Danny, Siobhan's father, who operates a fleet of fishing boats. Remy tells her proudly that Margaret is known up and down the coast for her wedding cakes and has even made a small business of it.

"So if you've a mind to marry, put your order in now – she's nearly a year booked."

"*Marry?*" She pulls her ring hand into her lap before he can see the telltale band of paler flesh, still noticeable. When she realizes he's only joking, she smiles weakly. "I should be getting back."

"Right." He stands. "You'll need brushes and rollers."

After she pays, Remy sketches a crude map to his house on the back of her receipt, extending an invitation to tea. "Drop in anytime. The missus doesn't get out much, chained to the cooker as she is."

When they load the dozen cans of paint into the car, Remy shakes his head. "That's a fair lot of work you've planned. Can I not give you the name of a man up your way?"

"Thanks, no. I'll be doing this job myself, Mr Conner." He scowls until she corrects herself. "Remy."

From the curb he directs her U-turn on the narrow street. Before pulling away, she leans out the window. "Thank you. And thank your granddaughter for the tea."

"Don't stay alone too long up there." He nods at the coast road. "Come back for whatever."

"I will." And she means it. Lise reminds herself to bring biscuits next time.

* * *

Driving through the village, she passes the lane where the Conners live. Once she's settled she'll call on Mrs Conner – Margaret – and get her half of the story.

It's what she's best at, other people's stories.

Along the coast drive she notices things missed on her few previous trips. A hand-lettered sign on pressboard is nailed to a split rail: *Two-Tailed Calf!* But the arrow only points to an empty field beyond a broken fence. There is a historical site marker at a mysterious mound of earth, but it doesn't indicate what sort of history it marks. Just a mile from her own drive she spies a break in the hedge and a gatepost anchoring a path. At the top of the hill the stone peak of a roofless building is just visible. Since there's nothing to suggest what lies above, she suspects it's something worth seeing. At the turn-in she parks and leaves the car.

Halfway up the steep path she stops to catch her breath, settling on a block of stone seemingly placed for that purpose. The view of the coast is expansive here; in every direction is a vista that is the Ireland of postcards: more sheep than people in a treeless quilt of pastures. The ruin of a crofter's cottage adds a picturesque reminder of the country's rugged history. To the north, the headlands jut through a bank of mist, and her hands fall to her sides, stilled by the sight.

The spot she's resting on could well be the exact place where Charlie had stopped to paint his sunrise, for the angle of the headlands slanting into the sea could only have been captured from this vantage point. She's within a matter of strides from where it was painted. That glowing canvas, still packed in its crate in the cottage below, has come full circle now.

Wind from the ocean makes a melancholy whistle, like the collective whisper of waves. Remembering Remy's seafarer's song, she shivers at the notion of dead men and mermaids, and climbs on. Gusts strong enough to hasten her upward lift several gannets into the sky, their wings casting shadows over her shoulder.

At the hill's crest, the land levels to reveal the first tier of a graveyard. There are two churches beyond. One looks to be eighteenth century and is abandoned. The other is ancient and crumbling. She circles the buildings to find there is no route or path other than the one she has climbed.

The ruined church has three standing walls, its doorway intact but low, as if built for people of an earlier age. The stone roof has fallen to a mossy jumble over the floor. She leans into one of the arched windows to discover a lichen-crusted altar, a Celtic cross fallen behind it, cracked among the stones.

In the ancient bit of graveyard she tries making out dates and letters on the headstones, but only slight impressions indicate that those buried had names at all. Many markers lean in the soil and a few are propped upright by stones; others have slipped so deeply into the earth that only a few inches show.

Across from the ruin, the newer church is boarded up and flanked by gravestones that are more modern, from the mid-eighteenth century onward. Several markers are from the 1950s, but only few have dates any later. One, marked Tom Donnelly, is as recent as 1969. In this section the names tend to repeat: Donnelly, Donnelly, Hurley, Hourihan, MacMurtry, Hourihan, Hourihan, Delaney. She watches for the name of her landlord's people, Kleege, but finds only one. Three graves are marked Conner. *Declan, loving son of Bernadette and Liam.* Two tiny, unmarked tablets between the parents might be the graves of Conner infants. These five souls may well be Remy's people.

The cemetery is a peaceful spot with an eye to the sea, out of earshot of the crashing surf. The quiet, along with the altitude, gives the impression of standing in the sky. Indeed, each time Lise moves from shelter to outdoors she feels overwhelmed by the moody expanse of sky, dwarfing the land like a torn sheet billowed over a green penny. In the course of one day she has witnessed mist dissolving into sunshine, sunshine darkened by a quick storm, then brightness again before more sodden gloom. This stretch of

Irish coast may not be the most welcoming, but its fast-changing nature suits her. Noticing the fog of her breath in the cold, she stuffs her raw hands into the pockets of her anorak and retraces her steps to the path down the hill.

After unloading the paint and supplies, she eats a cold supper and makes coffee to take out into the frigid last minutes of day. Walking to the low cliff, she eases down along the footholds to the sand. Light has been all but pulled from the clouds; only a fine skin of lavender remains. The gloaming. The saddest hour for her these days. Adam's name rises in her throat as she steps to the water.

When she finally looks up, all color is gone, night fallen like a boot.

Climbing the stairs to her room, she passes a window where the moon rises like an uneven ball of mercury behind the warped glass. She watches its slow climb into an opening in the clouds and recalls the phrase *to heaven's attic*. Where had she heard that? It sounded like something her father would say, but he'd said so many things that she's only now remembering after thirty years. He'd also claimed gap-toothed men were of superior wisdom – his decree whistling through the space in his own grin. She wonders if the hardware man, Remy, with *his* gap-toothed yawn and his tortoise face, isn't the local sage. There is a careless dignity about the man, a certain knowing in his eye. Surely she'll see him again, for in such a house as this there's often need for a bit of this or a length of that to hold the place together. If anyone would have stories – or histories – Remy would. He'd surely know about the old cemetery.

She lights the fire in her room and tears silver paper away from the boxed set of new sheets, an indulgence purchased on her first day in Galway, on one of the rare days she had allowed herself to imagine Charlie's arrival.

"Finest linen," the woman in the tourist shop had claimed, "woven in County Down." She'd been instructed to wash them with a touch of vinegar and to hang them out only on cloudy days or they would yellow, as if taking on color from the sun. As she'd paid, the clerk had asked, "Are they bottom drawer?"

"Pardon?"

"Bridal goods. A custom here is that a bride saves up the linens in the bottom drawer of her bureau, getting ready for the wedding day."

"Really? Do they still?"

"Not so much, I s'pose marriage isn't the dream it once was. It's all living together these days, isn't it? Even with the divorce legal now you'd think more would marry. But them that do now all register at the department stores." The woman shrugged.

"Bottom drawer…" Lise handed over her credit card. "Doesn't sound terribly hopeful."

When another customer stepped in, the clerk straightened. "So, these *are* a wedding gift then? Shall I wrap them?"

She'd barely hesitated, lying, "Yes. Please do."

The old bed is tall, posts grazing the sloped ceiling. As she tucks the sheets under the mattress she notices scars of age in the dark wood. Still, it is the best piece in the house, certainly the oldest. Plucking a small square of paper fallen to the floor from the box of linens, she reads: *Made in Portugal*.

After her laughter fades, she is suddenly enveloped by the quiet of the sleeping sea and the stillness of the house.

She eases between the new sheets and opens her paperback to read the same page twice, distracted by thoughts of the bed beneath.

How many children would have been conceived between its four posts? The book falls to her breast as she considers the past and what acts of love the bed would have hosted. Faces slowly shift into her imagination: men and women in dated nightclothes or with naked shoulders. She sees the women more distinctly: dour-faced, plain or fair, with expressions of rapture or endurance – perhaps even disgust – as their men move over and above them. Willing or not, the women would've rested on their pillows afterward in the very posture she now lies in. With a lazy grin at the thought of lovemaking, she dares imagine Charlie next to her, his head on the pillow. She lies for a languid moment before pressing the thought away, reminding herself of her uncertain imagination, which can turn even pleasant memories to misery.

And in her last moments of wakefulness, misery does come: she thinks of the certain suffering that happened here. Women would've labored to give birth in this bed; they would have writhed, grown ill, slipped under fevers and died. Some of these deaths would have been merciful and quick, and others not. Tossing on the linen sheets, she hopes some of those endings were peaceful, as much for her own sake as theirs.

She believes in spirits.

Chapter Two

There are times she believes Charlie is only a spirit – that their affair might have been an apparition. Her memories of their time together are otherworldly, unlikely scenes, beginning with their first timid exchanges that blindingly bright afternoon.

She'd arrived in Mexico alone. As she'd stepped from the plane, a warm wind ruffled her with damp scents of sea salt and greenery. The cab to Gerald's villa bucked over a highway laid over uneven scrubland. Most of the hour-long ride was spent with her arms splayed on the vinyl seat, her body propped like a tripod. By the time the driver finally found the villa, Lise was done in by travel; her neck ached, her bottom was numb from sitting and, when she dabbed at her eyes, melted mascara and grit came away on her handkerchief.

The taxi eased under an iron arch and along an avenue of sentry palms. At a circular courtyard she was deposited along with her luggage. She dragged her roller bag through a groomed patio anchored by a fountain.

Courtyard cobbles shimmered in the abandoned air of siesta hour. Heat pulsed from above to baste the adobe walls, chalky white surfaces that seemed to refract the very blankness of sleep. After the morning she'd had, she could use an hour of rest herself. Sighing, she settled to rest on the fountain's edge, taking in the unaccustomed hush and warmth. As she sat, her shoulders slowly softened, the tightness that had yoked her all morning thawing. Tipping her face, she marveled: only six hours ago she'd been in Toronto, shivering in the autumnal dawn while awaiting the airport shuttle.

She supposed she should find someone. Rising, Lise slipped out of her sandals and moved toward the only faint sound, jazz notes coming from a path opposite the main house. Sun stung her scalp until she entered the deep shade of the pathway. She followed a trail edged by plants with impossible leaves. Near a cleared space where the doorway to a square stucco building was propped open, she recognized the music as a Miles Davis tune. Her steps on the hard-packed earth approached dance, bare heels and toes tapping along. The name of the tune eluded her. Her feet on cold earth felt delicious, vaguely immoral.

She knew the building was a studio before stepping inside. Odors of linseed oil and solvents laced the scent of bougainvillea trellised over the door. The music was loud, but not jarring. Inside, a man stood with his back to her at a heavy easel, wholly absorbed in his work.

Lise frowned, trying to remember if Gerald had mentioned a painter.

The man's head was tilted in concentration; a spattered rag hung from the fist curled at his hip. Lise tilted her own head in the same manner to better see the painting he scrutinized. Just as she was thinking she should clear her throat or at least knock, she was stilled, not only by the painting on the easel, but by the many others along the walls: a dozen large seascapes in shades of salmon, grey, and ocher, with underlayments in vibrant blues and bronzes of sheer color, all applied with slashing movements of surf and tide. The effect was such that she leaned to the doorframe. The surface of the water looked soothing, yet dangerous. The paintings were as harmonious and discordant as the jazz on the stereo – similarly executed in crashing notes.

Lullabies and crescendos. A memory of different music rang just out of range, a tune she scrabbled toward with closed eyes. Where else had she felt deceptive and binding comfort give way so suddenly?

When the answer came, her eyes opened in wide amazement at the paintings. The towering pipe organ in the cathedral near her childhood home. The hours she'd endured in that cavernous church, lulled by wafting incense and the sound of missal pages falling. One minute she'd be lost in her own juvenile world, numbed by the drone of Latin Mass and, just as she would begin to drift, the organist would bear down and Lise would be jolted upright and pinned to the pew with fear, thunder tones coursing through her small chest.

How odd that a few seascapes would pull forth such peculiar, such long-forgotten moments. More odd that they suddenly made her want to find saltwater to wade in.

She turned to the painter, who was still unaware of her. *He* looked benign enough, crouched in a pigeon's attitude, head jutted toward his work. His bare foot swayed over the floor, sand falling lightly from its sole. She rapped at the doorframe.

Had she smiled when he turned, or had she only felt like smiling? There was more edge than surprise in his voice, as if he was resigned to frequent interruption. "Yes?" He squinted against the brightness behind her. "Can I help you?"

She took a step in so he might see her in his own light and, raising her voice against the music, apologized. "Hello. So sorry to interrupt, but I'm looking for Gerald or Clarice?"

The painter held up a finger and leaned away from the easel to lower the volume of the stereo. "Gerald's gone inland. You must be the anthropologist's wife."

"Um, archaeologist, actually."

"Sorry. That Stephen fellow, right? He and Gerald left for the site early this morning." He peered at her, his next words nearly inaudible. "He would have a wife like you." Lise read his expression as one between a smirk and a smile but hadn't a clue what to make of the comment. She decided to ignore it.

"And Clarice?"

"In the village, maybe." He shrugged. "Or in her room. She's always everywhere at once, but then one can never find her." He wiped his hand and took hers in a loose handshake. The more he said, the less idea she had of his accent, first wondering if he might be English, then changing her mind. She wouldn't have said the painter was attractive, but the moment he introduced himself she forgot his name, too absorbed in examining him. His long hair was sandy, the face beneath weathered and sharply angular. He was older than he looked from behind, perhaps fifty, with pale-blue eyes in creased temples. "Can I take you up to the house?"

She hesitated, wanting to make some comment about his work, but her mouth only opened like an empty pocket. She protested, pointing to his easel, where a base of dark shapes was emerging. "That's very kind, but I don't want to keep you from this."

He answered by peeling off his apron and finding a rag to wrap his brush. "Could use a break, actually."

Once outside, he didn't bring her directly to the villa but instead gave a brief tour, showing her the paths to the beach, the pool, and several small courtyards, all empty.

"Are there many of us?"

"You mean guests? Oh, Gerald's usual lot. About six or seven, all with kite-tails of letters after their names, PhDs of this and doctors of that." He leaned closer. "Barely a pulse among the lot."

"My husband." She shrugged.

"Is one of them." He struck his temple. "Of course."

"It's all right."

He grimaced.

"Really, it's OK." She laughed.

He steered her up a steep incline. At the top was a small clearing where two molting, tethered parrots pecked an empty feeding tin. They squawked at his approach.

"I've cut them loose three times now, but they keep coming back." He leaned close to one and whispered, "Coward." He dipped his hand into a bin and poured some seed into their tray.

"Perhaps they've nowhere to go?" When she held a finger near, one snapped his beak open to reveal a disturbingly thick, violet-colored tongue. She jerked her hand away.

"Perhaps no one else's stupid enough to feed them."

A few steps farther was a lookout. He motioned to a break in the palms where the Caribbean shone below. "There she is."

The expanse of sea spread out in a shocking aqua stain.

"It looks almost like a painting. It looks false."

"Sure, it's false, not a real ocean at all. Gerald had it shipped in. And dyed a color I'd never dare use."

When she laughed, he turned to assess her. After a few beats she tilted her head, staring back. He grinned. "Sorry."

"Don't be."

The lookout was small for two, and when Lise leaned out over the guard rail, she swayed in a moment of vertigo, reaching for the nearest tree trunk and closing her eyes against the drop.

"You all right?" He braced her by the elbow.

Her stomach pitched. "I just need a breath. I'm fine. Listen, I really don't want to keep you, and I really should find Clarice. She'll be expecting me."

"Right. You've had a long enough journey. Tour's over anyway. Let's get your things." He let go of her arm.

They made their way back to the fountain, where he insisted on carrying both bags. A manicured path led them through the back courtyard past the kitchen garden, where he rang the service bell under an arch.

When no one answered, he motioned her into a narrow hall of cupboards and through a pantry to a breakfast nook; the funnel of small spaces eventually opened up to a large formal dining room.

A broad-faced woman in a crisp blue uniform rushed at them, smoothing her coiled braid and muttering to herself in quick patois.

"Housekeeper," the painter whispered. He addressed the woman by her Christian name, Mercedes, and spoke in an apologetic string of Spanish, using exaggerated gestures and touching Mercedes's shoulder to press his points.

These two liked each other, Lise could tell, and even in her ignorance of the language, she understood they were joking. Then they began talking about her – she made out *siesta*, *comida*, and *gringa importante*. She assumed Mercedes was in charge of the house by the size of the ring of keys at her waist. The keys suggested she too was *importante*, allowed access where others wouldn't be trusted.

The painter translated. "Seems everyone is either out or napping, but Mercedes will take care of you. She'll get you something to eat, too. You look ready to topple."

She turned to Mercedes. "Thank you. *Gracias*."

"I speak some…" The woman held up a thumb and forefinger to form a small space. "Some little *inglés*."

Lise nodded thankfully and turned to take the handle of her suitcase from the painter. She reached out, noticing the squareness of his hand, how light caught in the bronze hairs, how flat and pale his nails were.

"You'll be all right now?" He didn't break his gaze until she nodded.

"I will. Promise."

The housekeeper watched the exchange before jutting her chin in the direction of a long hall. "Come, señora." The woman took the bag from Lise's shoulder, commandeered the roller bag, and hustled ahead toward the stairs.

Lise bent to retrieve her purse along with the items that had fallen out, a lipstick and her return airline ticket. When she looked up, the painter was moving away. She'd forgotten to thank him and would have called out, but she couldn't remember his name, so she silently watched him walk the length of the hall.

Mercedes was backing up the stairs, loudly banging the roller bag on each riser. "You follow now, señora?"

"Yes. *Sí*. Sorry."

At the landing, where the staircase split in two, Mercedes asked, "You share a room with your *esposo*, or you like your own?"

She had a choice? "Oh… my own, please." Then, as an after-thought she asked, "Will it be near his?"

"Near *whose*, señora?"

She slept through dinner and didn't see the painter again until the next evening when guests gathered for drinks near the pool. He was sitting on the steps of the shallow end with his feet in the water, a book on one knee. She couldn't make out its title.

Clarice looked very well, a bit more blond than usual, and happily at home in the villa, where she and Gerald spent several months each year. Casually dressed in a simple linen tunic and barefoot, Clarice still managed a regal air. Deftly orchestrating the hour in a role she reveled in – hostess – Clarice need only incline her head and guests followed her to the bar, in to dinner, or, as now, to be introduced to one another.

Lise noted that most guests were already either paired or clustered into groups, except for the painter, who seemed absorbed in his book, though he did glance up now and again from the pages and toward her, she was certain. Clarice followed Lise's gaze and asked, "Have you met?" Without waiting for an answer she called out and urged him over with a crook of her finger.

When he stood next to Lise, his dripping feet made puddles that seeped along the grouting to meet her own bare toes.

Clarice smiled proudly. "Everyone knows Charles Lowan."

Lise arranged her features and set down her glass, suddenly aware that the wrap skirt knotted around her waist had opened to reveal a bit of thigh.

He held out his hand. "Charlie'll do."

"A pleasure. Again."

"Yes. Again."

Gerald's villa was a philanthropist's hideaway. He and Clarice had sold their software company several years before so they could concentrate full-time on giving away the spoils. Among their local interests were an organic coffee co-op over the border in Belize, Lise's husband's ongoing excavation of the Mayan ruin fifty miles inland, and research into alternative fuels. From Clarice, Lise learned they were also Charles Lowan's devoted patrons; his paintings hung in their foundation headquarters in Brussels, and in their various homes. They had sponsored his exhibits in Barcelona and Paris and provided him a studio a few months each year.

The compound was set above the sea in gardens wrestled from scrubland, with tropical plants and palms imported from Honduras. The buildings were designed to appear colonial; the interiors had a quality of being shifted from one era to another. But the antique furniture was too old for the region, the architecture too colonial. The overwrought, overbuilt villa was like a movie set. And indeed, so removed from reality did her affair with Charlie seem in her memories, Lise saw it as if it were being acted out and filmed in cinematic excess."

During her first days at the villa Lise caught up on her reading and roamed the beach alone. Neither she nor Charlie mingled much with the other guests. Besides dinnertime, she rarely saw him in the villa, though she knew he had a room there. She assumed that he spent most of his time painting, by the continuous music pulsing from the studio. He seemed to prefer jazz, cello concertos, and old R&B, but when she wandered close enough she sometimes heard newer music of the sort her son liked: Frou Frou, Coldplay or Portishead. They encountered each other on the paths around the villa and on the steps leading to the beach, engaging in brief conversations that were laced with evidence they'd been watching each other.

He found an aloe plant and snapped off a length. "For your sunburn."

She shifted her sore shoulders and thanked him. Noticing his hands were clean of paint, she ventured, "You're not working.

Did you go to the village today?" There'd been no music from the studio on her way to and from the beach before lunch.

At the pool one morning she left her diamond watch and earrings on a table. She was dipping a foot into the water just as Charlie appeared on the patio. She quickly stepped in up to her knees.

He plucked up one of the earrings and tossed it in the air, deftly catching it behind his back. "Is your husband rich, like Gerald?"

The night before, over dinner, Clarice had joked about being younger than her husband by a day, claiming that one day and the fact that she was blond qualified her to be Gerald's "trophy wife". Lise looked at Charlie. "Why do you ask? Do you take me for a trophy wife?"

"Are you a trophy?"

Wading backward, she grinned. "Now you're trying to annoy me." Lise turned to dive under, knowing full well he would watch her swim the pool's entire length.

Most of the other guests had something to do either with Gerald's foundation or with one of its causes; a few were academics, like her husband, Stephen. But after a while they all seemed like extras whose faces made a collective blur once she had, consciously or not, trained her eye on Charles Lowan.

One evening, rushing out her door, she frightened him just as he was passing on his way to dinner. He recovered to joke, "Women terrify me."

She brushed by, smiling in the dark. "They should."

He followed her into the dining room and sat next to her, asking personal questions, most of which she shrugged off, claiming shyness. It was easier to answer his questions about Adam, and she tried to talk about her son without fawning. Charlie asked, "What's he like? What does he like?"

"Film. He has been addicted since he could walk, nearly. I remember once when he was only about two, he woke up from a dream but didn't know the word for 'dream', so he said, 'Nice nap, Mummy, saw movie.' Claims he's going to write scripts one day."

Charlie leaned in. "What sorts of films do you like?"

"Me? Oh, anything really good. I remember sitting up when I was a kid to watch the classics they always reran on TV – the black-and-white era. The great actors, you know? The dead ones."

"Like who?"

"Oh. Jimmy Stewart, James Mason, Burt Lancaster, Burton." As she ticked off more names, she noticed Charlie examining her hands. "Ava Gardner, Deborah Kerr, Myrna Loy, Bette Davis. That sort." She pulled her hands to her lap, away from his line of sight. "Are you listening?"

"I am. You like strong heroes and witty heroines who speak their minds. And you have lovely hands."

She blinked, not acknowledging she'd even heard his compliment. "Adam's favorite's Audrey Hepburn."

Charlie leaned back. "It sounds like you two are close."

Lise smiled. "Well, we're alone a fair bit, just the two of us, with Stephen gone so much. We passed a lot of evenings planted in front of the TV." She turned to him, her voice a false octave brighter. "Too many, but that's how it was. What's *your* favorite?"

He was looking steadily at her. "My favorite what?"

No one could have said they openly pursued each other, but it did seem they often found themselves alone in odd places at strange times. One morning she went out to film the village fishermen setting off for the day. Afterward she took a different route back to the villa, a rough inland mile that skirted the ruins of a temple. Turning her aim on one of the ancient terraces, she walked along, with her eye glued to the viewfinder. When Charlie cut into the frame, she nearly stumbled. He was sitting on the edge of a crumbling wall, looking up rather sleepily from his sketchbook. She found her voice. "You're out early."

"I thought this place would be deserted." Charlie hadn't combed his hair, and one foot was bare above a sandal fallen to the ground.

"So did I." Lise raised her rolling camera without thinking, catching his motion as their eyes met. She cocked her head, a gesture nearly identical to his. *The way he looked at her.*

"You don't mind, do you?" She took a step.

"Convenient device, that camera."

"What do you mean?"

"It allows you to be bold, when you're not, really."

She frowned. "I'm not sure about that."

"Aren't you?"

Walking back, she held her camera in the crook of her arm. Perhaps the camera did make it easier to move in the world; it gave her a reason to be places. It also gave her proof of moments, and of memories.

So many were lost. The reserve of memory where her father should have been was mostly a blank glare. She could remember the *feel* of him – could recall the crowding in her chest when in his presence. Through childhood she'd rarely strayed from the safe pool of his shadow, within reach of his stories, his lap, or the hand he so often settled on her hair. And while the rumble of his laugh echoed yet, Lise could not coax his face into frame, no matter how hard she focused.

But inside her camera, committed to film, Charlie's face *was* caught. Her lens had revealed a lover's glance. She'd seen it and would come to know it well: in his glimpses over the dinner table, his crooked smile whenever he opened his studio door to her, the look that made her spine feel suddenly unreliable. It was there, in just those few seconds of footage – the slight curl of his lip and the sideways nod. He'd known that early morning, days before anything happened, that something would.

* * *

In her room she fell to the bed. On her nightstand was a photo of Stephen and Adam, taken on Adam's seventeenth birthday. She didn't look at it but turned it facedown on her chest, trying to cobble together an image of Stephen without looking. She often tested herself with such games to challenge her flawed memory. Stephen's face was slow to form. Individual lines of jaw and cheek wavered; his eye emerged in slow color. Her husband's face gathered into a whole and Lise rolled to her side, a surprising tear absorbing into the linen.

When she'd begun dating Stephen, everyone had seemed to notice something she hadn't. Friends thought them a well-matched couple, a good *fit*. He was considered a catch – so intelligent, and with such a future. Even her mother had heard of Stephen's people, a known Montreal family. And he was so handsome that it was easy for Lise to imagine herself falling in love – she was so certain she would that when he'd suggested marriage, she'd accepted, unable to think of a reason not to. Besides, it was time. She was nearing thirty and tired of dating the rebellious types who were inspiring and passionate, but unpredictable and noncommittal. Stephen, on the other hand, was serious and safe.

Their marriage had started out as hopefully as any. Tracing backward, she could remember one of the instances of real happiness that had peppered their first years: the afternoon she'd told him she was pregnant. Walking into his cramped office at the university, she'd leaned over his desk, full of news but making him guess.

"Is it smaller than a bread box?" He pushed his glasses up over the crown of his shaggy blond hair.

"Much smaller. For now."

"Something that grows then? OK. Animal or vegetable?"

"Animal."

"Tell me it's not a puppy."

"Definitely not a puppy."

It was then he noticed her hand tracing a light circle over the front of her skirt. He'd jumped from his chair, picked her up, and spun her, knocking over a pile of papers. "A baby! I'm going to be a father?"

For the next months she'd had much of Stephen's attention. He'd doted on her through the pregnancy and seemed oddly grateful. In a reversal of roles he was suddenly in awe of *her* abilities, humbled by the amazing feats of growing a baby, giving birth, nursing. He was proud of her, and though Lise knew any woman could do what she'd done, she hungrily lapped up the attention, sensing it was short lived.

Between her new motherhood and Stephen's rise in academia, they were slowly pressed into nearly separate existences. He was gone several months of each year, visiting various archaeological sites or conducting field study abroad. When home, he was consumed by his university work, writing lectures and articles.

Lifting the frame from her chest, she examined the photo. Against the backdrop of flowering dogwood, Stephen wears the half smile he reserves for photographs, one hand resting on Adam's shoulder in a paternal attitude. He's impeccably groomed and younger-looking than his forty-eight years; his face is a mix of intelligence, entitlement and the ease of a man comfortable in his own skin. These traits are suggested in tiny explosions of color – a thousand pixels making up Stephen's face. But there is no clue of his inner life. The picture in her hand more or less portrays most of what Lise really knows of him.

She came upon Charlie at the lookout, leaning against the guard rail and out over the sea. Too far. She spoke softly so as not to startle him.

"Thinking of jumping?"

He was smiling, but his eyes were grave. "Not into the ocean."

She paused. "So, not suicide?"

"Nah, I'm too much of a coward for that." He met her eye. "Could *you* kill yourself?"

"I'm too fond of myself to consider it."

"I see that, but if you had to, could you?"

She looked out over the cliff. "If I had cancer or a brain tumor? Sure, in a New York minute."

He looked puzzled.

"The amount of time a New York cabbie takes to honk once the car ahead of him stops."

"Ah, no time at all, then."

"Right."

Pages of a letter were secured to the table with an oversize tropical seedpod from some plant whose Latin name was too long for Lise to remember. On a sleeve of stationery held to her knee she was responding to the letter, from Leonard, her best friend back home in Toronto. They'd been close since university, and he'd helped land her the job at the Film Center where they both worked. She scribbled over the thick paper with a green pen, using too many adjectives to thank Leonard for taking Adam shopping for school clothes in her absence. It seemed she was often thanking Leonard for performing one kindness or another, if not for her, then for Adam, who still called him "uncle". Indeed, during Adam's childhood Len had been around nearly as much as Lise's own brother, Paul. In the past several years, Len had stepped in to provide a male presence during the birthdays or holidays Stephen missed. But more often he was just there, stopping by unannounced to hang around, read the paper, or relieve Lise of her apron and salvage whatever dinner she was attempting. He regularly stayed the evening to watch videos, usually ending the night by carrying – and later steering – a sleepy Adam to his bed. Len kept his own coffee cup in her kitchen and knew his way around her house as well as she did. He'd taught Adam things she couldn't: how to press a shirt properly, how to square-knot a tie, and, more recently, how to dance.

Adam, anxious over a date, had shown up at Leonard's door with a CD of the sort of music that would be played at the school's Harvest Dance. Leonard relayed the incident in detail in his letter.

I said, "OK, I'm the girl," and he said, "Tell me something I don't know." But after a few turns around the kitchen he wasn't leading, and he couldn't keep a straight face, so I switched and said, "OK, fine, I'm leading." So I put my arm around him and snugged him in at the waist – you should've seen his face. He said, "Watch it, big boy," and we both fell apart. He did fine after that. Queer Eye for the Straight Teen – *think that would fly, Lise?*

Leonard *was* a marvelous dancer, often escorting Lise when she needed an arm to hang on to for this or that wedding or function. They were often mistaken for a couple until some comment or mannerism gave Leonard away. Lise bent over the letter, managing to describe the decor of the villa, which Len would find gauche and ostentatious. But the beach, she assured him, was plain old sand, and the other guests were just as beige and dull – except for one. She was effusive over Charles Lowan's paintings but faltered over a physical description of him... *the opposite of tall, dark and handsome?* Chewing her pen end and staring off across the pool, she was about to add more when Charlie himself emerged from a fern-choked path opposite the pool.

Lise blushed, pretended to sign the letter, and slowly folded it away in the time it took him to reach her. He slumped into the chaise next to hers, still wearing his painting clothes – khakis rolled up over his pale ankles, and a dark T-shirt with two ocher fingerprints marking the middle of his chest.

He looked tired, and the lines around his eyes were more deeply etched in the sunlight. A sudden urge to reach out and touch his temple overtook Lise. Unsure what to do, she rose, focusing on the paint smudges on his shirt, which were centered precisely over the shallow at his breastbone.

She stood mute a few beats before blurting, "I... I'm getting juice. Would you like some? You want ice?"

Her sandals lay forgotten and the patio tiles burned her feet, so she had to hopscotch along, certain she must look like an idiot. And in the kitchen she muttered into the freezer, her breath making clouds as she reminded herself aloud, "Nothing has happened." More composed by the time she found glasses and a tray, she took the shaded route back to the pool.

When she handed Charlie his glass of juice, a bit sloshed out onto his wrist. He absentmindedly raised his forearm and pressed his lips over the skin.

She sat. "How's the painting?"

"Nothing today." There was a timbre of exhaustion in his voice. "Too hot, I suppose. I can't seem to get going." He turned. "How about your work?"

A fleck of pineapple pulp was still caught on the flat plane of his wrist, at the pulse point.

"My work? Isn't terribly interesting. I raise money for a film center. Writing proposals and organizing fund-raising events. That sort of thing."

"Do you like it?"

Her eyes drifted back to the bit of pineapple. "I suppose so. It's just a matter of asking for money." She fluttered her hand. "Very much a trophy wife's job."

"Right. Sorry about that." He stretched out on the chaise. "Actually, I was wondering about your real work. Clarice mentioned you make documentaries, and you're always carrying that old camera about."

"Right. My device."

"Sorry about that, too. I must annoy you very much."

"Not as much as you might think."

He hung his head in mock penance. "I deserved that. Are you working on something now?"

"Nothing today. Same as you."

She'd hoped the time away might restart her imagination, that she would find new ideas for a film while in Mexico. But since arriving she'd only been visited by a tropical sleepiness, and a strange disquiet whenever Charles Lowan was near. It was true she hauled her camera about, but she had only turned it on a few times. Her inspiration had stalled months before, and she wondered if she wasn't drawn to Charlie's company in part for the confidence he seemed to have in his own talent. But now, in the torpor that seemed to have shrouded the villa, he seemed as restless and uninspired as she.

She told Charlie how she'd begun, after discovering an old eight-millimeter German camera in a second-hand shop. "It came with a case of raw film I knew was too old to be any good, but I used it anyway, and it turned out quite beautifully – all these sunspots and weird burns. It wasn't sepia, and it wasn't quite color either, but something in between, more ambered, like *time*. I used that film up long ago, but now I have the technology between the lab and editing to make my new footage look just as old."

He smiled. "I imagine the irony of that isn't lost on you?"

"It's not."

She described her first shorts, "learning films", she called them, and how students at the Film Center taught her how to cut and splice, how to lay in voices and music. She bought an old studio audio kit and experimented with sound to age it, rerecording tracks over a cell phone or against the hiss of the boiler room in the Center's basement. Her first piece was twenty minutes of Adam playing outdoors in winter: skating, building a snow fort. She accompanied these scenes with Welsh Christmas carols played on a tinny piano, along with an old recording of Dylan Thomas thundering lines from *A Child's Christmas in Wales*.

In Toronto she'd filmed tiny vignettes in the Indian markets, drawn by the immigrant women's gestures; the movements of their hennaed hands, the grace they made of buying a tomato, the way the carmine smudges at their brows shifted as they haggled over fishes. The best market was part of an old train depot, with a whole aisle devoted to spice vendors. This she filmed from above on a catwalk, and from its vantage point the mounds of spice and seeds were disks of warmth – pale cumins and shocking curries, pepper in shades of madder red and orange, mustard seeds in taxicab hues.

One morning her lens focused on a boy below dressed in a black-and-white soccer shirt and striped pants. His movements were a stark animation against the slow color of the milling crowd. She followed his mop of coal-colored hair as he tormented the vendors, pretending he would stomp into their precise mounds of spice before darting away. His bare feet were brown-topped; light-colored soles as his game took him from edge to edge; he pushed saris aside as though swimming through bright stalks of silk. Complaints were uttered in his wake, baskets jostled on bangle-bright arms.

In Lise's viewfinder the boy was an errant zebra at a sleepy costume ball. He jumped suddenly and his foot came down so hard in a cone of alum powder that a wide cloud rose, setting all nearby to coughing or cursing. The vendor shouted and reached through the burst of white to claw at the striped pants.

Her laughter shook the camera, so the final frames of the boy jogged among the sari hems as his last sprinter-fast footfalls were recorded: *white foot, brown, white foot, brown*. Then he was gone.

She quickly climbed down to the market floor and eventually located the boy's mother, who gave her name as Mrs Kali. Lise explained what she did and the sudden inspiration she'd had while on the catwalk. Mrs Kali regarded her with disbelief. "You want to film *my* boy? Whatever for?"

After a week, Mrs Kali agreed but warned that her son Raj was incorrigible, saying that if Lise could catch him for long enough to start the project, she could go ahead – provided it didn't interfere with his studies.

A year later, her market project, *Raj*, was entered in the Toronto Film Festival. It was a story of immigration seen through the eyes of the eight-year-old acclimatizing to his new surroundings, with most scenes shot at his height, and, when she could keep up, at his speed. The accompanying narration was in the voice of a female, presumably his sister but actually a friend of Adam's, a sable-eyed girl with the requisite accent.

After the film was shown and Lise had won the best cinematography award for short film, one of the judges, a journalist from New Delhi, took her aside and gently chastised her for the choice and portrayal of her subject. He did not use the word *exploitation*, but she felt it spelled in the space between them as the medallion grew cool in her hand. The journalist had said, "You will understand one day. You should make a film of yourself – then you will know."

"I'd like to see it sometime." Charlie was leaning eagerly forward. "What else have you done?"

She found herself telling him, surprised at her ease. She rarely spoke to Stephen about her films. It wasn't that he didn't encourage her; Stephen simply had other things on his mind, his own work being so much more serious. "I did a documentary on an eighty-year-old dressmaker evicted from her shop by the Preservation Alliance, that's one. Then a short piece on a dairy farmer who'd adopted twelve abused boys. I did start one piece that still haunts me – for a month I followed a couple of carnival travelers who were teaching their youngest daughters the art of picking pockets. Twins, they were probably the family's most valuable asset, you know, for the confusion they were able to make during thefts. They were beautiful girls, about ten years old, seasoned thieves already, and becoming such good pickpockets that I never did figure out how they did it, even on film. Over and over they got my pocketbook, sometimes my watch, and sometimes both at once. They were brilliant. But when I showed up to do final interviews, their trailer had disappeared, and that was that. So I never finished, but I've never stopped wondering about those girls… Lula and Camilla." She bit her lip and looked up at Charlie, expecting his drowsy profile, but his eyes were full on her. "There were a few others, but I won't bore you."

"Bore me?"

But she was talked out. They sat awhile, quietly watching the progress of a gecko following the sun to the hottest tiles, testing the checkerboard of terracotta before settling to bake. After a while she mused, "You'd think it would know by now that the hottest tiles are always the darker ones."

"Perhaps it doesn't see as well as you do." Charlie laughed. "Hell, I wish I could."

Sitting back, she framed Charlie in half shade, her gaze climbing to the hard line of his jaw, his deep temple and too-broad forehead. He would be considered plain by most.

"You choose what you see, I suppose."

He considered her a long moment before touching her arm. "You should, you know."

The nails of his fingers were rimmed in ocher, the same color pressed into the fabric of his shirt. The weight of them on her skin was light, acute.

"I should what?"

"Do what that journalist suggested. Make a film of yourself."

When he pulled his hand away, she felt marked.

"Elle?"

She froze. No one had called her that for a very long time. It took a moment for her to reply without her voice cracking. "Yes?"

Three young maids came each day from the village a mile away, and some mornings she watched from outside her room as they walked the path from the main gate.

At the fountain they put on aprons and tied their braids together while laughing and talking. By the time they reached the kitchen garden they would fall silent, ready for work. One morning the routine changed when the youngest of the three waited for the others to go in. She then rushed around to the front of the grounds and skipped down the beach path.

Lise skirted around the villa on the second-floor balcony to see the maid cross the expanse of sand to the water's edge, where she slipped off her shoes and stepped into the surf. Ankle deep, she stood very still.

A few moments passed with the maid lost in some reverie. Lise couldn't recall her name, was about to lose interest in the old game of following and watching, when a plaintive tune floated up.

Ah, yes, the girl who sang. What was her name? Eva, Flora? Always singing in the courtyard off the laundry; even while hanging sheets and towels she hummed through the clothespins held between her lips. Flora, she was sure. Flora, with her feet in the sea, her hand drifting to touch her cheek, was a moving sight.

It struck her then. *The girl is in love.*

Was it that easy to recognize? In her bathroom Lise lingered at the mirror, examining her own face. She'd not always considered herself pretty but had somehow felt more attractive as she'd aged, her features stronger than when she was in her thirties. There were minute differences between the halves of her face that made her surprisingly unphotogenic. One brow arced slightly higher than the other, and her upper lip was a millimeter fuller on one side. Her cheekbones were good, and her grey eyes set wide, bridging the nose she blamed on her mother for being too French. Her skin had held up, more or less. She wore her russet hair swept away from her face in a twist.

She dropped the straps of her nightgown, and the thin cotton fell to her hips. Her breasts were small, the right nipple edged with a fine half-moon scar from a biopsy. She was reminded then to examine herself, mentally counted the days of her last cycle and lifted one arm at a time to go through the paces, feeling the soft tissue with practiced fingers. Nothing. She nodded a silent thank-you to the glass.

Her arms were firm and her stomach was a taut swell. Back in Toronto she went to a pool every other day to swim a mile. She was able to dismiss her body as one well cared for, and until recently had had little reason to think of it as more than a soft shell to dress and tend.

When was the last time a man had looked at her with desire? Her friend Leonard often claimed she was a "stunner", but he didn't count. When she wore make-up or a dress Stephen liked, he often said she looked pretty, but after so many years she no longer expected words such as *beautiful* and *lovely*.

But Charlie believed her to be both. It was unspoken, but she knew. He'd called her Elle. And staring at her image, she considered the selective eye of love, how what you wish to see offers itself up on the surface of a body, on the planes of a lover's face. Words she'd spoken to Charlie echoed: *You choose what you see.*

The light rap on her door startled her. She hastily pulled the fallen nightgown over her breasts.

Stephen was away in the jungle.

Surely Charlie wouldn't be so bold?

"Señora?" The voice was female, young.

Lise saw her wild eyes in the mirror and laughed. It was only one of the maids. Flora, no less.

Chapter Three

Upon waking, Lise finds her fingers clutched around the bedpost, as if to feel the storm's rise through the cottage, the floor, the bed. The usual blue lull of dawn has been punctuated by waves and winds from the North Atlantic. Pulling her exposed hand under the bedclothes, she warms it against her stomach. With her nightgown sleeve she makes a mitten for her other hand and reaches for her water glass, where a thin wafer of ice floats. Lise balances the ice on her tongue until a cold ribbon melts down her throat. The fire in the grate is all but dead, and for a moment she considers tossing in her unread paperback, if only for a flash of warmth to dress by. Remy has given her the name of a man nearby who still cuts and delivers peat. She's called twice, but three days have passed and the man hasn't come by. There's coal in the sheep shed, but she'd rather shiver than deal with the filth and smoke.

She bolts into her clothes, jogs down the stairs, and finds a basket to collect driftwood. Leaving the cottage, she finds the sun has broken weakly through a tear in the clouds to gild tips of waves. With her camera under one arm and her basket swinging from the other, she wades the dew-heavy sea grass, soaked to her shins. At the beach she steadies her camera to record the surf and the flotsam in the shallows. The sand is littered with debris from the storm: skeins of seaweed, a tattered nylon sail, a dead tern, and the business end of a broken oar. She wedges the camera in a crevice of the cliff and circles along the ledge above so that when she climbs down into frame she is a far figure on the beach. Moving forward, she plucks up anything burnable, including the oar. By the time she's near the camera, there is enough wood collected for a few hours of heat. Night waves have borne in a basket's worth.

These days she accepts such small offerings without question. It's the larger windfalls that confound her. How she's come to live on this shore, in this plain house, for instance. When she'd told the estate agent she hoped to lease a seaside house near the headlands, he had looked at her with genuine pity. He'd wanted to help, but Americans and Germans had been snatching up all leases on the coast as far up as Donegal. But he would have a go, he promised.

He took the name of her hotel and called that very evening. Standing on the lobby carpet with his folders fluttering, he told her about a family who'd placed their mother in a nursing hospital. The relatives were at a loss over what to do with the old woman's vacant house. "I spoke with the oldest son today, just after my appointment with you. They're willing to let."

He had photographs, which he laid on a table in the dining room, warning, "Now, at first look the place might seem a bit bleak."

She stared at the slope of rocky hill and the house set starkly against overgrown gorse. The stone well-house and old sheep barn were missing half their roof slates.

The house. Her hand fumbled toward the neck of her sweater. "I know this place."

"Ah, so you've driven out that far?"

"No. Someone described it to me. I... I've imagined it."

The estate agent said nothing, but she could feel him straighten.

They'd gone for lunch in the village, but Charlie, noticing the sign for palm readings and tarot, had steered her away from the restaurant and through the woman's door, laying down his money before Lise could protest. Of course she'd been skeptical – who wouldn't be, trading pesos for a glimpse of the future?

But the house in the photograph was the same house, surely. She recalled the woman's exact words: *A plain house, stone, near large water, high waves. Not a handsome house.*

She sank to a chair, not trusting her knees. There were other photos, of the inside – a warren of square rooms, cluttered and small, but with windows to the sea. The last photo, taken from some high point, showed the whole property from afar, emphasizing its remoteness: a low cliff and a fingernail beach curving into the ocean, and the huddle of swaybacked buildings sprouting from rock and gorse. Lise looked up at the estate agent. Destiny was such a strong word. Was it fate or coincidence she'd found this particular man to ask after a house? She had simply seen his sign and had not hesitated to walk through his door.

Charlie had urged her to trust her intuition, and things would come. She's thought him simplistic at times, even foolish, but more often lately wonders if he isn't right. Perhaps embracing destiny is as simple as moving along without hesitation, entering whatever doors beckon.

The estate agent cleared his throat. "Right, then." He showed her the location on a map, tracing his finger along narrow secondary roads until he ran out of land. "It's maybe too rustic? A bit rough for someone like yourself?"

"Myself?"

"Ah, well, you know..." He glanced at her cashmere sleeve, her manicured nails.

She supposed she still bore the look of affluence that a life with Stephen had provided, but the money that brought her to Ireland was her own – finally taken from the small trust her father had left. It was money she'd long considered stained, and she'd actively ignored it, save once a year when she handed the unopened bank statements over to her accountant. The money had accrued over the decades to a surprising sum, enough to start anew with few worries, at least for a while. She dug in her handbag for the new Bank of Ireland checkbook.

"How much?"

As whips of hair sting her cheek, Lise peers into the camera's lens, wondering what will be detected in her gaze. After retrieving the camera, she walks toward the cottage, holding the still-running machine to her chest. Glancing down to the viewfinder, she spies her own image mirrored in a window of the cottage. She focuses on the glass.

The changes in her are obvious, even in the warped windowpane. Her stride is more deliberate, her face more open. Most days she feels some command over her life, over her imagination. Today the clouds are high and the ocean pulses in her precious camera. She winks at her reflection.

But then, as if to dash her mood, the weather shifts, ushering in more steel-bottomed clouds. Another storm, moving like a lid to cut the morning in half.

Walking forward, Lise appears in full frame. She's filming herself making a film. As the sky shutters to grey, the camera whirs and clicks to a stop.

"Make a film of yourself," the journalist and Charlie had both encouraged. But neither had offered any compelling reason. Really, she'd rather film the house and hills from a distance, perhaps from out on a boat, so the buildings could bob into focus from some far prow. Remy might know where she can hire a boatman.

She makes a trip back to the path to retrieve her basket of wood and hauls it, along with the camera, into the kitchen. After building a fire and brewing tea, she unloads the film inside a black, lightproof bag. The blind movements of her hands are certain over the angles of the old camera. The action reminds her of Charlie's hands – how perfectly they had known her contours under midnight bedcovers.

Once the film is safely in its canister she slides it out onto the table. Finding a Biro, she hesitantly prints the word *Me* on the label, staring at the blocky word. The very idea. Really, how much footage could she take of herself traipsing through Irish weather? Would she set up the tripod by the hearth and endeavor to fashion some sort of monologue against the romance of burning turf – and say *what*?

She shoves the canister into a far cupboard with its label face-down, intent on forgetting it.

Coming out of the market, she tries waving to Siobhan, but her arms are weighted with groceries. Rushing and dressed as if for a date in a tight skirt and a leather jacket, Siobhan slips ahead to cross the street, dodging a motorcycle with the ease of a cat, cigarette smoke tagging over her shoulder. Lise follows at a discreet distance, stepping into a doorway once when she thinks Siobhan might turn around.

At the door of Mertie's Pub, Siobhan smoothes back her seal-short hair, wincing as her leather cuff catches on the eyebrow ring. She spits her cigarette out before ducking inside.

Reaching the door, Lise nearly turns back. There's no good reason to follow the girl, but she still sometimes falls back on the childhood game without thinking. At Mertie's stoop a dozen pairs of rubber boots lean amid ruined bits of fishnet and a smatter of cigarette ends, Siobhan's still smoldering, with lip prints of glossy lavender. Directly left of the door, a ramp slopes down to the pier, where gulls ride a wind sharp with sea rot.

Inside the pub, the air isn't much better, but at least it's warm. The coffered ceiling is so layered with generations of smoke the oak is onyx black. She stashes her groceries in the snug and waits for her eyes to adjust to the dimness. Siobhan is perched on a barstool at the far end, leaning from a man holding on to her arm as though she might slip away.

Lise narrows her eyes. The man is twice Siobhan's age, darkly handsome, wearing a new suede coat and shining loafers. The topmost buttons of his shirt are undone. The man seems vaguely familiar but she cannot place him in the village. Certainly he's no fisherman, not with those clothes. Whoever he is, he's picked a fine trysting place. She squints to his hand to see if he's wearing a ring – he would be married, of course. Why else would he meet Siobhan in such a place?

The man's stance and his grip on Siobhan's arm rankle Lise. She considers marching over, but just as she decides to, the man suddenly lets go and turns to the bar in resignation, lifting his pint. Sighing, Lise looks away. The girl's affairs are none of her business. Hoping she might leave without being spotted, Lise eases halfway off the barstool, but the barman has appeared, asking, "What'll ya have, miss?"

Not wanting to seem rude, she asks for the first drink that comes to mind. "Port, I guess." Not that it matters; she won't drink it in any case. Fiddling with a book of matches, she watches the bar while the bartender struggles with the cork. The place is full of ragged fishermen, wrapped around their pints, spent from the day's labor. A sudden tap on her shoulder startles Lise.

Siobhan's smile is sweet, yet vaguely suspicious. "Slumming?"

"Ah. I s'pose so." Lise shrugs. "Saw you come in from up the street."

"So, that was you? I thought I felt a ghost." As Lise's drink is placed on the bar, the girl plucks it up. "Come join us. I'll introduce you to one of our more infamous locals."

"Thanks, but I was just leaving."

"Sure." She hoists Lise's glass. "So you've ordered this as take-away, right? C'mon. He doesn't bite."

The man stands at their approach and Siobhan presses Lise forward. "So, this is her."

He looks bemused. "Her?"

"Our woman! The one I was telling you about?" The girl slaps his sleeve. "The *Canadian*, Dad."

Dad? Lise's eyes widen.

"Ah, sure! Siobhan's mentioned you." He holds out a hand. "Pleased."

"Hello." She sheepishly allows him to pump her hand too vigorously for too long. With the two of them side by side, Lise sees it's obvious. Siobhan's dark beauty is mirrored in his chiseled profile, which is the very frame for Siobhan's softer features. He is as male and harsh as the girl is plush; their dark-lashed eyes are an identical jade. The man's nagging familiarity explained, a sigh escapes with her relief – that he's *not* Siobhan's married lover, not the man she's pierced her body for.

His face is close. "So you're the filmmaker woman, then?"

She inhales. "No secret now, is it? And you must be Danny, Remy Conner's son?"

"Am, yeah."

Siobhan steps away as Danny asks Lise a rapid-fire round of questions about how she's settling in. Before she can make even one reply, Danny's eye shifts and he calls out over her shoulder. "Siobhan, come back here!"

Lise turns, following Danny's angry gaze, to see Siobhan glide out the door.

The door swings shut behind her, and Danny curses something under his breath.

"Why has she run off? Is she upset?"

After a bitter last swallow of ale he sniffs, "Well, she's a female, so..." His smile is thin. "Been downright ferrety since her boy-friend's left."

"Left?"

"Gone off to Boston." He tips his empty glass at the barman. "To make it big, I imagine. And Siobhan's some notion to follow. Won't get very far if I have any say. Wants me to pay, of course."

"You don't want her to go?"

"To Colm?" He raised his brow. "Not particularly."

"Why?"

"He's a musician, for starters."

"Is that bad?"

"Bad enough." He orders another round, though she's barely touched her glass. When she protests, she notices his eyes falling to the V of her pullover. A glint of gold at his own unbuttoned collar reveals a chain nestled in hooks of dark chest hair.

She'd only come in to talk to Siobhan, and now she's trapped in a seedy bar with two full drinks and a Tom Jones wannabe. Lise sighs. "And Siobhan's mother?" She casually buttons her jacket closed. "What's *her* opinion of the boy?"

He clears his throat. "Brigid? She's, ah… *gone*." His focus shifts to the bottom of his glass.

"Oh." She takes a slow sip of the port. "I'm very sorry." After a long silence she asks, "Forgive me, but Siobhan's so bright. Why isn't she at university?"

"Stubbornness," Danny grunts. "Sheer stubbornness. She was all honors, top five percent and accepted to Trinity. Came time to pack up for Dublin, she wouldn't budge, was in the thick of it with Colm by then. And where'd it land her? He's off to America while she's selling bolts and baling wire."

"Does she enjoy working for your father?"

"She might, he's so soft on her."

During Lise's few visits to the shop, she's noticed Remy's demeanor with the girl, at turns demanding and short tempered, then almost grudgingly affectionate and oddly protective. Looking at Danny, she cannot help noticing he is as tall and dark as Remy is stocky and fair.

Danny begins telling her about his business, a derelict fishing fleet he's rebuilt from ruin. "Three rotting trawlers and a few wharf buildings. Now it's a state-of-the-art fleet, five boats. I pull an average ten ton of skate and herring each week, all off to the European market." He rambles on in terms she doesn't understand, about tariffs, haul limits, and restrictions. "It's a tough life," he claims.

"Tough?" Danny is expensively dressed and seems well rested. She is about to challenge him when she sees he's nodding toward the tired-looking men at the bar. "Most of these fellows work for me. A few live the season up near you, at the caravan park. You know it?"

"I do." The haphazard community of rusted caravans and muddied paths is an eyesore marring the best stretch of beach road. She passes it on each trip into the village, and she nearly complains just as Danny crows, "That's another of my holdings. I live up that way myself. Not in a caravan, a course." He then goes on to describe the house he's hired a Dublin architect to design, down to the taps. Lise watches the door, hoping some acquaintance of Danny's might drift in and relieve her.

By the end of the hour, she concludes there is no such thing as a brief personal history in Ireland, and what Danny has most in common with Remy is that he can wax eloquent, at least about himself.

When Danny's cell phone chirps, he excuses himself to take the call outside. Before the door even closes, a nudge from her left unbalances Lise. A pock-scarred man with bad teeth grins closely. "Enjoyin' yerself?"

She leans back from the pickled-onion smell of plowman's lunch. "Sure. I guess."

"A course y'are. This is a grand pub. You're lucky to be here 'stead of down Gaffney's, where the tourists go." He pokes his finger in an arc around the place. "This is an *Irish* pub, original to the nails – no souvenir counter, no Van Morrison piped at you, no fancy salads and no feckin' *Riverdance* on the video. Let them Yank tourists have it over at Gaffney's."

"But *I'm* a tourist, sort of."

"Ah, yer not. You're out at Kleege's place with your cans of green paint and your wee Morris car." He takes a gulp. "I had one just like it. Heaters in 'em are shite. Same year – whatsit, a 'fifty-nine?"

"'Sixty, actually."

"You all alone out there? No kin?"

Draining the rest of her port, she's glad now Danny has insisted on a second. "I've a son. Back in Toronto."

"Well, bring him on in when he comes round!"

She raises her glass, twisting her mouth into a smile. "Sure, I will."

The old man jerks his head toward the window, where Danny paces, talking on his phone. "That one wearing you down, is he?"

"Not for lack of trying. He's all right, just bragging."

"You might want to get out your camera for Mr Danny Conner – he's a story in himself. Told you about his fleet, a course. I got an earful of that. Next he'll ask you if you want a tour of the coast on a Sunday when the boats are idle."

"Why would he do that?"

He looks at her with pity. "You'll see then, if you're of a mind to go, that the boats are all named *Brigid*. *Brigid One* through *Five*. All after the wife."

"That's a touching memorial."

"Memorial?"

She lowers her voice. "How long since his wife's gone?"

"*Memorial?*" he repeats, hitting the bar with his palm. "So Danny's a widower now, is he? Your man'll say anything!"

"His wife's *not* dead?"

"Lord, no. Only moved to Dublin. Quite alive." He leans in. "Wouldn't abide his philandering."

"But he let me believe—"

"Course he did."

She frowns at the window. "And how long ago did his alive wife leave?"

He scratches his stubble with yellowed nails. "Oh, two years, now. Maybe less."

"Still, he must have loved her, to name the boats so?"

"Surely. Brigid's a grand girl, but Danny with his head so far up his own arse didn't know that till she'd packed it in."

Danny fills the doorway, his voice booming as he ushers a patron in. Lise's new acquaintance snatches up his pint, warning, "He's not above taking comfort where he can, miss."

"Ah, well… thanks for the heads-up."

"Heads-up it is." He slips away.

She gathers her groceries and meets Danny halfway down the bar.

"You're leaving?"

She holds up her bag, lying, "Ice cream."

"Oh. You met Mertie, then?"

"Him? Nice old fella, very chatty."

"Acts like he still owns the place."

"He doesn't?"

"No. I do."

She half laughs. "You've a regular monopoly here."

"Listen, if you're of a mind to see the coast, I've a nice trawler."

"Thanks, but I'm painting my kitchen this Sunday. But I imagine we'll meet again, Danny."

His tanned brow furrows. "Right. Well, anytime. The boat's always ready, so whenever."

On Sunday she tells Remy about meeting Danny. Remy confirms that Brigid is off in Dublin, and sighs as if his son's personal affairs are a source of ongoing exasperation. They sit at his usual table in the dining room of the Arches Hotel as he gulps coffee, which Margaret won't allow him at home. Over breakfast he's noticed Lise sniffing at her arm and scowling. She explains how that morning she'd gotten up in the dark and blindly pulled on clothes from the wardrobe. The smell of mothballs had trailed her halfway into town before she realized the cardigan she'd put on was Mrs Kleege's. Though she stuffed it into the boot of the car, its odor still clings to her blouse.

Mrs Kleege's daughter has come to take away a load of furniture, but too much of the old woman's personal life remains for Lise's comfort; every drawer and cupboard yields the history of a stranger.

"The cottage is lovely, Remy. Or could be, but I still feel like a visitor. What do you suppose the odds are Mrs Kleege will recover enough to return home?"

"None at all. She wouldn't know tea from piss with the Alzheimer's, and she's on her second hip, so she'll never climb those goat stairs you've got out there." He winks. "Not in this life, anyway."

"Do you think it'd be all right for me to clear away more of her things?"

"Jays, for what you're paying you'd think they'd send out a butler and maid to do it for you."

"You know how much rent I'm paying?"

He shrugs. "It'd be twice that if you were a Yank."

As she leaves, the old man bows his head back over a school exercise book to scribble something, wholly absorbed.

After she hauls out Mrs Kleege's remaining possessions, she starts cleaning, serenaded by the blasting stereo. The work is strenuous but goes fast, with sudden, satisfying results. The air clears after her sweeping and washing. The rooms lighten noticeably after the floors are stripped of old wax to reveal clear pine.

After a few days most of the rooms are bare and nearly ready for painting. Lise finds a piece of board in the barn and paints it with wide lashings of the tints Remy has mixed. Dragging the board from room to room, she checks in occasionally to see how the different hues will look in the changing hours of daylight.

After painting the entryway a foamy blue, she stretches the kinks from her neck and washes her brushes. A trip into town will be a break, she thinks. It's been days since she's spoken to a soul, and she's meant to visit Remy's wife for weeks, introduce herself to the woman she's heard so much about.

She writes *spackle sandpaper paint thinner* on her palm and shrugs into her rain jacket. Halfway up the hill, she lets the car roll backward down the drive and goes inside to pluck up one of the fresh reels of film that has arrived from Dublin. Hoisting her camera bag from its corner, she mumbles, "God knows what I'll get in this light."

A drowsy rain taps the roof of the little car during the drive. The village is dreary, boxed in by mist. Inside Conner's, the activity and light are riotous by comparison. The three boys who usually loiter at the pier have escaped the gloom to crowd the one aisle devoted to automotive supplies. No one seems to mind they are all three smoking. She grabs a plastic basket and chooses what she needs to finish her walls, along with fresh floor wax, and a night light for her bathroom.

She tries making small talk with Siobhan while paying for her things, but the girl is nearly silent. As soon as the transaction is over, she ducks into an aisle and resumes her task of tagging boxes of wood screws with a pricing gun.

Lise follows, shifting the parcel on her hip. "Your father tells me you've a boyfriend in America?"

Shooting a tiny tag onto a box, Siobhan frowns. "Did he now? Well, Colm'll hardly be my boyfriend much longer if he's in America and I'm here, now will he?"

"Can't you visit him?"

Siobhan snorts, "Sure, maybe in a year – if I keep working my backside off in this feckin' dump. But he'll have someone else by then."

"Oh, come on."

Siobhan faces her. "He's in a *band*. Colm won't last a month fending off those American girls, all fawning over his accent, buying him stupid vodka drinks." She mimics a nasal American whimper. "*Ooooh, Coooolm, you have such an adorable accent*, and *Oh, Colm, can I touch your horn?...*"

"Siobhan!" Her laugh is stifled under the girl's wilting glare.

"I'm serious!"

"Well, if he loves you, surely he'll wait." She's told herself the same thing countless times but, stating it aloud, Lise hears how hollow the platitude rings.

"Wait? Right, and I put a fiver out on the sidewalk and it'll be waiting there when I leave here tonight?"

"Not all men are alike, you know."

"Yeah, not all men are like my father."

Or mine. She blinks back the thought. "Siobhan… what do you want to do?"

"To go to the States!" she moans. "But I've only half the fare! And even if I had the rest I can't show up relying on Colm to pay my way once I get there."

"Maybe I could talk to your father?"

"Ha. Talk to *this* for the good it'll do." The girl aims the pricing gun at her. "Haven't you your own affairs to tend to?"

She shrinks. "I do."

Wanting to offer some comfort, she touches Siobhan's shoulder, only to have her hand shaken free. Lise steps back. "Well, if you ever want to talk."

Siobhan ignores her and goes back to blasting labels rapid-fire.

Remy is busy at the back of the shop. In her furious cleaning of the cottage, she's misplaced the paint receipt with directions to the Conners' house. She waits for him to sign a delivery bill before venturing, "I was thinking of stopping out to meet your missus?"

"My Margaret? Oh, God love you, girl, she's been keen to meet you. And I've a page I'd wanted to bring round to her at the lunchtime, but I've six cases of cabinet fittings coming, so I'll be lucky to eat at all, but don't tell her that." He limps to his workbench and pulls out a folded page from his exercise book, slips it into an envelope, writes *Wife* in a looping scrawl. He presses it into her hand. "Tell her I'll be half-six, today." He winks. "Tell her it's a madhouse here. Remember, second right on your way out of town, third house, red postbox."

She buys a cone of carnations from the market and drives to the lane of cottages. Third from the corner, Remy'd said. The house is whitewashed, with red trim. Red plastic geraniums bob at the window boxes. As the knocker drops she smiles, noticing the neatly worded sign under the blue enamel: *Casa Conner*. Hand-painted just beneath is *M. Conner – Cake Maker*.

Remy had described Margaret as lovely, but when the door is opened, Lise is stunned. Margaret has strands of bright silver woven through her jet-black chignon, and white skin precisely creased with smile lines around shockingly green eyes. Her open grin is set with perfect teeth, and her voice emerges as a tune. "Here's our woman then! Welcome!"

Margaret is the grandmother in fairy tales, Lise thinks, stuttering, "H-hello." It's an effort not to stare at the elegant hands bidding her in.

"Remy's just rung five minutes ago, so the tea's near ready. And look, you've brought flowers. Lord, I would've put on a dress if I'd known our pretty stranger was coming to call. Get in, come in now out of this filthy day!"

She is hustled through the hall to a new kitchen, where her coat is peeled from her and shaken. Margaret apologizes for the weather as if personally responsible.

The kitchen is three times the size of the formal parlor they've passed through. "Remy added on," Margaret explains. "Here, y'see, this whole wall is storage. He's magic with the cabinetry, should've been a furniture-maker."

The chrome oven is commercial, flanked by a vast stainless-steel island and two refrigerators. Everything is gleaming and modern, in contrast with the smell that permeates the room. Wafts of cinnamon, clove and juniper recall Christmases past.

Margaret puts the flowers in water while Lise looks around the kitchen. Shelves of clear glass jars are filled with currants, dates, dried cherries and lemon peel. Above the broad flour bins are enough bottles of dark brandy and rum to stock a pub. Opposite the industrial space is a small nook, quaint with upholstered armchairs and a china service set out on starched linen.

"Remy says you were kind enough to bring out his lines?"

"Lines? Oh, his page. Yes!" She pats her skirt pocket and pulls out the envelope.

"Let's see what we have today." After reading, Margaret smiles and lets the page flutter to the counter. "Just a few today. He must be busy down the shop. Every day I get a few. Usually about this or that, some small thing from the day. This morning, with the rain, it was his hands, couldn't do up his own jacket. So I had to for him. Here, you see?" She offers the note.

> *Hands gloved now in crêpe of years,*
> *Ease this rough brow*
> *with silken care,*
> *affix the buttons o'er my heart.*

The poem is dated with small numbers in the corner. Lise looks up. "That's quite lovely."

Margaret nods and eases the paper from her and opens a drawer full of similar notes. "But it wouldn't do to say I showed today's – he hates the arthritis."

Lise peers into the drawer. "These are *all* his?"

"Oh, yes." Margaret laughs. "Years and years' worth. More in boxes about here and there. Some he doesn't even bother dating, as they're no part of the songs."

"Songs?"

"Songs, poems, it's hard to say. He'll put them all in order one day, so he says."

"And he writes them for you *every* day?"

"The old fool thinks I'm his muse or some such nonsense." She tests the teapot with the backs of her fingers, blushing. "It's just Remy's way."

Remy, *a poet*? And married to graceful, gorgeous Margaret. Lise recalls faint words of advice, delivered in her father's voice: *Look harder, Roo. People are so much more than what you see.*

"You'll take milk, then?" Margaret smiles. "These scones are just from this morning, so nearly fresh."

* * *

Margaret is eager to hear about Toronto, the journey over, and how Lise is finding the cottage. Lise sinks into the soft chair and soaks up the warmth and tea. Before Margaret has a chance to ask about family, Lise tells about the storm that kept her tossing under the cottage eaves a few nights before, how several slates were torn from the roof with such force they hove into the wet ground to stand like small headstones.

The old woman shakes her head. "Good Lord, you must be a brave soul, living all alone out there."

"Brave?"

Margaret's voice is pitying. "Such solitude, no comfort but your own…"

There's no way to explain, but Lise has begun to think of the solitude as the cure she hadn't known she'd needed. That it is precisely her own comfort she needs.

After tea, Margaret shows her the rest of the house, pointing out the many things Remy has crafted, even picture frames on the mantel. Their wedding portrait shows them from the shoulders up: a young Margaret stunning and pale, and a half head taller than Remy. He's equally pale, and both look relieved, as if they've just survived something harrowing.

In the next photo, a group in Sunday dress stands on church steps. A more robust Margaret is holding a wailing infant in a long lace dress.

"Danny?"

"The same. Always bawling, always hungry, that one. Screamed through the entire christening. The priest joked he might be a 'Protest-ant'."

Two dark-haired girls are linked on the bottom step below Margaret. "These two must be relations?"

"My twin sisters, Mary and Ruth. They live in Castlebar, married to brothers. Martin and Reggie, so it's Mary and Marty and Ruthie and Reggie."

"Are you close?"

"Ah, sure, once. But twins? They're so like glue to themselves, aren't they?"

Noticing there are no ancestral pictures, she wonders if displaying the dead is bad luck in an Irish house. She nearly asks but then is distracted by the many photos of Siobhan at different ages: toddler, schoolgirl. A Communion portrait shows her full faced and innocent. On what looks to be her eighteenth birthday, Siobhan's hair is long, her brow unpierced. Next to it is Danny and Brigid's wedding photo.

Lise rises on her toes to better see Danny's wife. "She's beautiful." Brigid, freckled, with auburn waves spilling from a crown of daisies, has her arm looped through Danny's as if she'll never let go.

"Our Brigid? Indeed." Margaret sighs. "A real Irish rose."

Drawn back to something awry in the christening photo, Lise notices an odd slice as if a part was cut out.

"Come on, now." Margaret's voice is an octave higher as Lise is pulled away. "Let me show you the cakes."

In a glassed porch off the kitchen, Margaret opens the wide doors of a deep oak cupboard. Alcohol fumes press them back a step.

"That's right. You can get a headful just standing there. D'ya know those poor monks making the brandy up at the abbey can become terrible addicted without taking a drop? On account of being in those hot cellars breathing the fumes all hours. Seeps right through into the blood."

The cakes are lumpy, wrapped in muslin stained from the fruit and brandy. Each soaks in a shallow cask.

Margaret nods. "There they are, drunk as monks."

As if they aren't unappetizing enough, juniper berries scattered over each have darkened to resemble rodent droppings.

"That's one of the secrets, the berries there. Cross yourself, now, that's not to leave this room."

Lise dutifully crosses herself, surprised how automatic and quick the motion is. Her brother, Paul, when crossing himself, would always mumble, just out of their mother's earshot, "Spectacles, testicles, wallet and watch." Lise frowns at the cakes, wondering if he still does.

"Not very gorgeous, are they?" Margaret winks, shutting them away. "But here's a few near finished."

Beneath the bank of windows sit cakes in various stages of decoration. A few are two tiered, but most are single disks, iced a creamy yellow or pale green. Four have been finished, the lumps and uneven edges hidden, their imperfect shapes smoothed under Margaret's touch. Groupings of tiny sugar flowers form wild gardens over hillocks of glaze. Lise blinks at the cakes. They are Irish hillsides and glens.

Off to the side, sheets of parchment are covered with decorations Margaret has fashioned from sugar and egg: irises, thistles, lilies, roses of all hues. There are tiny stone fences and lengths of miniature hedges and stepping stones and minute birds to complete the edible landscapes. A magnifying light swings out from the wall over an array of tools that look more like a dentist's than a baker's. Slim bottles of professional food dyes stand ready on wire racks.

Margaret's endeavor has less to do with cake-making than art, Lise realizes. As the old woman passes the extraordinary cakes, she absently speaks to each, reminding them to whom they belong and when they'll be consumed. "Yer for Colleen Farrel and Tommy Gardner, Friday." She winks. "I've put on a wee yellow daisy for the baby that's coming, no one the wiser." She smoothes patches of icing and fusses over a hedge with a narrow tweezers. At the next cake she mutters, "And you, the fancy tier, for fancy Kit O'Hara and Seamus Trask, Friday as well." Reaching the smallest cake, Margaret tsk-tsks. "And you, poor thing, will be eaten by Mary Ross and her cheap fiancé down Galway." She affixes a horseshoe to lean against a sugar fence. "Poor Mary'll need this extra luck…"

"First cake I ever made was a disaster – my own wedding cake, at that. Looked worse than it tasted, if that's possible. Remy told me his only ever lie over that cake – claimed it was the most delicious thing he'd ever eaten." Margaret begins humming. As Lise watches the old woman minister over this cake or that, the sun comes out to flood the glass porch, illuminating Margaret's face.

Lise sees now she was right to follow her instincts and lug her camera into town despite the dim morning. She moves into the light-washed area of countertops. "Mrs Conner, Margaret, you know I make these little films?"

"Yes, Remy's said. That sounds like a nice hobby."

"It is. And I just had an idea. Watching you working, and now with the sun in this room, I was wondering – would you mind very much if I filmed you awhile?"

"Whatever for?"

"I'm not sure yet, but this is just so…" As she searches for a word, she follows rays of streaming sun, and Margaret follows her gaze. Before Margaret can protest, she sees perhaps what Lise does: each wedding cake a story, with decorations lying about as if plucked from dollhouse gardens, the room bright with yellow light.

"Ah, it *is* pretty, isn't it? And isn't it so, that a person can't see all what's around them until a fresh pair of eyes comes along to show it?"

"So, I'll get my gear?"

"You meant *right* now?"

She nods toward the window, the tenuous daylight. "Yes, actually, while I can."

"All right, then. Sure, you'll make me famous. But let me run a comb through this mop?"

Passing through the parlor, Lise fetches her keys from where they were left on the mantel, next to the christening photo. Light catches an odd edge under the glass. The picture had been altered – a man standing next to Margaret cut away, leaving only a severed suit shoulder. The next person, a priest, has been spliced closer.

As she reaches the front door she hears Margaret's singsong voice.

"The secrets stay in this kitchen."

Chapter Four

The first time Lise was invited to the studio, it was difficult to shake her sense of trespass. Charlie's tables were strewn with notes and sketches, books lay open, and photos and letters hung clipped like laundry to a wire. Dozens of objects were arranged in small vignettes – seashells scattered randomly over shelves and sills as if the surf had tossed them there, vintage inkwells weighting the corners of a drawing to keep it from curling. Stopping at a low table, she looked at Charlie with a question in her eye before touching anything. When he nodded, she reached out to the colors of pale brain corals, a ring of rusted keys from another era, a set of calibrated bronze spheres, and several inexplicable green-glass rods. She ran her hands over the white curves of what she thought was a sculpture before realizing it was some manner of bone: the half pelvis of a large animal.

When she recoiled, Charlie smiled. "Bull."

"I might have guessed. You didn't bring all these things with you?"

"Only the books. Everything else just turned up – either on the tides or in the flea markets in the village, sides of the road... I'm a bit of a junk hound, I'm afraid."

He held out a saucer of sand-polished pebbles. Without thinking, she opened her hand so he could pour them into her palm.

Tubes of paint were arranged by hue on rolling metal tables. With her free hand she picked up the open tube of cadmium red, briefly holding it to her nose. "Smells like you could eat it."

"Well, it's French, so..."

A quick glance passed between them before she stepped away to the corner where a stack of blank canvases leaned like dominoes.

Charlie followed, a tradesman's pride in his voice as he described how the linen was hand stretched and then coated in pure-white lead for the smoothest surface. Lise rattled the pebbles in her hand. Each blank canvas was as blue-white as a square of glacier. She turned and asked, "Was there snow where you grew up?"

"In Wales? Sure, sometimes."

Bending, she placed the pebbles in a spiral pattern over a canvas laid flat to dry on the floor. "If you were to spread these dark stones over snow or ice, they would absorb the heat and sink in to leave perfect holes, no matter how cold the air."

"Really?" He crouched and realigned the pebbles. When he stood, letters making up the name Elle spilled darkly over the white. "Like so?"

"Sure, like that." She swept up the stones in a quick motion. When she tried to hand them back, he folded her fingers closed.

"Keep 'em. Take them back to winter."

Shrugging, she let them cascade into her skirt pocket, a cool rattle against her hip. She swiftly moved to a table of glass jars, where sable and boar's-hair brushes were grouped by size. Some were so delicate they seemed no more than a few twisted eyelashes; others were the size of buds, some nearly the breadth of her palm. Tins of thinners and linseed oils with German labels stood ready. Soft rags were folded in clean stacks. Charlie's standards were evident everywhere she turned. Lise had been in studios before, but this one held something more than the trappings of a painter.

She took in the many canvases. "All water, all oceans. Why not people, or still lifes?"

He raked at his stubble. "Objects are too simple, and people are too complex. I can place myself – my abstract self, anyway – more easily into a seascape. Once I get a sense of whatever cove or beach I'm on, determine what mood the water carries, then I'm free to add my own interpretation, my own impressions. I couldn't do that with a model or an object. D'you understand?"

She touched a corner of a nearby canvas, his signature a near-illegible sienna slash. "I do. Your moods. They're all here, aren't they?"

As he ran a hand through his sandy hair, Lise saw he had grown suddenly shy, perhaps a bit unsure.

A closer look at the paintings revealed how each sea, beneath its hard strokes and bold colors, was tempered with subtler hues, more delicate notes. Perhaps Charlie was a gentler creature than she'd first imagined? She turned suddenly. "You must sing, or play an instrument?"

"God, no. Any pitch I have is in these."

At the large canvas, still wet on its easel, she stepped back and completely unfocused her eye until all detail gave way to composition, line, and light – a technique she used when setting up shots through her camera lens. Letting the dusky seascape slowly reform, she took in the semi-beached remains of a boat, bare ribs casting gloom over the water.

"It's rather somber, isn't it?"

"It's a dirge. I started it before you came, but now I'm too cheerful to finish – I've run out of angst. Here's my latest." He steered her to an unfinished canvas clamped to a smaller easel. "I've only just started this one. It's a bit lighter."

It was the beach she walked before dinner each evening. He'd painted the ocean as blue as it had been the first day when he'd shown her the lookout; the surf was azure and turquoise sea foam – all colors he'd claimed too daring to use. Lise recognized the angle of shoreline and the rise of low cliffs in the distance. Besides the brighter colors, the painting was unlike the others in that it included a small figure: a woman, bent in an *f* shape, shielding her eyes as if to glean something in the surf. Most of the figure's face was half-blurred by a sweep of sun-rusted hair. The hem of her skirt touched the water, the draping of bright yellow cloth familiar. Her breath caught. "That's me!"

"It is."

Heat prickled between her shoulder blades. "I thought you didn't paint people."

"I made an exception."

The sudden dryness in her mouth kept her from responding. When Charlie disappeared into the alcove kitchen to make tea, she stared at her small, still-wet image.

It could mean nothing, of course. He might simply have seen her on the beach and decided to include her on a whim. She forced herself to move on to look at other paintings, trying to concentrate while Charlie plugged in the kettle and rummaged for cups.

Under a skylight she crouched near a stack of heavy artists' books. Volumes of Italian drawings, oils by French masters, and several impressionists. His influences? She chose a volume embossed *Courbet*. Her hand was trembling as she flipped through the pages, letting the book fall open.

The first plate held a terrible darkness: a pond in a deep wood with stags locked in battle at its muddied shore. The animals were desperate-looking, as if prisoners, not creatures, of nature. She sat down cross-legged and pulled the book into her lap. It was a frightening scene, yet held a haunting beauty. The colors were muted and calm, and a far horizon of light pulsed through the canopy of trees, neutralizing the savagery. She leafed forward to other paintings, glad for the distraction of the book, glad to hear Charlie busy at his task, distanced for the moment. The slight tremor in her hand stilled.

One page surprised her as if she'd stumbled upon a secret room. A woman's naked torso was flaunted in melon light – thighs, stomach and one breast in frame, with sturdy thighs open to reveal her sleeping sex, only the faintest line of highlight suggesting the gloss of clitoris.

It was a lovingly wrought image, if a hint disconcerting in its omission of a head. Its title made her grin: *Origin of the World*. She was examining the details of pubic hair so fine she wondered how it was painted. Charlie's voice made her jump.

"Lemon, or milk?" He crouched beside her with two cups.

"Ah, plain."

He set the tea on the floor next to her, nodding at the color plate. "Enchanting, that. Don't you think?"

"Well, I suppose. She's a bit objectified, though." Quickly thumbing back to the stag painting, she mused, "What I wonder is how a painter goes from this" – she fanned the pages forward to the nude – "to *this*."

"Oh, I'd imagine it was the other way around. I'd say she drove poor Courbet into the woods."

The tea was too hot. "It must have been quite risqué, posing like that, back then. I wonder if she felt depraved."

"Or idolized. We don't know if she was *just* his model."

"Courbet's lover? Then this painting would've been their secret?"

"A lovely secret, if that was the case."

She cupped her face, still warm. "This painting was probably never meant for our eyes at all."

"Don't be so sure. If I could paint like that, I'd want the world to know."

"Maybe you would, but would *she*?"

He gave a sideways grin, meeting her eye.

She closed the book. "Why are we drinking tea in this heat?"

"Because I've run out of beer."

Charlie took the volume from her hands and began leafing through it. Within a few minutes he was engrossed.

Closing her eyes and leaning against the cool stucco, she listened to the ocean push itself forward. The Courbet painting flashed across her lids. She wondered if the artist could have truly loved his model, to paint her without a face.

She opened her eyes to Charlie's own work – his many painted oceans, which now, in her discomfort and the heat, seemed to swell toward her. Nearby, the new painting showed her own form bent at the sea. Charlie and Courbet had both painted a woman with her face obscured…

Her sense of trespass drifted back. Perhaps she'd seen enough art. "I should go."

Charlie clambered to his feet and pulled her up. For a moment, they stood close.

"Thanks." She broke away to gather the teacups. He watched her run water in the sink and wash the few dishes. The ease with which he took each cup from her suggested a domestic familiarity. She hurriedly wiped her hands on the towel he offered and walked to the door.

"Charlie?"

They stood at opposite sides of the room, each in the same uncertain posture, as if ready to step closer.

Like the rest of the villa, the studio seemed from another era, heavily beamed, with rough walls and vaulted brick, and in the middle of it stood Charlie, who with his wild hair and nondescript clothing might have been transported through an age himself. Surrounded by his timeless seascapes and the odd archive of objects, Charlie seemed happily rooted. With her hand on the door, Lise ventured, "You were born at the wrong time."

"Maybe." He shrugged and smoothed his hair back. "Maybe so."

Stephen phoned later in the day from a clearing near the dig. He and Gerald had hiked a mile to a high spot in the jungle in hopes of getting a better cell phone signal, but the connection was still punctuated with pockets of dead air. She and Clarice took turns shouting into the phone.

"Yes, I've arrived!" Lise gripped the receiver. "Right, yes, the trip was fine. Adam's fine. We spoke this morning. He's fine! Me? Swimming and reading, mostly. Reading! At the beach. No, the *beach*. Never mind! How's the excavation coming?"

She covered the mouthpiece and winced up at Clarice. "He says 'Excellent', or 'Excrement', I can't tell. He says they may finish soon. I give up." Lise handed over the phone, laughing. "Someone named Gearhole wants to speak to you."

Clarice backed into the pantry, shouting endearments at Gerald, the cord trailing her.

When Lise ran into Charlie in the hall, she didn't meet his eye. "Hi."

"Hi. I heard you laughing. Were you on the phone?"

"Stephen and Gerald called. Seems they'll be back soon."

"Oh. How soon?"

"I'm not sure."

He crossed his arms. "How did you two end up together?"

"Pardon?"

"Sorry. I mean how did you meet?"

She leaned against the wall. It was an innocent enough question. "We met twice, actually."

She'd first been introduced to Stephen at a Glendon soccer match during her senior year. Her courses were in fine arts, his in graduate sciences at McGill in Montreal. He was only in Toronto a few days, visiting his friend Carl, who dated Lise's friend Sandra.

"After the first time we met I barely remembered him, but then a few years later we were thrown together at a dinner party with the same couple. Carl and Sandra were married by then, with kids. It was an obvious setup. We laughed about it." Her tone was matter-of-fact. "They had these two little girls who toddled out to say goodnight, adorable, and there was this moment when Stephen and I looked at each other – the whole family thing didn't look so bad, at least not from the other side."

Charlie nodded.

"Is that the kind of thing you're after?"

Such questions, especially when mingled with the oppressive heat of afternoon, sapped Lise's energy. She had taken to lying down after lunch like everyone else, but seldom slept. She found the word *siesta* had a lovely ring to it. Daydreaming in her shuttered room was as good as having a dream.

Rising at dusk, she was late for dinner and a bit groggy. Charlie ignored the other guests and sat boldly next to her, handing her salt and bread she hadn't asked for. He continued his barrage of questions, and while she found most of them amusing, some stung. When he guessed she had been a lonely child, she defended herself. "Well, I spent a lot of time by myself, but doesn't every kid? I wasn't lonely, exactly; I was watching."

"Watching?"

"People. I sort of spied on people."

"Who?"

"Everyone. My brother, the neighbors, my mother. I even followed strangers sometimes."

"Why?"

She laughed. "I haven't a clue. I suppose I thought I'd find someone with a story, or maybe a secret. I wanted to see where they'd go, what they'd do. I wanted to be intrigued, I suppose." Lise shrugged. "Childish."

"And are you lonely now?"

After folding and refolding her napkin twice, she looked up, no longer caring what her expression might reveal.

Breakfast was served outdoors. Lise was picking over the buffet, balancing a plate of melon and a cup of coffee.

"That's all you're having?" Clarice had appeared next to her.

"Breakfast isn't my meal."

"I'm a bit off myself. But it's only a day or two now."

"Pardon?"

"Until they come home."

"Oh. Right. You must miss Gerald."

Clarice considered Lise. "C'mon. Let's go to the patio."

Lise followed the blond swing of Clarice's hair, moving away from the other guests, who were silently scattered among tables and engrossed in magazines or the week-old newspapers delivered to the villa by post.

"Here OK?" Clarice didn't wait for an answer but settled at the edge of the pool and swung her tanned feet into the cool water. She buttered her croissant, then delicately tore it to bits.

Lise took tiny bites of melon and sipped coffee. After a few minutes she cleared her throat. "Clarice, what do you know about Charles Lowan?"

"I've been thinking of asking you that." Clarice took a gulp of juice and looked into the glass. "You know, I've been all over the tropics, but nowhere is the orange juice as good as it is here." She inhaled deeply. "Listen, sweetie, there've been lots of women here over the years. You're the first Charlie's taken notice of."

"Really?" Lise knew as she spoke that her voice gave her away.

"Lise." Clarice sighed. "Just be—"

"Be what? You were about to say 'careful', weren't you?"

"No, I wasn't. Fine. I'll tell you what I know, but it isn't much. Charlie's not a reckless man, and I doubt he has many skeletons – at least from what I know of him. But he's so very private, I sometimes suspect he means to be isolated, alone. He'd deny it, of course." Clarice squinted into the sun. "I know it's none of my business, but what about Stephen, Lise?"

Lise shrugged. She hadn't allowed herself to think of her husband, didn't want to.

"Well." Clarice tipped her face, inhaling deeply. "It's going to be hot again today."

The day did grow dreadfully warm, but Lise braved the beach under the cover of a wide-brimmed sun hat and a linen shift worn over her swimsuit. The stretch of sand shimmered under the blur of heat, so she found a wedge of shade under a palm trunk. After a few restless minutes she settled and began digging in the sand with a scallop shell, delicately burrowing around a length of half-buried driftwood.

The bone-white shape reminded her of the ice man. When she'd been a child, a prehistoric man had been found near a glacier, preserved in a stratum of ice. He'd been chipped out in a great block and hauled to a Swiss laboratory. Her father had followed news of the discovery for months and brought home scientific journals and newspaper clippings, which Lise read over his shoulder. Experts had pieced together the man's life and discovered, among other things, that he was a vegetarian, that his leather garments had been sewn by a left-handed person, and that his calluses and musculature suggested he was some manner of farmer, an early agrarian. The cause of his death was determined to be a skull fracture acquired during a fatal fall.

Lise had been fascinated by the idea that mere ice could preserve such detail. So much about the man was known that she thought it disturbing. How awful, to be dug up and probed by scientists – men who could learn so much from a body but cared nothing about the man's thoughts or emotions, or his last moments of fear as he plummeted.

She was patting sand back over the driftwood when Charlie crouched next to her and said, "You're looking far off." He handed her a chalky blue shell. "What are you thinking of?"

"Oh, ancient stuff. There was this ice mummy found when I was a little girl. My father and I used to read about it." She leaned away, gripping the shell and shifting deeper into the sand.

"You lost him, didn't you?"

She knew he meant her father. "The ice man?"

"Don't be coy."

"'Lost' isn't quite the word. He was alive; then he was gone."

"Were you… were you angry when he died?"

She bit the inside of her cheek and shrugged the question away.

"Lise—"

"Lots of children lose their fathers, Charlie. I barely even remember…" But even as she spoke, Lise fought the tug that could drag her back over the jagged moments of that afternoon.

She'd felt for her father's pulse, swallowing against the sick taste rising up her throat. Easing his last letter from the typewriter, she shivered. And she'd shivered reading the letter, too, violently cold even while crouched in front of the bright hearth where she would burn it. She'd poked the black scroll of it until ash rose in a vortex – his last words twisted away in curls of smoke. Her fingertip, she remembered, had streaked the numbers of the dial as she telephoned for help. Lise could occasionally glimpse such images, but felt nothing but the cold.

Her hand was suddenly stilled. She realized Charlie was pressing it between his. "You're shaking."

"It's getting chilly."

"It's not," he said softly. "What happened?"

"He died. Listen. You don't want all this." She tossed aside the shell Charlie had so carefully chosen for her.

He handed her another.

Stephen and Gerald returned a day sooner than anticipated. Most everyone in the villa grew excited when the filthy truck and two Jeeps roared through the gates. The early arrival clearly meant good news regarding the dig. In the deepest cavern of the half-buried Mayan temple, they had discovered the cache of ritual pieces Stephen had long suspected would be there, more than a hundred artifacts. Even at a distance, Lise could read the triumph on his face. He was speaking to the official from the Bureau of Antiquities, who was supervising the handling of the objects. There was also an official translator from Mexico City.

Charlie was nowhere to be seen, though surely he would have heard the commotion. Lise wondered if he'd deliberately stayed away.

She watched her husband from a distance. Staff and guests lined the drive to watch as the students and hired laborers carefully unloaded the many crates. She waited unnoticed for an hour before retreating back into the empty villa. In her room Lise drew her drapes against the sight, against the euphoria she could not feel.

Stephen located her much later, on the path near the kitchen garden.

"Hello." Her arms were folded over the chest of her sundress, so that when he hugged her, her elbows awkwardly caught his middle.

"Isn't it great?"

"It is. Finally. I'm so glad for you, Stephen."

He'd spent years on the project, had begun researching only a few years after Adam was born. He'd barely finished his site work and a text on Iroquois burial mounds in Quebec when he'd begun trekking to Mexico. Other, lesser projects came and went, other chunks of time were spent working under senior archaeologists. But the Mayan project was solely Stephen's. He'd poured so much energy and time, so much thought, into his work, Lise had to admire his dedication. Whole seasons were spent poring over survey maps, aerial photographs, logs of previous searches and regional histories. Standard luggage on their few family vacations had included composite renderings, cell phones, and, more recently, laptop computers with GPS. For the past few years, Stephen had been completely engrossed in the Mayan ruin, all of his time eaten up with the bureaucracy of the Mexican government, university approval, and fund-raising. At the beginning she had considered his many trips away a necessary sacrifice and had endeavored to occupy herself and Adam until he returned.

Stephen's face was full of apology. "We have to go to Mexico City in a day or two, to get permission to take examples to Los Angeles."

She smiled crookedly, certain she was not included in his "we". "Why LA?"

"The lab there has the best carbon-dating equipment. Gerald's chartering a plane. Just a small one. I'm afraid only the crates and two of the students can go."

"But that's wonderful."

"Yeah. But this hasn't been much of a vacation for you, has it?"

"It's fine. Really." She looked him in the eye. "It's what I'm used to."

Before he could respond, Gerald trotted up, winking and giving her one of his crushing hugs. "Sorry to steal him away when we've just arrived, but I need him in the study for a minute."

"Go on, then." She kissed Gerald's cheek and patted her husband's arm before waving off the two men.

Stephen knocked on her door and peered in, scanning the space and frowning at the narrow bed. "You've your own room?"

"It's where they put me," she lied. He'd just begun to step in and close the door when Flora interrupted with a timid voice from the hall. Stephen was being summoned again, this time for a phone call.

Later, during dinner, Stephen sat at the head of the table and held forth on the dangers and difficulties of the days in the jungle. He relayed accounts of unearthing the various masks, bowls and tools. He had shaved and soaked off weeks of jungle grime to expose his deep tan and the lighter crow's feet at each temple. Lise saw his body was fit from the work and he'd grown a bit shaggy and less academic-looking. He'd refused Mercedes's offer to trim his hair, gone quite blond from the sun. She noted this new handsomeness as if from afar, noted also that it failed to stir her.

The chair next to hers, Charlie's chair, was occupied by one of the students. She hadn't seen Charlie all day. Neither had Clarice or the maids. She wondered if he was eating in the village.

After dinner there was a sort of informal exhibit. The entire population of the villa filed through the kitchen garden to see the objects displayed on long tables. They leaned over the numbered items, crowding the space, wanting to touch. The servants seemed very curious but held back a few steps behind the guests.

Lise stood quietly near the wall with Mercedes and Flora, wondering if the women felt some birthright or connection to these treasures about to be spirited away by the gringos, but their faces revealed little.

The studio windows were dark. Charlie still wasn't around. Picking her way back, she detoured down to the path to the beach, where the crescent of sand was deserted save for a few couples walking in the dusk and some youngsters feeding driftwood into the orange sparks of a beach fire. She sighed and climbed back up to the patio, where guests had settled. Lise kicked off her sandals and took a glass of wine before sitting at the shallow end of the pool.

"Want to take a walk down to the beach?" Stephen was leaning over her.

"I've just come from there." When she splashed her feet in the shallows, drops of pool water landed in her wine glass. "Besides" – she raised her glass – "I was planning to get drunk."

"You don't like being drunk."

"No. *You* don't like me being drunk. You say I get too quiet, then I go to sleep."

"Right." He sat down, took off his own shoes and eased his feet into the pool. He clicked his glass to hers. "Well. Cheers, then."

Around midnight she made her way upstairs, guiding herself along the rough stucco of the stairwell. In her room she drank water and paced until she felt sober. When she curled into a hammock out on the balcony with a novel, the print wavered, making her woozy. She closed the book but stayed outside, knowing that if Charlie did come back, he would have to pass her way. Enveloped in the tropical dark, swaying ever so slightly, Lise realized how taxing the harsh day had been: too hot and too bright. She concluded that night was much kinder, even with its chill. Sometime during the night she woke very stiff, with the skin of her arm quilted by the hammock's pattern. Rubbing her arm and walking back past the doors of the sleeping guests, she noticed Charlie's sandals had been left outside his door. He hadn't gone for good, as she'd feared.

When she emerged from her room at noon, the staff were running in circles preparing for the celebration dinner Gerald had requested. He and Stephen would be setting off for Mexico City the next day. Lise offered to help and was sent for extra hanging lights for the patio. While the gardeners set up long tables, she and Clarice decorated the fig trees with strings of lights and made small talk. Neither had mentioned Charlie since their morning by the pool.

After they finished, Clarice talked her into a quick shopping trip to the village. "Please? I saw this dress you'd look smashing in. C'mon, Stephen will love it."

They drove to a little boutique on the tourist end of the village, where she reluctantly allowed Clarice to make a gift of the dress, which was short and black and held together with a number of tropical-bright yellow and green straps. The dress was overtly provocative and much better suited to Clarice, who knew how to move in such a garment.

When they returned to the villa it was siesta time, but Lise wasn't at all tired. Tossing the dress box onto the bed, she changed and hastily tied a sarong over her swimsuit. She would go to the beach, and if Charlie wanted to find her, he would.

When she came down to the party, Stephen took in the dress and her painted lips and nodded approvingly. "That's better."

Her lids felt oddly heavy under a coating of mascara; her ribs were cinched by the architecture of the dress. Trying to keep her voice light, she asked, "What do you mean, 'better'?"

"More like yourself."

She felt less herself than she had since arriving in Mexico. Even the bracelet on her wrist felt like a prop.

During pre-dinner cocktails she took a cigarette from a pack left at the bar and slipped away to a corner. Realizing she had no match to light it, she was about to move back toward the crowd when a hand reached through the palm fronds, offering a familiar lighter. She laughed. "Charlie!" Pressing the greenery aside, she whispered, "Where've you *been*?"

"Sulking. Are you all right?"

"Yeah. I'm not sleeping well."

He stepped out. "I know. I saw you pass my window as it was getting light."

She frowned. "You were up? You should have come out."

"I did. I thought you were sleepwalking. I only watched until you'd made it to your door."

The dinner gong rang. They shrugged at the same time, and Charlie made an "after you" motion toward the table, murmuring, "That's quite a dress."

"Ugly, isn't it?"

He grinned. "Yes."

Dinner was a loud affair with many toasts. She and Stephen were seated next to each other. Clarice had hired a trio of musicians to roam the patio with their guitars. When they noticed Stephen's arm settle briefly over Lise's shoulder, they drifted over to serenade them with a love song. As the lyrics wore on, Lise concentrated on a candle flame, praying Charlie wouldn't turn to see Stephen's fingers tapping the rhythm over her bare arm.

After the table was cleared, dessert was served with cognacs and coffee. Fresh glasses and demitasse cups appeared on the linen. Later, cigars, liqueurs and narrow flutes of champagne were pressed around. Gerald had pulled his best vintages from the wine cellar. All around Lise, people were getting happily drunk.

The trio settled in a corner of the terrace, and guests partnered to dance. She fought a sudden desire to lay her head on the table.

Gerald appeared, bending to offer his arm. "Dance, madam?"

"Oh, Gerald, I can't."

He slurred, "A courshe you can!"

"No. I mean, really. I got too much sun today – I'm practically boiled."

"You do look a little flushed." Stephen pushed himself up, using the table edge. "C'mon. I'll take you upstairs."

"No." She sprang up. "This is your party! You stay and celebrate. I'm just going to have a bath and take an aspirin."

"Right, well, it is eleven o'clock, after all."

"Sorry."

He brushed her mouth with a rough kiss. "Get some rest, then."

Nodding goodnight to the other guests, she passed Clarice, who winked approvingly, but then clucked, "You're *not* going up already?"

"I am." She yawned hugely and hurried from the patio. As she reached the loggia, an explosion of laughter made her turn back. Gerald and Stephen were locked in each other's arms, swaying in an exaggerated tango, each clenching a Cuban cigar sideways, like a lit rose.

She walked along, tugging at the waistband of the dress. A moving glint within one of the dark arches startled her until she realized it was the glow of Charlie's cigarette. He didn't move from the pillar he leaned against, only bowed slightly, raising his glass to her.

Noise from the party edged under the pillow over her head. An hour later Lise got up, pulled on a robe, and stepped into her espadrilles to creep down the outer staircase.

Music and voices drifted over the high wall separating the front of the villa from the rear. On the servants' side, along the kitchen path, she heard lower, more serious voices from behind the courtyard door, locked and guarded since the artifacts from the dig had been secured there. Stepping up on a cistern, she steadied herself with a thick vine and peered over the wall.

Charlie, still in his dinner jacket, stood with the gardeners, Mercedes and the hired guard. All were huddled at the long tables, examining the tagged and numbered items. With a battery torch, Charlie washed a beam of light over each item and then listened intently as the servants quietly discussed the artifact; one or another of them seemed to know a bit of the history or significance of each object. Under one table was a crate of lesser finds: common household utensils and broken crockery still crusted with lime or dried earth. Charlie reached in and pawed through, pulling out as many items as there were people surrounding him. He put something in his breast pocket, then placed the rest of the items on the ground. Rising from his crouch, he looked directly at Lise, as if he knew all along she'd been watching. His eyes locked hers while the servants stooped one by one to slip their choice into waistbands or under aprons. Charlie turned his flashlight off so that only dim starlight washed the courtyard tiles, so only their eyes were visible.

Guitar chords from the party mingled with murmurs as the Mexicans quietly slipped away. The music serenaded Lise's slow climb up the steps and along the balcony to her room, where the theft played through her mind and followed her into sleep, so that by dawn she had to convince herself the scene wasn't a dream.

A movement outside her door woke her completely. Someone tried her latch and, finding it locked, shuffled away, coughing.

She brought Stephen's shirts to Flora to iron, and in broken Spanish managed to request that the girl pack Stephen's suitcase, a chore Lise usually performed herself. As Lise turned out the laundry door, Mercedes walked in with a look of disapproval, asking, "You not go to Los Angeles, señora?"

"No." She looked squarely at Mercedes. "I'm staying here."

* * *

She went to the fountain in the afternoon while the Jeeps were being loaded. Stephen found her there. His scuffed leather duffel pulled down one shoulder and he held a briefcase in his other hand. When he spoke, his voice was hoarse. "We've just finished packing up."

Lise's hand was held under the water's surface, pressed to the bottom over green and silver coins. "Is something wrong?"

"Several artifacts are missing."

"Really? Actually missing, or just lost?"

"Well, they didn't walk off."

"Stolen, then. Anything important?"

"That's the weird part. What's gone is so common... worthless, really." A horn blasted at the gate and he inhaled. "That's us, I'm afraid."

"Have a good trip."

He took a step. "Listen. This will all be over soon, right?"

"This? You mean your work?" She shook her head. "I don't think so, Stephen. It's what you love." Lise reached out to touch him, to show she wasn't angry. "I've only just realized how much of your life this really is."

"Lise." He looked tired, as he often was at the end of one of his projects. But he would rally, as he always did, and in a few months he would revive to fuse onto the next thing.

"When this dig is finished and you've written all the articles and dotted all the *i*'s, you'll start another."

In the pause they looked at each other, and for an instant Lise thought they might connect a moment to see, in some simultaneous revelation, that it was time to forgo the pretense and admit that their future would be an exact mirror of their past. But just then a car horn bleated. Stephen closed his eyes, dropping his head. "Shit. They're waiting."

"I know. Don't worry. It's fine." And though he hadn't asked, she added, "*I'm* fine."

When his hand pressed her shoulder, she closed her eyes. When she opened them, he was gone.

* * *

Staring into the water long after the rumble of vehicles had faded, she watched her silhouette waver in the basin of hopeful coins – a hundred wishes had been made there and forgotten. Digging in her skirt pocket, she found a newly minted coin. With no idea of its worth, she tossed it among the others.

Clarice walked slowly up the drive. Even tearful she looked elegant. "I wondered where you were. Have you been sitting here this whole time?"

"Oh, Clarice, don't cry. They'll be back soon."

"I'm not used to it the way you are, Lise." She dabbed her running mascara. "Gerald and I have only been separated a few times."

She squeezed Clarice's hand. "You'll get used to it."

"I will not." She sat down and glanced into the fountain, to the new coin. "Dare I ask what you wished for?"

"Don't."

She took a shaded path through dark foliage to where strains of an opera wept through Charlie's open windows. He stood at a high drafting table under a lamp, sketching with quick, sure movements. A cone of tungsten light isolated him from the recesses of the studio. When she stepped from the palms, he raised his head as if sensing something. After a moment he sharpened a pencil and went back to work. They were no more than ten feet from each other. Neither reacted to the shrill noises of a volleyball game floating up from the beach below. Strange, she thought, how solitary she and Charlie seemed, in the midst of everything.

She sat next to Clarice during dinner, assuming her host might need cheering, but Clarice was upbeat, announcing halfway through the meal that she'd decided to follow Gerald to Mexico City, and that she'd be leaving in the morning. "To surprise him." Clarice kissed Lise's cheek hard. "You'll help hold the fort?"

* * *

The next afternoon, Lise found the studio door ajar. Charlie motioned her in without a word. He was wearing street clothes, a loose shirt over linen trousers and rope sandals.

"You're not painting?"

He shook his head. "I thought you might be going to the airport with Clarice, and I had this weird idea she'd convince you to go along. I was going to walk to the village and get drunk."

"But I'm here." She smiled and turned to the painting of herself on the beach. "You've finished?"

"Just last night."

More detail had been added: the stretch of her arm, her hand reaching toward something under the surface, just beyond her grasp. Minute strokes had filled in her profile.

Charlie stepped close behind her. "See your neck there? I had to rely on memory for that." He reached out and trailed his finger from the arc of her shoulder to the base of her skull. "I see now I got it right."

Individual hairs of her scalp shifted under his touch. "It's a good likeness."

"I was just ready to sign it." He chose a delicate brush and two tubes of grey. After looking more closely at the color of her eyes, he shook his head and opted for a darker tube. "Odd, isn't it, how eyes change one day to the next."

Lise said nothing, only watched as he bent to paint *C. Lowan.* He straightened.

"I saw you at the fountain yesterday, after your man left."

She nodded.

"You don't love him, do you?"

"I thought I did."

"Sorry, I needed to know."

She looked at the door. "I can't stay. I promised Clarice I'd help Mercedes and the cook plan menus for the next few days." At the threshold she took his hand, turned it over to smooth the red-blond hairs at his wrist. It was the first lingering contact she'd allowed herself. It felt as she'd imagined it would. Better.

Halfway through dinner she excused herself. The guests seemed to be holding their own, and Charlie hadn't come – earlier she'd seen his note telling the cook he wouldn't be eating. She wasn't hungry either. She took a bottle of limeade to her room and drank it sitting cross-legged on the bed, watching out her window as the sky dwindled to quarter light.

Charlie had been forthright with her. But what did she really know of him? He was gifted, he thought her beautiful and he was a thief. Of his past she knew very little. But couldn't he say the same of her, for the many questions she'd only half answered? They were nearly strangers. But the way he looked at her, the way his hand had perfectly cradled hers, did it matter?

For the first time in the villa she fell quickly, deeply asleep.

She woke in darkness. After showering, she pulled on a nightgown that was too good for sleeping in, feeling its silk sigh over her ribs and hips. Covering her bare shoulders with an embroidered shawl, she slipped out onto the balcony, listening for signs of life.

Feeling each tile underfoot, she crept along, barely breathing until her hand found the wood grain of his door. The latch made only the slightest noise. Following the sound of his breath, she settled herself lightly on the edge of the bed. When she found her voice, she whispered, "Were you dreaming?"

He knew exactly where her hand was. "I still am."

Their first moments were tender, but Lise soon grew anxious. Her own body seemed suddenly unfamiliar; an odd tightness constricted her chest.

She pulled away and sat up.

Charlie said nothing as her hands slipped from his. Minutes passed with only a ribbon of breath between them. As if from far off, as if from above, Lise could see herself – half-naked and curled away from Charlie, her hands folded into fists. And she could see Charlie too, his patient concern, his careful watch over her, as if she were something rare.

When he touched her again, it was to wrap her in the shawl. His arms encircled her and his chin lightly balanced on her shoulder. With his cheek to her ear, he began gently rocking her in the dark. They swayed until her breath evened and her head rested against his shoulder. He rose from the bed and helped her to her feet.

Was he sending her away?

He slipped his arm lightly around her waist and turned her in a waltz, humming a tune so quietly there was no telling what it might be. As they moved through the louvered shadows, he brought her hand to his mouth and kissed her palm before pressing it over his heart. As he hummed she felt the tones change in the chambers of his chest. Their dance slowed, her light exhalation filling the shallow above his collarbone.

The shawl was wrapped around both of them. When they let go, silk rippled down to pool at their feet.

Chapter Five

Danny Conner seems thrilled she's accepted his offer, although Lise has made it clear over the phone that the cruise is to gather footage – it's not a jaunt, and certainly not a date. To ensure there's no misunderstanding, she insults him by offering to pay for the petrol.

She drives to the pier early, sets up her camera and lines up a shot in her viewfinder; all five trawlers bumping against the slips, all with *Brigid* emblazoned on their sterns. When Danny comes out of his dockside office, he grins at her old car parked next to his new Land Rover. "You drove here in that?"

"And I'll get home in it too."

Brigid II, as promised, is clean, freshly washed, with droplets rolling across her spar-varnished trim. Below deck is a tiny galley with an ell of cushioned seating around a table. There is a cramped toilet Danny calls the head. *Brigid II* was a fleet boat, he explains, but he's converted it to suit his own use, sport-fishing. She sees no sign of fishing gear and surmises which sport he means after ducking her head into the sleeping cabin. Backing out, she stifles a giggle. Only a man who has seen too many Bond films would have furnished his trysting place so, with a velvet bedspread, a marble Venus on the half shell, recessed lighting and a headboard covered with a smoked mirror. She pulls the door firmly shut.

He's brought "a little something" Margaret has sent along after hearing Lise is Danny's passenger: salmon cream and cucumber on fresh rye, a salad of cress, grown in her own cold frame, walnut pâté and gingered pears.

"You'll thank her for me?" She watches as he wedges the lunch containers into a tiny refrigerator crammed with beer.

Danny adds his own offering, pulling two cartons of Michelob out to make room, light and regular. "Six for you, and six for me." He opens two bottles and hands her one.

Noticing her boots, Danny shakes his head disapprovingly and rummages through a locker full of women's deck shoes, tossing her a pair.

She wriggles into them. "Perfect."

On deck they get ready to launch, hoisting up dock buffers and undoing ropes ringed around little anvils bolted to the deck. "Cleats," Danny corrects, over-enunciating.

"Cleats," she repeats, hissing the s.

In the pilothouse he turns a key and pushes a button, and the engine rumbles to life.

As they leave the pier, she secures her tripod, running safety wires to either side of the fore rail and to the hatch.

Beyond the jetty the prow slices easily through low swells. The village and then the harbor grow small in her lens. Farther out, the swells grow to gentle rollers. She asks Danny to swing in closer, and he angles the boat more landward. Several miles north, he throttles down the engine, taps on the glass and points to far hills, where a lane of roofless cottages are planted into the hillcrest, the spine of a ruined village. On the slopes below, hundreds of sheep are pastured. She pans her camera along the abandoned village and over the vast herd, strewn like wedding rice.

Danny comes out of the pilothouse and tells Lise to aim higher. In the viewfinder his finger points to the highest peak, where a rambling salmon-colored house rises like a blemish. She's about to comment on its ungainliness when he claims, "There's my place."

"Big." She can think of nothing else to say.

Danny is as good as his word, taking her farther north to her own beach. He tries to explain the formula for converting miles into knots, but she is so excited to see her own stretch of coast that she can't concentrate. They swing in close where she can film her cottage and the hills beyond. Danny waits for her to clip in a new reel before curving away to approach from another angle.

The two small islands that seem so mysterious from her beach are a disappointment close up – barren ramps of granite skirted with algae. She would like to walk them, but Danny shows her there's no good landing place.

Down the coast they drop anchor in the cove fronting the caravan park Danny owns. On the grassy stretch above the beach, she counts nearly thirty caravans, each so close to its neighbor a bottle could easily be passed from one window to the next. Laundry is strung to dry close to the charcoal grills wafting smoke that stinks of rank meat and lighter fluid. Up the slope beyond the boundary marking Danny's land is another cluster of caravans, vintage, in varying states of disrepair and windowlessness. One is hooked up to harness hitches, and another is bereft of wheels altogether. The rubbish around these older wrecks is impressive, the laundry more colorful, adding cheer to the refugee-camp air. It's like a small village, Lise thinks as she turns to Danny. "Who?—"

"Travelers," he sniffs.

"Like Gypsies?"

"Squatters."

On the beach below, an aluminum can rolls in a tide pool, and plastic-bag tumbleweeds have snagged on the legs of plastic chairs to billow like jibs. Children zag furiously along the sand in a game of tag, grabbing at one another's scarves and making shrieks of the pitch all children seem to acquire at water's edge. *Brigid II* is anchored close enough that Lise can make out faces through her long lens. She zooms in to isolate a middle-aged couple, immobile on their campstools. Both are wrapped tight in anoraks, eating chips with stony expressions aimed slightly away, as if avoiding the other's eye. They remind her of herself and Stephen during their last months together. She refocuses, asking Danny to hold the boom out over the water. "Would you?"

"This is a thing, isn't it? Looks like a squirrel on a stick."

"The fur makes a sort of windbreak, to keep out the sound." Lise reaches to adjust the microphone.

"What's this film about, anyway? My mother says you were in her kitchen this week and last to film her working over those damn cakes. Said you were asking after her and my father. It's not about *them*, is it?"

He is talking nearly into the boom. She turns almost imperceptibly so that Danny is just in frame, the beach and the unhappy couple visible over his shoulder.

"I haven't a clue. Maybe *love*, if anything."

"*Love*! Well, then why be asking an old woman?"

She laughs. "And why not?"

Danny rolls his eyes.

"Should I be asking you, Danny?"

"Sure, maybe I know something."

She aims straight on. "Tell me about love, then. What makes it work?"

"Work? Succeed, like?" He thinks a moment. "I s'pose it's mostly a matter of saying the right things at the right time, isn't it? Remembering the right dates and buying the proper gifts. Keeping them happy."

He seems so pleased with his answer that she can only sigh. "Have you a girlfriend now?"

"A girl? I'd say I've one sort of regular" – he wobbles his hand – "and a possible second."

"Second? Never mind. When was the last time you *really* fell for someone?"

"Ah, that's history."

"Brigid?"

He looks away. "Yeah."

"Why'd you fall for her?"

He stares over the waves until his jaw loses its edge. "I dunno, lots of reasons. I remember this certain smell she had, you know, like something new. And those gorgeous legs that went on forever. We met at a dance down in Cork, and after one turn around the room with her I couldn't swallow." He scrutinizes Lise. "But you seem the skeptical sort. Maybe you don't believe in love at first sight?"

"Maybe I do." She remembers stepping through Charlie's door as if it were that morning. When he'd turned from his easel, something shifted in her throat and she thought, *Now here's someone*. And the look he'd given her. Danny's eye holds a similar look when he speaks of Brigid. In a softer voice she repeats, "Maybe I do."

"Well, that's what it was. After her I couldn't concentrate on anything, any*one* else."

"And what's she like herself?"

"Well, I couldn't say now, could I, since she's off me."

"What happened?"

"I s'pose she wanted something more, I guess, or maybe less – I'm not very good at the kind of talk women want. I've other needs, if you know."

"You mean sex? I'm wondering about *real* intimacy, Danny."

"You're awfully bold." He frowns. "You're in bed with someone, believe me, *that's* intimate. Maybe you shouldn't analyze so much. Might do *you* good, to just... seems yourself could use some."

She blanches. "Some *what*, Danny?"

He glowers at the camera as if just remembering it. Lise lowers it but leaves it running, so only Danny's shoes and deck appear in the viewfinder.

"So you loved Brigid, but were you friends?"

He stares at her. "That's such shite. Married 'friends'."

"Why's it shite?"

"You answer questions with questions, you know that? I've plenty friends, I didn't need another at home." Danny's foot taps angrily, centered in frame.

"Margaret and Remy are great friends, I'd say."

"Ah, they're just used to each other. Besides, they're old. What else's left to them?"

"Maybe their best years?"

"Good grief."

"All right, so you couldn't be friends with Brigid?"

"Christ, no. I was in love with her." He's genuinely irked now, jabbing his finger toward the high peak where his house stands. "I didn't build that for any friend, but for a wife. Brigid had no lack for anything. Anything! The fecking paint hardly dry, and her bags were packed." He shook his head. "Women. We give you everything, and it's never enough, never what you want."

"Did you ever ask – what she wanted, I mean?"

"Now you're after lecturing me – Christ, you sound just like her. She wanted more of one thing and I more of another. End of story."

She discreetly presses the *Off* button. Danny silently hands her the boom and turns away.

The trawler rocks and they eat lunch in near silence.

When Danny bends to catch a paper napkin blowing across the deck, a thin gold chain falls free of his shirt, a delicate wedding band caught in its links.

He meets her eye as he tucks it away. "You asked what she's like? Well, she's smart as anything – a nurse, and a damn good one. And witty too, great sense of humor on her – like Siobhan on a good day."

"She sounds lovely."

"And patient, now that I think about it. So fucking patient." He looks away. "She put up with her share, I suppose. Had good enough reason to go, in the end."

Like Siobhan, he flinches when she reaches for his shoulder, but he doesn't jerk away.

They have coffee and Margaret's pears for dessert. When she asks about the coast and the abandoned village near his land, Danny becomes more spirited. "That settlement was abandoned fairly recently, only about forty years back. There're other emptied villages along the coast, either burnt out or cleared." Danny launches into the sad and violent history of the area, recounting tales of much earlier times, when abbeys and churches were destroyed by Vikings. He can list what lands within his county were disputed by which crowns. Shaking his salt-clogged pen, he charts Cromwell's bloody path on a map he draws over his napkin. He knows details of the famine that shock her: over a distant hill in one mass grave more than three thousand of the starved are buried. He can recount what tribes of families either emigrated or died out.

Danny reminds her a bit of Stephen. So full of facts: more at ease in knowledge than in matters of the heart.

She hands him another beer. "You and Stephen would get on well."

"Your husband?"

"Ex-husband."

"You miss him?"

"No." They both laugh.

"So you weren't friends either?"

"You've got me there, Danny. No. We weren't, and he wouldn't be wearing my ring on a chain."

"What happened?"

"It was more what didn't happen. Then I left." It's her turn to go quiet. She hunches into her collar while Danny clears away the lunch scraps. After he winches the anchor up, he disappears into the pilothouse to restart the engine. When it's roaring he sticks his head out.

"C'mon in here. You'll freeze out there."

"I'm fine. I want the air."

Danny shrugs. "Hearty sort, huh?"

At the rail, she slides to the deck to sit, draping her legs over the bow. Icy spray needles through her stockings. As the boat meets heavier water, she remembers to watch the horizon. To avoid becoming seasick she keeps a bead on the land, letting her center move with the swells – advice she'd tried giving Charlie on the night they'd nearly drowned.

Charlie had suggested the charter. They chose the evening cruise because it left from the pier at the far end of the village, where they were less likely to be spotted. Guests at the villa would be eating dinner at that hour, and those who might be out would never visit this seedier side of the village, full of cheap *mercados*, street vendors and beggars.

The evening cruise was meant to be romantic, with hors d'oeuvres and dancing. The brochure tempted: *Deluxe Sunset Cruise*. Lise and Charlie were joined by twelve Americans from a package hotel – couples from places like Fort Wayne, Raleigh and Minneapolis. Several were sunburnt and tired-looking, and one young bride appeared ill even before they were under way. Milling on deck, passengers introduced themselves in various drawls and, once assembled, were given waivers to sign and life jackets that no one put on. They were served warm champagne in plastic flutes and were directed to the banquet table, where cheese curled on squares of rye, and mushrooms were wrapped in undercooked bacon.

Lise didn't care. She was just happy to be able to hold Charlie's hand in public. The paper plates and diesel smell seemed a small price for that. They toasted the newlyweds, and then, more quietly, themselves.

About forty minutes into the cruise, the first gust came. Charlie was talking to an engineer from Vermont when a fluke of air lifted a plastic chair and vaulted it over the rail. Skirts billowed comically. Hats were caught in midair. Passengers swayed and steadied themselves. There was laughter and in a moment it was forgotten. The yacht continued on course.

The steward frowned at the chair bobbing in the wake. He cleaned up spilled champagne and a scattering of crackers.

Puzzling in the direction of the gust, he dropped his mop and called out something to his mate. They stood at the railing with binoculars, staring as if transfixed at the fast-moving cloud bank on the horizon.

One of the stewards shouted and the captain came out and watched the approaching storm through his binoculars for a full minute before giving the order. As soon as they began putting their life vests on, a swell from seemingly nowhere tilted the deck a full thirty degrees. Stewards scurried about, grabbing people as they fell. As the boat righted, passengers' laughter was thin and nervous. Everyone fumbled to fix the straps of their orange vests.

The squall came so fast that by the time they were ushered below deck the boat was already heaving. The cabin was a low-ceilinged lounge set with small cocktail tables bolted to the floor. Long upholstered benches flanked the room under banks of portholes. Rain churned over the glass, reminding Lise of a washing machine. As the boat veered into waves, the engine roared, propellers bucking free above the water.

Passengers clung to whatever or whomever they could. She was wedged on a bench between Charlie and a heavyset midwestern woman. The three of them managed to keep up some banter those first few minutes. When the boat wrenched sideways, the bride across the aisle became ill. Her husband tried prying her from the vomit-spattered life vest, but one of the crew stopped him.

In spite of the engine's roar, they came no closer to land. Lise's hand became numb from clutching the table to stay anchored. When a silence fell behind the waves and rain, the crew looked at one another with wide eyes. The engine had died. A junior steward backed up against the steps. They all leaned, straining to hear as the captain turned the starter. It ground once, twice; then the motor shuddered to life for a few seconds before cutting out.

Charlie had gone completely quiet, his arm clamped around her. When she saw his fear, she began to whisper the sorts of calming things she might say to Adam during a thunderstorm: "It's OK. Just a stupid storm. Just God making a fuss." But she knew it was more than a stupid storm. She'd sailed with her father and Paul on Lake Ontario, in weather only half as rough, where they'd had a few close calls but had never encountered waves like those battering the cruise boat. To capsize in Lake Ontario meant exposure and hypothermia in freezing water. Her father had solemnly explained how freezing was quick and merciful. As peaceful, he claimed, as the death of the man in the Jack London story, the one who couldn't keep his fire lit and finally gave up his struggle, closing his ice-lashed eyes.

But the warm Gulf waters of Mexico would not provide any numb or merciful end. Sharks would assure some agony. Lise shuddered.

There was a flurry of instructions in rapid-fire Spanish. The hatch was pried open and switches were thrown. When one of the crew jumped into the bilge compartment there was a distinct splash as he hit standing water. Charlie blinked at her once, stony faced, then looked away to stare mutely out the porthole. She turned his chin to see his eyes oddly focused. *Shock?*

She'd heard that distraction sometimes helped shock victims. She should talk to him, tell a story or recite some poem. None came. Charlie had been hounding her for details of her childhood, but she'd half-jokingly denied ever having one. There was convent school, and summers at the family cottage on Lake Baptiste, but even those times seemed too soft-edged to conjure. So instead she offered up moments from Adam's childhood – those were clear.

"He called me 'Muddy' for years, a combination of *Mummy* and *Daddy*, I suspect." A slight pressure from Charlie's hand urged her on. "Once, in his room, he was doing something he shouldn't have – I can't remember what. Anyway, there was a photograph of me on his bedside table. He'd put Silly Putty over the eyes, two little dots of it pressed over the glass – to blind me, so I couldn't catch him misbehaving."

They rolled and pitched for what seemed an eternity but might have been only a few minutes. She wove Charlie's fingers through her own. "The thing about Adam" – she looked out the porthole – "whenever I was lonely, he just knew. He would be very sweet. When Stephen was away he'd beg to sleep in the same room, like Bert and Ernie. Years later he asked if Bert and Ernie were gay, like Uncle Len." She laughed. Charlie didn't.

Rain came sideways at the vessel. The carpet on the cabin floor was soaked through, and portholes leaked ribbons of seawater. She drew in a great breath as more water lapped in under the main hatch. Someone had pulled out an inflatable life raft. Folded, it was the size of a case of beer, filthy and mended with patches. It didn't look as if it would inflate, let alone float.

The crew gave frantic instructions for how best to get off the boat should it begin to go down: "Hold hands, stay together and jump as far as you can from the boat. Swim to land. If the boat goes down, swim to land, yes?"

Charlie turned at the words "goes down". Several passengers gave in to hysterics; the bride whimpered. With the next pitch, Lise's forehead met the sharp edge of the porthole. She cursed. Charlie, more alert now, pulled her head close and pressed his mouth to the knot forming at her temple. As she blinked away the pain, the engine died a third time. One of the crew crossed himself, and she understood the gesture to mean that the boat, regardless of its size, couldn't stay upright without power in the twenty-foot swells. When her head began to bleed, Charlie applied pressure with his palm. She winced, not in pain, but at seeing his hopelessness. He knew too.

A deeper pain choked her. *Adam*. She imagined him motherless. She thought of the people who loved him: Paul and Monique, his cousin Ritchie, his grandmother Phoebe. Stephen, of course. Fighting for some assurance, something to take with her, she pulled one memory of his childhood forth and she leaned into Charlie's side, murmuring, "I found him once when he was about four, in the middle of the night, in the kitchen, hiding under his blanket, with Cheerios rolling out. And I remember a stream of milk along the floor. His little hand came out to try to dam it. I asked him what he was doing. He explained that he was hungry but was afraid of the kitchen – he didn't like the way the appliances looked back at him. So he'd made a tent to eat in. He was so young, yet had figured out how to get what he needed and feel safe. When I lifted the blanket, he offered me a spoonful of cereal." Would Adam remember such moments? She hoped so. All she had of her own father was a voice. Not even a photograph survived. She'd destroyed them all in a fit of what her mother had assumed was teenage grief. She rested her head on Charlie's shoulder and clung, sorry there was so little history between the two of them to mourn. Only half aware of what was happening, she saw the crew dry the spark plugs and pass them back into the engine compartment. The starter ground; the motor sputtered hopefully, died, then flooded. By then she had given in completely, and begun whispering endearments she hoped Charlie could comprehend.

But just as she'd given up, the engine caught and came to life. Lise held her breath, could feel Charlie holding his. The cylinders chugged to a full growl, and then suddenly they were moving, cutting the waves, veering left. One of the crew sank to his knees in either relief or silent prayer. No one spoke. They were leaning, swaying, listening for any hesitation from the engine.

By the time the boat docked, the squall had dissipated to a mere downpour, and passengers wobbling down the gangway gazed skyward as if the pelting rain was the loveliest of sights. Lise was giddy with relief, and the entire crew was grinning as they helped people ashore. She barely felt her steps on the pier. She would see Adam again.

Charlie's only words as they moved to solid land were "I love you. I love you."

* * *

There were no taxis. They didn't care; they were happy to walk the two miles, would've walked two hundred. The warm rain washed blood from Lise's hair, and Charlie wiped the diluted orange from her cheek. They held hands, pulling each other through puddles, laughing. When he grew serious, Charlie thanked her for the stories she'd told him on the boat.

"Oh, those were easy stories."

He squeezed her arm. "Tell me the hard stories, Elle, the ones you keep."

She stopped and turned. Even in the dimness she could make out his expression. "I will."

Nearing the villa, bedraggled and still shaken, Charlie asked what music she would like played at her funeral. He whispered into her wet ear, "Which songs, sweetheart?"

"That's easy too." She named them.

In the studio he taped a square of gauze to her temple; the cut was not as deep as he had feared. Lise put the kettle on. Noticing that Charlie was still trembling, she helped him peel off his wet clothes and wrapped him in a sheet. He settled on a stool so she could dry his hair. When the sheet fell to his hips, she winced – even when they had made love he'd not seemed so naked. In the harsh overhead light she saw how the skin of his chest stretched taut over ribs. His hands and wrists seemed an exaggerated masculinity on his slim frame. He was as smooth and lightly freckled as a youth. And with the towel half over his face, he seemed only a boy.

She pulled the towel away and with her thumbs tenderly pressed his eyelids closed. Kissing his forehead and brow, only her lips touched him. When he reached for her, she folded his hands aside. Her lips grazed his; her tongue tested the bristles of his mustache. As his mouth opened, she traced his inner cheek and the keys of his teeth with her tongue. At the cleft of delicate flesh between his gums and upper lip, she paused. Charlie remained still under her motions. She had tried to be this way with other men, but they always took control, took over, to kiss or touch the way *they* wanted. Charlie was letting her give, allowing her into the soft recesses of his mouth, the tender inner slope of his lower lip.

With only the lightest touch and gentlest kiss, Lise seemed able to lift Charlie toward her, to buoy him.

Months later, Charlie claimed in a letter that just such memories sustained him. That during their separation he was able to work these moments into images so clear he could paint from them, finding his recall for her so acute that it seemed there was some repository at the corner of his eye storing her images. He admitted that on his loneliest days he would imagine her lips at his collarbone and, repeating her name like a mantra, would climax to the memory of her hands smoothing his rain-tangled hair.

Relative to drowning, the perils of a love affair seemed inconsequential. Since their lives had been spared, they decided to live them.

Charlie abandoned his seascapes and began to work from her. Afternoon light slanting into the studio became his cue to rise from bed to begin sketching. At first he drew only parts of her – arms, one shoulder, the slope of a breast, the taper of an ankle. Later, when he began his studies of her face, he drew from all angles, caught all her moods: impatient, post-coital, amused, serious, silly. In one drawing she would appear needful, and in the next, sated and content.

He mused that the beginnings of love were simply stages of one person being revealed in the other's light, the best of their traits rising. "The marvels of us." Charlie had laughed. She laughed, too, but didn't try to define it. *Marvels?* At first she thought he meant the physical marvels, for her body did feel new when wrapped in his arms. Lise imagined herself cloaked in a finer skin and knew his side was the best place to stand or lie next to. Her lips were swollen, her hips ached, her flesh was alert and tender. The mattress that had been in a far corner was pulled to the center of the studio to become the low arena where the rest of life receded to a point beyond concern. Time distended in the languid hours. She'd known sex as pleasure and, at its worst, as an obligation, but had not considered it a form of expression, had never recognized her own body's eloquence.

Wriggling upright to examine Charlie's drowsy lids, she found the tiny beat at his temple, and asked, "Is this what all the songs are about?" Tracing the pulse points of his body had taken up the morning, her fingertips following the blue sap that ebbed under the plane of his wrist. He solemnly nodded and she covered the top of his foot with hers. "Have you been like this with others?"

He shook his head. "I can't explain. Something opens" – Charlie pulled her hand to the base of his throat – "here."

Lise understood. For her, there was a weird cord that stretched from the back of her neck to her womb. It triggered a desire yet was oddly distinct. Sexual, but innocent.

While posing for Charlie, she drifted, listening to the ocean until she dreamed of it washing over her. The closer she edged toward sleep, the clearer the liquid music became – lyrics in a dead sea-language, tempting her to the depths. A remembered bit of Homer's *Odyssey* surfaced – the mermaids: sirens, who enticed clumsy mortals with promises of eternal grace. The pose Charlie had arranged Lise in was similar to a mermaid's lazy posture, hip sunk into the mattress, her feet tangled together. She imagined giving up her grip on land to slip seaward, lakeward, under waves, under ice. To sink and fuse with the bottom. She dreamed Charlie was an oceanographer, an explorer charting her with his thumb and finger splayed like a compass, his hand walking the swell of her hip. Her throat opened to become a sea channel, a glacier. He mapped her mouth as a cove, her spine an ice ridge. In slumber the boundaries between the hemispheres of north and south blurred. Humidity and marsh water met cold currents to pulse toward opposite oceans, one aqua blue, the other laced grey with ice.

Chapter Six

Lise's eyes opened to Charlie holding a charcoal. Her mouth was sour with sleep and even before she woke fully, her focus blurred with tears.

"Elle? What's wrong?" Charlie folded forward to kneel close, gathering her to him. "What is it?"

She cried openly. "I'm a *mother*. Adam's mother." His name was a hard draw, a pull of undertow. Her shoulders heaved. "I can*not*, cannot be doing this."

"You mean *us*? Oh, Elle."

"I can't do this to Adam. Who could betray their child?" It wasn't a question for Charlie. She was asking herself, and the answer nearly pulled her back under some cold surface: *My father. He would have, was ready to, but died trying.* With salt tears she soaked Charlie's sleeve through.

"Elle. Adam's not a child."

"I'm not talking about his age. It's not that simple."

Charlie's face was halved in light. It was a face she'd never laid eyes on until only weeks before. In that moment she knew that not to see it again would mean less of a life. The night of the cruise she'd told him she would leave Stephen immediately if Charlie asked. Now she wasn't as sure.

His hand cupped her jaw. "Tell me."

"If Adam were to know about this." Her arm swept the space, the bed where she slumped, the easel with its half-drawn nude. "That I'm—"

"Human?"

"Charlie. It's more. Something happened. A long time ago. My father…"

When Charlie stiffened, Lise quickly shook her head. "No, no. Nothing like that. It's just that sometimes children *can't* forgive." He nodded and looked away, but not before she caught the pain in his eye. Charlie deserved more, and hadn't she promised to tell him the stories she'd kept? And couldn't he, of all people, be trusted? Lying back on the pillow, she decided.

"Lie next to me?"

Charlie sighed. "You needn't explain, Elle."

"But I do." When she began, they were both looking up through the skylight, Lise clinging tightly to Charlie's hand, as a child might.

In the villa she paced the tiles of her room. The heat was terrible, even with the ceiling fans rocking at full speed. She paced the darker, cooler halls until Mercedes stepped into her path.

"Señora, you need something? I make you a cold drink?" The woman peered into her eyes. "Maybe you don't sleep so good?"

"I sleep!" When she saw the housekeeper's concern was genuine, Lise quickly repeated, more softly, "I sleep."

She found her sandals and bag and left the villa, walking the road to the village. At the town square she slipped into the tourist center and used the pay phone to call her brother's house in Toronto.

Adam answered with a gravelly "Hullo?"

"Hi, sweetie."

"Hey. What's up, Mom?"

"I was just calling to see how you are."

"Ah, same as I was this morning."

"Oh, right. I called, didn't I?"

"Yeah, you did." His next word was muffled with a cough.

"I heard that. You said 'sunstroke'."

"Ha."

"Not very ha."

It was an old routine, the *Winnie-the-Pooh* vernacular that had infused their banter when he was young, but more recently was met with sighs or silence. When, she wondered, had he begun to grow away from her, from their too-tight history?

"So, what are you doing today?"

"I told you, burning CDs and studying for stupid calculus – *ridicalculus* – that I'll never use in life. And Aunt Monique is helping me with my French. She's taking Ritchie and me to a movie in an hour. Do you need to write this down, Mom?"

"Adam, don't be… I just called to say hi, and to see how the studying is going."

He fell silent. After he'd failed two subjects during spring semester, the school counselor had ventured that such sudden turns were often rooted in stress. He'd asked – rather boldly, Lise thought – if there had been any trouble at home. "There's never been trouble," she'd snapped.

The school year had begun just as Lise was scheduled to leave for Mexico. She'd seriously considered canceling her trip, afraid that Adam wouldn't get a good start. Her brother thought differently. Paul and his wife, Monique, had planned their autumn with Adam in mind and had been looking forward to his stay. When Lise voiced her concern over Adam, Paul suggested that the change might do his nephew good.

"C'mon, Paul, when is change good for a teenager?"

"You can't smother him, Sis."

Surely she'd never smothered Adam. But when even Adam balked at the idea of her not going to Mexico, she'd given in and packed.

Adam cleared his throat against the faint crackle of the line. "I'm studying, OK? Right now, in fact. Mom, I gotta go."

"Listen—"

"Hey. Say hi to Dad?"

She wound the phone cord around her finger. "Sure."

The line cut to a dial tone. A youth standing nearby was patiently bouncing on the balls of his feet. When she replaced the receiver, he moved closer. "Pardon, ma'am, you finished?"

The boy was barely older than Adam but appeared to be traveling alone. He shifted his heavy backpack and pulled a blond dreadlock free of a strap.

"I am." As she sidled out of the booth she touched the boy instinctively, reassuringly, as a mother might touch a son.

Another clear moment of Adam's childhood fixed: They were standing patiently in line at the butcher's shop one autumn afternoon. He'd learned a palindrome in school that day and was attempting to relate it.

"A what, sweetheart?"

"You *know*, a platendom."

"I don't understand."

"A pallydream?"

Suddenly her number was called and Lise was too busy ordering veal to listen. He tugged at her sleeve twice before she'd impatiently shushed him. His shout silenced the customers and the butcher. Adam's voice rang in the large space, "Madam, I'm Adam!"

That proclamation stretched through time, his young voice hoarse with conviction. He knew who he was.

Along the square, restaurant staff were setting outdoor tables for the night, laying candles and cutlery on linen as mariachi bands tuned. Among the local girls strolling in their evening ritual, she saw a familiar face: Flora, arm in arm with another girl. Flora's unbraided hair fanned nearly to the hem of her short skirt. She wore high-heeled sandals, and her lacquered toenails shone as she and her companion passed under a streetlamp to approach the patio of a corner restaurant.

A handsome, sloe-eyed youth in a waiter's uniform struggled to set right a garden torch leaning in its base. Flora stopped a few steps short of him and shyly waited. When the boy looked up and noticed her, his brow softened and he straightened. A moment of solemn lust passed between them before the spell was broken

112

by Flora's sudden giggle. The two volleyed a few words. The boy plucked an orchid from one of the table arrangements and leaned over the low rail to offer it. Flora clutched it tightly to her breast and stood mooning until her friend finally pulled her away from the scene.

The young man shored the tilting garden pole as he watched the girls turn the corner and sashay out of sight.

How simple their love looked to Lise, how free. The boy was undoubtedly the one Flora pined for at the water's edge. First love? Moving away, she laughed aloud, realizing the boy was, quite literally, holding a torch.

Charlie shook his cramped hand and backed away from the easel. Lise rolled, grateful to be released from her pose, and unfurled herself in a yawning stretch. She peeked at the latest drawing while Charlie was occupied, bent into an armoire, searching for something. She heard a rustle and peered over the easel to see him pull out a square parcel and unwrap its layers of muslin. He brought over a small painting delicately framed in gilded wood.

"I've been keeping this for years."

She stepped back to the mattress and sank down, balancing the frame on her knees. The seascape was composed of simple elements: a headland cutting into the water like a great stone plow and a sunrise, shattered as if the sky had been struck by a similar blade. It burned with color, every essence of the place washed in fiery hues. She held it up. "It's extraordinary. Where is this place?"

"The edge of nowhere, really, some tiny place on the Irish coast – I can't recall which county or village, but it's written under the paper backing."

"This sky."

"You like it, then?" His grin was boyish.

"Of course I do! It's amazing. Here, where the air is moving… how'd you do that?"

"I've no clue. I hardly remember painting it."

"No. Really?"

"Really." He kneeled next to her naked hip. "I'd been driving all night and came across this place. The light was insane. I couldn't get my easel up fast enough, and once my brush hit the canvas, the oddest thing happened – I got sort of *taken* in." His hands moved as though trying to winnow meaning from air. "Then I just painted and painted, and the whole time I had this overwhelming sense of calm, if I had to name it. Of suddenly being where I was meant to be, of knowing who I was. D'you understand?"

"I do." Her voice fell away. "I did, once." Lise pressed an ear to her cupped palm, as if listening to some distant sound. Charlie's moment had come to him as sight, while hers was a song composed of gongs and trills and voices slipping out of range. Only an echo survived, a cold aria that faded to silence whenever she tried wresting it from her past. The attending tones of a Canadian midnight came back clearly – lake wind whistling, the rasp of ice under a boot, her ear ringing with cold and the timbre of her father's voice, so masculine and out of place among the others. He'd been telling her something vitally important, and Lise would give anything to remember what, but all she owned were shards of a blue night, as cold and black as the painting in her hands was warm and light. She took a last look at the sun-shot canvas before handing it back. "But you have this, Charlie. Your amazing sky. You know how beautiful it is?"

"I do." He pressed it to her. "Now I want you to have it."

She tried to put it back into his hands. "No. You can't just give this away."

When he wouldn't take it, she laid it on the bed. "C'mon, Charlie. This is one of those rare gifts you get in life."

He laughed, bending close. "And how many of you will I get?" Before she could protest, he rose. "Really, I want you to take it."

In the quiet of the studio the sunrise glowed up at her. She dressed while Charlie made tea.

She thought of the shoe box packed deep in her closet back in Toronto. Inside were cigar-band rings, grimy valentines, Cracker Jack charms, ticket stubs from theaters and rock concerts, bits of jewelry and the odd matchbook from a restaurant or bar – mementos of boys and men, kept for what emotional value they once held. Some of the items had been accepted with mixed feelings, some with gratitude, others with a sense of due reward. One gift was the result of a dare, a compact of face powder that she had challenged a boy to steal for her. She doubted that boy, a man now, would ever have kept the peace-symbol key ring she in turn had stolen for him.

Remembering Flora and the orchid the waiter had given her, Lise imagined the girl pressing that flower into the pages of a Bible or some cookbook. Years from now, Flora might cradle the brown velum petals and remember feeling beautiful.

Were such keepsakes – bought or stolen, expensive or cheap – validations that she'd satisfied desires, performed well the steps of love? She'd never need such proof from Charlie; what was between them was elevated above any of the relationships represented in her sad shoe box. The offer of the painting was gesture enough; the gift itself perhaps too dear.

Charlie had busied himself around the studio. His movements seemed nonchalant at first glance, but Lise noticed his shoulders drop, the set half smile on his face. Uncertainty hung in the space between them, where only an hour before they had made love. She dressed and reluctantly lifted the painting, wrapping it in her shawl.

Stepping forward to kiss Charlie, she faltered, only grazing his jaw.

She hurried to the villa on the back path, hoping no one would come along and ask about her package. Clarice was back from Mexico City, but Lise had been avoiding her, staying away from the villa or anywhere she might encounter her hostess alone.

At the stairs to the balcony, something stopped her. The painting she held – *hid*, to her sudden shame – was no token: it was a precious gift. She pulled the shawl from the canvas and stared at the painting. It was magnificent. She turned around and hurried back to the studio, not caring who might see, hoping it wasn't too late to accept the painting with some of the grace Charlie had given it with.

He was standing where she had left him.

"I forgot to ask. What's the painting called?"

"Nothing. It seemed foolish to try to name it."

Pointing to the plateau of the headlands, where the grass washed gold under the burst sky, she asked, "There. Would you meet me there in a few months' time?"

They embraced, happily unaware, for the moment, that a few months would stretch to so many.

Mexico was no place to end her marriage. She and Charlie were as discreet as they could be. Secrets were one thing, but deception another, and neither could muster much stomach for it. Lise worried they'd be found out – that she or Charlie would slip, make some mistake.

And they did. At the beach, as she sat on a chaise drying her hair, Charlie lifted the wet curtain of it to kiss the small crescent at her hairline, now healing from pink to white. He whispered something she was too rattled to hear, for at that moment Flora had bounded out of the palms and onto the sand. As soon as she saw them, the maid bent as though adjusting the heel of her shoe, giving them time to break away from each other. But of course she had seen.

Their many absences from the villa would have spoken volumes, if anyone were paying attention. With irrational hope, Lise assumed no one was.

They stole a quick embrace in the upstairs hall near the stairs as two other guests suddenly emerged from their rooms. Charlie stepped back, smoothing his wild hair, and Lise quickly dug in her straw bag as if looking for something. The woman smiled knowingly when moving past them to descend the stairs. Charlie muttered a greeting as her professor husband followed. When Charlie thought the couple was out of earshot, he boldly added, "Now, when they start going on about the flan or mango tart or whatever dessert is tonight, I'll point to you over my coffee and say, *That woman's taste puts this all to shame.*"

"Charlie," she rasped.

His comment had resonated in the stairwell so that the man – Lise suddenly remembered he taught poetry at Berkeley – paused on the riser, cranking his head to look squarely up at both of them. She took her hand away from her mouth long enough to quote, "*Love is a dead-sea fruit that turns to ashes in your mouth.* Who wrote that, professor?"

He frowned in response and continued down the stairs.

These were the sorts of mistakes they made.

Later, lying in bed, she wondered who might suspect.

Charlie rolled to face her. "The guests might think something, but only the staff know for certain."

"The staff?"

"Sure. People leave clues about themselves, don't they? They know everything. The maids, anyway. They know who is under stress – from any number of signs, say, how tangled their sheets are, or how violently their cigarettes are stubbed out."

"Yes, but—"

"They'd know who's in the bottle, or addicted to pills. Who's dallying. For instance, I imagine they know you've not been sleeping in your own bed."

She sat up. "But I've mussed it every morning!"

"Who's your maid?"

"Flora."

"Right."

She sighed. "Is 'dallying' even a word?" Her fingers tapped over his broad forehead. "And what do they know of *you*?"

"Nothing much, I might be a ghost for how often I'm in the villa. And they don't dare come in here." He looked around the studio at the many sketches, her shawl draped over his chair, cups and glasses set about in twos. "It's a good thing. This place is a bloody novel."

"Ah. But *you* can do no wrong in their eyes, can you, Robin Hood?"

"Sometimes, Elle" – he winked – "sometimes things need to be shifted into the proper hands."

"As I'm now in yours?"

His smile faded. "That's not funny, Elle."

Charlie had a point: the servants probably did know, but it was the other guests she feared, people of Gerald's sort – sharkish business types. Or the academics like Stephen, trained to observe. Most guests stayed only a week or two before being undone by sun, unaccustomed idleness and too much fresh air. Every week taxis pulled up to unload similar faces to replace those departing. Lise knew none of them posed any real threat, but still, she couldn't help imagining dramas where Stephen was alerted and sent her packing; though he didn't possess that sort of passion, he did have pride, and in her mind she imagined some magistrate bringing down his gavel to take away her rights to Adam.

The other unthinkable scenario was that she'd never see Charlie again.

She made Charlie sit across from her during dinner so he wouldn't be as likely to touch her. The first time she wore the sea-colored silk dress, Charlie leaned over the tablecloth, admiring the cut of the silk and the amount of shoulder it revealed. "Now, *that* dress was made for you." In a low voice he added, "Bring that to the studio later. And what's in it. Bring all of that."

"Careful," she pleaded quietly as he filled her glass. "I think Mercedes saw your painting in my room today – the door of my armoire was open."

"Then we must be more careful about where we hide our gifts."

She had nothing as nice as a painting to give him, but when he stole into her room that midnight, she offered a small gift: an old CD with the song she'd rediscovered.

"Joni Mitchell. Also Canadian," she'd claimed, proudly handing it over.

"Ah, like Rocky and Bullwinkle."

"Rocky and Bullwinkle are from Minnesota."

"Not Canada? Who would've guessed?"

She sniffed, "Famous Canadians – I bet you can't name two."

"Pish. I can do better than that. Margaret Trudeau, for one." His brow furrowed a moment; then his face halved in a smile. "And all those mounted police she must have been so fond of!"

She patted him. "Very good!"

* * *

Such inane conversations come back nearly word for word, not because anything they said was so fascinating or witty, but because of the ease they had with each other – that's what she needs to remember.

A cold, wet spell traps Lise in the cottage for several days. In the morning she writes long letters home, describing to Leonard her encounters with the Conners; most of her rambling paragraphs feature Siobhan and Remy. She taunts Leonard with physical descriptions of Danny, the ruggedly handsome Irish sailor. *Need I say more? Did I mention the mirrored headboard on his "pleasure" boat? Alas, Len, he's straight as a rod. You'll still come visit?*

Bracing herself, every few days she tries to write to Adam, but spends more time chewing the pen than putting down words. She tosses any letters with even a hint of pleading or sorrow and

119

starts over, revising multiple times before committing his pages to envelopes. Pulling forth history, she adds details and what stories she can recall, introducing Adam to the grandfather he's never known.

In the quiet weeks since she arrived in Ireland, the desperation Lise felt in Canada has been tempered by distance and time. She's stopped struggling to quell her memories and is able now to allow all thoughts and acknowledge them, however clouded or pained.

Of all the stories she's ever been told, watched on screen, or endeavored to make herself, she understands that only those that unfold naturally endure. And now when she listens to Remy telling his tales, she thinks, *Ah,* that's *how it's done.* Uncertain how her own story will unfold, she's come to accept the gaps as part of its fabric. Remy reminds her there are no neat endings, but if she steers her course and aims true, what's meant for her will come.

She continues the mindless tasks of scrubbing walls and repairing cracks in the plaster. She's just patched nail holes in the two ghostly squares where portraits of the Virgin Mary and JFK hung side by side, as if they made the ideal couple. She absently hums 'Hail to the Chief' off-key while sanding moons of crusted Spackle. A 1958 Saint-of-the-Month calendar is peeled from the plaster, one page falling to her feet. March's pinup, St Francis de Sales, is one Lise has never heard of, so she looks him up, finding he is patron saint of writers. She tacks him to the space above the tiny desk where she pens her letters, so that his gilded face peers over her shoulder.

From the paint Remy has mixed, she chooses the same buttery green as the middle stripe of the silk dress. In the dining room she brushes the walls by hand in lazy strokes, thinking of Charlie painting her. As she drifts from one memory to the next, the hue of the plaster changes under her brush, and she remembers the gecko in Charlie's studio changing its skin to match the blue wall.

In spite of the weather, she visits the hillside cemetery again, this time lugging a trowel, a potted azalea, and a plastic water jug.

Searching the rows, she finds the most derelict marker and traces the few shallow hatches of illegible letters. The earth of the grave dips like a hammock. Whoever was buried beneath is dust by now, so long dead even the stone has forgotten his name. The grave has a view to the sea. It will do.

After pulling up weeds, she digs dirt from a moldy heap behind the tiny shed, hauling it back to the grave in shovelfuls. When the shallow is leveled she sows handfuls of grass seed, patting them into the damp loam. She pours water from the jug into the hole dug for the azalea and sets the plant in gently, hoping it's not too early, too cold, for it to take root.

Lise has never actually seen her father's grave, has never spoken to his spirit or laid a flower down in grief. She wonders if he will humor her, hopes he finds this borrowed grave suitable. When she goes to put her hands together, she finds the posture of prayer too self-conscious. After he'd died she'd forsaken any notion of God. She'd sat dumbly through her religion classes when she bothered showing up at all; more often she'd joined other truant Saint Agnes girls to smoke in the rectory garden, learning crude jokes in French and how to inhale without coughing.

Her modified prayer stance is a crouch on her heels, with dirty hands on dirty knees, her eyes opened. If she keeps the grass watered, the shrub alive… perhaps by the time the azalea blooms, more tangible memories might open to her as well.

On her way out of the cemetery she stops at the Conner plots and tidies them, plucking up the wrapper from a Cadbury bar; the smell of chocolate still clings. Remy's been recently.

She'll come back and film a few frames of the Conner graves and the vistas beyond them. For the first time in months, she is thinking more seriously about work, wondering if the footage she's collected of the Conners might not gel into something solid. No concrete direction has come to her yet, but she knows that if she keeps at it, the thread pulling it all together will reveal itself.

* * *

Lise finishes painting the last dining room wall just as the afternoon light begins to fade. The headlands canvas lies facedown on the dining room table, its paper backing mended where she'd torn it to find the name of the village. She hangs the painting on the wall, still slightly damp. She shifts the frame a fraction and stands back to see whether it's straight.

If one could disappear into a painting, Lise has nearly managed. Outside the window is the very coast Charlie had been taken in by, was compelled to paint; and in doing so he had lost himself in a pure moment. She need only turn and look through the warped window-pane to compare the headlands from this lower angle. In the hour of twilight, the distant cape has grown blue, indistinct from the sea.

The other paintings are still in their crate. Once the parlor is finished she will hang them all there, as if in their own small gallery. The packing label and customs form claim there are eight paintings, no doubt a misprint, for she remembers only seven. But then she'd been so upset the night of the exhibit – she'd expected to find Charlie and instead was confronted by her own image, his paintings like a wall of mirrors exposing her, reflecting so much more than mere flesh.

Stephen had followed her to the gallery that night, had seen the paintings, and had raged.

Adam had seen them too. No letter she might write him could convey her regret over that.

She mistakes the sound of a knock as the clatter of a loose roof slate and so ignores it. Her hammer-taps on the paint lid echo oddly, out of sync. A moment later she realizes the rapping noise is coming from the kitchen door. Peering into the hall and out the small back window, she sees a parked car losing its outline to the dusk. Wiping hands on her paint-spotted shirt, she steps warily to the vestibule. *Who on earth?*

She clicks the latch and cracks the door an inch. "Hullo?"

"You alive in there? I've been at the knocking for five minutes but you keep the bloody door locked like this is bloody New York."

Lise opens the door. "Siobhan. What are *you* doing here?"

"And cheers to you too." The girl steps in, smoke rank in her hair. "It's a forty-minute drive up here to West Bumfuck for such a greeting?"

Lise laughs, motioning her into the kitchen. "Sorry. You caught me off guard. I don't get many visitors up this way."

"Yeah. I can see that. You look like you've just swallowed your teeth." Siobhan shudders. "The place isn't haunted, on top of everything?" Holding out a fat parcel tied with twine, she lets it thud to the table. "I'm out here on account of this reek."

"What is it?" She hefts the package. Its smell is intense, but not unpleasantly so – a briny fish.

"Gram Maggie says it's some kind a grouper they don't usually get here anymore, but my da hauled it up today and if you'd seen Gram's face you'd have thought she won the lotto. It's called scud or scrod, something like scrotum. Anyway, you're to cook it right away in half seawater, half wine, with the lemons and some seaweed."

"Oh. That's very kind. I don't think I've any lemons…"

"Right, well, Gram remembered there's no lemon trees out here in Far Bugger either." Siobhan pulls one lemon after another from the inner pockets of her wax coat. A half dozen roll across the table. "But everyone knows you've got the wine cuz Tommy at the ShopRite says you nearly cleaned him out." She speaks toward her chest while struggling to rezip her coat.

"He did? You're not leaving? Take off that coat. You can't drive all this way and turn back. You'll stay for dinner." She nods at the unopened crate atop the fridge. "There's Tommy's wine. Hand me that screwdriver, please."

She pries open the case of merlot and lifts out a bottle. "We'll have a bit of this. You're my first ever guest. There must be some tradition here for sharing a drink on such an occasion?"

"You share a drink here on the occasion of having a pulse. But just a bit, like, I'm driving. D'ya know that was the first full case of wine Tommy's ever sold to anyone not having a wedding or a wake." Siobhan scans the room, past the paintbrushes soaking in the stone sink to the table where a paperback is held open with a plate holding a half-eaten sandwich.

"Seems neither of us has any wild Saturday night plans, does it?" She sings, "*Saturday, Saturday, blah blah blah, Saturday, Saturday night's all right*! Now there's some songwriting. And who's the nancy with the weird glasses sang that, again?"

"Elton John."

"Right. Still ahoof?"

"Alive? Sure." Lise forgets there are twenty-odd years between them. She points to jelly glasses on the drainboard, and Siobhan lifts the two largest. Lise grips the bottle between her knees and grimaces as the cork twists out with a *plip*. She fills the glasses, then raises hers. "Here's to it."

"To your new home." Siobhan clicks her glass and shakes her head. "Word in town is, besides your being a wino, that if you're not already daft, living out here you will be in no time. You'll be nutters, hoarding newspapers and eating seagulls before summer."

"Oh, really?" She laughs. "And what do they say about you?"

"Plenty." Siobhan peeks into the dining room. "So, do I get the grand tour? I can hardly go back without a full report."

They circle through the rooms to the front hall, where the girl bounds ahead up the narrow staircase. At the door of the bedroom she calls back down, "Aha, you're waiting on someone! There's more candles than church up here."

After a beat Lise shouts up, "They're in case of storms."

"Storms my arse." She pounds down the stairs. "Lavender scented." She winks. "S'OK. We've all got our secrets. Yours is safe with me."

To Lise Siobhan's moods seem as unpredictable as Danny's, shifting one minute to the next, one meeting to the next. During their last encounter the girl had been surly and withdrawn.

After the glass of wine, they don jackets and scarves and take the bottle outside. Siobhan steers her car to the edge of the slope and aims its beams toward the beach, where she's certain they will find the proper type of seaweed for their dining. "The slimy lot." Siobhan wrinkles her nose. "Like wet feathers." They stoop and search mostly by feel in the shadows, plucking up bits here and there. Passing the bottle between them, their fingers cast comically long shadows from the headlights. Though the bottle is half empty well before the bucket is half filled, Siobhan declares there is enough seaweed.

They fall to the sand and lie back to see stars have come out to brighten the sky. Lise asks after a constellation she doesn't recognize.

"Oh, right, this isn't your sky, is it? Well, Grump knows all that shite."

"Grump?"

"Remy. I'm told I couldn't say 'Granddad' when I was little, only 'Grump', and everyone thought it fit well enough – anyway, he knows all the stars, even bought one a few years back."

"Bought one?"

"Money down the hole. You *know*, you buy a star and have it named for a loved one – supposedly it gets printed up on some chart. A complete rip-off. I could fly to the States and back on what he spent just to name a phony star for Gram Maggie. It was three hundred quid or some nonsense. Bleeding anniversary gift." She grunts and points out a string of weak stars. "You see that constellation – those five in a row there, kinda drooping?"

"Sort of. It's so small, and a bit dim."

"Course it's small! That's your Phallus Minor." Siobhan elbows her, howling. "Sure, size doesn't matter!"

They throw bits of seaweed at the crabs drawn by the headlights. Siobhan grimaces. "They still do it. I know for a fact."

"Who? Does what?"

"Gram Maggie and Grump. They go at it still. Can you believe?"

She offers the last of the bottle. "And why not? That's rather sweet."

"Sweet? I'd say it's rather disgusting." Siobhan drinks, then squints into the bottom of the empty bottle. "He's got hair on his back like a bath mat. I've *seen* it." Her shudder turns to a shiver and she pulls her arms tight. "Jesus, can we not go in? We'll freeze our tits off out here."

Climbing back to the house, they fall twice, snorting. Inside, the kitchen is too bright, so they turn off the overhead and set to preparing the meal by candlelight. Lise throws the fish and halved lemons into a pot with the seaweed and lights the gas. Half of a second bottle of wine goes into the concoction.

In a moment of clarity she plucks Siobhan's car keys from the counter and hides them in the egg compartment of the fridge. Siobhan flips through Lise's CD collection, moaning at the names Loreena McKennitt, Máire Brennan, the Chieftains. "Ah, you've all the *Oirish* dreck, don'tcha? Aha, here we are!" She holds up the jewel cases with Janis Joplin, Aretha Franklin and Sarah Vaughan. "You've these at least."

The girl cranks the volume and they sit across from each other, bobbing to the music, singing along, each daring the other, drop by drop, to fill her glass so high that wine pillows just above the rim before spilling over.

"It's called a meniscus."

"A men-*what*? It's a feckin' wine bump!"

It becomes a betting game, Siobhan winning three pounds to her one. "Brilliant." She rakes in the coins. "At least my money worries are over."

They stack their winnings, ignoring the fish burbling on the cooker. The bottle falls and rolls empty along the floor, necessitating the opening of another, which they find hilarious.

They argue over who are the best female vocalists.

"Can the dead be included?"

"Sure. Then I vote for Edith Piaf, and you can include Janis."

"OK. Alphabetical order? Aretha, for starters."

"Patsy Cline," Lise offers.

"Ella."

"Billie Holiday."

"Bonnie Raitt."

"All bad girls!" Siobhan pounds the table.

"Wait, Ella wasn't a bad girl—"

"She wasn't Mother Teresa."

"Gimme one of those cigarettes. Madonna? No, wait… Marlene Dietrich!"

"Couldn't sing her way out an open door. Like you."

They sing 'Baubles, Bangles and Beads', 'Like a Virgin', and 'Respect'. Siobhan rocks back, her chair knocking open the cupboard where Lise's audio gear is stored. "Wassis gadget?"

"Tape recorder."

"Perfect. We'll record a concert!" She presses buttons until the machine whirs. They sing 'Me and Bobby McGee', and since Siobhan doesn't know 'Angel from Montgomery', Lise must sing it alone. Siobhan laughs until tears stream. By midnight they are singing songs they don't know, smoking up Siobhan's Marlboros.

When they run out of songs, they start telling jokes, clutching each other over the kitchen table when they can't remember the punch lines.

Siobhan half reclines across the table. "Ah, you're not near so tight-arsed as we first thought, Miss La-di-da-aren't-I-mysterious."

"Me? Mysterious?"

"Yup. Mysterious wino-hermit." Siobhan claps at her own hand but misses. "What didja s'pose we'd think?"

Lise blows a smoke ring, amazed she remembers how. "I dunno."

"Well, whoever you are, or why ever you're here, you're not so bad." Without lifting her head from her forearm, she raises her glass in a toast, adding, "Especially for someone almost my father's age."

"I think I'm older, actually."

"Jesus, you're not?" There is such shock in her voice and such genuine pity that they both start laughing until they forget why.

It's easier to feed the fire from the floor, so they slide from their chairs to prop themselves against the press, pelting the hearth with lumps of coal and slats pulled from the wine crate.

"Any more of that mer*loy* stuff?"

After uncorking another, Lise asks, "Your Colm – how long since he's gone?"

"Ah. Lemme count. Seven weeks and three days…" She closes one eye to focus on the kitchen clock. "Sixteen hours and twenty minutes. But now, that's just a guess."

"Does he write?"

She pulls a cell phone from her vest. "Text messages." She presses a button and *Mss u drlig* pops up on the tiny screen. "I miss him too." Siobhan's face, already flushed from the wine, deepens a shade. "I'm ready to chew me own arm off, you know? I dunno how the nuns do it, that celibacy bollocks, I mean." The girl pokes vigorously at the coals until sparks jump.

"You're crying."

"Well, fuck, I s'pose I am, like."

"Why don't you just go to him?"

"Money, a course. It doesn't grow on trees. Even if it did, we've no bleedin' trees, have you not noticed?"

"He's gonna find someone else, I know it."

"Siobhan, it's only a bit of time. He's back in six months, right?"

"That's right. Six months too late. If I had the fare I'd be gone tomorrow." Siobhan wearily hoists herself up, mumbling, "I need the loo."

"Hmm." Lise is half listening. She's staring past the table to the line of coat hooks where her purse hangs. As Siobhan's footfalls thud up the stairs she gets up herself and moves around the table to the hall.

Lise is back in front of the fire when Siobhan returns to plop down next to her.

"Where were we?"

"Talking about Colm."

"Hand me that bottle. I'll shut up about it now; you wouldn't pity my lot."

"And why not? Maybe I've a similar lot myself?"

"So, you *are* waiting on somebody. Tell!"

Tell? She leans toward the girl, considering what a relief it would be to let it all out. Keeping Charlie a secret for so long... There've been times she's been sure she'd burst with it.

Siobhan elbows her. "Gwan, then, tell me 'bout 'im."

"Charles Lowan." It felt lovely to say his name. "Well, for starters he's a painter. We met in the Yucatán – you know, it's that hump on the east coast of Mes... Mes... *Mex*ico."

Describing that first afternoon, how her senses had expanded to take in all the newness – the texture of the air, the heat, the smells, everything around her a hue brighter. There was the prickly excitement of arriving somewhere exotic. "When I first saw Charlie, I really only saw his back first, and his paintings – but still, I thought, *Now here's someone.*"

Siobhan stays quiet as Lise manages to describe how Charlie's hands felt on her: a degree warmer than her own skin, more alive somehow than other men's hands.

"And the first time we made love... I mean *the moment* he was inside me? Well, I knew my life was changed. Forever."

Siobhan's warm shoulder feels solid, encouraging Lise to go on. "And leaving him there, at that awful little airport was like... like *death*. But I had to go, didn't I?" Her next words are a whisper. "I had to. I have a son. Did you know I have a son? He's younger than you by a few..." She turns as Siobhan's dark head dips heavily forward. There's no way of knowing how long the girl has been asleep.

Nudging her awake enough to pull her to her feet, Lise gets an arm around Siobhan's waist and guides her through the hall to the parlor, where she aims her toward the sofa. Struggling to take off the girl's boots, Lise falls backward nearly into the hearth.

When Lise opens her eyes, she's leaning against the brickwork, her leg asleep. Hobbling upright, she notices the air has grown oddly close. Staggering to the front door, she opens it and leans out, holding onto the jamb. A line of daylight has begun to brighten the water. Leaving the door ajar, she turns back inside and climbs the stairs, followed by wafts of cold air. She's oblivious to the slight noise from the kitchen. The fish boiling away, the pot's lid knocking gently.

Chapter Seven

As she retreats under the covers, a slow consciousness settles over her like ash. A burnt smell in the web of hair across Lise's cheek recalls perfect smoke rings launched over the kitchen table. Her temple throbs and her eyes shift so painfully that she imagines a set of walnuts. A hangover. *A doozy*, her father would claim. Easing her arms into a bathrobe, she hopes her memory of an aspirin bottle in the kitchen cupboard is real. Opening windows, she breathes blasts of ocean air, then leans on a sash, mumbling, "Dreadful," but for the first time in Ireland she is grateful for another grey day.

Downstairs, the sofa is vacant and the blanket folded. The kitchen has been tidied, candle wax scraped from the table and slats from the wine crate stacked at the hearth. The floor's been swept, and five empty bottles line the drainboard. The back door is wedged open with the ruined pot, its lump of fish tarred fast to the bottom. Siobhan's car is gone.

But hadn't she hidden the car keys? Lise laughs. She had, surely, but Siobhan had been sitting right at the table, in full view. That mystery solved, she tackles the note left on the kitchen table.

Thanks for the craic – and the tea and beans!
S.

She knows *craic* means company – or something like it. Perhaps *tea and beans* means wine and talk? Remy will know. Remembering their breakfast meeting, she looks at the clock and moans. In less than an hour she's due at the Arches Hotel, with no chance of canceling, since it's her idea. She's asked to film his furtive

Sunday ritual of caffeine and cholesterol while Margaret is off to Mass.

In the bathroom she cringes at her small-eyed reflection clutching the aspirin bottle with both hands. Standing in the shower until the water runs cold, she tries recollecting details of the night before. She and Siobhan had talked nonstop, but she can barely recall a word.

Taking only what she can carry in one trip, Lisa loads the car and drives into the village, gripping the wheel. On Arches Road, dozens of cars cram the narrow street in Sunday traffic. Muffled hymns and organ music compete from the two churches on either end of the street, creating a stereo effect. Parking directly in front of the hotel, she ignores the zone marker and lugs her cases up the steps.

The lobby is empty, and Remy is the only patron in the dining room, where he's bent scribbling into his school exercise book.

More lines to Margaret? She coughs so as not to startle him.

"I know you're there." He doesn't turn. "You're late."

"And you're cross."

"No more than usual."

She sets her camera down and slumps across from him. Out the window the lane is quiet.

"Seems we're the only two heathens not in church."

"Three." Remy nods toward the bored-looking waiter.

"Do you ever go to Mass with Margaret?"

"That's a door I don't darken 'cept for weddings and funerals, but don't get me started on the church." He focuses on a spot between her eyes. "Sore head?"

"Very." When she squints, a slight weight shifts on the bridge of her nose. She's still wearing her sunglasses but makes no move to take them off. "Your granddaughter's a bad influence."

"Haven't seen her today. Usually she's off to church with Margaret, but she didn't come by this morning. Now I know why. Bad influence indeed."

After a few gulps of coffee, she rigs Remy with a tiny microphone. "It's good of you to do this."

"Good? It's a mean bastard won't share a story."

She sets the tape recorder between them on the table. Digging in her bag for an audiotape, she finds one has been used and marked *Kitchen Floor* in unfamiliar handwriting. Staring at the cassette, she dimly recalls Siobhan's fiddling – God knows what nonsense is recorded on it. She crams it into the side pocket and gets a fresh tape.

There isn't much light, and she's forgotten her meter, so she can only turn on her camera to *Auto* and hope for the best.

The waiter brings a fresh pot of coffee, glancing suspiciously toward the camera. "Breakfast?"

"Oh, none for me, just coffee. And water. A liter. With ice, please?"

The waiter gives her a look but returns to place a glass bowl of ice chips before her with a flourish. Overkill, she thinks, and thanks him accordingly, with a bow. She fills her water glass, chip by chip, until the spoon grows cold in her hand. While Remy eats his buttered oatcakes and bacon, the ice fuses together, cracking in tiny fissures: the sharp corners of the chips soften when she pours water over them.

Remy watches her, his knife and fork going still. "When you're finished building that, will you be drinking it?"

"Pardon?"

"Never mind." He nods at the camera. "Know what this film's about yet?"

In a cupboard back in the cottage, reels with stories and interviews of Remy, Margaret, and Danny have begun to accumulate, but Lise remains unsure how the scenes within might weave together; besides, she has no footage of Siobhan at all. "Oh, it'll come to me." She breathes in the coffee steam. "You were going to tell me about some of the wedding customs here?"

"Weddings. But before the weddings can happen, there's a fair bit of shenanigans. You know about the dowries?"

"A bit. I saw a film made here – I think it was called *The Quiet Man*."

"Good Lord! John bloody Wayne dragging Maureen O'Hara over the gorse by her hair – and her happy to burn up her dowry and cook his grub at the end of the day? That's Hollywood, for you, isn't it so? A decent Irishwoman would've murdered him."

"Dowries?" She steers him back to the subject.

"Right. My own mother had a dowry that became a bit of a story. Was a sore subject in our house till the day my father dropped." Remy leans on his elbows and looks from the camera to her as if addressing two people. He seems as at ease in front of the lens as a seasoned actor. "Three days before my mother, Bernadette O'Toole, became a Conner, she arrived here with ten dairy cows she'd raised and tended herself. Herded them twenty miles down the coast road. Her people were well known as breeders, so my mother knew cows, but nothing 'bout the trading of dowries. And being naive so, she thought she was bringing her herd into the marriage with her like a bunch of pets. A course soon enough the lot of them got settled on her new sister-in-law to become *her* dowry, so's *she* could marry the lad on the neighboring farm."

Remy tapped his temple. "Cows have stellar memories, and they well remembered the voice and scent of my mother. They ruined the fences nearly every day, trying to get back to her at milking times. My mother hadn't any babies yet, what with not being settled in her heart; and having to chase her own cows away each day didn't make matters pleasanter. It didn't take long for those broken fences and lovesick cows to cause bad blood between my father and his sister's new husband. But as history's witness, wives tend to get what they want in the end, and my father was forced to buy back the herd, for exactly the price of the gasoline tractor he had been saving for, so it cost him that, plus plenty of humiliation down at the pub."

Remy shook his head. "Out of sheer stubbornness he never did own a tractor, even when he could afford to. Each time he went to hook up our horse to the old plow, he'd tip his hat to my mother and growl, 'Oi'm off to buy the bleedin' cows now, Bernadette.'"

Her forehead stung when she laughed. "So that's an Irish dowry?"

"One of the last."

"So, Margaret didn't have one?"

A dark look passes over the old man's features. "Christ, no. She come with the clothes barely on her back and twin sisters in tow. Anyway, her father'd drunk up anything they had 'cept some broken-down boats and that bit of pier Danny's fixed up. The old sot would've been known as a rock man, those days."

"A rock man?"

"Someone without land or even a fence." Remy barely pauses. "Ah, now, since we're on fences, another story comes to mind." He pours more coffee into her outstretched cup. Remy's stories seem to lead one into the next, backing in and out of subjects.

"Now this happened years past but sticks with me yet. Back when I farmed – before the leg got too much – I went to Castlebar one day for a special battery for that sort of fence that shocks the livestock. So, I explain to the shopkeep – a gnarly git who wouldn't give the time of day – that it only takes one jolt. After one jolt the sheep stay off, see? Sheep are just smart enough that way. But I have a dozen lambs and the battery is dead, and these new ones need to have the shock to learn themselves. So the old piker goes off and comes back with a replacement battery, and mind you he's not said a word to me until I'm paid and nearly out the door, when he lifts his head just long enough to say, 'I knew a man who married *twice*.'"

After a moment she nearly sputters coffee down her blouse.

"Ah, see now? You're not so slow." Remy pats her arm.

"Gee, thanks." She wipes her chin.

"And will *you* marry again?"

She squints suspiciously. "Maybe. If the right man came along."

"And will he?"

"He might. But he'd have to come along, now wouldn't he?"

"You mean come *here*?"

Ignoring his last question, she taps a fingernail along the rim of her cup, considering the idea. To *marry*? To commit to cherish Charlie in the way Remy cherished Margaret? She exhales. "Sure, then, if he comes here, I'd marry him. But not in a church, not that again."

"Good girl."

When Stephen had proposed, they'd only been together a few months. Lise was at odds over her future as it was, unsure whether she wanted to continue teaching or go on to graduate school. But those concerns became secondary when her mother was diagnosed with cancer. Lise hadn't entirely made up her mind about Stephen before her mother began plotting the traditional wedding she'd always wanted for herself, having been a war bride.

A date was set. The small guest list swelled, so the venue had to be changed. Things grew beyond Lise's control. She wanted to suggest to Stephen that they just live together, since neither seemed really sure, but by then the wedding had become her mother's swansong. As it turned out, the cancer was far more advanced than initially thought, and there was no luxury of time. The wedding date was moved up and, before Lise had time to think, she found herself in the middle of a gaudy, choreographed ceremony, with her frail mother hanging on her brother Paul's arm. The wedding had been an unreal pastel affair blurred by tears and haste.

The first weeks of marriage were taken up with nursing her mother and facing the grim business of death. Stephen was consumed with his postgraduate studies. After the funeral, they packed up for Lake Baptiste, where Stephen finished his dissertation and mastered the barbecue while Lise mourned and took brooding pinhole photos of waterscapes. In the evenings they ate quiet meals and made love after sunset, usually in silence. That summer was uneventful, unremarkable, and Lise would recall it as the best time of their marriage.

By autumn, Stephen was offered three different assistant professorships. When he chose the position in Halifax, she was thrilled – mostly at the idea of living near the ocean – and she was happy enough to quit her job teaching middle school. Having assumed she'd find work once they settled, Lise was only able to get on a roster for substitute teachers. In their row house near the campus, she took on Stephen's share of the household responsibilities and fell into a mindless domesticity of gardening and cooking. Stephen worked all hours, writing, teaching and correcting student papers. Lise helped with research on the manuscript for his first book – a study of the indigenous tribes of Quebec. Entering his notes and research into the computer, Lise felt purposeful and relieved. She didn't have to think much about herself, about anything. For the time being she was Stephen's helpmate, but she didn't mind, assuming that one day the tables would turn and she would finish graduate school, while Stephen took *his* turn at filling in the gaps.

But just before Christmas break that year in Halifax, Lise discovered she was pregnant. The first time she'd felt Adam move, all the attending instincts and hormones kicked in, and she became happily complacent. After Adam was born, one post led Stephen to the next, each more prestigious and demanding than the last. They moved four times in ten years. Lise became an expert at dismantling and packing up homes and re-establishing the family with as little upheaval as possible. Stephen gratefully left it all to her. When they moved back to Toronto, Stephen settled at U of T, as a specialist in indigenous archaeology.

Lise took stock of her life and was shocked. She'd become the seasoned wife of an academic, but little more. Years had sped by unchecked and, besides her time with Adam, there hadn't been much joy. She'd not consciously given up her plans but had simply set them aside. Scrambling to make up for lost time, she took the first job offered – a position below Leonard at the Film Center. In two years she worked her way up to admissions director, then development director. It was good work that placed her nearer to filmmaking, and she had her camera by then.

"Misery loves company, doesn't it?" Remy's booming voice jolts her.

Lise's reply is curt. "I never said I was *un*happy. Just not *very* happy. There's a difference."

Remy looks at her. "I was only going to say, married people seem to want everyone else married too. Can't abide the idea of someone alone."

"But you're very happy to be married."

He clears his throat. "*I* am. I don't know how those poor bachelors do it, with only themselves all day, not to mention all night. Course it's better now for the unmarried than it used to be. There's some nasty customs here in Ireland for those avoiding the altar. You've not heard of Shrovetide?"

Lise shakes her head.

"It's a sort of open season on the unwed." As he hunkers forward, she glances through the camera's viewfinder to check the frame.

"This happened not so many generations back, in Margaret's family – to a cousin, name of Colin Rafferty, a well-off bachelor, salted three years in a row."

"Salted?"

"Right, on Salt Monday – not to be confused with Chalk Sunday, mind you, but similar like. A fella would get salted for failing to marry by spring, by what's called Shrovetide. The salt was to preserve him till the next year, but I don't know the meaning behind the chalk, except to mark the person being ridiculed. We Irish are geniuses at assigning shame. Anyway, God help the poor sod that misses being engaged by Lent, and Colin Rafferty was one. A bright lad, but terrible shy and a stutterer in the bargain. He was in love with a girl but barely had the nerve to speak her name, which, unfortunately, was Connie. So, he could barely propose, even though C-C-Connie was a bold girl, giving every chance. Still, he couldn't rouse the nerve nor get his tongue round her name. Come three years into it, Connie had already seen him salted the two times and your girl there got angry to have to wait another year. Colin saw then she'd given up on him. So, young Rafferty walked to the peak of the headlands and never walked back. You've seen the sign for Rafferty's Road up your way? Well, until I was a lad the road was called Rafferty's Leap."

"Poor man."

As Remy launches into another tale, she finds her concentration fractured between too many stories and the headache knotting behind her eyes. Fixed on the old man's hands, she notices how steady they are. His wedding ring is thin and beaten, as if he's never taken it off. Remy has offered very little of his own history but has provided such small evidences that it is his devotion to Margaret that sustains him.

The ice in her glass has melted to a few floating shards that tap her teeth as she drinks. She interrupts Remy, reaching out to touch his wedding band.

"It's not about the rings, or the dowries, or the poetry, or even the lovemaking, is it?"

His brow hitches at the mention of sex, but after a beat he smiles. "What're you after?"

"What love *really* is. What do you think, Remy?"

"Love?" He waves the word aside. "What's love but trust, anyway? That's the realest – and rarest – thing, at the end of the day." He peers at her. "But you already know that."

* * *

Trust.

When she first agreed, she thought it simply Charlie's idea of a lovers' game. But reaching up to feel the blindfold fast over her cheekbones, she had misgivings. She was too warm in the afternoon stillness, and dizzy from having been spun in place. Charlie had already darted away, his footfalls underscoring her abandonment. She took a few woozy steps in what she hoped was his direction, patting the air for anything familiar. Varnish on the studio floor was tacky; her foot lifting made the sound of an orange being peeled.

He had moved again. She could sense him – the air just beyond her stirred, and she cocked her head in hopes of catching his scent. If she was quiet enough, she might even hear him breathe. The air was rife with heat, a stripe of it slanting over her thigh to suggest she was near a window, but which window? She held out a palm to detect the direction of a breeze that smelled of the sea. Noises from outdoors mingled with those inside; leaves rustled, the pool filter hummed. Air lifted a drawing tacked to the wall and it fell to scrape against the rough plaster.

Humidity whispered through the glass louvers and into a space where the air was moving and slightly tinged with Charlie's smell. He was watching, certainly. As she thought of how his eyes focused with such intent whenever he sketched her body, arousal stretched within to rise to her throat. Touching the hollow between her collarbones, she noted the dampness of her skin. Resting fingertips between her breasts, she gathered more beads of perspiration and reached out, thinking she might tempt Charlie with her scent.

No. It was too early in the game.

A missile of movement disturbed the air near her shoulder. Some small object pinged to the floor a few feet ahead. He'd thrown it, of course. Her eyes narrowed behind the blindfold. "Red herring," she declared, her voice loud in her ears. She stepped away from where the object had landed to a space where tropical mildew and paint smells were intense, some airless corner.

Certain she was near an easel, Lise reached her arm to sweep the air. The arc of her index finger met the surface of canvas and the cool slickness of still-wet paint. She brought the smudge to her nostrils, trying vainly to determine its hue, for surely indigo smelled different from violet or ocher. There were so many conflicting odors: hibiscus, bitter palmetto, her own oils, stale lemon cake from the morning's tea. Firmly pressing her finger to the center of her lower lip, she left a print. Only Charlie would know the color now.

When something tickled over the top of her foot, she froze, then gasped. Ugly, feather-light centipedes were commonplace around the studio, often skittering out from burrows in the blistered timbers. Lise hopped in revulsion and fumbled to yank away the blindfold, but a breeze blew the thing back over her foot and her shoulders softened – it was only something light, inanimate. She crouched to retrieve a tumbleweed of dust, pulling it apart to reveal the textures within: pencil shavings, a seedpod, sand, a thread; a bundle of miscellany under her fingertips.

Sounds amplified. It seemed to her that one sense diluted the next: were she to pull the blindfold off, she would lose the delicious move-ment of air, lose her new ability to isolate smells and sounds. She'd read of people becoming suicidal after losing their sense of taste or smell, and could understand now how blindness might be preferable, unable to imagine not being able to smell Charlie, taste him.

An unmistakable noise made her grin – the creak of a small bone as Charlie's foot arched, his toes turning on the floor. In her confidence she turned and took bold strides, bounding toward the sound. She grabbed out and caught the soft crook of his arm, her palm rasping up his forearm to clutch at his shoulder.

She skidded on something slick, and her stomach lurched at the idea of crashing into unknown space. Her knee hit Charlie's leg, and as they toppled she took in the smoothness and temperature of his skin, felt how the hairs on his shin drew flat under her kneecap. He smelled vaguely of lime and the small cigars he smoked after dinner.

Charlie grunted as he hit the floor. Lise's knee and elbow struck the cement a fraction after, her sharp cry startling them both. Her chin slammed to his sternum as she landed atop him. His breath caught, then seized, the wind knocked out of him.

Lise rolled to her knees, ignoring the rip of pain in her leg to crouch over him. With palms to his temples, her fingertips crept blindly into his hair, working the weight of his skull until she could knit her hands into a cradle.

"Charlie, *Charlie*. Are you all right?"

He didn't answer.

"Charlie!"

When his thumb met her lip, she remembered the paint smudged there.

"Azure," he managed. She knew he was smiling.

They stayed that way, his head in the hammock of her palms, until her question folded the stillness.

"What is this?"

There was no hesitation as the weight of his head shifted toward her. He pulled the blindfold down to meet her eyes.

"Trust."

Later, the bruise on her shin would be incorporated into one of his paintings. It was that single detail that most affected her, overwhelmed her – eclipsing the nudity. He'd portrayed all her flawed humanness in a bloom of delicate olive-blue and yellow, a bruise so realistically wrought it made her wince.

The first time she posed for a full nude, she saw the uncertainty in Charlie's hand, the charcoal hovering above his sketch pad. Three quick drawings were begun, then abandoned. He cursed as he tore up the last attempt, apologizing, "Sorry, it's a long time since I worked from a model."

"Perhaps I'm too naked."

"Maybe."

"We'll try again tomorrow?" She reached for the green stippled dress and lifted it. As the hem fell over her hair, Charlie backed a step away. "Wait." He came forward to still her arms. "Hold that, just there." The frustration in his voice gave way. "It's the dress. I have it. *We* have it."

142

And so it was the dress – or more specifically the act of Lise dressing – that inspired him to paint seven actions, some demure, some seductive, a few even awkward. The study she most vividly recalled was the one of her hands twisting to reach behind her shoulder blades to button the dress. It had been the most difficult pose, but she'd made the best of it, standing in sessions of more than twenty minutes in near contortion. When Charlie finished, she let the dress fall and stepped out of it, massaging her sore wrist. "When you go, take this dress with you. I'll never wear it again."

"I wouldn't want it."

"Why not?"

"Without you in it?" Lise saw grief cloud his eyes: he too was aware of the dwindling number of days left to them.

For one week they worked into the evenings to reach the goal of one complete drawing. The studies later became invaluable to Charlie, when he painted the series. Each image of her was depicted exactly life-size, yet the paintings seemed small when hung in the expanse of the gallery where they were eventually exhibited. Small pieces, *masterpieces*, one critic would claim, boldly suggesting that in painting her, Mr Lowan had distinguished his career. Future commentary invariably assigned his works to three distinct periods: Early Seas, the Dresser, and Later Seas. Another critic who faithfully followed Charlie's career remarked with burning irony that in his Canadian debut, Charles Lowan had made his truest work – but only after he'd lost himself.

Charlie often gave her gifts. One morning she found a chain with a saint medal looped around her teacup handle.

"What's this?"

"Saint Catherine of Bologna. Found her in the flea market and thought of you. Her feast day is the same as your birthday, so she's your ideal patron." He fixed the clasp behind her neck and settled the medal between her breasts. "You're in good company now."

She touched the Latin inscription edging the oval. "What's she the saint of?"

"Artists."

"You should have her for yourself."

He winked. "I can always steal another. Besides, you'll need her."

What he meant – what they both knew – was that the months ahead would be tougher for her, surely.

She kissed him. "Thank you. Now, what can I give you?"

"Oh, I dunno, a bit of hope for us?"

She smiled and pretended to sprinkle something over his head. He pretended to rise under it.

* * *

When patrons begin filling the hotel dining room, Lise realizes Mass is over, that she's been listening to Remy for more than two hours. Absently rubbing the surface of her medal, she idly looks out the window to see staggered lines of people on Arches Road.

Remy coughs. "Four cups of coffee, you're still barely with us?"

"I'm here."

He points to the chain twined around her fingers, the dangling medal. "Keepsake?"

"Uh-huh."

"From the man you'd stand up with?"

"Yes, actually."

He lifts his glasses for a closer look. "Which Catherine is that?"

"The Italian, from Bologna." She leans over so he can see the inscription. "You know Latin?"

"Enough." He squints. "It says, roughly, *Create and rejoice in your labors*. You know who she was?"

"A patron to artists, and something else. Temptations, I think. That's what my friend told me – *Charlie* told me."

"Ah, so he has a name. Good. Yes, Catherine was all that, and a great documentarian as well. She illustrated sacred scripts and the

144

like, every bit as good as our monks with their Book of Kells. Also did something important for the Italian painters of her time, if I recall. After her grave was dug up and her still fresh as a rose, she was posthumously sainted."

"How do you know all this?"

"Have you not read *Lives of the Saints*?" Remy even remembers a few of Catherine's seven canons: "Let's see, there was diligence, trust in self, and remembrance of passion."

"You have a lot of theology for an atheist, Remy."

"Theology, mythology, all the ologies are nearly the same – just stories. But I'm only agnostic; atheists have no faith."

"But you do?"

"Sure." He winks. "You carry some faith in that medal, am I wrong?"

Lise shrugs. "Oh, I dunno, faith in an object?"

He looks at her squarely. "Sure, in an object. Why not, if it embodies the possibility of faith? If you've an ounce of faith, just about any object can become the talisman to guide you."

"So if you believe—"

"*Truly* believe? Then half your work's done; it's life makes the rest happen. Take care, though, that you don't rely too much on the symbols of faith. D'ya know our own Siobhan believes herself fated to the boy Colm, on account of the hole of Kilmaolcheader."

"The hole of what?"

"At the churchyard there's some old pillar with a hole in it, and it's believed that when the fingers of a him and a her meet through it, they're fated to marry. So the girl swears she's engaged." Remy points to his eyebrow. "Granted, her choice of engagement ring is a bit odd."

"So she *did* pierce her eyebrow for a man."

"Boy, really. But right so, just before you came. She was a desperate girl those first weeks. She's better now, though, don't you think?"

Remembering Siobhan's tears of the night before, Lise only shrugs.

Remy huffs, "Colm's no match for her, regardless. So life will take care of the rest. She'll forget him soon enough."

"Will she?" It's been an exhausting morning, and Lise sees the reel of film is nearly spent. The meeting's over.

The entire ride home, something about Siobhan and Colm nags her jumbled, caffeinated thoughts. The hangover still grips as she thinks, *It'll come to me*. Edging in the cottage door, she drops her case just as the phone begins ringing.

She skids into the parlor. So few people have the number that there's a good chance it's him. She grabs up the receiver. "Hello."

"Hello?"

"Adam!"

"Ah, no."

"Stephen?" She drops into a chair. "Oh. You sound so alike now, I can hardly tell who's who. What is it? Adam all right?"

"Fine. Listen. I just need your address."

"For?"

"Adam's entrance forms for university."

She rattles off the address. "Is that all?"

"Not quite. The real estate agents here have determined a market value for the house. My lawyer's sending along the offer for your half."

She sighs. "Just have them send the paperwork." The house is the last bit of property to settle, and the most personal, but Stephen's tone is quite businesslike.

"All right, then." He was about to hang up.

"Wait! How is he?"

"Adam?"

"Yes, *Adam*."

"You mean he doesn't call you?"

"You know he doesn't." Unable to control the wavering in her voice, Lise presses the phone to its cradle before he can say anything else.

Chapter Eight

When the car pulls up, Lise is arranging store-bought pastries on a plate. Quickly crumpling the waxed bakery sack, she tosses it to flare in the hearth before rushing outside. Margaret is her guest and subject of the afternoon's filming.

"Margaret! How was your drive?"

"It's not the N15, is it? I'd forgotten how far! And I used to *pedal* out here and back… hard to believe now." With hands on her hips she surveys the cottage and outbuildings. "Lord. The place hasn't changed a stone in forty years."

"Would you like to see the beach?"

"Indeed." Margaret skirts ahead of Lise around the corner of the cottage. Taking in the view, she sighs. "Just as I remember."

At the end of the sandy path, Lise offers the old woman an arm to help her down the slope, but Margaret waves her away to climb down on her own. Once on the sand, she rubs her hands and nods toward a low cliff hemming the horseshoe beach. "My first kiss was just over by that rock."

"Really? You and Remy?"

Margaret laughs. "Heavens, no. Peter Kleege. Maeve Kleege's nephew, from the North."

"Your first kiss was here?"

"Ah, yeah, I don't know how we managed it – Maeve with those falcon eyes always swooping in from nowhere." She blinks. "*Ah*, Peter. Good-looking boy… eyes like that sky."

"He was your beau?"

"Well, not properly. That wouldn't have done. He was only a summer boy, y'see, sent down by his people, who feared he'd fall into some black doings in Derry." Frowning, she adds, "A very long time ago, all that. I often wonder what became of him. Smart dresser he was. Had his own car, and always money enough for the cinema or to stand a pint. Back then I never wondered how, but after he'd gone off… well, he'd one uncle in the IRA and another in the RUC, so who knows what he'd got up to." Margaret squares her shoulders. "Oh, we used to love to swim out here." She steps out of her shoes and wades in, unaware of her stockings. When Lise turns to see her, it's too late; the old woman is in nearly to her knees. "Margaret! That water's freezing!"

Rain from the night before has frozen in depressions, so that the beach appears littered with jagged, tin-bright shapes.

Margaret shivers and slowly looks to Lise. "It is rather arctic, isn't it?" The hem of her dress has darkened in the water. "But smell that air!" She grins as she plods out of the surf.

Lise sniffs obediently. Out over the water are the two islands Danny took her to see on his boat. "Margaret, see those islands, the two humps?"

"Ah, sure. We called them His and Hers – you see there, the one looks like it's got a bosom. Those are still the same." Backtracking to where she's left her shoes, Margaret steps into them, lifts her wet hem, and bemoans the state of her legs. "Ach, would you look at these posts! New spots and veins every week, it seems. At least the sea doesn't change, does it? Just watches us land here as babes and limp away with our hair gone white."

"But you're not that old, Margaret."

"Well, not so old as yer Kleege woman, but not so far behind either. Do the seals still come round?"

"What seals?"

"Pity. Used to be rafts of 'em. Goodness, it *is* chilly. How about that cup of tea?"

Lise follows Margaret into the cottage and stops to hang the wet stockings her guest has peeled off and left in a puddle by the door. Margaret walks barefoot through the rooms, ignoring

Lise's suggestion to sit by the hearth and warm herself. Instead she gazes around in admiration, taking in the stripped floors, the new cushions and the scrubbed walls. "My, it's certainly changed in here. It was never so nice when old Maeve had the place. Good on you for sweeping out the gloom. It's nearly a home now, isn't it?"

"It's coming along." She quickly shows Margaret the upstairs, and as they descend the steps, a pitch from the kitchen grows to shrillness. "Kettle's boiled." Lise leads into the kitchen. "Tea."

Margaret nods approvingly as Lise rinses the teapot with boiling water. She heaps in three teaspoons of loose tea, is about to put in a fourth when Margaret edges close, wrinkling her nose.

"Three brews a perfect pot. Odd numbers are best. The luckiest things in life come in threes, fives and so on, don't they just?" She winks. "'Cept marriage, a course – one's not enough there, and three's an awful crowd."

"Right." Lise quickly turns to the cupboard, her voice thin as she pretends to look for sugar. "Three is a crowd."

There are cream rolls and cinnamon buns for tea. When Margaret bites into one, she nods. "Ah, sure. These'll be from McIntyre's. But you needn't have fussed so for me. I'm sure whatever you'd have made yourself would do."

"Believe me, these are much nicer than any I could make. Never got the hang of baking."

"You don't make your own bread and such? Oh well, you'll come down to my kitchen for an afternoon and I'll show you a few easy things. And how was your fish Saturday last?"

"The fish. Oh! Yes. I meant to thank you. It was… OK. I might've overcooked it a bit."

"Tch. I told Siobhan to tell you – ten minutes, no more, the slightest simmer."

After tea they move into the parlor, where the camera is set up. She's put out a decanter of sherry and two glasses, remembering Remy's mention that Margaret liked a dram of something in the afternoons. If it makes her less nervous before the camera, all the better.

"There's where you'll sit. And we're all ready. You'll talk just as you normally do, Margaret. Try your best not to look at the camera. Right?"

"We're starting so soon?" She adjusts the still-damp hem over her knees and looks straight at the lens. Margaret's gone to the trouble of a Sunday dress, but as she smoothes her hair back, Lise notices she's wearing two different earrings. When it's pointed out, Margaret turns red with embarrassment.

"Dear Lord! My brain is hardening and here I'm supposed to be giving my memories – well, that's how reliable I'll be." She pulls off the clips, one silver orb and one garnet crescent. "Remy swears I've been dotty from the beginning, but I've only pretended to be when it suits me. And now I'm like that boy who cried wolf – I can't always remember the telephone number to the shop, and I make hash of the silliest details." She crossly tosses the mismatched earrings into her purse.

"Details don't matter, Margaret. I'm only after stories."

"Ah, well, *those* I have." She relaxes a bit and leans back. "Most the old days I remember. Or if it's a recipe you're wanting, those I know from heart."

"Then I'll only ask after the recipes and stories." The camera is quietly humming. "How did you meet –" Peter Kleege's name is on the tip of her tongue; he'd obviously been Margaret's first love, but some instinct stops her. "How'd you meet Remy?"

"Mm. People round here don't *meet*, so much. Just sometimes you notice them harder than others. I don't remember actually meeting Remy. He was always limping about, whistling. An odd boy. Thoughtful."

"Thoughtful – yes, he bought you a star, didn't he?"

"He did! My star." She dips into the shopping bag at her feet. "See, here, I've even brought my map of the sky, like you asked." She takes out a folded chart and spreads it over the table. "Oh, and here's the family picture album, too. There might be something in there you'll want to use in your movie?"

"Sure. If you could leave it – just for a day or two?" She points to the chart. "So, about your star?"

"Oh, it's just the sort of thing Remy'd do, to show his feelings in a different way, romantic like. He fancies himself that." She taps her finger along the chart. "And here it is – see my name there, just this speck! He was so proud when he gave me this. I know it's a bit foolish, but I'd rather have this than some ordinary treasure. Queer, isn't it, that every woman alive seems to want a diamond to flash, or pearls for her throat? But the notion that a man might please any girl with the same gift! Where's the imagination in that? Remy wouldn't be so common thinking. Maybe *odd*'s more the word. He'd say *different*. He'd say lots of things."

"He does talk, doesn't he?"

"Streaks. Better than radio most nights. But if you tried to take it all in, he could wear the ears off you – all those facts of this and that. Sometimes he recites."

"His poems?"

"His. Others'." Margaret eyes the sherry.

"Oh! Sorry, let me pour you some." Lise fills the small glasses. Margaret holds one aloft, toasting. "To the poets, then." After a polite sip she frowns. "Ever notice the poets're usually men? Women haven't the leisure, of course. Only a man would make the hours for such nonsense."

"But Remy's poems aren't nonsense?"

"No. But it's only a hobby anyway. Says he's no good at it."

"Can you recite any he's written for you?"

"A few. I may not be able to remember what was yesterday's date, but there's this one poem I won't forget, because it was the first time we…" She looks up slyly. "The first *time*."

"I see. Well, you needn't—"

"Oh, heavens, it wasn't dirty, just the opposite like. I remember he'd brought me these plum branches just blooming and smelling like evening." Her eyes mist as she absently sips sherry. "*Just* like evening. Oh, he'd waited so long. Such patience he had all those months; then home he came with those twigs held together with a bit of twine. Down on his knee he went, reciting,

From evening's blue-lit branches cut,
Blossoms pilfered in pale twilight,
Cast petals over this anointed hour,
This anointed night.

"I *have* remembered it! Oh, and those were pretty flowers, too. Better than anything from a shop. I found later he *had* stolen them – from the rectory garden, no less! – but I never said a word. He gave me that poem on one knee, like some knight, kissing my wedding ring. That was an evening." Her tone shifts. "Ah, yeah. He was very gentle with his kisses. I'd expected him to be hungry like, from the wait. But his hands were so... his touch so light, almost like he feared he might leave marks..." Margaret's focus is cast somewhere far beyond the window. "Well, when Remy took my hair down I did feel like a girl in a poem. Loved like." She folds her hands into a bridge under her chin. "And he was very funny, too, laughing at how the freckles on my back made a pattern like stars, how blue and thin the milk was."

Milk? Lise straightens from behind the camera, puzzled and about to form a question, for surely she's missed a word – she so often does when preoccupied behind the viewfinder. "Pardon?" she says, but her voice falls away at the sight of the old woman, her eyes shut and her fingers touching her own cheek, as if remembering Remy's hand there.

"And he gave me a song afterwards, sang me to sleep."

"Margaret, did you say—"

"What, dear?"

Lise, seeing the tears, reaches for a box of tissue. "Nothing. Here, take one."

After Margaret pats her eyes, the remoteness in her voice dissolves. "That fool. He's brilliant at making me cry even when he's not around! Ah, some of his lines can still make me laugh or cry – other things too." Margaret holds the sherry glass to her collar. "Believe it or not, he used to write some very racy lines – could put together a lovely page not using one nasty word and still take the legs out from under me. What's the word, *suggestive*?" She shakes her head. "And where in the world have those letters got to? Oh, I'd hate to think of Siobhan finding them."

"You imagine she's too innocent?"

"Ha! She wouldn't understand, is all. Don't all the young people now know more about sex than doctors? Yet so little about love, even less of how the two fit together. Besides, the idea of us, like *that*? A girl doesn't like to know such things about her grandparents. It's bad enough with her teasing. She's the only person alive can embarrass Remy. As a joke once she called him a horny tortoise. Course I expected him to yank her bald, but he only turned a shade of that paper and set his spoon down."

"So he's not so fierce, for all his barking?"

"Remy? Soft as butter."

"He is a bit nostalgic, isn't he?"

"*Nostalgia*. Might be a disease for how it sounds, like something that would settle in the lower back." Margaret's tone clips into practicality. "Who has time to waste thinking about old beginnings when there's middle and ends to attend to!" She looks squarely into the camera. "It's not so much what happened then as how things turned out."

The statement vaguely echoes something Remy had said the very first time Lise asked about his courtship. Lise can barely imagine Margaret and Remy young, or how they had ever come to make a pair. Had they been drawn together, or thrown? She poured another two measures of sherry into Margaret's glass, peering at her. She'd said "milk". Clear as a bell. "Why did – *how* did you know you'd marry Remy?"

"I got the dish."

"Dish?"

"Divination."

"Pardon?"

"I'll show you." Margaret gets up. "Here, you sit in my chair, and now leave that camera running, right? Have you four saucers in that kitchen?"

"Sure."

"You stay put and, when I come in, you shut your eyes tight."

"All right." She reluctantly shifts into Margaret's chair. From the kitchen come sounds of plates being taken from the cupboard, the tap running, a ping of metal and the back door opening, then closing. She feels the unblinking eye of the camera and turns to call out, "What's this divination going to tell me?"

"Your future, of course. Eyes shut tight, now?"

She nods as Margaret moves into the room and places something on the table. "One more trip and we're ready. No peeking!"

There is more scrabbling, then footsteps and the rattle of china saucers being set down.

"I feel a little silly."

"Psh. Women here have been doing this for centuries. Now, this's how it goes. There are the four saucers in front of you." Her hand is taken and guided to touch each rim. "You're to settle on one, simple as that."

"And if I choose the wrong one?"

"*You* don't choose, dear. It's your fate; it chooses you. Now, here we go. Just one, mind you, and don't touch what's on the saucers, only the rims. The first one that feels right, you stop at."

Her hands are guided again to the edges of the saucers. She touches each, lingering at the last before moving back to the third.

"Can I choose two?"

"Don't be daft. And stop thinking."

"I'll try." Since Margaret seems to believe in the game, Lise decides to go along. Her fingers waver between the third and fourth

154

saucers as she tries emptying her mind, listening to the sounds of the house: the leather chair creaking beneath her, wind moaning in the gutters. Just as she's nearly forgotten what she's doing, her fingers shift to settle on the cool lip of the third saucer.

"Oh. This one."

"You're sure?"

"I am." She laughs. "Just not sure *why*."

"Grand! Open your eyes now."

The saucers hold odd bits: a mound of salt, clay chips, a puddle of water and a metal curtain ring from the kitchen window. "I've chosen water?"

"Brilliant choice. Here, you see the others? The salt? That represents wealth. Clay means early death." Margaret crosses herself quickly. "But you barely touched that one. And the fourth plate, with the ring, where you hesitated, that foretells a marriage, as you might guess."

"And water?"

"Means a person will emigrate over a sea." Her grin is broad. "So you'll be staying with us, then!"

"I will?"

"I knew the moment I got out of my car. You look just right standing near this house."

Margaret isn't the first person to predict her settling at this place. Lise looks out the window to the desolate sea, waves chopping at the shore. Live here? When she turns back, Margaret is dumping the bit of clay into the hearth. What faith she must have had, giving destiny over to a game. Lise nods at the plates. "And *this* is how you decided to marry Remy?"

Margaret looks at her sternly. "Absolutely. I was scared witless, thinking I'd get the clay for sure. But I got the ring, didn't I? And here we are, forty-some years later." She nods from Lise to the running camera, grinning. "And see now, you're in the film as well!"

"So I am."

155

As they clear away, Margaret scans the room again. "I cannot get over it. The place has really come round." She picks up both sherry glasses. "And you're all unpacked save for this crate. Goodness, what have you in there? A treasure?"

"Just some scandalous paintings."

"Sure, sure." She raises her glass and drains it. "Bless your heart."

Once in her car, Margaret rolls down the window. "Lord, I nearly forgot. You've not seen Siobhan?"

"No. Not since Saturday... well, Sunday, actually, we were up rather late." The nagging feeling she'd had coming from her meeting with Remy edges back, as if she's forgotten something vital. "She's not called?"

Margaret shrugs. "Ach, she's probably off to Dublin to see Brigid. Thing is, she should've been in the shop today."

"Does she do that, just go off?"

"Used to, now and again, but now with Colm gone to America she mostly mopes about here. I'll stop by her place and see what's what. But sure that's all – she's maybe left a note, or Danny'll know where she's gone. Maybe I'll phone Brigid myself later." She grasps the steering wheel to back away, muttering.

Lise politely watches the car, waving until it disappears over the rise. The second it's out of sight she bolts into the house.

In the parlor she opens the photo album Margaret brought and pulls Conner family photos from the sleeves. Remy's handwriting is neat in the lower corners, where he has dated the photos, just as he dates everything, down to his grocery lists. She lays the photos facedown, glancing from one set of numbers to another, and notices that the date on their wedding picture conflicts with the date on Danny's first birthday portrait.

It doesn't take much to piece together the story Margaret has inadvertently laid out for her. Certainly it wasn't unusual or even noteworthy that Margaret might have been pregnant before marrying Remy. But there's something else... they married in autumn, yet Remy had brought her plum blossoms the first time they made love. He'd kissed her wedding ring that first night; at least that's how Margaret remembered it. An autumn wedding. Fruit trees, *plum trees*, bloom only once, in spring. Remy had laughed at the blue milk. Breast milk.

Lise sits back on her heels, puzzling. Unsure what, if anything, she's discovered.

* * *

During their last days together in Mexico, Charlie nearly persuaded Lise to stay on until Stephen returned so they might face him together, but the notion was too frightening. She still imagined that Stephen, so brilliant at making things happen, might also prevent her from going home to her son.

"I can't stay, Charlie. Adam needs me."

"I understand that. But when will we see each other again?"

"In a few months. I'll just need time to sort things out."

"And in the meantime? Just carry on as usual?"

"No, Charlie, there isn't any *usual*. Not anymore. We just carry on."

He reached for her, sighing.

They continued their work in the studio. She was still posing, half-clad in the green stippled dress. He'd already stopped making any drawings that included her eyes. When she saw his final sketch, the sadness made her want to tear it up. "Do I always look so tragic?"

"No. See these earlier drawings? You glow."

"To you, maybe."

He showed her drawing after drawing. "That's you. And this, and this – gloomy, sexy, happy, whatever. I'm only someone you've been brave enough to show yourself to."

When he said that, she nearly lost her will. "I can't leave here."

"Yes, you can."

She faced him. "This *is* real, isn't it?"

"If this isn't, I don't know what is." His fingers twined in her hair. "I *will* wait, you know."

They drove south toward the Belize border to a village with a restaurant Clarice had recommended. Throughout the silent meal, Lise couldn't shake her despair. Their last day was fast approaching. She memorized Charlie's palm, squared its heft and broadness against hers while their uneaten food grew cold.

As they left the restaurant, a man loitering outside offered them a tour of a sea cave. At first Charlie waved him off, but then the man said something she half understood, *agua de fósforo.*

"What'd he say?"

"He claims water in the cave glows phosphorescent."

She stood back, hoping Charlie would have the sense to walk away. But he had heard of the cave, had even tried to find it himself. "C'mon. It'll cheer us up."

"Shouldn't we be getting back?"

"He says it's miraculous." His smile was wan. "We could use a miracle."

They followed the man's truck a mile or so through a strip of jungle until the road dead-ended at a secluded horseshoe beach. They made their way down a slippery path to the cavern entrance. When she stalled, Charlie turned back.

"Take my arm."

She swallowed. "Do you think it's safe?"

They crouched along a cool passage. Water dripped from the low ceiling. She gripped Charlie's arm and kept her eyes on the wavering beam of the guide's flashlight. They passed a tidal pool, and the cavern opened onto a massive chamber where they stood on a crescent of sand surrounding a tiny lagoon. The water wasn't glowing, and for a moment she was certain they'd been led into some trap. She glued herself to Charlie's side. When the guide turned off his light, she braced herself. Bandits would jump them; they would be robbed. Or worse.

But as the moments ticked past, there was only a dripping quiet as their eyes adjusted to the dim light. She blinked as the cavern walls took form in the slight glow from the pool. The longer they stood, the lighter the cavern became. The rough dome above flickered in the reflected light of weak green fire. The water itself seemed a trick, the glow brighter in the depths, as if someone with a colored torch swam underneath.

Charlie gazed up to the dome of stalactites, where drops of water poised at their tips like tears. When he let go of her to step up on a ledge for a closer look, air swirled coldly around Lise's bare neck.

Displaced and chilled, Lise was suddenly looking at the back of her father's head, a cloud of breath huffing sideways with his words.

It was winter at Lake Baptiste. She and Paul stood flanking their father and all three were looking up to the deep cottage eaves, where a row of dangerously large icicles strained the gutters. Lise had always imagined the two sides of the roof as a great pair of wings over the cottage, and that day the wings were adorned with a crystalline fringe made achingly beautiful in the February sunlight. Her father feared the ice would bow the gutters or create ice dams under the shingles above to flood the attic rooms. She was surrounded by the sound of dripping and disturbed by the unfamiliar tone of worry in her father's voice.

"See, if I try breaking them off, they'll dent the gutters or maybe break the windows. Any ideas for how else we might get them down?" Lise found it sad they had to destroy the pretty icicles, but her father wanted it done, so she put her mind to it.

Paul wrinkled his nose. "I dunno, Dad. How about we start a fire under them?"

Their father pretended to consider the idea. "Sort of close to the house for that, Son."

"*I* know, Daddy!" Lise tugged his sleeve and pointed halfway up the slope of the roof to a dormer window. "What if we open that window and poured boiling water down in the gutters? Wouldn't the icicles just let go?"

"Hmm." Her father was rubbing his chin. "That's not half-bad, Elle. Not bad at all."

She grinned at her brother, who began to glower back just as a wild groan and a terrible metallic snap rent the air. Lise saw only her father's gloved hand as it caught her arm to fling her clear. As she was spun sideways and hurled downward, there was a crash and a china shatter, followed by the rush of something heavy skimming the air next to her lowered head.

"What? What was that!?"

Charlie jumped down from his perch. "Just tide washing out from the next chamber. You all right?"

She blinked and nudged in closer to him. "I'm fine."

"Beautiful, isn't it?" Charlie wrapped an arm around her. When he felt her trembling, he whispered, "Cold?"

"Yeah, a little."

Their guide nodded up at the dome.

"Ask him what makes it glow."

Charlie spoke, then listened intently as the guide answered. "Ah, *sí. Sí.* He says people have many ideas. Some say it is spirit light, ancient, from souls sacrificed to Mayan gods, or drowned fishermen, or pirates killed here. Others claim it has white magic, that this water can heal wounds or mend broken souls."

He listened another moment and faced Lise. "The religious believe a miracle makes the water glow – that the cave filled with holy tears on the feast day of Guadalupe."

"*Sí.*" The man spoke very rapidly as he continued, his eyes shining.

Charlie translated. "Of course, there is a scientific explanation, very simple, he says. But – and now this is a question he is asking *us*

– should magic always be explained? Should we know the answers to every mystery God lays before us? And finally he suggests – wouldn't we rather leave this place tonight having chosen our own explanations?" Charlie spoke again, looking intently at her, though still speaking Spanish. Both men nodded enthusiastically, then laughed.

"What did you say?"

"I agreed, and said the best mysteries are best left unexplained."

"*Amor*." The guide tipped his hat.

That she understood.

When they reached the car, Charlie began to take out his wallet. The man stepped back abruptly. "No. No, señor." They had a rapid conversation during which Charlie put a hand on the man's shoulder and thanked him several times.

The guide bowed and murmured, "*Duerman con los angelitos*," before ducking into the dark cab of his truck. Lise looked to Charlie, who translated the phrase as he steered her to the car. *Sleep with angels.*

"Charlie, why wouldn't he take any money?"

"Because he wasn't a tour guide. He'd watched us in the restaurant and thought it might do us good to see the cave."

"Who was he, I wonder?"

"His name is Martinez. He's here from Guadalajara visiting his sister. *Padre* Martinez – he's a priest."

She thought back to her moments of wariness and panic, feeling small. "You knew to trust him from the beginning, didn't you?"

"Sure." His look was pitying. "You didn't?"

During their last few nights at the villa, they slept little and poorly, falling into fitful dreams only near dawn. In sleep, Lise held Charlie so securely that to get up to use the bathroom he had to ease away from her, limb by limb. "Poor Elle," he whispered.

Once she woke to find him kneeling just over her, his hands hovering a few inches from her shoulder, his palms close enough she could feel a slight heat as he traced the air over her flesh. She rolled, groggy. "What're you doing, Charlie?"

"Collecting."

"Collecting what?"

"You."

Flora was sent to find her. She rapped timidly, venturing, "Señora? *Teléfono... es, ah, su esposo.* Señor Stephen?"

She tied her robe together and opened the door, a finger pressed to her lips, nodding to where Charlie lay sleeping. "Shhh."

Flora was wide eyed. "*Sí, sí. Comprendo,*" she whispered. "*Comprendo.*"

She followed the girl to the kitchen, where the tiles were cold under her feet. "Stephen?"

"Hey. They took forever getting you. Sorry to drag you out of bed."

"Don't be. I was up... I was out."

"Oh? Mercedes said you were asleep."

"No."

"Well, anyway, I just talked to Adam, caught him before he went off to school. He said you hadn't called for a few days. I was just wondering if everything is all right. You OK?"

"I... I might have eaten something. Either that or it's the water. I'm fine now though. I'll call Adam this morning. How'd he sound?"

"A little droopy. Probably misses us more than he admits."

Us. She inhaled.

"You there?"

"Yeah. This phone. What else did he say?"

"Oh, you know Adam. He hasn't much to say these days. Listen, you should have Mercedes or Clarice call the doctor."

"Stephen."

"At least take some Imodium, and drink plenty of water. Bottled."

She looked at her hands, wishing he wouldn't be kind. "I will. Clarice says you've left Mexico City. Are you in LA now?"

"Yeah. I'll fill you in later. It's going well."

"That's wonderful."

When she looked up, she saw Charlie was walking toward her down the long hall from the dining room.

"Say hi to Clarice. Is that painter still there?"

Swallowing, she watched as Charlie reached the arch of the breakfast room door. "I think so."

"Anyone else interesting come?"

"I don't really know."

"Oh, right, you've been down. Well, get some rest, then. I'll talk to you soon."

"OK, bye then." Charlie stepped into the kitchen.

Stephen paused. "Bye. Love you." He said it casually, like *Have a nice day*.

"Ah… me too." She winced and held down the clear button until a bloodless dent marked her thumb.

Charlie was standing no more than a foot away, looking sleepy.

"I woke and you were gone." He nodded at the phone. "Stephen, right? You said 'me too'. Me too what?"

Her eyes closed. "He said, 'Love you.' It was automatic. He says it all the time."

"Is it automatic to respond?"

"Yes."

"Does he mean it?"

"He might, but I don't *feel* it. Listen. He only called to tell me Adam is lonely, or a little off. I forgot to call him yesterday."

She took both Charlie's hands in full view of Mercedes. "Please don't look at me like that."

"Like what?"

"Wounded. Can you see now, Charlie? This isn't so simple."

He tightened his fingers around hers. "I know it's not."

The kitchen was a maze of sharp edges, of cool stainless and ceramic tile. She leaned hard into Charlie's warmth.

The day before she was to leave, Charlie rolled up the drawings of her and slid them into a heavy cardboard tube. When he pulled a suitcase from the closet, she sat up. "You're leaving too?"

He looked drained. "I can't stay with you gone. I changed my ticket."

"When? Not today?"

"Tomorrow. My flight's just after yours."

"So. We'll go to the airport together?"

"Yeah." He kissed her forehead. "Let's not say goodbye here."

They walked to the far side of the village, close to the pier where their near-fatal cruise had launched. They found a small restaurant with a shaded patio, but just as they were being seated, Charlie pointed across the street. "See that sign?"

"Which one?"

"*Tea Leaf Reader.*"

"Charlie."

He took her arm. "C'mon, we're not really hungry anyway."

They entered a dark enclosure piled with egg crates. Fees for tarot and palm readings were posted on the wall. A barefoot boy with light eyes urged them in. Charlie touched her shoulder. "Don't talk too much – just listen."

"You do this often?"

He winked. "Now and then."

Her eyes adjusted to the dimness in time to lean away from a thin cat, which was hissing and poised like a wicket. "At least it's not black," she whispered.

An old woman draped in a confusing arrangement of dirty sweaters and scarves rose from her chair as the cat sprang in the air between Lise and Charlie. It captured a small lizard and pivoted, proudly dangling the creature from one claw.

"Señora, tea or tarot?" The old woman's English was oddly accented.

Charlie pressed her forward. "Both."

"You." The tea leaf reader motioned to Charlie with her jaw. "Wait in the street."

"Charlie" – Lise spoke through her teeth – "do not leave me here."

"Seems I must." His eyebrow hitched. "She's rather strict, huh?" Then he was gone.

"Sit, señora. We have tea." The woman croaked out an order to the boy in a language Lise didn't recognize. Dark eyes raked over her. "We are Romany. I am Madam Magda. Give your hand."

"But I wanted tea leaf and tarot."

"Tea, yes, palm, yes. No tarot for you." The woman was wearing a sock as a glove, with holes cut to expose a snarl of fingers that she rapped down like a mallet. "Your hands."

Lise obediently laid a hand down.

"Both. Palms up."

Madam peered at her palms, poking along the various lines and roughly turning her wrists. When the boy came in with the tea, the woman ignored him.

"You have one child – he has good humor, but some darkness coming. This winter, the coldest months" – she shook her head – "will be very difficult, for both the boy and you."

"Difficult how?"

"Mostly your own doing." She didn't explain, and her tone was nearly bored as she rattled off additional remarks over her hand. "Long enough life. Double fate line." She scowled suddenly and spoke emphatically. "You are unsettled with old business. Finish it." The teacup was pushed forward. "Drink now."

The tea was barely warm. Lise could only hope it had been boiled. In the candlelight she saw the woman had one frosty cataract.

Madam watched her drink, and rapped her hand again, motioning her to give over the cup. "You finish? Good. I begin."

"OK, I—"

"*I* begin." Madam studied the contents of the cup for less than five seconds, sat back and stared straight ahead, pointing a gingerroot finger to her stomach. "You are going to be ill, here. It will begin in the heart and spread to your belly." She shrugged. "But you can heal when you want. Remember this."

Her eyes were screwed shut. "Right now there is something pulled from you – a shield or a veil. Like ice, nearly. You've been hidden under this... but you can leave it for good – you need to. Do not hide underneath. It's no place for you."

The woman's eyes opened, shifting and blind, as if in a dream. "But there *is* a place, a house maybe. A house with poor chimneys. It has an eye to the water, a plain house, stone, near large water, high waves. Not a handsome house, but happy. It can hold you. You will find this place only when you stop seeking."

"Is there a man?"

The woman sniffed. "Don't ask what you already know. There are two. You stand between. Wait for the music."

"Music?"

"Women singing, making clouds with their song." She put the cup down and stared at Lise. "Any questions?"

A shiver climbed Lise's neck. The cold breath of singing women? Stored somewhere in her history was a similar image, too deep to dredge. Lise shook herself.

"Questions? Ah, I'm not sure... Wait, yes – my son. You mentioned darkness, difficulty. What did you mean?"

"He is on his path, not yours. It is his own difficulty." For the first time her sour face breaks a smile, showing surprisingly healthy teeth. "He has sun in his future. Two children will come, two grandchildren. Both black-haired."

"But my son is blond."

"*Black*-haired." She stood up. "That's thirty pesos."

* * *

She emerged into dusty heat to find Charlie smoking. She shielded her eyes and motioned him in. "I'll say she's strict. Don't keep madam waiting. And don't contradict her."

After he ducked into the doorway, she leaned against the building to finish his cigarette. *Thirty pesos!* She ground the butt under her sandal and crossed the street to wait in the shade.

A half hour passed. She couldn't imagine what was taking so long. By the time he finally came out, Lise was impatient and warm. "What did she say?"

"Nothing much."

"You were in there long enough."

"We had things to talk about."

"Don't be cagey."

"All right. We talked about you."

"Me! She was with me for all of ten minutes. What could she possibly know?"

"That you're a skeptic. But that you'll come around."

"Oh please. What else?"

He looked at her. "Everything."

Her footsteps on the flagstones were deliberate. She carried her sandals, wanting to remember this walk on the soles of her bare feet, her final walk to Charlie's door.

The studio was nearly empty. The seascapes were crated near the double doors, with his dealer's name and address stenciled in red. The sturdy tube of drawings leaned against a canvas duffel bag and his carry-on. The tables were cleared, his collected objects either returned to the sea or given away.

Lise noticed her own footprints on the dusty floor. They would soon be swept away, along with such other small evidences as an auburn hair caught in a glass louver; a grapefruit peel scalloped by Charlie's fingernails; her lip-prints dulling the rim of the best teacup; a silk thread floating from the hanger where her sea-colored dress had hung.

When she said his name, her voice broke in the emptiness. *Just as well*, she thought, sinking to the mattress. *Words are useless now*.

For the first time they were silent as they made love. Tried to make love. They would begin, become overwhelmed and roll from each other, perspiring. Though each was desperate for release, neither could climax. She settled for sobs; Charlie settled for kissing her eyes.

He told her coastal raindrops sometimes fall as salty as tears. The leaky skylight – a black square above where she and Charlie slept – admitted one drop that met her cheek as she turned away.

Rain trickled to the corner of her mouth. She fell into a dream where she gathered drops in a teacup. The cup filled and spilled over as she tried to reach up to dam the hole where drops fell, fast, then faster. But she couldn't reach the skylight. The hole opened to wet night. The corrugated tin roof rang with applause. As the studio doors blew violently inward, bed sheets caught in the air to rise and veer away like seabirds, leaving her and Charlie exposed and naked.

To her horror, Stephen rushed in from the rain, dragging Adam with him, sputtering and pointing to where she and Charlie lay.

All she could do was implore, *Go back, go away*. But her voice seized in her throat.

Charlie woke and gathered her, his breath warm on her neck. "You were crying. You were dreaming."

"I wasn't dreaming. I was wide awake."

"No, you weren't. Go back to sleep." He kissed her damp hair.

She tried to sleep, but her eyes kept opening to the skylight and the rare rain tapping there. Charlie told her a children's story in Welsh, hoping the droning of an unfamiliar language would soothe her. It didn't.

* * *

At dawn they took extra feed to the birds. The night's rain had glossed every leaf and soaked each tree trunk. Dust had been washed from the air, so all seemed pristine and vivid, the foliage more green and the ocean more falsely blue than it had appeared the day she'd arrived, the day Charlie had taken her up the same path. The parrots' heavy green heads toggled at Charlie's approach. With his pocket knife, Charlie cut the tethers from their blue legs. He poured seed into the tin, warning, "Now, when this is eaten up, no one will feed you. So you'll have to go then."

She watched the parrots peck while Charlie made ridiculous flapping gestures, trying to show them what to do. She pulled him back. "Oh, Charlie. Just ask someone else to feed them."

"No good. They might, for a while, but then they'd just forget." Turning back on the path, Charlie shouted at the birds, "Go on!"

They walked the beach. Wading in the shallows, they tossed cereal to the angelfish and schools of pearl-colored needlefish. She pelted Charlie's legs with handfuls until his ankles and feet were swarmed. He smiled broadly as tropical fish raised gooseflesh on his calves. They ventured out waist-deep, where she sprayed the rest of the cereal in a circle around them both. As the bits sank, hordes of blue, gold and white fish rushed them, slipping between the columns of their legs, gliding against them with feathery tails. Charlie's eyes grew wide as the blurred colors warped under the surface. She and Charlie tried to touch the fish, but they darted in all directions.

She flung her arms around his neck and pulled her knees to his chest. "One's bit me!"

"Where?"

"Behind my knee!"

"Does it hurt?"

"No. It was more like…" Taking his earlobe between her teeth, she nibbled. "Like this…"

After the fish swam off, they waded back toward the villa.

"You *will* write?"

"Of course." She planted her chin on his shoulder, her eyes welling. "It's just hit me – the reality, I mean. We've only a matter of hours, Charlie."

"Do something for me?"

"Of course."

"On the plane, don't think of the rest of today, only this morning."

The shore was deserted save a dozen pelicans strung along the pilings spiking out of the shallows. "One more thing." He pointed to the bench at the very end of the pier. "We need to walk out there."

"Why?"

"Because if I was to ask a girl to marry me, that's where I'd do it."

Back in her room, she was too rattled to manage packing on her own and had to call Flora. The girl helped find cardboard and twine and properly wrapped Charlie's painting of the headlands. They moved around the room in static silence, folding clothes into luggage.

Footsteps in the hall halted at the door, and Lise turned at Clarice's voice. "I brought you these." She held a prescription bottle in her hand. "I know how you hate to fly, so…" She set the pills on the bed and backed up to the doorframe, her arms folded. "You're all packed… for home?"

"Of course home, Clarice. Where did you think?"

"I didn't think anything, Lise. Sorry, you seem upset."

"I'm not." She looked at her friend – all the awkward moments she must have put Clarice through this past month. "Listen, I should explain."

"Don't. I've seen the way you two are together. You needn't say a word."

It seemed she'd only looked down for a second, willing herself not to cry, but when she raised her head, Clarice had disappeared.

An embroidered handkerchief was pressed into her hand. Lise was about to lay it away when she realized it wasn't hers. Flora met her eye, nodding solemnly. "For you, señora. I hope you like. I make it for you."

Dumbfounded, Lise leaned toward the girl. "I didn't know you could speak English. And so well!"

"Not *so* well. My boyfriend had school in Ohio. He teaches me a little, yes?"

Lise smoothed the handkerchief over her palm. Her initials were twined among a vine. "*Gracias*, Flora. It's very beautiful. *Gracias*."

"You are... *welcome*?"

"Yes. *Sí*, welcome."

"Ah." The girl smiled and backed out of the room, a suitcase knocking against her knees.

Lise packed her gear last, distressed to find most of her film had been destroyed by salt air and heat. She tossed it away except for the one reel still safe inside her camera, the reel with the few frames of Charlie the morning she'd found him sketching at the temple ruin. The morning he'd looked straight into her.

She gathered all her remaining pesos and folded them into an envelope and began to write Flora's name as the taxi blasted its horn. Lise faltered, the *r* laid jagged under her pen.

* * *

Staring at the final *r* in *Margaret Conner*, Lise traces the tiny letters printed in white on the night-colored chart of stars. Near Margaret's name is a tiny speck, a pinhole of light from some far galaxy: the star Remy had bought.

She lays the chart down among the flutter of Conner photographs with their mixed-up dates along with the one photo she's discovered after searching Maeve Kleege's boxes left in the sheep barn. In a sleeve of loose snapshots was the yellowed image of a youth in a beret, who she believes is Peter Kleege. On the back of the snapshot is the year, 1950, and the initials *PJK*. Between these photographs, Margaret's unintentional slip and plain facts, such as the proper season for flowering plums, Lise has pieced together a reluctant conclusion, certain now that Danny was born several months before Margaret and Remy consummated their marriage. That Danny is not Remy's son.

Margaret had revealed just enough, her memories shaken loose with sherry and nostalgia. Normally Lise would chalk up the comment about blue milk to an old woman's confusion and leave it at that. And perhaps that's exactly what she should do.

But her intuition is too strong to ignore. And there was Margaret's wistful look when telling of her first kiss with Peter Kleege on the beach. The story's a bit too intriguing – if the Kleege boy had been involved in something up in Derry, the IRA or something criminal, as Margaret ventured, perhaps her family hadn't allowed a marriage. Or perhaps Peter Kleege had his way and then left her in disgrace? Sitting until it's nearly dark, Lise considers the weight of such a secret – in such a place as this.

She searches the photograph for similarities to Danny – any hint in the jaw or cheek that might tie them. The boy is dark-haired, handsome, with eyes full of certainty, but the snapshot is so faded it's hard to find an edge to his features. Placing the picture among the others, she shudders, not because he might be Danny's father, but because of the eerie sense that the young man in the photograph is dead, that she is surely looking at a ghost.

Chapter Nine

For a moment, Lise is confused by the glow from her digital clock: the same phosphorescent green as in the underground lagoon. She lies still until shadows form around familiar objects: a floor lamp, the posts of her bed, Mrs Kleege's hulking wardrobe.

The memory that has nudged her from sleep comes clear – the elusive bit that's been nagging her about Siobhan. A memory of Flora has jogged it free – the maid's shy "*Gracias*" when Lise handed over the envelope of pesos. As she pulls on layers of T-shirt, flannel shirt and cardigan, gaps of her drunken evening with Siobhan close. She feels her way down the stairs and along the hall, the cottage still dark. Outside, the moon is a thin scythe about to shear the hills. Lise slogs through dew-wet grass to fetch an armful of the turf that's finally been delivered.

The kitchen is icy-damp save for an arc of warmth near the hearth. Flames jump a minute after the turf is laid over the surviving embers, gilding the room with light. Her audio kit is where she's stowed it in the press, and the tape marked *Kitchen Floor* in Siobhan's handwriting is tucked into the side pocket. She sets the tape recorder on the table and snaps in the cassette before sliding down to a chair and pressing *Play*. At first it's difficult to separate voices from music, the sounds of fire crackling and the fish boiling on the stove. She fast-forwards to the end to find what she's after. The sound quality is poor, but then Siobhan wouldn't have known how to set the machine properly. She shuts her eyes and turns her ear so close her hair brushes over the dials and buttons.

"*He's gonna find someone else, I know it.*"

"*Siobhan, it's only a bit of time. He's back in six months, right?*"

"That's right. Six months too late. If I had the fare I'd be gone tomorrow."

Siobhan's voice borders on exhaustion. The tape hisses a moment of silence, and then she says, wearily: *"I need the loo."* A few seconds later her boot heels can be heard tapping the linoleum and fading, followed by softer noises of Lise struggling up from the floor and moving about. The snap of her pocketbook clasp is clear, followed by a long pause and then the unmistakable tear of perforated paper. The final sound is a neat *zip* after she put the check into Siobhan's jacket pocket.

Lise lays her head on the table. *So. There it is.* After retrieving her purse from the hall, she dumps its contents. In her checkbook a blank has been torn away; the misspelled scrawl of *Soibhan Conner* inked in the register.

Tipping her face to the ceiling, she wonders how she will tell Remy and Margaret she's funded Siobhan's flight. She cannot think of facing Danny.

She reaches the shop just as Remy has unlocked the door and is flipping the *Open* sign.

"Can we go in, please?"

"Is something wrong?"

"Sort of. It's about Siobhan."

"You know, then?" He steers her in. "I'd been ringing her flat all hours since she didn't show up the shop Monday – finally went round last night and found the note."

"Is she in Boston?"

"She is. Though I can't imagine how. Colm couldn't have sent her the fare, so Christ knows how she managed it."

"*I* know." She holds open her checkbook to Remy, pointing to the stub.

He scratches his neck. "You've spelt her name wrong – it's *i* before *o*." After a moment he sits heavily.

"I'm so sorry, Remy. We'd had an awful lot of wine. I don't

remember it all, only that she was so miserable and that I wanted to help her."

He looks again at the amount. "That's generous help, rather more than the airfare, I'd say."

"Right. Enough for tea and beans, too."

"Pardon?"

"Never mind. She didn't ask me for the money, if that means anything. It's completely my doing."

Remy exhales, for once seeming lost for words.

"Danny will be furious, won't he?"

"Furious enough. But it's Margaret who'll be in ribbons. She's never liked the look of Colm, claims he's no match for Siobhan."

"Why?"

"Dunno. Women's intuition, I s'pose. We'd best go to her, then, break the news."

"You're angry."

"I am."

She sighs. "I'd be."

Outside they climb into the Morris Minor and drive through the evening in silence.

The Conners' parlor is a relic from the fifties; the horsehair chair makes Lise's legs itch through her chinos. Sheer olive drapes cast an ill hue over the room, which is obviously reserved for formal callers. Nervously winding the fringe from a tapestry pillow between her fingers and wondering if she'll ever be invited into the Conners' kitchen again, she strains to hear Remy's voice in the hall, where he's on the telephone to Danny. Danny's voice can be heard shouting over the line. Remy mumbles a reply Lise puzzles over until realizing he's speaking Irish. Margaret nods, comprehending but not offering any translation. Lise's name is peppered along a string of vowel-laden words. Wincing, she presses back into the cushions.

Margaret creases and recreases the handkerchief between her palms. Since being shown the check register, she's not spoken a word.

"Margaret, I know I'd no right. The thing is, Siobhan was so unhappy."

Her gaze doesn't move from the grate. "And haven't we all been, one time or other?"

"I'm not making excuses, Margaret."

Margaret looks up, finally. "Ah, sure your heart was in the right place. Still, it was a rash thing you did."

Remy returns from the hall. "Danny's at full boil." He turns to Lise. "But Siobhan's a determined girl, he knows that, even agrees she would've found one way or another to get at Colm. 'Twas only a matter of time, anyway."

"For what it's worth, I'm very sorry."

He meets her eye. "It's worth something."

Charlie held her hand in the taxi to the airport. She hadn't realized she was repeatedly apologizing until Charlie finally pressed a finger to her mouth.

"Stop, Elle. Please stop saying you're sorry. Of course you have to go home. I didn't imagine this any other way."

"I know. Still, I'm—"

"Don't." The car sped through low scrubland, a lunar expanse of pitted clay that stretched for miles. Neither said much, but occasionally Charlie would point to something out the window or lift her hand and kiss it. She leaned against the door and looked hard at him, watching strands of ginger-colored hair skip across his forehead. He looked calmer than he was; the uneven pressure of his fingers riffed across her knee like static notes.

Just north of Playa del Carmen a tow truck and police van blocked the road. Debris from an accident was cleared away. The taxi driver cursed vividly, leaving the vehicle twice to check progress on the road ahead. Lise brightened at the thought that they might be turned back. She allowed herself the fantasy of missed flights, of one extra night with Charlie. But soon the driver returned, giving them a solemn thumbs-up.

By the time they were dropped curbside at the airport, they were a full hour behind schedule. In the chaos of unloading luggage, Charlie momentarily misplaced his tube of precious drawings. Panic drained his face of all expression until the tube was discovered hanging on Lise's back, its strap tangled with the strap of the tote flung over her shoulder. The porters became confused, didn't understand they were flying on separate planes. Their tickets were examined, and they were pressed through check-in, and Charlie rushed Lise to the gate with only minutes to spare.

It wasn't the goodbye she'd hoped for. It was horrible enough to part at all; why couldn't they have a few quiet moments? There was no time to sit with hands twined, no time to cry. She needed the bathroom; her face was streaked with perspiration and her palms slipped damply along the package held to her chest – Charlie's sunrise.

"I can't believe this is happening. Come to Canada."

"And do what? Skulk around until you're free? That's no way to start." He wiped tears from her jaw with his thumbs. "You know that."

When the PA system announced final boarding for her Air Canada flight, Lise felt the floor underneath might fall away. Clutching Charlie's arm, she pleaded, "Listen, I'll take the next plane. Please, Charlie? There's over an hour before your flight leaves. *An hour.*"

"No." He kissed her wet lashes and gently pulled himself free, steering her to the tarmac. Her passport and boarding pass were taken by blurred hands as Charlie whispered, "I love you, Elle." When she turned, he was backing away, attempting a smile.

The ticket agent patted her arm. "I bet you'd like to take him with you, eh?" The Canadian accent startled Lise. She nodded, swallowing.

* * *

After the plane took off, she swallowed two of the pills Clarice had given her. For the first hour of the flight she constantly checked her watch, noting the time when Charlie would be boarding, when he'd be airborne. Could he possibly be as miserable as she was? She tried to concentrate on the cloud patterns outside the window, taking some comfort knowing he would be looking out at the same clouds, at least the same sky.

She was so unaware of the effect of the sedative that when the flight attendant came to gather the litter and her plastic lunch tray, she was amazed. She hadn't remembered eating.

Charlie had asked her to remember the morning, and she did, thinking of the slow walk to the pier, picturing his grin, the boyish nervousness as he asked, "Will you marry me?"

"Marry you? If I could? In a New York minute."

There'd been no hesitation then. She pressed her temple to the cold window. *Marry him*? How? The tiny portal revealed a sky expanding to infinity. It was easy to visualize their two planes as specks – one speeding north to Canada, and the other east, over the curve of a cold ocean. Charlie would be somewhere over the unforgiving grey. She wondered if he was reliving the moments of the morning: his proposal and her flippant answer. Had he realized yet how impossible it all was? Pulling the shade against the view, she pressed herself deep into the narrow seat.

When she woke, people were standing and pulling luggage from the overhead bins and putting on coats. Weren't these the same passengers on her flight to Mexico, more than a month before? Perhaps they'd never taken off? Had she invented Charlie and the elaborate fantasy of a love affair in a dream? Had his question on the pier also been imagined?

The proof was in her arms, his painting held to her chest. It was real.

* * *

Her sister-in-law and her nephew were waiting in the arrivals hall. She scanned faces in the crowd for Adam, stopping short when she realized he'd been moving straight toward her, that she'd looked right at her son without registering him. He was dressed out of character – a leather jacket over a long sweatshirt, and heavy motorcycle boots, but something besides the clothes was different. Lise realized with a jolt that she had expected a young boy, not a young man. She'd remained dry-eyed the whole flight, but the moment Adam touched her she began weeping.

"Wow, Mom. That glad to see me?"

"Oh, I missed you!" She tilted her chin. "My God, you're so tall."

"Nah, you're just shrinking." He swiveled his ankle so she could see the chunky heel of his boot.

Ritchie slouched forward. "Hey, Auntie Lise, can I grab your bags?"

"Thanks, Ritchie."

Monique kissed her on each cheek. "Welcome home!" When Lise stepped back, Monique made a motion to take the painting.

"No. I'll carry this. Thanks."

"What is it?"

"Oh, just a seascape I bought." As she spoke, she understood the words were the first of a hundred lies she would have to tell.

As the boys walked ahead with the luggage, Lise kept her gaze glued to the back of Adam's neck. Monique looped an arm through hers. "Paul sends his apologies. He had a meeting. Rough flight?"

"Uh-huh. Turbulent."

"That all? You look wrecked."

"I am." She shrugged. "Thanks for having Adam all this time. Was he OK?"

"He was a good sport. Mostly." Monique squeezed her arm. "He missed you."

Lise sighed. "I was gone a lifetime."

Indeed, walking through her front door felt like stepping into another life. When the alarm system sounded warning beeps, she stared at the numbered panel until Adam reached around her to punch in the code. "Jesus. Earth to Mother – forget your own birthday?"

"Don't say 'Jesus', Adam."

"'Christ', then?" Adam made a show of hoisting all three bags from the stoop and taking the stairs in twos. She looked down the hall, slowly walking its length to the kitchen. At the very back of the house she opened the blinds of the windows overlooking the garden and unlocked the French doors.

Her homecoming ritual has always included a visit to the garden, regardless of the season. Lise would check the far beds and shady corners for any changes, duck among the arm-like branches of the trees to take in the sweet rotting smells of ruined fruit.

Through the window she could see her favorite tree – a clumped river birch – dangling its last leaves. The rest had fallen in coin-colored drifts over the curve of the brickwork path. Ray, the man who helped with the heavier chores, had been by to wrap the more tender shrubs in burlap and had trimmed the perennials she'd last seen in full bloom to blunt stalks. The English ivy had changed from deep green to a rust red nearly identical to the brick walls it clung to. Under the arbor, chairs tipped forward to rest on the edge of an iron table, where small green pears spilled from a wire basket. Gazing out at the space, she saw her time away measured by real change; nearly an entire season had slipped by.

When she and Stephen bought the brownstone years before, the garden had been a blight of dead grass and untended trees. Lise had torn up or cut away everything but one mature larch. With that lone tree as a starting point, she redesigned paths and beds, transforming the narrow city lot into a shaded labyrinth, planting everything herself except for the trees. She'd laid each flagstone, had tucked moss between each crevice.

The garden was more carefully tended than any room in the house. The first time Leonard saw her in it, happily up to her elbows in compost, he proclaimed it her boudoir, challenging, "You do know the meaning of the word, right?"

"Of course. A woman's own room… a den of sorts, right?"

"Nope. A place to sulk."

Sulk? Lise hadn't believed him. He was right, though – she'd looked it up. To her, the word *retreat* seemed more apt. When gardening she could always count on a few hours of peace; dirt – the feel of it, the smell – calmed her. Plants needed so little of her.

Attached to any future with Charlie was a list of parallel, in-evitable tolls she'd already begun agonizing over. The emotional upheaval to Adam was foremost, too raw to think of, but there were the secondary difficulties and sacrifices – an uncertain future, relocating, giving up the comforts of the house she was standing in, the lifestyle she'd lived, the few friends that were more Stephen's than hers, perhaps even her work. But Lise hadn't considered her garden. The idyllic composition of her green boudoir blurred through the fog of her breath on the window. As the next disturbing thought occurred to her, her fingers slipped from the doorknob – of all that would be left behind, she'd miss this garden most… perhaps even more than her marriage.

Turning back into the house, she settled at the kitchen table, glancing guiltily out the window just once while picking through mail. Unable to get even halfway through the chore, she got up, lowered the blinds, and made an aimless loop through the rest of the house, flicking on lamps to erase the shadowed corners of the high-ceilinged rooms. Mrs Hobbs had been in; plants had been watered and pinched, glossy periodicals fanned over the coffee table – cinematography magazines, archaeological and horticultural journals, museum newsletters. She separated them into two piles: her own and Stephen's.

In the foyer she heard the stereo in Adam's room thump to life two full floors above. She dragged her thumbnail along the wainscoting of the hall past the den, the lavatory and the small pantry. Stopping at the house's most unusual feature – an antique telephone box wedged just under the rear stairwell, converted for wine storage – Lise opened and closed the glass door several times, considered opening a bottle, testing her ragged thumbnail against her teeth. Perhaps it wasn't a good idea, she realized, remembering the sedative she'd taken on the plane. She slumped back into the kitchen. Surely she'd find something to do there. They'd need food, of course.

She tilted her face toward the music above and waited for the song to end. In the lull she shouted up the back stairs, "Adam! Come down, please!"

A minute later he thudded down the polished treads in his socks, jumping down the last steps into the kitchen. "You called?"

Her pen was poised over a list. "I'm going to the grocery store. Want to come?"

"*No es necesario*. Aunt Monique shopped this afternoon before doing the airport thing. We're stocked." He opened the refrigerator to show milk, eggs, greens, deli cartons and a covered dish. "See? She even brought over this casserole for dinner."

"Oh." She sat back and watched Adam take a yogurt from the side door. He peeled and licked the lid before gulping directly from the carton. Wiping his mouth on his sleeve, he eyed her. "You're not gonna yell?"

"Too tired."

"Yeah, your eyes look weird. Couch? We can build a fire in the den; it's cold enough now."

They watched the last half hour of *The Thin Man* and ate Monique's risotto directly from the dish with dueling forks. During commercials, Adam compared his white forearm to Lise's tanned one, and she asked about his time with Paul and Monique and how things were in school with first-semester exams approaching. She kept up the questions to prevent him from asking too much about her trip. There was no energy for lies.

At midnight she woke with a start to a clang. Adam was hanging up fireplace tools, and the television screen was rolling credits to another vintage film. "What did we watch?" She got up from the sofa, wobbling. "Hitchcock?"

Adam caught her arm. "*Vertigo*."

"No, really."

"*Rear Window*."

"Right, right." She smiled and leaned in. "Thanks, monkey. I guess I'm home?"

"Beddy-bye for you, Mom. You're a noodle."

In the morning she showered and dressed, cinching herself into undergarments and pulling tights over the tan lines at her thighs. Her hand lingered over the curve of her hip, which Charlie had traced countless times. When Adam rapped on her door she yanked the zipper of her skirt, catching the flesh at her waist. "Shit!"

"Mom? You OK?"

"No! Yes! I'll be right down."

Making breakfast, reading the paper, walking with Adam to Summerhill Station – all seemed actions from a half-forgotten script.

She shifted the awkward parcel of Charlie's painting under her arm. Adam carried her briefcase as far as the station steps, where they went their separate ways, she to the southbound train, and Adam on foot to school. He handed over her briefcase and tapped her parcel. "What's that?"

"A painting. I *told* you."

"Ah, *no*, actually you didn't." He backed away a step, both hands in the air. She was about to apologize for her tone when Adam looked over her shoulder and his arm shot up in greeting as he shouted toward a girl his age. "Gotta fly." He jogged away, calling, "See ya ta-night."

At the Film Center she was greeted like a lost soul, plied with coffee and fresh pastries bought especially for her return. Someone had even hung a gaudy *Welcome Back* banner over her door. She had photographs of the villa and showed them to the more curious of her co-workers, hoping the obvious luxury of the villa might corroborate her claim that for six weeks she'd done nearly nothing. To her relief, Lise found that Leonard was in meetings until noon. Of all the staff, he was the one she wasn't ready to face. He'd see immediately that she wasn't herself. Most of her morning was spent away from the administrative wing. Weaving in and out of the editing labs and the soundstages, she asked students about their projects and took unnecessary notes. In the reference library she filed stray videos and magazines and even cleaned the fridge in the student lounge, a chore so grim the staff only joked about doing it.

In her office she carefully hung Charlie's painting and began composing her first letter to him – rambling, dull reportage of the details of her return, the oddness of it, the void of missing him already.

At lunchtime she walked to the Allan Gardens to sit alone in the Palm House. Finding herself in front of the goldfish pond, she sank to a bench and stared at the fish.

Only the day before, she'd stood in the sea with Charlie to feed the fish. Only yesterday he'd asked her to marry him.

Her clothing seemed an unaccustomed weight on her body. Her shoes felt tight and too warm, and suddenly the conservatory air was too close and too thick to breathe. She grabbed her coat and made for an exit. Rushing toward the door, she didn't notice the orange plastic cones boldly lettered *Caution*! Lise needed to reach

184

the cool air on the other side of the door. A few swift strides from the exit, her foot met wet tile, skimmed and launched her leg up and away. Her other foot followed in an identical scissor kick. She was airborne. For an instant she was suspended like a magician's assistant during the hoop trick. Facing upward, she caught a clear glimpse through the great dome's curved glass panels – the sky beyond was a blue bowl, a lovely cloud-riddled bowl cupping her. For a fraction of an unforgettable second she was weightless, afloat. *Ah*, she thought, *such color*! Then, with a blink, she was on the floor, splayed and breathless on her back. Unblinking and wondering if she might have broken her arm, she stared through the glass to the sky, a thought cutting the pain for a second, *Charlie should see this*.

Holding her elbow, she struggled to sit up, wanting childishly to howl. A maintenance worker had flung down his mop and rushed at her, alarm ringing his mouth. He helped her to her feet. "Ma'am, you OK? Ma'am?"

She tested her footing and broke away from his support. She plucked up her bag from the floor and pressed on to the door without responding. The man's tone changed when he called after her, "What? You didn't see my sign?"

Outside, she rested on the steps, tasting blood from the rough tag where she'd bitten her lip. She wasn't hurt but was halfway back to the Film Center before she stopped shaking.

Back at her desk she took out the letter she'd begun for Charlie, tore it up, and began anew, describing the conservatory and the fishpond and recounting in great detail her fall, the wonder of it, and the sudden hard reality of the pain after it. It was a rather apt analogy, she thought, for their parting. The day, she wrote, seemed endless and bleak, despite the autumn sun. Unable to describe more, she signed off with *Missing you*.

When Leonard rapped on her doorframe, she quickly closed out the document on her screen and swiveled, making her voice bright.

"Hey, Len."

"What's happened? Karen said you were limping?"

"Nothing. I fell."

"Falling isn't nothing. Why haven't you been in to see me?"

"Well, look at me." She pointed to the rip in her sleeve, her bruised elbow.

He leaned over the desk and squinted at the swelling over her lip, gingerly touching it. "You *are* a sight. Let me take you round the corner to Hal's for a glass of first aid. You could tell me all about your trip."

"One glass wouldn't be enough, Len. Can I have a rain check?"

He frowned. "Maybe tomorrow, when we can go somewhere proper?"

"Not tomorrow." Turning back to face the computer, she said, "How about next week? That'd be better."

"Next week? Sure, Lise. There anything you need?"

"Thanks, no."

But when he began backing away, she blurted, "Len, wait. Yes, I do need something. Something to do, please. Something complicated."

Adam talked her into attending a martial arts film festival at Harbor Center. For three evenings she was glad to sit in a dark theater with two hundred youths as the screen flared with eruptions of kung fu punctuating the plot-free stories. On the weekend she began rearranging closets and cupboards, hauling boxes of old clothes and toys to the hospital thrift shop. In the garden shed, she noticed the tools needed reorganizing. Things she wouldn't normally spend time on kept her from thinking too much: arranging the CDs, clearing out old documents and programs from her laptop, alphabetizing seed packets.

She made a dinner date with Leonard for the evening Stephen was due home. Normally she'd have met his plane, but this time she only left a message on his mobile, apologizing with an excuse of urgent business with Leonard. Of course their dinner was neither urgent nor business, but she'd put Leonard off long enough. She took him to his favorite restaurant and tried to engage him in small talk, asking about his new house, how his furniture fit into the new space and how his cat was adjusting.

"How's Garbo?"

He scratched his goatee and leveled a look at her. "She's OK. How's Stephen?"

"The same." She glanced at her watch. "Probably landing about now."

"And you?"

"Oh, you know."

He leaned in. "No, I don't *know*. You've been avoiding me, Lise. And since when do you shut your office door? You gonna tell me what's going on?"

She pinched both earlobes hard between thumbs and fingers, her habit when having to relay anything difficult. "I'm going to leave Stephen."

"Oh. *Oh*." He sat back. "When?"

"You're not surprised?"

"Not really." Leonard ran a hand slowly over his smooth head. "But wait, this isn't just since you got back?"

She shook her head.

"Oh, cupcake. What happened down there in Mazatlán?"

"Yucatán," she corrected him. "You might want another drink, Len."

It was after ten when she got home. Stephen's luggage was piled at the foot of the stairs. She followed laughter to the kitchen, where he and Adam were fooling around, finishing up the dishes and flinging towels at each other with loud snaps.

After she apologized for not being able to pick him up, she asked after his flight and his dealings with the museum in Mexico and the people in LA. She nodded as if listening with interest, then sat down to watch Adam open the gift Gerald and Clarice had sent along – a set of clay skeleton puppets.

"Cool. I'm gonna hang them over my bed." He lifted the wooden crossbars and made the skeletons dance along the table.

"They aren't exactly toys." Stephen began explaining rites of the Day of the Dead.

Lise stood. "Stephen, lighten up."

He looked at her squarely. "Sorry?"

"Never mind." She walked to the sink, as if she meant to.

When Stephen took up his side of the bed, she felt her body stiffen and her stomach ache. After three sleepless nights next to Stephen, she placed the nagging familiarity of her nausea. In the months following her father's death she'd suffered a persistent and undiagnosed ailment. She'd been given noxious tonics and kept home from school to spend days curled on the couch, protectively clutching her middle and watching daytime television. She came to know and dislike all the characters on *High Hopes*, her mother's favorite soap, preferring *Strange Paradise*, a poor version of the American show *Dark Shadows*. In later years she would always feel slightly ill at the mention of these old programs.

Two of Clarice's pills were enough to put Lise to sleep each night, but within a week of Stephen's return the bottle was empty. One afternoon she left the Center early and saw the family doctor, who flatly turned down her request for more sedatives. He assured Lise that if he treated her stomach ailment, sleep would follow. She began to argue; but without telling him the whole story, without mentioning Charlie and her situation, she had no explicable cause for the type of anxiety she was having. She told him she might be depressed, thinking he would give in then, but he only urged her to consider therapy, writing out the name and number of a woman who practiced near her neighborhood.

Frustrated, she slouched out of the clinic, tossing the crumpled slip into a bin at the car park. She didn't want to *talk*, didn't need to sit in a stranger's office and pour her heart out.

She only wanted to replicate the numbness of her flight back from Mexico, the blanket haze Clarice's Valium had provided. She needed rest, and sharing a bed with Stephen felt so much like acting that she couldn't relax long enough to let sleep come.

For a few nights she waited until Stephen was asleep and took refuge on the couch, at first uneasy that she'd oversleep and Adam would discover her there. Then she hit on the idea of leaving the television on. If either Adam or Stephen found her, it would appear as though she'd only fallen asleep watching a film.

Throughout her days, Lise was aware of the time difference between her and Charlie. The hours only emphasized the distance between Toronto and Cardiff, a city she couldn't picture in a country she'd never visited. He'd described his studio as a damp half floor in an old British gasworks on the Taff River. At different times of day, she would try to visualize Charlie – during the mornings, he might be having lunch, or working. As she sat down to her dinner, Charlie would be going to bed or reading, perhaps even writing to her.

His letters arrived at her office, but she usually saved them to be read in the Palm House at Allan Gardens. In spite of her fall, she often went back to sit in its privacy and tropical warmth. As it grew colder, Lise found it terribly difficult to adjust to the weather, had never experienced such dread at the prospect of winter.

Her preferred spot was near a pool of lazy, tangerine-colored carp, where the air smelled faintly of the path to Charlie's studio. Here she sat among familiar plants to pick listlessly at her lunches. She lingered over Charlie's letters, and while they weren't very long – usually only a page – he always included a small line drawing in the margins. His most recent letter included a self-portrait inked on the envelope's inner flap, which she'd carefully torn off and folded into her wallet. Charlie wrote that he was painting all hours, that filling time with work kept him sane. He hoped the same held true for her.

But Lise couldn't work, certainly not in the way Charlie seemed able to. She hadn't turned her camera on since the morning she'd filmed him drawing at the temple ruin. After hours, when the Center had closed, she developed that bit of film and locked herself in the screening room to watch its three minutes of the long walk along the wall of the ruin, followed by those precious seconds of Charlie looking up from his sketch pad. She replayed the film in slow motion and made a copy in case the original was lost. She watched it over and over, awaiting the shift when the stone wall led to his grin. It was the best thing she had, this one moment, his eyes clear on her.

She had his painting too. Its clean sunrise made a stark contrast to the urban haze outside her office window. Gazing at it, she could drift into romantic daydreams in which she and Charlie were together and free to walk such landscapes. Whole afternoons could trickle away until someone tapped on her office door, when she'd shake herself back to the moment and pluck up a pen, or place her hands on her keyboard in a posture of industry. The work she failed to accomplish at the office was brought home, where it was vital she stay busy. Her briefcase bulged with files she dumped out onto the kitchen table next to her laptop. Adam often did his homework at the counter island, and his nearness anchored her, comforted her, even his annoying groans over pages of calculus or his foot tapping to the muffled beat of whatever music pulsed from his earphones.

Stephen continued work on the Mayan find, returning briefly to Mexico with a photographer to re-examine and document objects. He wrote and rewrote texts to accompany each item and was also writing a long account for a popular magazine. When he was away, Lise slept ten hours each night. The couch had taken its toll on her lower back, so she shifted back to her side of the bed, simply denying the probability that Stephen would eventually touch her.

Her stomach continued churning and she began to lose weight. The one good thing about impending winter was the bulkier wardrobe that hid her thinning arms. Stephen didn't notice her weight, nor did he comment on her odd sleeping habits or her sudden interest in twentieth-century painting. He mentioned very little, to her great relief.

Having searched for the same volume of Courbet she'd seen in Charlie's studio, Lise settled for an inferior version, disappointed with its reproduction of the nude *Origin of the World*, poorly reprinted in black and white, with the model diminished to only a quarter page.

Charlie had given her two of his own exhibition catalogues, which she kept in a bottom drawer, only taking them out to peer at the small images when Stephen was away. She looked up Charlie's contemporaries to find few were as accomplished, and none was as talented – at least not in her mind. His peers seemed unable to capture the grace and aggression of the ocean the way Charlie did. He'd told her once that the sea had possessed him in the same manner she now did. She recalled his description of making the sunrise he'd given her, how during the hours of painting it he'd been taken in. She wondered, with mixed emotions, if he still felt taken in by her.

Heavy volumes covered her bedside table. She pored over the plates until Stephen complained, "I cannot sleep with this light on all hours."

"Well, one of us should get some rest." She gave him her sleep mask, which served two purposes: he fell asleep more quickly and it quelled her suspicion that he was watching her. Once he was asleep, she was free to ease the medal of Saint Catherine out from her nightclothes, its warm oval soothing her as she rubbed it like a worry stone.

Though there was a clear channel of space between her and Stephen in bed, he still sometimes rolled toward her in sleep, so she would jerk awake. How long, she wondered, could she cling to the edge of the mattress, her stomach burning?

Leonard insisted on outings, a quick lunch one day, clothes shopping another. He had a better eye for fashion than Lise, so she allowed him to choose a few dresses.

"The green striped one you wore last week is great, but frankly, Lise, it's way past season." He handed her an armful of warmer garments in jersey knit and wool.

When she came out of the changing room, he lifted his tiny glasses to scrutinize her waistline. "Hmm, you've dropped a size." He spoke to her in the mirror. "You pick up some bug in Mexico?"

"Please. Don't mention Mexico."

"Why not?" He cocked his head, working his goatee. When she dropped her gaze, he took her arm and turned her face to him. "Stephen doesn't even know, does he? You haven't told him yet?"

"No."

"What are you waiting for?"

"The right time."

Stephen complained she was being antisocial and, since it was his only real complaint in weeks, she placated him by inviting Paul, Monique and Ritchie over for dinner – an overdue thank-you for having kept Adam while she and Stephen were away.

Once they were seated in the dining room, Monique looked over the walls and asked, "Where have you hung that new painting? The one you had on the plane?"

"What? Oh, that. I'd forgotten about it. I don't even think it's unwrapped."

"We bought a painting?" Stephen was carving lamb.

"Just a sunrise."

"Well, I'd like to see it."

"Actually, I'm not sure where it is. It could be at the office, I think."

"You think?" Adam raised his fork. "Mom, I saw you carry it to the train."

"Adam, don't talk with your mouth full." She turned to her nephew. "Ritchie, you like asparagus, don't you?" When she reached for the dish, her hand shook visibly.

After dinner, Paul called them into the living room and opened the mysterious box he'd brought along. Inside were old movie reels and a green projector with rough sides, scorched brown where the bulb was housed. She took the reels one by one from their frayed cardboard sleeves and tried reading the faded labels.

"What are these?"

"C'mon, Sis. You don't know?"

Adam peered into the box. "What's on them, Uncle Paul?"

"Proof. That your mother and I were young once."

"They had cameras back then?" Adam moved his fist in a hand-crank motion and made a whirring noise.

Paul eased the projector onto the coffee table. "That white wall will work as a screen if we just take down that mirror. Ritchie? You're tallest."

After Ritchie got the mirror down, they all took seats on the couch or floor, except Stephen, who stood at the door, edging aside when Monique came from the kitchen with a bowl of popcorn. Monique sat and patted the empty seat next to her. "Grab a spot, Stephen."

"That's OK, Mo. I've got calls to make."

Adam turned. "C'mon, Dad. Just one reel?"

"Fine." He did not sit.

As test frames ticked off the seconds, Lise had no idea what she was about to see.

The shoreline of Lake Baptiste flickered onto the screen, the woods across the bay reflecting blackly in the water. The camera then panned across the end of the fishing dock. Ten seconds of wobbling ensued before the camera was steadied on a picnic scene at the beach. The first person in frame was a chubby little girl bent over a pail, seriously at play.

Paul laughed. "There you are."

Lise straightened, inhaled.

Monique pointed to her shirred and ruffled swim costume. "Haute couture."

"I was only four."

"You were fat!" Adam was on the floor, leaning against the couch near her knees.

Paul turned. "Nah, she was *cute*."

"Thanks, Paul. I *was*, wasn't I?" The camera circled her as she played, digging and pouring. Lise stared at her younger self, the round face framed with curls. The metal shovel in her hand, she remembered, had been bright orange; its color seeped through memory against the dull black and white. Recalling the toy's rusted edge – how she'd rubbed flaked bits onto her knee to tint the skin and the bloody flavor on her tongue when she'd licked it away – she was amazed. The feel of that shovel's hollow stem seemed indelible upon her palm, making her wonder how very selective her memory was.

She watched, unblinking, her handful of popcorn uneaten and cold. As a boy came into frame, Paul laughed suddenly and pointed to the static image of himself. At eight he'd been all arms and legs, running alongside their dog, Shake. Boy and dog barreled toward the camera, kicking up sprays of sand before Paul fell to the blanket in a heap. Their mother, in pearly, winged sunglasses, wore a demure swim costume trimmed with a bow at each hip. She leaned quickly away from the dog.

"That Grandma Annette?"

She let Paul answer, following the motions of her mother's thin arms digging in the picnic basket with one hand, fanning away some insect with the other. What overlaid the images jolted her

– the *look* of the footage. The blurred edges, the sunspots and burn marks, the grain – all were elements she endeavored to imbue her own films with.

She turned to her brother. "Paul, have we ever seen these?"

"Sure, lots of times, when we were little. Dad used to haul them out about once a year."

"You're sure?" She'd never seen these films. Certainly she hadn't.

As the screen went white, Adam asked, "Uncle Paul, where's our grandpa?"

"Running the camera."

Paul clipped in another reel, and an indoor scene ticked into focus, darker than the last, the living room of their old house, now Paul's. She was seven, and Paul about eleven. They were near a Christmas tree, in their pajamas, laughing and kicking the debris of wrapping paper and discarded boxes. They vamped for the camera; then both bent to pick up the same toy. Their heads clacked together with such force that everyone watching the film gasped. The camera jogged as Lise's small body shot backward. For a second there was a tilted view of her furiously rubbing her head, her mouth silently stretched in pain.

Her father *was* there, his reaction evidenced by the rough pitch forward and the abrupt stilling as his camera was set down. They watched what he'd seen: little Lise in distress. His legs entered the frame, and a pair of hands swooped down to lift her away. The camera ran on, trained on the empty corner of the living room, exactly as she remembered it, with nubby chairs and sofas with blond, conical legs, the fern-patterned drapes she used to hide behind, and the grass-cloth wallpaper that smelled of dry hay. After a few minutes it became clear the family wasn't coming back.

"Adam, see that stuffed giraffe on the floor?"

"Uh-huh."

"Her name was Gams." She sighed. "Odd I can remember a

toy's name but none of these scenes." Picking up the next reel, she wondered what other moments might be revealed.

Paul took it from her and glanced at the date. "Well, you'll remember this one."

The scene opened to a summer day under the shade of the boulevard trees, giants she had climbed, long since felled by Dutch elm disease. The street was lined with shark-finned, two-tone sedans.

Ritchie sat up. "Hey, that's just outside our house."

Adam leaned forward. "Those cars are sweet."

The angle shifted from the avenue to the sidewalk, where Lise was struggling to mount a brand-new bicycle. A man's forearm fell into the frame, holding the bike seat steady. Once she was on, her father's hand – for it must have been his – covered the gap of flesh between her T-shirt and shorts. Ritchie pointed to the disembodied arm. "Is *that* Grandpa Hart?"

Paul squinted. "Yup, that's him."

"That bike's a tank."

"It was beautiful." She didn't remember being taught to ride it, yet here was the proof. "Shhh. Just watch." The Schwinn had been blue with yellow streamers at the handgrips, a jack-of-hearts playing card bent among the spokes. Whoever held the camera trotted unsteadily behind, just far enough to reveal a flash of her father's short sleeve, the nape of his neck and one sturdy shoulder. Though wobbling, she gained enough speed that her father's hand came unglued from her back. He stumbled forward to give one last push, and she was off. Her father stopped, resting his hands on his hips as she pedaled away. Halfway down the block she turned back to look at him. The bike turned into the grass, where she tumbled off, popping quickly up to show she wasn't hurt. Her father's shoulders rose in a shrug. As he turned toward the camera, a wide grin halved his profile, and suddenly, unfairly, just as he was about to face them all, the screen went white, the end of the reel ticking an echo of the playing card in the spokes of her blue bicycle.

Her father's face had been irretrievably wiped from Lise's memory. Her sob surprised everyone in the room. Instinctively she turned to Adam, his startled expression in the projector's light. Stephen took one step from the doorway and stopped.

When her brother pressed her hand, she shook her head. "I hardly remember him, Paul. Not even his face."

After the reels were packed up and the table was cleared, they gathered at the door to say goodbye. Lise handed Paul his coat, asking suddenly, "Do you think Mum and Dad were happy?"

Paul looked puzzled. "You mean with each other? Well, sure."

"No. I mean *really* happy."

"Sis, I never really thought about it. They never fought."

"C'mon, Paul. Lots of unhappy couples never fight."

"That's true." Monique smiled at Paul as she slipped into her coat. "It takes passion to fight. Isn't that so, *cheri*?"

Lise crossed her arms. "But *you* two are still in love."

Paul cleared his throat a beat too late. Lise's words rang in the foyer. Adam looked slowly from Stephen's face to hers. After everyone had shuffled out and she'd locked the door, Lise turned back into the foyer to find Adam and Stephen both staring, both waiting.

She rushed upstairs, through the bedroom to the bathroom, where she was sick. After twenty minutes, Stephen knocked. When she didn't answer, he opened the door to find her perched on the edge of the tub holding a cold washcloth to her lips. The room smelled of vomit.

"You're *still* not feeling well?"

She nodded. "My stomach." She rose and rinsed her face. "I'm going to try a few nights in the guest room, if you don't mind."

"Is there... Lise, do you think there's some reason you're sick?"

"A reason?" She sidled out of the small space. "Sick is sick."

"I think we should talk about what you said downstairs."

"Stephen, please, I'm very tired." She gathered pillows from her side of the bed and walked down the hall.

* * *

The bitterness in her stomach grew. Leonard noticed the vials and bottles of remedies collecting on her desk. He stood in the doorway while she chased spoonfuls of plain yogurt with swigs of Pepto-Bismol.

"You should go home."

She scraped the noxious pink from her tongue with a napkin. "I feel better here."

He stepped in and closed the door. "It's no good, Lise. You need to do something."

"You know what Adam said to me the other day?"

"No."

"He suggested Stephen and I should do something together, take a trip to somewhere romantic. To 'shake things up', he said. He's playing matchmaker for his own parents."

"That's pretty sad, Lise."

Lise looked up at her friend. "I know."

Chapter Ten

When Lise stops by the Conners' house Sunday morning, Margaret is tearfully winnowing through a box of Siobhan's old school papers, reading old essays and taping bits of childish artwork to the front of the icebox.

"It's Sundays are the worst," Margaret explains. "Siobhan's usually the one takes me to Mass. I was just about to walk down to the late service."

"I'll take you."

It takes some convincing, but Lise is finally able to make Margaret believe she *wants* to accompany her. Outside, Margaret ducks into the car. "Have you no scarf?"

"You still need to cover your head for Mass?"

"Oh, I s'pose you're fine as you are. How long since you've been?"

She hates to admit, "Since Adam was baptized."

"Lord." Margaret pats a hand over her heart. "But what of confession? You must go to confession now and again?"

"Well…"

"Tch. You should; it's a great relief, absolution. No need to carry around the weight of sin." She sniffs, "It's not as though you're some fallen woman."

Lise smiles, puts the car in gear.

"Look at our Siobhan now – the girl has her fun, maybe not all on the up-and-up, and when Saturday comes round, she tells Father what she's been up to, says her penance and is freed of the burden."

"Is it really that simple, Margaret?"

"Sure. If you've true faith."

"Do you go to confession yourself?"

"Of course. Grant you, my sins are so boring I forget them myself. Sometimes I'll go in and make up one or two, just to give Father the business." Doubt clouds Margaret's eye. "You don't suppose…"

"Suppose what?"

"That Siobhan's going regular to Mass there in Boston?"

"Boston's full of churches, Margaret."

"But is she going?"

As they crawl through the Sunday congestion on Arches Road, Remy can clearly be seen in the hotel's wide dining room window, his profile hooked over his coffee cup as he taps his pencil over its rim. He's staring into the pages of his notebook.

Margaret sighs. "Every Sunday he puts on those bifocals and that fusty cap to sit right there for all the world to see he'll not be caught alive in church."

After parking, Lise opens the boot and pulls out the scarf she's kept there for visits to the windy cemetery. Tying it under her chin, she grins at Margaret. "Ready, then?"

Since Siobhan's flight, Lise has noticed little change in Margaret, but Remy seems suddenly older, more tired. He misses Siobhan more fiercely than Margaret, though he's too stubborn to admit it.

When Lise visits the shop on Monday, he's gnarlier than usual, blaming being shorthanded. To fill Siobhan's position he's hired a local fisherman for the low season, but Remy grouses, "Thick as a plank, can't tally his own fingers, and wouldn't know which end of a spanner to pick up."

"Could I help?"

"You can't fill Siobhan's shoes, if that's what you're offering. You're not sarcastic enough. Besides, she's the only one can make sense of the new stock system in the computer."

"I might be able to do that."

The shop telephone rings, but he makes no move to answer it. "You want to do something useful, you might go about forgiving yourself for writing that check."

She looks again toward the ringing phone. "You going to answer that?"

"No." He crosses his arms. "Where's your camera these days? Shouldn't you be at work on this film?"

"Since Siobhan's gone I just don't feel right."

"The world's not stopped. Come in tomorrow with your camera."

"Here? Why?"

"You'll see. Nine o'clock."

When she arrives at the shop, Remy has already set up the front corner as a sort of stage. "See, people are in and out of here all day. I imagine a few might be convinced to say a word or two into your camera there."

"About what?"

"About their own sweethearts. Of how they met their spouses and such."

She's skeptical but humors him. After she sets up her tripod and opens her thermos of tea, Remy unlocks the door to let in the few waiting customers. He seems so pleased with himself and so suddenly cheerful that she hates to point out the ambush quality of his scheme. Indeed, most customers regard her suspiciously even before Remy explains she's making a film.

The woman paying at the register sneers, "What's the theme? *Love?*" She rushes away with her wood wax, muttering, "Nonsense!" at the door. Others decline as well; in the first hour the only customer Remy's able to coerce is a farmer with a large debt on his account.

The man crosses his wrists over his crotch and stands so the lens aims squarely at his midsection. Remy presses him. "*Sit*, Jimmy, and tell us how you met Betty, then."

He fumbles backward and sits. "Met? Well... ah, we met in a cinema. It was a matinee, I remember, a-cause it was sunny out and dark as pitch inside. I had a bit of trouble getting my eyes – you know how, on a bright day coming indoors fast? So I felt my way along the aisle and sat down, hard like, right on the girl." His eyes dart nervously from the lens to Remy. "I couldn't tell you what was playing, only something with top hats – a musical, I think. Is that what you're after, Remy?"

"Fine, fine. That's grand, Jimmy. Then what?"

Jimmy frowns. "Then nothing, we married is all."

After Jimmy slips out of the shop, obviously embarrassed, she hands Remy a chocolate bar from her purse. "It's a very interesting idea, Remy, but you see how this might not work?"

"Give it time, woman. It's only the morning."

In the hours before lunch, not a soul can be persuaded to share their story. Lise unwraps her sandwich, venturing, "I can't blame them. I *am* a stranger here."

"Stranger? A good half of them believe you're a distant Conner cousin."

"They do? But you correct them, right?"

"No. I only let them assume, since most do anyway. People will provide their own fill when a gap opens – it's easier than asking after the truth. There's your difference between being curious and being inquisitive." He nods out the window to a matronly woman in tweed bustling up the street. "And here's one now who can yammer all day and never ask a question. Mrs Bonner. She'll have a word for you."

Mrs Bonner is a small-mouthed woman with steely curls tight to her head. She is willing to cooperate, but Remy and Lise must first endure a litany of complaints: her spleen, the rain, the state of Arches Road and the pollution from the lorries causing rust on her peonies. After half an hour and two cups of tea, Mrs Bonner finally sits and gives her full name and her husband's. To Remy's question, she replies, "Ah, sure! Robert saw me outside the dentist, waiting for my bus. He walked up and gave me his handkerchief. But I didn't take it, course not. Him being so forward like that. Young men were, especially in those days." She narrowed her eyes. "Handsome girls had to watch out for ourselves, you see. So anyway, Robert – he called himself Bobby back then, but that's hardly a proper name, now is it?" She shakes her head. "Anyway, he walked right up to me, spat on his handkerchief and reached out to wipe my chin. Wipe it! Well, I was so shocked I couldn't move. Here I'd been so numbed from the Novocain I couldn't feel the blood there. In any case, I wasn't myself, so I showed him the tooth in my coin purse, and he took me for an ice cream. Now that would've been November, I reckon, because the pictures of our Mr Kennedy were just going up, God rest his soul, and I remember there being one in the dentist's lobby." Mrs Bonner barely takes a breath. "Bonners were a good enough family – sure, I could have done better, but Robert showed promise. I knew I could straighten him into some form, so after we married…" By the time Mrs Bonner lets go of her purse handle to jab a finger at the camera, Remy is yawning openly.

"That's fine, Mrs Bonner." Lise smiles and comes round the front of the camera to shake the woman's hand.

"But I'm not finished, miss. You can't only want *just* how we met?"

"Yes, that's all, actually."

The next subject, Mr Edgar, is as brief as Mrs Bonner was long winded. In his clipped accent he growls, "How we *met*? Me and Doris, you mean?" He bends to glower toward the lens without sitting. "Can't remember. Don't care to."

As he taps his cane out of the shop, Remy explains, "Unionist. He's fewer friends here than you, and he's been mucking about thirty years."

The truant boys from the quay edge in, having heard that someone was collecting stories.

"Whadya pay, then?"

"Not a pence." Remy crosses his arms.

The boy named Reg pushes his companion forward. "Do it for the piss, Paulie."

Paulie sits. "First girl, like?"

Reg snorts, "No, first *sheep*, eejit."

Lise ignores Reg. "Yes, Paulie, first *girl*. Just start with her name."

"I didna know her *first* name. She were me maths teacher, Mrs Culligan. Still fancies me since then, when I give her my best in the cloakroom..." Paulie snorts, sees Remy coming his way and begins to scramble. Remy pushes him none too gently toward the door. Paulie's companions don't follow. Reg slips quickly onto the vacant chair. "That thing running?" Then he stutters dramatically into the lens, "Me c-cousin Kathleen, but we only k-kissed. Is a c-c-c-cousin a sin to k-kiss?"

Reg is pulled up by Mick, who bends to leer into the lens. "*Girls!* I'm no nancy-boy, no quare, but I know well enough to stay away from some fishy girl." He steps back, making a universal hand motion. "Prefer me own fist, right?"

There's a clamber of heels as they flee, Remy roaring and slamming the door after them. Their shouts and boot falls drum down Arches Road. Remy and Lise look at each other a moment, then burst out laughing.

A bright-eyed and bustling woman, Mrs Carlyle, comes in to buy upholstery tacks and agrees to sit but warns she's in a hurry. "How I met my husband? You mean my now one, or the others? I haven't time for all. I'm on number four with the Donnelly curse. Ah, but you're not from here, so you wouldn't know the story, would you, miss?"

"Well, no."

"You see, after I was just myself, Sarah Donnelly, I became Mrs Harris, then Costello, then Grange and now Carlyle." She ticks off on her fingers. "Hunting accident, lorry accident, pneumonia. The curse has passed down six generations of our women." For a three-time widow, Mrs Carlyle seems very cheerful. "My daughter Maire now, didn't she think she'd beat the curse by not marrying, and isn't the man she lives with in hospital as we speak with a gangrenous arm?" She holds up her bag with the tacks, popping up from the chair. "I've work to finish, or I'd talk all day, but the truth is I can't keep the misters separate enough to tell you how I met them, not even Roddy, my now one."

After Mrs Carlyle leaves, Lise sighs. "*There's* a story."

Remy revels in his brief role as director, urging customers to sit straight, to speak up. Lise introduces herself in case they don't already know her name, but most do.

While Remy is in back, an old man who seems lost wanders in, pretending to read the tidal chart at the door. She can smell alcohol when he edges closer. "Remy about?"

"Just in back. He should be right out, though."

"I hear you're taking stories about how people here mate up or some such thing?"

"That's right."

Remy clomps out from the aisle, sees the man, and stops to mutter, "Jesus wept." His sigh is followed by a dull greeting. "Hullo, Kenny."

"Your woman here says you're wanting stories, Remy. I was nearby, down Mertie's, so I'm glad to oblige, but was wondering... Ya see, I'm a tad short today and the next round's waitin' on me like."

"Right, Kenny." Remy opens the register to extract a ten-pound note and places it in the man's waiting palm.

"Ah, bless you." Kenny faces the camera. "Now *what's* it you're after?"

Remy crosses his arms. "How you met your bride."

Kenny rubs his forehead. "Oh yeah, I should remember that, sure now. How I met Theresa... How I met..."

Lise looks to Remy, now leaning over the register. "Take your time, Kenny."

Kenny sits, crosses and uncrosses his legs three times. "A course I remember. The year, anyway. That was 'fifty-five, I think. Yup." He leans forward, temples clamped between fists as if he might squeeze out the memory. "Theresa. She was my mother's Saturday girl, for the laundry and whatnot. She ironed a shirt for me to wear to a dance I was taking another girl to." He seems pleased to have remembered, but his smile fades quickly. "Theresa. We had forty good years. A great girl, yeah… a great girl… Christ, Remy, have you a tissue on ya?"

A middle-aged farm couple peer shyly from the aisle, hoping to slip out unnoticed, but Remy fetches another chair and steers them both to sit. The wife speaks first.

"We met at a church supper."

"No, Katie, it was a church jumble sale."

"It was a supper, love."

"Sale."

"Supper."

"Randall, you've not remembered one birthday or anniversary without being reminded in twenty-seven years, so how in Christ would you remember how we met!" The woman goes shrill. "I'm *telling* you now, it was a bleeding supper!"

Randall's neck goes the color of a beet as he faces the lens. "We met at a church supper."

Remy grins, exposing the gap in his teeth.

By the end of the long day, word has swept the village and a few more people come around to offer their stories. Whether Remy's intended to or not Lise cannot know, but he's introduced her into the tight society of the village, person by person, story by story. Lise may be an outsider still, but perhaps less of a stranger.

When he insists she sit down herself, Lise balks.

"How I met Stephen?"

"Nah, the other. The *one*."

206

"Oh." She sits and looks at her knees. When she tilts her chin up, Remy nods encouragement.

"I met Charlie in his studio. I just walked in and there he was. I think I'd been waiting for him for a long time, Remy. I just didn't know it."

* * *

Adam walked into the kitchen, where she was curled around a cup of rice tea, a plate of greens pushed aside. The Chinese herbalist on Bathurst Road had changed her diet to raw foods and teas. She plucked at the monotonous meals, her jaw aching. To maintain her weight, Lise had begun drinking protein shakes loaded with peanut butter.

Teasing in his brand of sympathy, Adam nudged her. "Shall I spike your soy milk?"

When she didn't answer, he affected Eeyore's maudlin whine. "Is it the dreaded *meno-paws*, Motherest?"

He could still make her laugh.

"No. Look outside there, Adam. Seems winter's here." In the garden, bare branches framed a view of grey clouds. "Thanksgiving's next week."

"Will Dad be home for it?"

"I s'pose."

"Leonard coming?"

"Uh-huh. And Paul, Ritchie and Monique."

"The usual suspects, then." Adam glanced warily at her plate of greens. "And will you be roasting one of those tofurkeys, or do we get a real bird?"

"Real."

"Can Aunt Monique cook it this time?"

Stephen found her packing up books and the rest of her things from their shared medicine chest. "Dr Wu said I should get plenty of uninterrupted sleep, so I'll be staying longer in the guest room."

He followed her down the hall as she carried her reading lamp. Her alarm clock and a photo of Adam were already settled on the bedside table.

Stephen leaned on the bureau. "Just like in Mexico." His tone stopped her.

"What do you mean?"

"Separate rooms." He nodded at the box of medicines on the nightstand. "But now you've got a reason."

In the guest room she had privacy, could lock the door to reread Charlie's letters and write him long replies. He'd accepted a temporary teaching post for the second semester at an academy in Berlin. He would begin soon, just after the New Year. In his letters he no longer questioned Lise about her plans, though he repeated his promise – he'd wait for her, no matter how long. She stopped at a line from his last letter: *I've understood your need to go slow, especially now that I know about your father, but the past and the present are very different.*

But Charlie was only human. She need only look at the calendar to know, if the tables were turned, she might've given up by now.

His warmth pressed along the length of her spine, and she coiled back to meet his spoon shape, his knees snug behind hers. When his lips found her neck, she sighed and snuggled toward his heat, turning her face to inhale his smell.

Her eyes opened and she stiffened away from the body touching hers. Pulling the sheet around her, she sputtered.

"Stephen! What are you doing?"

He turned on the light, waiting a long moment before answering. "It's been months, Lise."

She blinked against the brightness. "What are you thinking? Couldn't we have talked about this first?"

He rolled away. "Right. My mistake. I should've made an appointment to make love to my wife."

"Stephen."

"You have something to tell me?"

"No." What she meant to say, what she had so often rehearsed, was *We need to sit down and finish this properly.* Instead she blurted, "It's the middle of the night and you sneak in here? It's—"

"It's *what?*" he shouted.

"It's creepy!"

He bounded to his feet and punched his fists into the sleeves of his bathrobe.

She looked down at the disheveled bedclothes. Stephen stood there nearly a minute, giving her a chance to say more. When she didn't respond, he spun out of the room, his feet pounding the distance between rooms. When the far door slammed, Lise winced. And though she knew he wouldn't be back, she went to the door and locked it. Turning the latch, she was overcome by regret. She'd had her chance, had let it slip.

With her back to the door she slid to the carpet, staring up at the ceiling. Adam's room was just above. *Be asleep*, she prayed. *Please be asleep.*

She padded into the dining room, following the smell of coffee. The light in the room was wrong; her gaze was pulled to the window, where she saw that a veneer of early snow had coated the garden. Stephen was outside, sweeping the pathway with deliberate, stiff motions.

There was a carafe of coffee on the table amid sections of the Sunday paper. She poured herself a cup, disregarding Dr Wu's advice, and pawed through the paper until she found the home section. She listlessly skimmed the pages, glancing up every few minutes to assess Stephen's progress as he worked his way nearer to the house.

They could talk now. They had to. She got up and reached for the door, was ready to call him to come in when Adam slouched into the dining room carrying a bowl of cereal. He mumbled,

"Morning," and fell into a chair. He opened the entertainment section and anchored it with his bowl.

Lise sat. "You sleep OK, Adam?"

"Not really." He ran a hand through sleep-spiked hair. "Some stupid dream. You were in it, yelling something."

"Really?"

But Adam was already scanning the showtimes for films.

"New film by the guy who directed *Trainspotting*. Wanna go?"

"What's it about?"

"Plague." He shrugged. "End of the world."

"Sounds great. Let me think about it."

A few minutes later, Stephen came in, kicked off his snow-covered tennis shoes, and sat.

For twenty minutes the room was hushed with Sunday morning lull. The clock chimed once; papers rustled across the table; her pen whispered over the boxes of the crossword puzzle. She wished she'd turned on the radio.

Adam pushed his chair loudly over the hardwood, snatching up his empty bowl. "Well, enough fun for me." He looked from Stephen to her before turning away.

"Where're you going, Adam?" But he was already in the kitchen, his spoon clattering into the sink.

Now. They had to talk. Stephen watched as she carefully folded the newspaper. The sound of Adam's door slamming was her cue. "Stephen?"

He gave her a burning look, pushed his own chair back and stood. "Enough fun for me too. I need a shower."

With her chin on her arm, she gazed out at her white garden. Since she'd parted from Charlie, nothing had gone as she'd imagined it would. It had all been so clear to her in Mexico, in the warped reality of the tropics. She'd imagined returning to Canada to make neat, businesslike cuts to her life, mend this and clip that. But each time she considered making a move, inertia swamped her or illness set her back. She should go upstairs, face Stephen and force him to listen. Words of the old Romany woman came to her. When she'd asked about the men in her life: *There are two. You stand between.*

Perhaps what she really needed was to step away from both.

Her stomach pitched with the acid of black coffee as Lise remembered the seer's other proclamation, which at the time seemed inane: *You are going to be ill.* And her assurance, *But you can heal when you want.* Lise swallowed the sourness in her throat.

As the winds off Lake Ontario grew bitter, the humid warmth of Allan Gardens conservatory made it that much more of a refuge. She stayed until well into the afternoon, until dusk darkened the snow-covered hedges outside and lights flickered on. As the view outdoors dissolved, Lise was sealed inside with the smells of tamarind and earth. The many panels of window glass become mirrors, foggy with condensation. Looking higher in the dome, Lise saw a woman reflected from a great height – a well-dressed, haggard-looking woman sitting in the exact posture she was in.

Her father's face wasn't the only one she couldn't conjure. For a moment she hadn't recognized herself. Before leaving the Palm House, she looked up once more at her small image, recalling the words: *Sometimes a thing cannot be truly seen until you step away from it.* Had Charlie said that, or her father?

* * *

Spring in Ireland, she's found, isn't much different from winter – only somewhat less damp, a knot less windy. The thermometer climbs, but anemically, sometimes even spurting up for a jacket-shedding hour. Remy limps alongside Lise on the sand, reciting the cures for a broken heart. *Remedia amoris*: "Hold a stone close, and your blood will seep into the stone, and the stone into your blood. The blood then becomes stone, so will your heart, and you'll stop bleeding."

The thought prickles between her shoulder blades. "Hope I never need that one."

"Here's another, then. Stuff your ears and blindfold your eyes one hour for every month your loved one held you in thrall. When you take the cloths away, however many hours or days later, you'll be blind to the lover and deaf to his words."

"That's almost worse."

"'Tis the kindest, really. Others involve revenge, poison, exile, even burning – and isn't that irony, now, to scar your dearest memories. But then love's shining blade goes deep, doesn't it?"

"Sorry, did you say 'exile'?"

"I did. Jays, do you never tire of staring your eyeballs over this pot of waves?"

She took his arm. "I suppose I don't."

When the weather is dry, only a cramp of hunger will drive her inside. With the idea of making a real path from the cottage to the beach, Lise has begun collecting flat oval stones, each several pounds apiece, heavy enough to round her shoulders when carried. Finding a dozen can take hours. On the grassy plateau she takes her time, pressing each stone into the sandy soil to slightly overlap the next, like scales of a serpent slipping from the house toward the sea.

When she stands and presses her fists into the small of her back, she sees only her progress, not the long labor ahead. Laying the path is similar to working her garden, but since there is no crucial season for planting stones, there is no rush. A day's work can yield less than the length of a stride. Some days she toils with no real progress, redoing sections or shifting the direction of those stones already laid. Night waves toss up new stones, which she gathers before high tide. Lise has discovered that once her eye fixes on the idea of a certain shape and size stone, all else blurs from sight.

Sometimes she'll drop to a crouch and push aside seaweed or sand where invariably the perfect stone lies waiting.

Able now to let her intuition lead her, she takes what's offered, without question.

In mid-spring the ocean is only barely warmer than when she'd arrived in Ireland. As she wades in nearly to the tops of Mrs Kleege's leaky boots, her feet grow immediately numb, but the shallows often reveal a treasure among the broken shells and foam. This morning it's a soft shape rolling whitely among pebbles. Pulling up the sleeve of her sweater, she quickly plunges her arm into the surf to extract an old teacup.

Its form is intact, but its thickness is uneven; one side is nearly translucent, and its footing is uncertain when she sets it down. Glaze is worn away to expose a chalky texture of fired porcelain. It is a whimsical object; the sea has rarified it into an impressionist's teacup.

Filled with tiny cone-shaped shells from her pockets, it becomes a gift. Heading back to the cottage with the cup wrapped in her sweater front, she decides to send it to Siobhan in Boston, as a reminder of home. Remy calls America "the other side", telling people, "Siobhan's gone over the other side," as if she's forsaken her home team.

Siobhan's written Lise twice now and has called Margaret a half-dozen times. In the kitchen, Lise flips over the first postcard, showing the exterior of an American-style Irish pub.

Dear Hermit,
Boston is dreadful cold, but at least has LIFE. The accent has landed me a job in this tourist bar – shamrocks printed on the glasses, and the whole place painted a green not found in nature. Colm works all hours in the clubs. I miss you all. Real letter to follow. Sorry about the hot water you're in with my father.
Your fugitive,
Siobhan

* * *

If she were healthy, she'd have the energy to face Stephen. Lise threw away her medicines. If it were a simple matter of will, as the Romany woman had claimed, then she would get well.

Back in the office she put away Charlie's letters and packed his painting of the headlands, hanging a calendar in its stead, a chart of real days to remind her that precious time was passing. Her letter to him was brief: *I've real work to do now, Charlie. I'll understand if you cannot wait, but I need to tell Stephen in my own time, then try to make Adam understand. I don't know how long that might take.*

Parked in the Loblaws lot, she was digging in her purse for her grocery list and inadvertently pressed the speed-dial button on her cell phone. There was a distant trilling, and then from the depths of her purse a tiny voice called, "Hello?"

What? She fumbled to fish the phone from her bag. "Hello?"

"You there?"

"Stephen? Sorry. My phone… I must have pressed the wrong—"

"What do you want, Lise?"

"I just said I didn't mean to call."

"Then I'll hang up." Weariness laced his voice. The efforts of avoiding each other had exhausted them both; since the night he'd come to the guest room they'd barely spoken. She suddenly felt a rush of pity – for Stephen and herself. Neither deserved such unhappiness, but she'd been too cowardly to approach him with the truth.

How odd her phone had just gone off. But perhaps that was how things happened, she thought. If you didn't move forward on your own, something intervened on your behalf. Lise took a breath.

"Stephen. Don't hang up. Listen, we can't keep doing this."

"Doing what?"

"Being polite." She pulled her foot back into the car and shut the door. "When I get home, we need to sit down and sort this out."

"Why wait? I'm sitting right now."

"Fine. Let's talk."

He cleared his throat. "Lise, did you – have you been seeing someone?"

"Stephen."

"Fine. Don't answer that. You're unhappy, and you've been ill, but whatever's happened is in the past, right? So we can fix this."

"Fix? Fix our marriage? It's not broken, Stephen; it's finished." As the silence stretched, Lise saw there was no option. Her unhappiness and fears for Adam were no excuse for avoiding the truth. "I want a divorce."

"I know." His voice caught. "I've known for a while. One favor – it's so close to Christmas. My mother's coming, and Adam doesn't need this right now. Can we wait until after the holidays?"

"Wait?" If Stephen could bear another few weeks, so could she. It was for Adam's sake, after all. "Sure."

Leonard was in his office. She edged in and shut the door. "I've spoken to Stephen, Len. I've told him I'm leaving."

"When?"

She shrugged. "Soon."

Len pressed the button on his phone that stopped incoming calls. "What did you tell him? How much does he know?"

"Not much, he didn't seem to want to—"

"So, you didn't tell him about the painter? That's bullshit, Lise." Leonard pulled his glasses down to the end of his nose and affected a German accent. "Lie on zee couch, please."

"No way."

"You never should have waited this long. It'll come back to haunt you."

"I have a son, OK?"

"You do." He frowned. "And you think Adam can't see through your act? Thanksgiving was bad enough, Lise. Will there be a repeat performance at Christmas?"

She sighed. "Stephen's mother is coming from Montreal. It will be her last holiday with us as a family. Len, are you angry with me?"

"Annoyed, mostly."

Lise perched on the edge of a chair. They sat in silence for several minutes. She'd been cagey with everyone, even her best friend.

"Listen." She told him about visiting the old psychic, recounting what the Romany woman in Mexico had said about her standing between two men. "But I had the feeling even then that Stephen wasn't one of them."

"Who else do you think she meant?"

"My father."

Leonard tapped his pencil. "I've known you for what, twenty years? You've never said a word about him. How old were you when he died?"

"Fourteen."

"And how did he die?"

"He was writing a letter and his heart stopped."

"Oh." He waited. "*And?*"

"And..." As long as she stuck to the facts, it was as easy as reciting a poem. She took a breath. "And I found him..." As she described the contents of the letter, Leonard got up to stand next to her. When he put his arm around her shoulder, Lise went limp. "Oh, God, Len, I don't know. I suppose my father *is* the other man."

"Sure he is. And you've been terrified of how Adam will react when you leave Stephen. Don't you see the connection?"

"I do. Adam may never forgive me."

"Oh, sweetie."

* * *

Lise identifies the rumble of Danny's Land Rover as it rolls to a heavy stop over the driveway of shells. She reaches the door just as he's about to knock. "I've been expecting you."

"You have?"

"Uh-huh."

"You've known, then, Siobhan's in Boston, living with Colm."

She motions Danny inside, but he won't budge. Shielding her eyes against the low sun, she steps past him and crosses the drive to lean on the hood of the Morris Minor.

"You've driven a long way, Danny." A month has passed since Siobhan's flight, yet Danny seems no less angry.

"You'd no business giving her that money."

"I know and I am very, very sorry for that."

"A bit late, I'd say."

"Yes, but... Danny, Siobhan was so unhappy – said she couldn't get on with any kind of future until she saw Colm at least once more. I know better now. I thought I was helping."

"Right. And the path to hell—"

"Is paved with good intentions. Believe me, Danny, if I could take it back, I would."

His hands are fists at his sides. "But you *can't*. You might assume what we need, but you barely know us. Yet you've swooped down here, worming yourself in—"

"I take full responsibility for Siobhan's leaving."

"Take responsibility? There you are again. *Take*. You offer nothing of yourself."

"Danny?"

"What?"

"If you won't come in the house, will you at least sit down and take a drink here outside?"

He shrugs, a motion Lise interprets as a yes.

She hurries inside to fetch him a drink before he changes his mind. While her tea steeps, Lise watches out the window as he drags a pattern into the driveway with his heel. On her way out she grabs the bottle and tucks a whiskey glass into her jacket. Once outside, she sees he's somewhat calmed.

The Land Rover's bumper is wide enough to hold the whiskey bottle and her teapot. She sets the glass on the bonnet near Danny.

The grill emits hot smells of engine grease and fuel. Danny plants his dusty boot on the chrome and stares at some point beyond her as he drinks. When his glass is empty, he takes up the bottle and turns it in his hand. "I hear how you're at the villagers now, in my father's shop, asking personal questions of total strangers."

"You mean with the film? That was Remy's idea."

"A regular voyeur himself, isn't he?"

She laughs. "He's much better at it than I am."

Danny scratches his chin. "You're right, there. He doesn't salt the open wounds, only listens."

When she raises her teacup, he automatically taps his glass to the rim, mumbling, "*Sláinte.*"

"To Remy?"

"Sure." His accent thickens. "To me da, then, bless and keep the aul' git's soul…"

As he looks out over the beach, Danny nearly smiles.

She examines his features. There may be no blood between Remy and Danny, but they've been father and son nonetheless. She feels a renewed guilt for her imaginings and suspicions regarding Margaret and the mysterious Peter Kleege. If Danny was conceived on the beach he now faced, it is none of her affair.

"Have you no father of your own?"

The question jolts her. "No." She scowls. "I mean yes. But he's dead."

"So, you're after borrowing mine?"

Pressing her toes into the crushed shells of the drive, her voice falters. "Remy's become a friend. If that's what you mean by 'borrow', then I have."

"I should tell you, then, that people here usually only borrow when they've something to lend in return." The look in his eye makes him seem certain she has nothing of value.

But maybe she does. "I only have what everyone else has, Danny. A history." As she leans back, amazed at what she's about to do, a smile comes with the irony – that Danny Conner of all people will be the person she tells her story to.

"History?"

"Remember telling me how you met Brigid in Cork? How you saw her and *knew* somehow?"

He balances the whiskey glass in the crook of his arm. "I'm listening."

"Well, I met someone too. A painter."

Beginning with the day she arrived in Mexico, Lise describes her first tentative steps into the studio, how ungrounded she'd felt after meeting Charlie. She tells Danny how it felt to be seen the way Charlie had seen her. She doesn't linger overlong on the romantic bits, instead recalls the hard moments of hesitation and guilt as she and Charlie began their affair, their paranoia at being found out, their distaste for the deception and risk.

Danny's not only listening, she realizes; he's listening with compassion. She's underestimated him. When the sky overhead darkens, Danny presses her into the house, carrying the bottle and the teapot. As they pass through the dining room, she stops to show him the painting of the headlands.

"That's his, that's Charlie's. Name of your village is written there on the back. It's this painting brought me here, as much as anything else."

"Ah, yeah. I've seen the place when it's like that." He stares. "In the early days when I used to go out on the boats fishing on my own, I'd sometimes find the sky all magic and light like so." He touches the canvas. "I should get out there again someday. It's easy to forget, you know, how such sights bring a person round."

After he builds a fire, he encourages her to continue, and she reconstructs the last days in Mexico. When Danny turns on a light, she blinks against the glare and tells about the agonizing months in Toronto, culminating with the icy night of Charlie's exhibit, how the paintings had jarred her awake, had changed everything. How they'd driven a wedge between her and Adam.

Danny nods. "That's a tough place. Christ, haven't we all made mistakes with our kids? It's the hardest job in the world, and so easy to make a complete bollocks of it. What happened after?"

"Then the ghost came." She leans in, hoarse from talking and suddenly exhausted. "Do you believe in ghosts, Danny?"

"No."

"Mermaids, then?"

He shakes his head. "Sorry, no."

She believed in them once. And is aware now of the exact moment she stopped believing and began forgetting with fervor: the moment her father turned away, slinking off into the arms of a mermaid, leaving Lise with only a song. A song she cannot remember the words to, but whose choir tones still resonate – a secret, sung by an ice chorus.

Danny speaks softly, careful not to startle her. "What'd your mermaids say?"

She shudders. "I dunno. I wish I did…"

Night has sealed the small cottage. Danny glances around the room, grown small with the hour. "So, you're here now. No wonder Siobhan calls you Hermit. And your man, then? The painter, will he be coming here?"

She cannot answer.

"Ah, you've talked yourself thin." Danny straightens.

"You all right?" When she feels a weight over her legs, she opens her eyes long enough to see Danny tucking the afghan under her feet. Even as she sinks, the weight of her silence lessens. "I'm better now."

Chapter Eleven

The invitation had grown dimpled and bent in her grip, but she couldn't let go. If she did, the card would launch from her palm like a bird, and the printed words would disappear in some cruel trick. She took her eyes away only long enough to peer out to the sky rimed with snow and dusk.

If months were assigned colors, if a calendar wheel was imposed over a palette, then December in Toronto would fall somewhere between delft and dirty yellow, the color of a bruise, the same hue as the shadow under her eyes.

Frost had grown a field of ice ferns on the glass walls of the Palm House. In the humidity and heat, Lise could imagine being back in Mexico, even as she scratched the frosted glass to collect ice shards to melt under her nails. She could smell the packed earth leading to Charlie's studio. Her route to their rendezvous took her through a tunnel of sentry palms and bougainvillea so deeply shaded that when she slipped into Charlie's arms, her neck and shoulders were always cool.

The invitation for the exhibit had arrived on her office desk with a stack of Christmas cards. She'd been quickly slicing open envelopes, barely reading. Each card was so like the next, with holiday scenes and hasty signatures, that when she came across one with a familiar view, so out of context with its shock of Gulf colors, she sat back. It was a reproduction of Charlie's painting of her on the beach – her far figure bending to the surf.

On the opposite side was the name of a gallery on Queen Street in Toronto, and the announcement *New Works by Charles Lowan*. Then the date of the coming exhibit. Barely breathing, she read and reread, at first thinking it a joke or a mistake. According to the card, Charlie would be in Toronto in two weeks, at a gallery less than a mile from where she sat.

But that was hardly possible. No one just had an exhibit. Exhibits took months of planning, a year, more. Charlie had never mentioned it during their time in Mexico or their months of correspondence since. Yet he would have known for ages. Other than to report his work was going well, Charlie had barely mentioned his painting. Lise's first thought was that some vital message had been lost in the ether of cyberspace or in the Canadian mail. She checked her computer first, scanning for unopened messages, but everything from Charlie was there, had been read. She dashed off a quick e-mail. *Is it true? You're coming here?*

Stashed in the locked drawer were his few handwritten letters, which she folded open and began reading in order. His first brief pages were composed with blushing efforts at poetry, and those she lingered over. More recent letters were less effusive, as if he'd begun to wear down; still, none mentioned an exhibit, which could only mean he'd deliberately kept it from her. Had he meant to surprise her?

Sweeping the letters back into the drawer, she locked them away. Her mind raced. Charlie was coming to Toronto. The windowpane above her desk was pocked with gritty ice. The soft snow of morning had clotted to sleet through the afternoon. As the last students left, driving through the gates, their car headlights made slow yellow smudges below.

She grabbed her coat and tucked the invitation into a pocket just as her computer chimed and the cartoon worm popped its head up to announce *You have one new message!* So soon? And so late? It would be 1 a.m. for Charlie.

Her smile faded as she read the subject line. *An autoresponse has been sent by the recipient.* It was only the generic holiday greeting and new address she'd gotten from him the day before. Charlie had mentioned at least twice that he'd be in transit over the holiday break, that between leaving Wales and arriving in Germany at the beginning of the semester, he'd be traveling and visiting friends. There was no way she could even get him a letter, there was no time.

After leaving the Center, she went to the Palm House, too excited and uneasy to go home. But the place was filled with too many reflections. Everywhere she looked, her hollow-eyed twin blinked back. One morning in Mexico, the same morning Flora sang to the sea, Lise had examined herself in a mirror, wondering if she was still desirable. That had been only a few days before she and Charlie became lovers. That all seemed a very long time ago, now, so long it was hard to remember feeling beautiful. In the reflection in the fishpond, her mouth made a wavering line. When the tail of a carp flicked the surface, her image gave way to rings of colored water.

In two weeks she and Charlie would be face-to-face. What would he see in her eyes now?

When she stepped into the house, Stephen met her in the foyer. "Where *were* you?"

"The office." Lise saw his doubt. Her face was flushed and her hair damp from the humid greenhouse air; if not for her pinched expression, she might look fresh from some tryst.

"I called there."

"I didn't answer. What's wrong?"

"My mother waited an hour for you at the airport, couldn't get a hold of anyone here, and finally had to take a cab."

"Oh, God, I'm sorry. Where is she?"

"With Adam. He's keeping her busy in the kitchen."

"I completely forgot she was coming today."

"You forget a lot lately. I've moved your things back into our room and changed the bedding in the guest room." His tone was flat. "Don't worry – I won't touch you."

"Stephen. Please. We need to talk, now. *Really* talk. Something's come up."

Anger deepened his voice. "Talk? Listen, Lise, I've been wanting to talk for months. And now my mother's here for Christmas. I'd wager it's your turn to wait."

"What does she know?"

"About us? As much as I do." He moved down the hall until his form filled the kitchen door. His tone shifted as he spoke to his mother. As Lise hung her wet coat, she inhaled, bracing to greet her mother-in-law, applying a smile.

"Phoebe. I'm so sorry."

Phoebe stood and opened her arms. "Ah, here you're home safe, that's what matters! And in one piece. I was afraid you'd had some accident in this weather." Phoebe wrapped her in a hug, smelling of talc and French cigarettes. "Grand to see you, Lise."

Lise could feel the smudge of bronze lipstick gild her cheek. "Good to see you too, Phoebe."

Phoebe frowned and took her by the shoulders. "You're not feeling well?"

"I'm fine. Fine, really. Are you settling in?"

"I am. And just about to beat Adam in cribbage. Care to watch?"

Adam snorted, "Sure, Gran. Let's make it for a dollar, then? I mean since you're gonna win and all."

"*Trounce*, I believe, is the word." Phoebe sat and rolled her sleeves to shuffle. "You're on. A dollar it is."

Lise managed to watch the entire game without making eye contact with Stephen.

Two weeks – that was how long Phoebe would stay. It was the amount of time until Charlie would arrive. She could manage.

Lending her nervous energy to the season, Lise wrote cards, decorated the hall banister with cedar swags, baked cookies, and took Adam and his grandmother shopping. Between preparing for the holiday and making sure Phoebe was entertained and meals were cooked, Lise found that the days passed more quickly than she could have hoped.

The day before Christmas Eve, Phoebe helped pick out a spruce tree, which Adam dragged three blocks home over the snow-slick walks. At home, Lise hauled down the boxed ornaments and the tree stand from the attic. Phoebe had already found the old Christmas records.

While Lise stood on the stepladder with a string of colored bulbs, Adam quickly wound an extra set around her legs and plugged it in so she was bound to the rungs by flashing lights.

"Very clever." From her perch, happily trapped, she watched Adam and Phoebe finish decorating. She heard the door to the basement garage open, followed by steps and the thump of Stephen's briefcase meeting the hall table. He'd gone to the campus every morning since his mother's arrival, even though most of the university was shut down.

"Adam, let me down, please."

"One more handful of tinsel, OK?"

"*Now*, Adam."

The Bing Crosby carol on the stereo came to an end. When Stephen entered the room, she was tearing at the lights, shaking them from her ankles. Phoebe looked curiously at Stephen and then Lise before reaching up to help free her daughter-in-law.

Later, she and Stephen sat on opposite sides of the room, sipping eggnog and watching Adam lift the china angel from its cotton batting. He was tall enough now to place it on the treetop with an easy stretch of his arm. Tradition was that the holiday officially began after Adam topped the tree and flicked off the wall switch.

As the room fell to darkness, the lighted tree washed the space in cheery color.

Adam stepped over Lise's legs to sit between her and Phoebe on the couch. Grateful for the dimness, Lise looked from one face to another, pained with the knowledge that this gathering would be their last as a family. Phoebe's floury cheek was tilted onto Adam's shoulder, her eyes misting as *The Bells of Dublin* floated from the stereo. Adam had one arm around his grandmother, the other flung over the back of the couch. When Phoebe sniffled and eased a handkerchief from her sleeve, Adam snugged her a bit closer and murmured, "Gran, you're leaking." Lise met her son's eye and smiled. He winked back.

Stephen had shifted to face the tree. His profile – the jut of his jaw, the bend in his neck – had softened, at least for the moment. It seemed to Lise some of his anger might have given way to something else. Sadness, perhaps.

They were both so tired. Limping toward the end.

Lise blinked hard in the uneven light, fighting the warning sting of tears. There could be no crying now. There was wine to mull and oyster stew to make for carolers and neighbors who would be dropping by soon.

Late Christmas morning, Stephen took Phoebe to Mass, leaving Lise and Adam to themselves. While the ham baked, Adam cut and folded placards for the table, drawing caricatures on each instead of writing out the names. Leonard's card was unmistakable, a limp-wristed Lenin with his goatee sharpened to a point. Monique's had a heart-shaped face, huge eyes, and a Betty Boop curl. Paul was a grinning Saint Bernard.

Lise made Adam a sandwich to tide him over. She peered over his shoulder to see his rendition of Phoebe, with her teeth drawn as strands of pearls, matching her oversize necklace, for which they mercilessly teased her, insisting it made her look like Barbara Bush. Lise held up Adam's and Ritchie's cards, showing their exaggerated heads sewn onto the bodies of *South Park* characters. The cards for her and Stephen were only printed names. When she looked at Adam, he only shrugged.

"Sorry, ran out of steam." He rose and took the sandwich with a nod, turning into the den with a copy of *Independent Cinema* tucked under his arm.

She folded and propped the cards at each china plate, placing Adam's between her own and Stephen's.

Christmas dinner was quiet, everyone a bit subdued. Paul had a mild virus, and Len had had either too much to drink or too little and was less vivid than usual. After dessert they all gathered in the living room and opened gifts. Adam and Ritchie both received titanium-framed backpacks for the trip they planned to take through Europe over spring break. Phoebe, using the worn excuse that Adam was her only grandchild, had gone overboard again, giving him the newest model Sony camcorder and a handheld Global Positioning System to take along. Much of the afternoon was taken up with figuring out how to use the GPS. Stephen knew precisely how it worked, but made Adam figure it out for himself. Leonard offered an address on the other side of Toronto where he was going to meet a date, and Adam determined the best route. Lise raised a brow at him from across the coffee table. "A date, Leonard? On Christmas night?" He only shrugged and grinned.

When she walked him out, they spent a moment on the stoop. Lise rubbed her arms and blurted her news through chattering teeth. "Len, Charlie's coming. *Here*."

"What? When?"

"Next week. For an exhibit."

"You're joking."

"Cross my heart."

"Oh, God, and I won't be around. I'm going to Saint Thomas, remember?"

She kissed him. "I'll fill you in when you get home."

The dull days after Christmas were cold and grey and mercifully short. Everyone stayed close to home, even Stephen, who spent hours shut in his tiny office on the top floor across from Adam's room.

Phoebe and Adam took over the sofa in the den to watch his favorite films. Passing the door, Lise would see the two huddled in the light of *Brother from Another Planet* and *Down by Law*. They watched *Fight Club*, then *Desperado*. She heard Adam try to convince Phoebe of the merits of such films, defending the violence. "Yes, Gran, I know what *gratuitous* means. These are comedies, *especially* the bloody parts."

In turn, he watched a few of his grandmother's suggestions, Truffaut and Godard films, with plots she could explain to him.

Several days after Christmas, Stephen came down the back stairs to find her making dinner. He rubbed his unshaven chin. "I forgot, we haven't talked about the department party."

Her knife stopped halfway through the baguette she held to the cutting board. As head of his department, Stephen traditionally hosted the holiday event, an early-evening cocktail party held every New Year's Eve.

"Stephen, I didn't imagine we'd host the party this year, I mean considering…" She swallowed. New Year's Eve was the night of Charlie's exhibit. "Considering this isn't a good time. For anybody."

He blinked. "It's only a couple dozen people. And it's just a few hours." Stephen spoke slowly, as if to a child. "Besides, I've already sent out the invitations."

"Stephen!"

"You can do this one last thing." It wasn't a question.

"Right." It was out of her control. There was to be a party. Lise didn't take her eyes from the cutting board; she simply continued slicing, reminding herself to breathe.

She planned an hors d'oeuvres menu and made shopping lists. The party would go on as scheduled, but Lise would slip away to the gallery when the time came. The notion of consequence barely occurred to her. If it had, she would have pressed it aside.

Phoebe helped with the food. They spent an afternoon driving around to get liquor, deli items and fresh seafood. Lise was nervous to be alone with her mother-in-law, but they only talked about Adam and about her job, so Lise relaxed until they were nearly home, when Phoebe put a hand on her arm. "Adam says things have been rough."

"Adam did? Not Stephen?"

"Yes, he says you've been ill, and he notices things – children do, you know, sometimes even before we do."

"What? What has he noticed?" A mild panic constricted Lise's chest.

"Please." Phoebe frowned. "Had you thought I wouldn't see? I'm not blind, dear. Goodness, the look in Stephen's eye these days. And you, so distant. I couldn't help noticing the two of you didn't exchange presents."

"So, Stephen hasn't spoken to you?"

Phoebe shook her head. "No."

"I'm so sorry, Phoebe."

"I'm sorry too. But don't apologize. You've enough to deal with." Phoebe sat back, obviously waiting for Lise to add details.

"I know this visit's been difficult. But next time will be different." Lise engaged the clutch and shifted, considering the irony of her statement. "I promise. Look. Here we are, home."

Lise had an hour alone on New Year's Eve morning, before anyone was up. An hour to contemplate the idea: Charlie was here, somewhere in Toronto! She spent the morning cooking, humming, bending deeper into her tasks whenever anyone entered the kitchen.

Folding napkins, she thought of the cuffs of Charlie's white linen shirts, the soft sleeves she'd so often rolled to reveal his wrists. Arranging the flowers, she inhaled the green smell, so similar to the budding vines outside Charlie's door.

Phoebe commented on Lise's color, thumbing her cheek and remarking that she was looking rather better than she had been.

"Thank you." Lise turned before Phoebe could see the stupid grin she was grappling against.

As the hour of the party neared, she lined up bottles and wine glasses on the buffet. Out on the patio she filled ice buckets for champagne and pressed blue bottles of vodka into the snow. While hors d'oeuvres warmed, she left Phoebe to arrange the cold food and locked herself away for a long bath.

While soaking, she gave into daydreams of meeting Charlie. She envisioned him from afar, as though through a small aperture: their eyes would lock, all else would blur away save the color of his irises, the cracked-ice quality of fissures surrounding his pupils and the pupils themselves like portals.

After dressing, she climbed to the third floor and leaned into Adam's open door.

He was on his bed, ears encased in headphones as he read the screenplay of *Memento*.

"Ad? Adam?"

"Yup?"

When he pulled the headphones away Lise could clearly make out lyrics, but she didn't mention the volume. "I want you to go down now and help your Gran. And listen, I may step out later... just for an hour or so. A friend is having an opening down-town."

He yawned. "OK. But I'm going to another party later myself."

"Fine. Just be your charming self here until ten or so?"

"That works."

"Wear that V-neck I gave you?"

"*Mom.*"

After pulling the door closed, Lise stood still in the hall until she heard the first ring of the doorbell and Stephen's distant voice greeting the first guests. The stairwell split at the landing, so she was able to avoid the foyer by taking the narrow descent directly to the kitchen. Phoebe was garnishing a platter of canapés, a white apron over the sequined bosom of her dress. She'd pinned her silver hair up in a loose chignon, and her lips shone with an extra application of frosty peach. "You look very chic, Phoebe. Adam's coming down to help in a minute."

"No need." Phoebe placed a last sprig of green to a platter of tiny quiches. "I'm nearly finished." She took off her apron and picked up a glass of wine, toasting the air just as the doorbell sounded again. "Here's to it."

Lise wrapped chilled asparagus in paper-thin prosciutto. Stephen came in to fetch a beer for a guest. "Enough people are here I could use help with drinks." He frowned at her bare shoulders. "Where's the brown velvet you had laid out on the bed?"

"I tore the zipper." Lying and smiling, she picked up a tray.

"Well, you'll freeze in that." He swooped past, a bottle in each hand.

But what other dress could she wear to meet Charlie? The sea-colored silk fit less snugly than it had in Mexico but still draped in the right places. The cloth smelled vaguely of linseed and lime, of the hours spent posing in the studio.

As more guests arrived, she and Adam ferried coats upstairs to heap on the beds. She looped down the back way into the kitchen to pick up another tray, more toothpicks, the extra corkscrew. In the front rooms she pressed food and drink around before quickly retreating to the rear of the house. In the pantry she hastily picked from the trays, washing down bites of food with club soda, not wanting to eat but knowing she must. In her jittery state she had no desire for a drink, yet passing the foyer mirror, she noticed that she appeared glassy-eyed and drunk.

In an hour, she told her reflection, *in an hour I'll see Charlie.*

She made herself walk more slowly on her next round with hors d'oeuvres trays. The reception at the gallery would already have begun. Precious minutes were ticking away. It was all Lise could do not to fling her tray and run. There weren't enough people gathered yet that she could leave unnoticed.

When a number of university couples came all at once, she saw her chance. After turning up the stereo to drown the sound of the garage door a floor below, she walked into the kitchen hall, gauging the tap of her heels over the tiles. At the door to the basement she slipped out into the dark space. Descending, she heard Stephen's laughter, muffled by the thick oak.

In the frigid air pooled at the bottom of the stairs, she lifted her coat and gloves from the same hiding place as her purse. The satin lining of her coat was icy-smooth; Lise held it to her flushed cheek a moment before slipping her bare arms in.

Traffic clogged the core of the city. Bars and restaurants were crowded for the holiday and there were few parking places; the best she could find was blocks from the gallery. Walking against the wind, she was glad for her heavy coat, had no idea it had gotten so cold. She hurried and, turning the corner nearest the gallery, mumbled under her breath, unsure if it was the White Rabbit she was quoting or the Mad Hatter: *I'm late, I'm late, for a very important date.* In either case she felt a little silly, more so when she skidded on a slick patch of sidewalk when rounding the corner. Ahead she saw the sign for the gallery and made herself slow. To her relief, there were still people moving into the gallery and milling near the vestibule. A few hardy smokers stood outside, stomping to stay warm, holding wine-glass stems and cigarettes in gloved fingers.

Weaving among them, she tried to see into the gallery, but it was more or less solid with people. She asked the man next to her, "How's the show?"

"Good. Very good, in fact."

Suddenly she wasn't ready. "May I have one of those?"

He shook a Players from his pack and lit it for her. She caught his glance and gave a quick smile; for all the man knew, her hands were only shaking from the cold. "Thanks." Turning away, she paced between parking meters. She'd have her cigarette and then go in.

Once inside, she rummaged in her purse but couldn't find the invitation. After she hung up her coat, a gallery assistant approached her. Would she be asked to leave?

"Sorry, I was certain I had it." She shrugged apologetically.

"Had what?"

"My invitation."

"Well, *you* wouldn't really need one." The assistant's smile seemed to prickle across her bare shoulders.

Lise felt oddly self-conscious, asking before she stepped away, "The artist, Charlie... *Mr* Lowan, where can I find him?"

"Oh, you should see Mr Aroyan about that. He's our director, the white-haired gentleman with the grey suit, yellow tie. You can't miss him. He'll be in the second gallery."

Charlie's seascapes looked wonderful in their frames. Several red circles were affixed near titles, indicating the paintings had been sold. As she moved through the room, she caught the faint smell of oil paint and had to pause, her legs unsure. A waiter approached. She took a glass of mineral water and drank most of it before progressing through the crowd. Looking at the back of every man's head, she expected Charlie would turn toward her.

She'd daydreamed, anticipated these moments a hundred times since leaving Mexico. In her imagination, seeing Charlie would be a nearly still encounter, with time to see each other from afar, space to walk toward one another. But pressing through the crowd, she found herself turning in slow circles and realized that nothing, nothing turns out as you think it will. Here she was trapped between knots of people, straining to see over shoulders. Careful of elbows and wine glasses, she repeatedly excused herself, too overwhelmed to notice that people stopped all conversation as she passed. A man looked at her quite boldly, she thought, at least a beat longer than was polite. Touching her own face, grown warm, she wondered if she had smeared something across her cheek or nose. It seemed a space had grown around her suddenly. She looked down. Her dress was properly on. Her shoes were a matched pair.

A woman pointed to her. Lise began to smile but then realized she must have been mistaken for someone else. A tall man in grey pinstripes raised his chin. He held out his hand as though he knew her. Trying to peer around him, she missed his first name. Mr Aroyan shook her hand in a vigorous greeting. "How good of you to come." Lise smiled back. His accent was a melody; he was the man who would deliver Charlie to her.

"Thank you." She was puzzling over his enthusiasm but was too preoccupied to question it.

"You've worn the dress?"

"Pardon?" His remark barely registered. She wanted to get away from him; she wanted what she'd come for – to see Charlie. "Excuse me, but the artist, Charles Lowan, where can I find him?"

Mr Aroyan sighed. "Ah, yes, very unfortunate. His flight from London was grounded. Britain's socked in with bad weather, we're told. Sleet, apparently."

"What do you mean, 'grounded'?"

"Canceled, I'm afraid." Mr Aroyan nodded. "It's terrible, I know. But we're so honored *you* could come."

"Canceled? Did he… Was there any message?"

"Message? No."

"Well, is he coming later? Tomorrow?"

"I wouldn't say so. He'd only planned to be here the one night as it was. I understand he has some obligation just after the weekend – he's teaching somewhere, maybe?"

"In Berlin." Lise fought tears. "So he's not coming at all?"

"No."

People nearby watched the exchange, and a ripple of silence ebbed outward from where she and Mr Aroyan stood. "He's not here." Her voice conveyed such dejection that Mr Aroyan bent over her. "No, but these are, at least." Lise thought he might pat her as though she were a child, and she took a step back as his arm swept an arc along the wall, where at first there appeared to be a number of framed mirrors, each reflecting the colors of her dress.

Then she saw, and the breath she took contained no air. Her pulse thudded in her ears.

A few uncertain steps led her to the wall of paintings. Looking from one to the next, she recognized the compositions from the studio sketches Charlie had made, now full-scale paintings. She froze, faced with her own image, fixed in full, saturated color. "Oh," she whispered. "Oh, Charlie."

People watched her halting progress, their whispers followed her. Turning, she swayed toward the gallery director, who firmly braced her arm and mouthed words she imagined were in a different language. Her face was burning. At one painting she pointed mutely to a tiny placard on the wall marked *NFS*, looking to Mr Aroyan.

"It means 'not for sale'."

"Ah." Each of the paintings was flanked with the same placard. They were not titled but were simply numbered one through seven. She concentrated on those numbers and on each corner, where Charlie's signature made a small composition of its own. At the last painting she tilted her gaze. As she examined the images, she was unaware how heavily she leaned on Mr Aroyan's arm, unaware the strap of her dress had fallen.

Each painting of her was toned by depth or lightness of stroke. *Such colors*, Lise thought. Number seven was washed in somber tones of evening, her posture resonating sadness. Lise remembered posing for it during the cheerless hours of their last evening. This portrait was somehow the most intimate, despite its being the only one of her fully dressed. Her face was bowed, unrecognizable, her lashes downcast.

In fact, none of the paintings showed her eyes, she realized. In each canvas, the eyes that Charlie claimed to love were either closed or turned away. He'd often remarked on them, their warm graphite hues, making such claims as, "You've the softest eyes, blanket eyes." He'd joked while drawing her, "Bed-pillow eyes. I'm going to fall into them." When he punned "mesmer-eyes," she'd thrown a pencil to quiet him.

None of the paintings revealed Lise entirely; none revealed her identity. Like Courbet, Charlie had painted the woman he loved with a protective hand, never exposing her completely to the viewer.

"None really show me."

She was speaking to herself, had forgotten Mr Aroyan until he squeezed her elbow and responded, "I imagine Mr Lowan had his reasons."

Lise self-consciously crossed her arms, clutching the side seams of the sea-colored dress. By wearing it she'd revealed precisely what Charlie had endeavored to hide; she had announced herself as the model, the subject, the muse. Mr Aroyan had identified her immediately; so had many in the crowd, some still staring from her dress to her face. Had she worn the brown velvet, Lise would have passed through the room unknown.

Someone got her a chair. Mr Aroyan handed her a fresh glass of water. Where had the first gone? He pulled a second chair close to hers.

As Mr Aroyan spoke, she hungrily took in all he said – about the paintings, about Charlie. At each mention of his name, she inhaled. Mr Aroyan applauded Charlie's genius, claiming that the exhibit was already a great success. In softer tones he assured her he was as disappointed as she by Charlie's absence.

They'd been sitting long enough that most people had filtered out the door. Lise was still staring at the canvases, had refused an offer of wine. She hadn't thought of leaving, couldn't begin to think of going home, of going anywhere. As the light in the front of the gallery was turned off, a man called her name. The voice was not Charlie's, so she didn't turn. Two sets of footfalls neared as someone rushed through the main gallery, followed by the young woman who was Mr Aroyan's assistant, calling in a shrill voice, "Sir, *sir!*" A man burst into the second room of the gallery, his voice emphatic. "I don't *care* if the fucking reception is over!"

Stephen charged into the space, flushed and angry. In several strides he was above Lise, holding the invitation she'd thought was in her purse. Mr Aroyan stood abruptly, and the gallery assistant planted herself in the doorway, looking angry. Stephen's face was a heated scowl, and cold air wafted from him, borne in on the sails of his open coat. "I've just left a house full of guests to find you."

"Why?"

"Why? Christ, Lise, why d'you think?" Lise shivered as he pressed the invitation toward her like an indictment.

Mr Aroyan was suddenly standing.

"It's all right. He's my husband." Her words fell dully under Stephen's heavy breath.

Stephen followed her gaze to the wall of paintings and after a protracted moment made a garbled sound.

He stepped away to walk the length of the wall. His hands fell limp at his sides, and his legs had a wooden quality, as if he knees had locked. He glanced back once, at the dress Lise was wearing. Tipping his body forward, he peered at each painting.

When he was finished, he stood still a long moment, his face a mask. "Where is he?"

"He's not here."

"Fucking coward. I knew it was him." He jutted his chin. "I knew it was that Scottish bastard."

"He's Welsh," she whispered.

He stabbed a finger at the first painting – the one full nude. "Look what he's done! We've been humiliated."

Lise looked at her husband. "*I* haven't." Rising from her chair, she pointed along the wall. "That's me, Stephen. *Me*."

"What, tell me, just *what* were you thinking?"

"I wasn't. For once." His hand was raised toward her and for a confused moment Lise thought he might adjust her jaw, but then his hand fell.

"I'm sorry, Stephen. I should have told you sooner." She took a step toward the door.

"Where are you going?"

"I don't know."

But she did know. Lise walked calmly through the arch separating the galleries. Near the door she took her coat from its hanger and looked back once, to see Stephen hadn't moved, save his hands, curled to fists now at his sides.

Half an hour later she was at an all-night petrol station at the northernmost edge of the city. She'd fueled the car and had purchased a meager supply of groceries. With the motor running, she sat watching the windows fog and defrost repeatedly until she lost count.

As she left Toronto's outskirts, all grew dark, with only the occasional farmhouse window flashing from behind the trees. Snow gleamed pastel under the rising moon. She read the dashboard clock and shook her head. The shape of her life had changed in a matter of hours.

But hadn't her past led her on this precise course, to exactly this destination – this moment?

Her first New Year's Eve as Stephen's wife was spent at a boisterous party where the women wore boas and everyone grew drunk enough to rumba. Lise was the new faculty wife and didn't know a soul. They were barely through the door when she lost sight of Stephen. She moved awkwardly around groups, balancing a warm glass of ginger ale, finally settling in a corner to be chatted up by the dean's boring wife. Just before the stroke of midnight she broke away to search for Stephen. She finally found him deep in conversation with a male colleague. As the countdown to midnight commenced, she skirted a table to approach him. But he didn't stand when she reached him, only lifted himself a few inches from his chair as the bandleader boomed, "Three, two, one!"

As confetti flew and noisemakers whirred, couples around them stopped to embrace, kiss, wish each other happiness. Stephen pecked her cheek dutifully before sitting back down, turning again to his companion. With those motions – *rise, kiss, sit, turn* – the familiar numbness had fallen over her. It was a veil-like thing, a tattered comfort she could call up for just such instances. Behind it, she could be witness to almost anything yet avoid being affected by it. Backing away, she watched her husband and his companion toast the New Year. She knew as she turned that any other woman would be angry, would revolt, demand attention. But she wasn't like other women, as she'd not been like other girls.

She pressed the gas pedal. Her anger over that one stroke of midnight had been tucked away, never aired. She'd forgotten it, hadn't she? What possible good came of dredging up what was best forgotten? And weren't similar moments over the past eighteen years also denied? On the road leaving the city, Lise recalled instances of being slighted, of her needs being ignored by Stephen. Times she had been taken for granted by him rushed forth with such force Lise felt she could tear the steering wheel from its mooring. Oddly enough, she wasn't angry at Stephen. It was her fault, mostly. Stephen was who he'd always been: perpetually preoccupied and unabashedly self-absorbed. And she'd married him knowing it. Realizing that mistake on the night of that long-ago New Year's Eve, she'd simply stopped having feelings for Stephen to hurt. She'd had to. Adam was already on the way. It wasn't only Stephen she'd been numb to. Lise had taken refuge under the veil long before, had only shaken it off once – during her few weeks with Charlie.

The yellow stripe painted on the road separated the lanes of north and south, future from past. The drive to Lake Baptiste was a pause between the two. Concentrating on the motions of driving, she felt the weight of her foot lifting from the accelerator or brake, the turn of her wrist while steering.

After leaving behind the last small town on the route, the road narrowed. Pavement gave way just past the last sign of life, an old bait shop with a lone petrol pump and a ramshackle fishing lodge, now closed for the season.

At the cabin lane she turned at the *Private* sign to ease the car along the peninsula between low banks of snow. Shuttered lake cottages and boathouses strung along either side of the road. A movement in the brush caught her eye, and a small herd of deer turned to stare with garnet-bright eyes.

At the cottage's driveway she accelerated to break through a crusted bank of plowed snow, the car fishtailing into a tunnel of interlocking pine. The cottage windows glinted in the distance. The garage came into view, a square timber building still straight and dry eighty years after her grandfather had felled the trees to build it. License plates from the different provinces shingled the shed roof like a metal quilt. Thermometers with Canada Dry and Quaker State logos rusted under the eaves. A bone-white elk rack crowned the peak above the wooden doors. Beyond the garage and woodshed, lines of the gabled cottage were just visible in the moonlight. After shutting off the engine, Lise climbed out into purple air. The garage door was frozen to its threshold so that she had to kick and shoulder it free. Once inside, she felt along the tool shelf for the hiding place.

The rusted oilcan hid a spare key within, hung from a coil in its own chamber – her father's device, another of his secrets. He'd emptied the can of oil, removed its bottom and then welded two new bottoms on to create a false chamber with a spring latch. Such objects could jog him to life – if not his face, at least his voice. She could remember how pleased he'd been with himself, describing to his buddies down at the Mobil dock how he'd made the device or demonstrating it over beers at Walter's Lodge. She'd voiced her skepticism. "Daddy, how good is a secret when everyone knows?" He'd only laughed and set about making more trick cans, passing them around to others on the lake, so that if she had wanted, Lise could probably have found keys to most cottages along the east shore.

The key was so cold it stung her palm, with teeth worn so thin it was a wonder the tumblers of the lock could read such hints. *One last time*, she prayed, and held her breath. The latch gave with ease.

The cottage walls were fashioned of thick, squared timbers, but indoors the air was still cold enough to make clouds of her breath. She took a flashlight to the cellar, where the oil-heater thermostat was set just high enough to keep taps and pipes from freezing. She adjusted the gauge, turned the water-heater dial, and flipped the *On* switches for the pressure pumps and filters. Her movements were automatic and deliberate, each small task a plug holding back the hours of the evening.

Lifting her hand to a switch near the rafter, she watched her own small motion in the way Charlie might, focusing on the grace and frailness of her fingers. He had studied how her hands held a hairbrush, fell open on a pillow or strained to button the very dress she was wearing. She felt the silk catch slightly over her knee when she lifted her foot. Her body was a marvel, at least to Charlie, and what he'd made of her skin and bones...

Any one scene – the unsettling stares from strangers at the gallery or the look on Stephen's face – if she lingered on any one image for too long, she would unravel. Lise leaned against the warmth of the water heater and closed her eyes as the paintings came back to her.

The canvases depicted her in various stages of putting on the dress, a simple act made graceful, seductive and even childish under Charlie's brush.

The first, titled *One*, showed the studio's interior, its light fading under the weight of dusk. Through the window is a miniature homage to his seascapes, the last sun-tinged waves of the day rolling toward the sand in warm hues. Lise faces the window, utterly naked, the curves of her body washed with the same light as the waning sky.

Two: the same perspective, but this time the studio is racked with light. She is reaching for the dress, which is on a hanger and placed so that it obscures the window where the sea had been in the first canvas. Later, when coming back to this painting, she would better understand its significance: Charlie had turned away from the sea to paint her. *Three*: Lise is perched on a cushion with her back to the viewer; her body is in half turn, the dress draped over her arm, one foot half-hidden under her buttocks. A damp strand of hair curves a treble note near her shoulder blade. *Four*: a side view. Lise's body makes a Z shape as she lifts the dress, about to let it cascade over her. The bottom of her foot is dirty and her leg is in movement, the musculature of her calf stretching as she arches, hair tossed down over her back. *Five*: she is sitting on the floor, a hairbrush near her hip. The dress is unbuttoned to reveal her lower back, her spine and one shoulder blade. Hands twist behind to the lowest buttons, and her neck is craned as if she might somehow see behind. *Six*: the dress is on, but Lise remains seated, wearing one espadrille, the other canted on its side nearby. The cloth is pooled in her lap to expose her thighs, and her head is bowed as she examines the bruise on her shin, fingers just grazing the mark, her memento from the afternoon of the blindfold. The bruise is sickly green and blue, painted with such realism a ghostly ache revisited her leg when she saw it.

Seven: the only close-up, but with her head bowed and face half-obscured, so that only someone who knew her would recognize the curve of her neck, her lashes casting spiked shadows over her cheekbones. Her skin is flushed and her hands meet over the bodice of the dress, one hand poised protectively above a breast.

Back in the gallery, when she'd scanned the series from a distance, glancing from one painting to the next, she'd understood the portraits somehow contained a message meant solely for her. Charlie had relived their days in oil, articulating their story in the best and perhaps the only way he could. She recalled the small, amazing detail of the last painting: a small mirror hanging far behind Lise's bowed head reflecting another portrait, a miniature showing half of Charlie's face, his eye to the viewer, his look claiming, *This is what I saw.*

She climbed the cellar stairs, put away her few groceries, and took stock of what food was already in the cottage's refrigerator and cupboards. From the upstairs rooms she pulled comforters and pillows from beds and hauled them down to the sofa nearest to the hearth.

In the back hall she pulled on a pair of Adam's old boots to haul firewood from the shed. She would keep warm by staying in motion until the cottage heated up. Four trips later, there was enough wood to keep the fire going for a night and a day. When the last armload of birch was stacked, she wandered back outside.

Chapter Twelve

Lise barely felt the cold, though she knew by the squeal of her footfalls and the particular blue-black of the sky that it was well below freezing. Her gaze fell to a strange, fractured light at the lakeshore. Slipping down the last stretch of path to the beach, she discovered thin sheets of ice from a previous freeze had washed up to shore in layers like a plowing of glass, a phenomenon she'd seen only once before: an *ice shove*. She could only have learned that from her father – he'd known everything about ice.

Mincing her way onto the slick surface, she pried a triangle free and peered through it. The lights of the cottage distorted. She held the slab skyward, moved the mottled pane side-to-side, and smiled, whispering, "The moon is drunk." The ice slipped from her gloved hand to smash at her feet. Lise jumped as shards nicked at her stockings. Picking out another, she surveyed the lake through the thin frozen pane. Wisps of snow lay over the solid surface like the crests of flat waves. Holding the ice higher to the rangy line of pines across the lake, she dropped it on purpose, stepping back as it hit. The shatter rang.

Tossing another as she might toss a horseshoe, she watched it skim and cartwheel to crack into smaller pieces. She kicked whole sheets loose from the pile and shattered them in satisfying bursts of sound. Chunks exploded into shards. Breaking the thinnest piece over her head, she laughed, crystals catching in her fur collar to prickle as they melted down her neck. Moving along, she slipped and fought to regain her balance, her footing already tenuous in Adam's too-large boots.

Thinking of nothing but breaking more ice, Lise became bent on destruction. The action warmed and limbered her. Panting and giddy, she hurled piece after piece, each one becoming a wasted day from her past to be cracked in two or four, pent-up unhappiness to be broken like so many mirrors – the times she'd wanted to break every dish in the kitchen, every glass in the cupboard.

Prying the largest piece from the jumble, she hoisted it to her shoulder and hurled it with all her might. A muscle in her upper arm rippled with pain and she gulped a lungful of freezing air. Sinking to the ice, she cradled her arm, her weight balanced on knees numb with cold. She bit her lip to shift the pain away from her arm, wondering if she'd torn something.

Tears ran in warm ribbons over her cheeks as she half laughed, half sobbed into her collar. Moonlight cast a blunt shadow of her, rocking and howling like some madwoman. When the pain lessened, she looked up to see the moon centered over the ice, brightening the night so that she could make out small details, even the dial of her watch. It was nearly midnight. Her breath erupted in small clouds as she watched the progress of the second hand. Four minutes until the New Year. Worn out, she sat back on her heels and held her head in her hands. After a while she tested her shoulder. Finding she could move it, she struggled to her feet and glanced at her watch again. There was less than a minute left.

Stepping forward, she began counting backward: "Thirty-seven, thirty-six, thirty-five." As she moved onto the black ice toward the center of the bay, the sound of her countdown was crisply amplified, carried across to the far shore to ricochet along the cliff.

Each footstep took her farther from the wretched months since she'd left Mexico: the guilt, the ache. "Twelve, eleven, ten." Her voice rang back in an echo. "Nine… *nine… nine.*" Moving faster, she shouted, "*Eight! Seven! Six!*"

After four long strides she stopped. "*One!… one… one… one.*" The echo rang away like the end of a song, the end of something. Lise listened for the final faint strains, anticipating silence. But another sound swooped in, a familiar and frightening sound. Her body tensed with the sudden odd reverberation – a prolonged sound rising from the lake bottom that trailed away just beneath her feet. She looked down and then behind. Panic seized her. The cottage lights were pinpoints. *Too far.* How had she gotten this far out?

Her first tentative step toward shore elicited another sound, a low moan. As if in answer, another part of the lake emitted a groaning cry. The ice was cracking. Fear gripped Lise to wring cold from her limbs with a rush of adrenaline. Closer voices called, like women but not women – creatures chanting long, drawn-out notes.

She knew this song.

And she knew something of ice, its countless dangers, all the facts and phenomena her father had imparted in paternal warnings: *Never* skate or walk out alone. If you break through, turn around to climb out. When finding yourself on unstable ice, lie down. Lise sank slowly to her hands and knees, distributing her weight. Stretching her length, she lay prostrate, her limbs out. Ice fissured under her as she said a wordless prayer, closing her eyes to brace for what would come.

As she waited for the collapse, the back of her lids flashed another midnight. Her father had roused her from sleep, coaxing her from her warm bunk in the cabin to help her into a snowsuit. She couldn't have been more than seven or eight. She remembered her groggy reluctance as feet were pried into boots, hands into mittens. Carried half-asleep down the slope between the pines, she had pressed her face into her father's anorak, his neck the one warm crook in the cold night. She recalled his shaving-soap smell and the tickle of his fur hood, the rumble of his voice, promising mermaids would sing from below.

She'd been terrified at first, then suspicious, raising her head. *Daddy, a singing lake?* His breath warmed the shell of her ear. *Nothing to be afraid of, Elle.*

* * *

The next fissure made a resounding howl, followed not by the expected breaking sound, but by her father's distant voice: *The cracking only strengthens it, sweetheart.* He'd promised.

She lifted her head to see moonlight boring into clear ice beneath, where air bubbles were trapped to some depth, revealing that the ice was thick as a beam.

Every muscle in Lise's body went limp with relief.

Her laughter rose in a mist. As she lay her ear to the surface, the fragmented memories she'd so often tried to gather finally pulled themselves into a whole: that blue song, her awe as she heard a mermaid's ghost sing *Ping*, then another join in with *Tewww*. She could see them clearly, half-women with spun ice for hair, scales like dimes tapering from rounded hips to translucent fantails. Born of an eight-year-old's imagination, the mermaids had appeared around her in an unbroken circle to sing, blinking eyes of aquamarine under snowflake lashes.

What will they sing for me? she'd whispered.

Her father had crouched next to her, a gloved hand on her shoulder, his face hooded by fur. *Anything you want, Mitten.*

Anything, Daddy?

Your heart's desire.

What's a heart's desire?

A wish.

Oh. Small fingers clutched the fur at his collar. *Then you will always be my daddy.*

As the mermaids sang away the old year, her father retreated with fading footfalls, a beat behind the last full measure. The mermaids were once as real to her as he had been. She pushed herself up from the frozen surface and made her way back, melancholy tones fading from the throats of mermaids singing the last notes of an ice chorus.

* * *

Her camera is set on automatic and trained on Remy, gone quiet since she's finished telling the story. He is silent for so long that she's startled when he suddenly does speak.

"It's a fine story, what happened to you on the ice that night." He presses her hand. "It's important to tell, at least one soul. In the end, memories are all we have."

"Yes, but that's just it. It's only a memory. But you, you're a great storyteller, Remy."

"Nah. I'm a hardware man who only knows a few legends and a lot of hearsay, but see, you can cobble together a real story, with what you fit in that camera and what's inside there" – he points to her temple, then her chest – "*and* there. All you need do now is match up those pictures with what memories are inside you."

"But I've told you now."

"Tell your boy. He'll carry it longer."

"But my son—"

"We need to pass such bits on. Perhaps one day Siobhan will tell tales of me to her own children; then some new Conner will know something of me." He sighs. "You've only a story so long as someone sees fit to keep telling. If you don't tell, those bits go out with you when you die. The *shanachie*, the real storytellers of Ireland, they were the ones kept the memories alive here, but they're long gone now. Course you cannot tell a story without stepping outside yourself to see it different like." He looks at Lise. "Even those you keep for yourself, the secrets."

"I think I understand."

"And aren't you young people with your cameras making these films just the new breed of *shanachie*?" He smiles. "Sure if you didn't break through the ice that night, but not how you thought you might."

* * *

Before she leaves him scratching his lines to Margaret into a notebook, Remy stands to hug her. The contact is unexpected; the silvery stubble of his cheek and coolness of his ear are a sudden intimacy, out of character. Lise turns quickly before he can see her eyes.

After loading gear into the car, she lingers in front of the hotel with half a mind to go back inside and tell Remy the rest. Instead, she wanders across the street and down to the pier. Sitting on the cement bench, she tosses pebbles at the receding tide, wondering if what he says is true, that the unspoken bits die with you. She's never stepped outside herself to see the rest, but lately she has come to suspect that if she holds it too tightly, her own story might keep her hostage.

* * *

On her way home from school she'd bought a new record with her babysitting money. There was a Milky Way bar in the icebox, along with a Coke she'd hidden from her brother. It was Friday, a day to celebrate. Shifting her book bag, she gathered mail from the stoop and pressed her way into the house.

She was usually home before Paul, who had cross-country practice after school, and her mother, who spent her afternoons volunteering at the museum or clerking at the hospital thrift shop. The door slamming behind her cracked the quiet air of the house. Grinning, she kicked off her loafers and skated the hallway parquet to the kitchen on stocking feet. The Coke was still there, the bottle shining with condensation as she carried it up the narrow back stairs. Shut into her room with her books and record player, she savored unwrapping the album, the soft hiss the needle made as she lowered it to the first groove.

Simon and Garfunkel serenaded her reading of Whitman for literature class. She was nearly through 'Salut au Monde!' mouthing the words around caramel and chocolate, tracing her sticky fingertip over the words until she faltered over one she didn't recognize, *coptic*.

"Damn." She rolled from her bed and pounded down the front stairs. "Coptic, coptic, coptic." She skated along the hall to her father's study, where the mammoth *Webster's* lay open on its swivel stand. Her lower lip was sucked into the neck of the Coke bottle and she was letting it dangle, seeing how long she could keep it there with the suction. When she entered the room and found her father sleeping in his chair, she let the bottle fall into her cupped hand. He sometimes came home for lunch but was rarely so late getting back to the office.

"Hey, Dad."

She always remembered the next moments as if through some thickness, as if through ice.

"Dad?" In her rush forward she dropped the bottle, tripped over it, and skidded across the rough weave of the rug, unaware of the skin burning from her knees.

Before she landed at her father's feet, her mouth shaped the only word she had air for, "*No.*"

His hand was limp over the arm of his leather chair; the other rested near the enamel keys of the Olivetti. As if in mid-sentence or mid-thought, he had turned his chair toward the study door, away from the typewriter. To call out some last word? A cry for help? Her name?

He was slumped, but only slightly, eyes half-open, so that it seemed her father was only a little dead.

She pressed knuckles to her temple until her eyes blurred. The typewriter keys wavered under the blinding square of white paper. He'd been writing something, had begun a letter. She rose to her feet, fought dizziness to focus, blinking until words formed. *My dear Charlotte*.

Charlotte? She looked from her father's face to the letter. She'd made a mistake, he wasn't dead, only playing possum, and this letter was part of the game.

With an odd grin she reached lightly across so as not to wake him, easing the letter from the roller with a slow *tah-tah-tah*, her hand brushing his cool shirtsleeve. Her last contact with her father was to gently swivel his chair so that he faced away.

She sat on the couch and read the unfinished letter several times.

My dear Charlotte,
I'm leaving Annette. I've been unfair to take your patience for granted. Honestly, I don't know how you've managed this long, but I believe what we have together is worth the sacrifice, and if I can—

Later she would think, *Yes, it's true, what they always say about seeing your life flash before you.* Only she wasn't dying, and it wasn't her past she was seeing, but her future. The weird detachment she'd felt that afternoon would come to surround and protect her, because if she could find her father dead and then learn of his plan to walk out on his family, if she could bear all that and keep the secret of his deception – she could bear anything.

After reading his letter a final time, she stared a long while at the back of her father's head, concluding that the man kiltered in the chair was indeed dead but was not her father. An impostor, whose last act was one so removed from her real father's character that his lack of manners allowed him to come into her father's house, sit in his chair and die there. She never wanted to see that man's face again.

That was it. He'd written *if I can* and then died. One phrase she kept repeating aloud: *worth the sacrifice*. Stupidly turning the page over, Lise expected to find her own name typed there, along with Paul's, for surely they were the sacrifice he'd alluded to.

And their mother, of course. Her mother. Not wondering if what she was doing was wrong, she simply did it, her arms moving stiffly as a doll's. The fire in the grate was still sputtering. The whisper of the burning letter joined the hiss of damp maple as she watched sentences shrink in on themselves and curl. After the paper made a black scroll, she prodded it to ash with the poker, then watched her hand trying to shake the poker loose. Unable to let go, she scooted back on her behind, striking her side on the hard edge of the telephone stand. With one hand she dialed the operator.

They found her like that, curled into herself, like something burnt.

She would forever associate the smell of burning paper with death.

Later, someone applied salve to her knees, perhaps the same Benedictine nurse who made her swallow the pill that made everything grow soft. A blue-eyed nun in flowing white, whom Lise imagined, in the haze of the sedative, to be her father's lover. Charlotte even had a red enamel cross pinned over her heart as if she were a nurse.

Charlotte had cleverly arrived in the ambulance from the Catholic hospital to steal him. As the drug pulled Lise deeper, she saw the logic; Charlotte had disguised herself in the yards of a nursing habit to conceal the flowing tail, for doubtless, Lise convinced herself, Charlotte the mistress – though disguised as a nun – was also a mermaid. As Lise drifted into unconsciousness, this all made perfect sense.

She had expected to see Charlotte at the funeral and kept watching for some face obscured by black lace, but no such veiled stranger arrived for her to attack, no tearstained face she might expose. She'd even rehearsed in the mirror, spitting out, "My father would never, ever have left us for you!"

At the cemetery she refused to get out of the limousine. Her brother tried to coax her out, even bruised her wrist in his attempt to pry her grip free from the door handle. Her mother wept, then begged, but Lise wouldn't budge, and so they left her alone, breathing circles on the glass, watching the gates for the car that would bring the last mourner.

When guests filled the house after the funeral, Lise guarded the fire in her father's study, tossing bits of kindling onto the hearth while aunts and uncles, cousins and her father's business associates came and went. She nodded as their mouths made kind shapes, even allowed people to hug her, but always with an eye to the flames.

Over the next days she tended the fire unnoticed. Flower arrangements wilted to crisps and she added them to the flames. Newspapers and condolence cards were burnt. Using the side door closest to the woodpile, she brought in only what she could hide under the chairs. At night she sneaked down to sleep on the sofa, waking every few hours to pile on split maple.

A week later she returned to school. At lunchtime she'd raced home to feed the fire but found Rosalind, their day woman, and her mother, both in aprons, giving the room a thorough cleaning. They'd doused the embers, had swept the grate clean.

Lise staggered at the doorway. "What have you done?"

Her mother looked up from the hearth. "I've put the fire out."

"Why?"

"*Why?* Look outside. It's a beautiful, warm day. Goodness, with that fire going, this room was like a sauna."

Rushing at her mother, she began shrieking. Rosalind backed out of the room. Her mother caught her flailing arms and held her tight. "That's it, sweetheart. Let it out, now. Let it all out."

"I hate him," she cried. "I *hate* him."

She obsessed over Charlotte; feverishly stabbing pins into an apple-shaped cushion from the sewing box, she imagined jabbing Charlotte's eyes until bloody streams stained her cheeks. *Charlotte, harlot, home-wrecker whore.*

There was an ache, but no real pain. No grief, only questions. She pulled out the Ouija board and lit a candle in her room after everyone was asleep. With her fingertips on the plastic disk, she waited, but the pointer seemed cemented on its little rubber feet, refusing to divulge who Charlotte was.

Lise ransacked her father's desk, his files. There was nothing in his closets but clothes. The glove compartment of his car, the trunk, even his tackle box, all searched, revealing nothing.

Her brother grieved with an ease she envied. She would pass by the parlor or the kitchen to see Paul with his face to their mother's collar, his shoulders heaving as he produced the sorts of tears she didn't know boys could.

Their mother grieved more deeply, losing weight until a shadow was carved under her paled cheekbones. Memories would level her into a chair, cant her tall frame to the fence. She paused in open-mouthed distress, sometimes for several minutes before shaking herself back to the task at hand: cooking, pruning, folding clothes from the line.

The house expanded with the extra space left by Lise's father. Her mother emptied his drawers into charity bags, gave away meaningful items to his colleagues and friends. Golf clubs, ashtrays and hunting rifles left the house with these visitors; his war medals, fly-fishing rod and watch were kept for Paul.

She'd thought it morbid and asked her mother, "What's the difference between *memento* and *memento mori*?"

"I haven't a clue." Then, as if remembering her daughter, Annette offered up things from the open box at her feet. "Would you like his typewriter?"

"No, I would not."

"Something else, then?"

"Nothing." Lise folded her arms. "Wait. Maybe his dictionary."

In it she underscored the words *adulteress*, *mistress*, *paramour*. She didn't know there was an equivalent for the male adulterer

– had always thought *philanderer* was a nice man who gave away money.

Lise had heard stories of widows following their husbands quickly in death, as if dying was easier than learning to live without them. But her mother seemed healthy enough, and for the first time, Lise thought of her fifty-year-old mother as young, relative to other widows on their block. Their neighbor, old Mrs Kettle, had hung on long after old Mr Kettle died, slowly bending into the type of widow who mutters to canned goods in the Super Valu or shrieks at the paperboy.

With time, the red drained from her mother's eyes. Lise watched her mother closely for signs of recovery, relieved when her posture improved and her cheek softened with a bit of gained weight. Within six months, Annette had taken on extra volunteer work, joined a golf club. Lise finally relaxed the day her mother came home with her hair dyed a glossy auburn and cut into a pageboy, hardly a widow's hairstyle.

As her mother had struggled to salvage some happiness, Lise grew to understand her new duty as a daughter – to preserve that happiness, to preserve her mother's memory of the perfect family by keeping silent.

* * *

The moment she was home from Lake Baptiste, Stephen walked out the door with two suitcases and piled them in the trunk. When he came back for a third, she met him in the hallway.

"I should be the one going, Stephen. Listen, I only need enough time to pack some things and find a place. I shouldn't stay in this house."

Stephen looked at his watch as if he hadn't heard, and stopped halfway down the steps to the street, speaking in a dead tone over his shoulder. "Adam'll be home soon. We'll tell him together."

* * *

Adam didn't seem terribly shocked at the news of the separation. He stared at the kitchen table, his jaw set as he asked, "How long have you been staying together because of me?"

"Not long." Lise shrank a little in her chair, hoping it was the last of the lies, though she doubted he believed it. He would have noticed, during their last months together, how Stephen's anger and her exhaustion had tainted the air. And though he'd known she'd been at Lake Baptiste, he hadn't asked why. Lise had to wonder what was going through his mind. She would tell him about Charlie, of course, in time. The right moment for that would come.

Lise wouldn't have dreamed he'd find out on his own.

* * *

Remy puts a framed picture into her hand. "That's me fifty years ago." In the photograph he's sitting in a semicircle with several other young men, all holding musical instruments. Remy holds a fiddle balanced on his lame knee. He has a full head of curly hair, and the sleeves of his starched white shirt are rolled up over thick forearms. He hasn't changed terribly much, Lise notes, save the hair and his rounded back – his turtle shell, he calls it. His gaze is as intense as it is in the photograph, and he's smiling, but even when he was young, his smile seemed provisional.

"You're so young."

"Ah, we were kids; it was good craic. I was just eighteen there."

"My son's age." Her smile feels tight. Adam's birthday was a week before. Still, there's been no word.

They are in the Conners' parlor, waiting for Margaret to arrive home from Mass. She stands to place the photo near the baptismal picture, lingering at its mended line a beat too long. Remy notices, saying in a flat tone, "I see you're curious about that one, the one where the man's cut out?"

"Oh, was it a man?" She clears her throat weakly.

"You know it was. Sit yourself. I'm going to tell you a story."

She stiffens. "Isn't this one of those you should keep for yourself?"

"It is, but I'm telling you anyway. And I'll make this fast because I don't want Margaret walking in and hearing. She came home after being up your place that day you filmed her, she was upset like, but didn't know why. I figured she might have unknowingly let something or other slip, and then I found out she'd left our family photo album with you, so I guessed then what would be bothering the both of you, so I'm setting things right, d'you hear?"

Lowering herself into a chair Lise nods reluctantly. "OK."

"And it *is* just a story, all right?"

"All right."

"Years ago now, there's this young girl, and she's a little in love with a handsome boy who'd she'd maybe marry, if he asked, but the girl's father wouldn't have it in any case."

Remy delivers these facts with none of the color he adds to stories or conversation. "And the girl is nearly twenty, so the father sees it coming down the road regardless, if not this boy, then surely another, for this girl is very beautiful. And the father's a right bastard, a drunkard, and a widower with two more daughters to raise, and this one is helping with the little girls. Naturally, he doesn't want to lose her, so..." Remy takes a breath. "So let's say he knows a way to... ruin her. Ruin her for marriage."

"What do you mean, 'ruin' her?"

He looks her in the eye. "He interfered, he forced her—"

"No." She sits back, shaking her head. "Her own father?"

"Yes. Let me finish. So he... *does*." Remy stops, shakes his head. "Anyway, she's in trouble soon enough."

"Trouble – you mean pregnant? Jesus."

Remy holds up a hand. "But what the bastard doesn't know is that there's another young man about who'd take this girl in any condition at all, for how much he loves her. Any condition."

"So it wasn't Peter Kleege..."

"If only."

They sit in the silence of the parlor, in golden light from the grate, though Lise suddenly feels cold. When she reaches for Remy's hand, he clamps her fingers tight.

"I'd suspected you weren't Danny's father, but in the end it hardly—"

"Matters? That it doesn't. I've *been* Danny's father – that's all that counts. Margaret's father's cut out of that picture, yeah." He looks her in the eye. "It was our door she come running to after he'd had at her for the last time. It was my own mother who wiped her tears and took off her torn clothes to clean her up, finding her big bellied – the reason she'd been shut away so in that house. I went that very night with a hammer to kill him."

"But you didn't?" She swallows.

"He ruined it by being so drunk God's own thunder couldn't wake him, let alone a blow to the head. Killing a man out cold in his own piss is no satisfaction. I only took the twins, Ruthie and Mary, and got them safe away to their aunt." He nods to the mantel. "And I suppose you imagine Margaret cut him out of that picture? I did. That day of Danny's baptism was the last we saw of him. He was half-sober then, so I promised to murder him the next time I laid eyes on him. But the next day he turned up drowned in the nets off his trawler. I like to think it was no accident, that he had the decency to do himself in."

"So. You saved Margaret. You married her, kept her secret?"

"I saved no one. I only married the girl I loved – and as for secrets, that one's ours, hers and mine. All we have we own to-gether, even that. Sometimes Margaret forgets it ever happened. More and more these last years. I sometimes wonder if the brain doesn't conspire with the heart to bury such things deep, where they belong."

When the key turns in the door, they glance at each other. Lise quickly thumbs away a tear as the door opens, and Remy stands. When he calls out to the hallway, his voice has regained some of its bite. "For Christ's sake, woman, were you hog-tied down that church? We were just about to come drag you from the pew."

"Ah, you weren't. You're in here yapping like a dog, probably boring the feet off this poor girl with your old stories."

As Margaret bustles into the room, Lise stands and places her hand on the old man's shoulder, managing a smile.

"Nah, it's much worse, Margaret. He's shown me pictures of when he had hair and his own teeth, bragging about his rogue days."

* * *

Two days after Stephen left, the school principal called the Center to inform her Adam had cut his afternoon classes. Lise left work early and rushed home to find him in his room, splayed on the bed with his eyes closed and headphones resting on his chest. She stood at the foot of the bed for several minutes, unable to tell whether he was sleeping, or pretending to sleep. In either case, he looked pained. Lise wanted to touch him, feel his forehead, but she only backed away, softly closing the door.

An hour later he walked through the kitchen, where she was circling advertisements for apartments. He didn't respond to her hello.

"Adam, were you asleep? You want to talk?"

"No."

"You're not sick?"

"No."

"But the school called. I was worried. Where were you?"

"I should ask *you* that."

"Pardon?"

"Cut the crap, Mom."

"Adam!"

"You want to know where I've been? On Queen Street, in a gallery."

She laid the pencil next to her coffee cup. "You were *where*?"

"You told me you were going to a gallery New Year's Eve, remember? You told me a friend was having an exhibit, like it was no big deal. When I woke up, you were gone, Grandma was packing and Dad was going nuts. Then you didn't come home for days. It's not like I didn't know something was up. Dad even left this on the table." He pulled the crumpled invitation to Charlie's exhibit from his jacket and tossed it down.

Charlie's name was in bold type. It might have been her father's letter, for how she leaned away from it. "Adam—"

"So I went to the gallery. Today."

Her hands shook. "Adam. Sit down." His eye held hers for a moment, long enough for her to see that her son was consumed by the same confused disgust she'd felt for her father.

Instead of sitting, he placed both hands flat on the table and leaned toward her, speaking in the cold tone of a stranger. "You had an affair. I'm not stupid, I saw the paintings, I knew they were you."

Then he backed away, kicking one of the boxes of things she'd begun packing.

"*Please* sit? Let me tell you—"

"What, the naked truth?" His voice oozed rancor.

It was Adam who'd told her the Latin derivation of the word *sarcasm* – to tear flesh.

As he strode from the room, she stood, in ribbons.

Stephen contacted her only when necessary, always calling before he stopped by to retrieve something from his desk or closet. When not discussing Adam or details of the separation, he was mute. She had no idea how angry or indifferent he was, and realized she might never know.

Adam barely listened to her and rarely spoke more words than needed to get through the business of a day, asking for his phone messages or curtly letting her know where he'd be. Her questions were responded to with one-word replies.

He spent most evenings with Stephen but did not mention what they did or which restaurants they ate in. All Lise could do was act normally, do the same things she'd always done around the house: be home by five to make dinner, knowing he wouldn't eat it. But she was certain, though Adam was no longer a child, he still needed a child's reassurance that his own world wouldn't be tilted, that things wouldn't fall apart.

During breakfast, their one meal of the day together, Adam had taken to wearing his headphones to the table, his look daring her to object.

Lise would pull work from her briefcase and pretend to read the scripts or proposals in front of her or seem to be listening to the CBC on the kitchen radio. They cleared their own dishes like strangers in a cafeteria, preoccupied and self-conscious. Lise began sorting and packing her things: books, clothes and the odd objects that had once meant something. Boxes began to accumulate along the perimeters of rooms. Adam lived more outside the house than in, coming and going like a boarder. And when he was home, only steps away from her, the span of a kitchen table, or in the car sitting only inches from her, he couldn't have been farther, couldn't seem to *get* far enough away. The few times she'd tried to touch him, he'd stepped deliberately, slowly away. It was a pain in her arms not to reach for him.

The silence was oppressive. Leonard came frequently in the evenings, staying on after dinner until Lise either began yawning or stopped crying, or the wine was gone. One particularly late night they were in the den, going over documents Stephen's lawyer had sent. Adam came in, long past curfew, and walked by the open door without a word. He went through the kitchen and directly upstairs.

It was one thing for Adam to ignore her, but he'd never been rude to Leonard. She started to get up from the desk, but Leonard caught her arm. "He's *seventeen*, Lise. This won't last."

"God, Len, I hope you're right."

She shopped in Kensington Market for the type of vintage shirts Adam liked. She left flyers and schedules for concerts and films for him, and complimentary tickets. These items were all left untouched, moved from his bed to a neat pile near the door. Upon discovering them there, Lise realized how pathetic she must seem, bribing her own son. She didn't expect forgiveness, but if she just explained everything honestly, Adam might understand. Since he wouldn't talk, she tried composing a letter. After several drafts, she crumpled the sheets, jamming them into the bottom of the kitchen trash. It wasn't a matter of not being able to choose the right words. She simply didn't own them.

She looked at a few apartments but in the end accepted the repeated invitation to stay with Paul and Monique until she could form a more permanent plan. Paul had inherited their parents' house in Rosedale and had lived in it since he and Monique had married, twenty years before. At first she didn't savor the idea of being in the old house, of intruding upon her brother and his family, but Adam had always been comfortable there. He was close to Paul and adored Monique. Ritchie was more like a best friend than a cousin. He'd be better off there than alone with her in some bare apartment.

Once it was decided where she would live, Lise finally sat down to write another letter, the one she'd put off for weeks. She addressed the envelope in care of the academy in Berlin and laid two sheets of cream paper on the table.

But after *Dear Charlie* and twenty futile minutes, her pen still dangled over the blank page. There was so much to tell him – how her eyes had opened in the gallery, how she finally trusted his love for her. But over and again words eluded her. He might have guessed at her reaction to his paintings, but she couldn't burden him with the rest. Charlie didn't deserve the pain of knowing that he'd unwittingly precipitated her rift with Adam, and Stephen's fury. Charlie would be so devastated to know what despair his paintings had wrought, especially given the lengths he'd taken to conceal her identity...

In the end, the letter was reduced to a note:

The exhibit was lovely. Stephen and I have separated and I am alone now, weaving myself back together, taking the time you urged me to. I haven't forgotten us; you know I won't. But I have to think of Adam, for now.

She signed with her initials, erased them, and wrote *Elle*.

After the exhibit came down, Mr Aroyan called to say the crate of paintings had been packed up, were ready to ship. He asked where they should be sent.

"Back to Charles Lowan, I suspect." She started giving Charlie's Berlin address, but he interrupted her.

"Oh, I have that. Mr Lowan instructed that these paintings go to you."

"Oh?" The phone was warm at her ear. Out the kitchen window she saw a lip of snow curl at the edge of the patio table, the stem of one brown pear poking through.

"Are you there?"

"Yes. Send them in care of my brother. Have you a pen, Mr Aroyan?"

Details of the separation were negotiated through Stephen's attorney. The only issue Stephen was willing to discuss directly was Adam. He too wanted as little upheaval for their son as possible, so when Lise suggested Stephen keep the house for Adam's sake, he seemed willing, even eager. There had been talk for years of Phoebe's spending more time in Toronto. For a moment, Stephen's hand unclenched. "Right. Mother loves the garden, and the guest room's empty now."

In the civil confines of the lawyer's office it was determined that for as long as she resided with Paul, Adam would stay with her during the week. His weekends would be spent at home with Stephen. They didn't address permanent custody, since Adam was so near his eighteenth birthday. Graduation was only a few months away, and for the spring holiday he'd be with Ritchie, backpacking in Europe.

Her brother and Monique helped her move in on a chilly Saturday afternoon. Lise found herself in the very room she'd occupied until going to university. Standing in the doorway, she set down her suitcases with mixed emotions, feeling as if she'd just arrived home after a time away. Part of her wanted to turn, flee. At first it was disconcerting to be in the house. The air was somber with memories, and it took several days before Lise felt at ease. Her sister-in-law implored her to treat the place as her own, but Lise preferred her room and the kitchen, not wanting to be in Adam's way. Family sounds drifted from below while she read or perused the same faded tulip wallpaper in its four neat, never-changing fields. She'd often counted the printed flowers – 2,730 – right to left and top to bottom. Sometimes, on those days when she was home sick from school, she'd counted backward.

A vague, sickroom aura still permeated the space, emphasized by the enamel bed and the terrazzo bathroom floor in hospital green. Lise didn't mind. In fact she felt her time in this house was meant to be a time of recuperation.

Although Adam could have had his own room in the rambling house, Paul – having noticed Adam's behavior and the amount of time his nephew spent alone and sulking – decided the boys should room together, a means of folding Adam more firmly into the family. An extra bed was moved into Ritchie's room, and Paul made an extra effort to involve Adam in evening activities Lise herself avoided.

A week after they'd moved in, Paul came to her room and sat on the edge of her bed. Lise laid down the magazine she'd been reading. He had such a thoughtful expression on his face that she couldn't hold back a grin as she remembered one of his old names. "Hello, Captain Sensible." As a child, Paul rarely did or said anything without first mulling and considering, sometimes for outrageous amounts of time.

"You know, Lise, there're worse things than being sensible."

"I know. Sorry, Paul, you just had this look… I think I know why you're here." She'd already decided to answer any questions Paul might ask about what led to the separation. He was her brother, and she was a guest under his roof. "I guess I owe you an explanation." She sat up.

"About your marriage?" He shook his head. "That's none of my business. I just wanted you to know that whatever is going on between you and Adam—"

"That's a bit more complicated."

"I see that" – Paul nodded – "but whatever it is, I'm sure it'll pass. He'll be fine. It's you I'm worried about, Sis."

"I'm fine, Paul."

"Like hell."

Lise sat up so her face was level with his. Growing up, they'd not been terribly close; the gap of years between them had been just wide enough that they'd led nearly separate childhoods. Teasing had been their main means of communication; he'd been "Mommy's Pauliewog," and she was "Daddy's precious petal" – names they'd often mouthed at each other with sneers. When she became a teenager, Paul was nearly grown up, and by the time their father died, Paul was ready to go away to university.

During their mother's illness, they'd forged a friendlier alliance, often making uneasy jokes about becoming orphaned.

Around that time they realized they actually liked each other. By then they were both married and would soon become parents themselves.

She was about to insist she was indeed all right and hoped to leave it at that, but the words that roiled up were an unexpected admission. "I'm a bit lost, Paul."

"Yeah, I can see."

She looked around the room. "It's so weird being here."

Paul smiled. "Believe me, I know. I sleep in Mom and Dad's old room – in the bed I was probably conceived in, for God's sake."

Lise pulled a face. "Eww. But they only did it—"

"Those *two* times," Paul chimed in to finish, and they both rolled their eyes at the old joke. Just then the boys banged up the stairs. Lise stood, rewound the knot of her hair and smoothed her skirt. "I should go help Monique with dinner." When she turned at the door, Paul was still sitting on her bed, leafing through the magazine she'd abandoned. "Hey?"

He looked up. "Yeah, Sis?"

"Thanks, Paul. For everything."

He grimaced. "Let's don't have a flavored coffee commercial."

"OK." She snapped off the light, leaving him in pitch, ignoring his bark as she shut the door.

After dinner she wandered into her father's old study to find Adam and Ritchie sticking pins into the mounted wall map of Europe. Each colored pin represented places they would visit on their trip, still months away. Ritchie planned to study architecture, so his pins were planted in cities where they could see great buildings. When he stuck a red pin into Prague, Adam nodded in agreement. He'd read of a vast studio there that once made Nazi propaganda films but now produced features. Though there were already four pins planted, Ritchie was poised with a fifth.

Adam moaned. "We've only got two and a half weeks, Ritch. Three cities, right?"

"So let's pick five – that way we'll have two backups."

Lise approached the map and pointed to the three pins planted at Rome, Paris and Barcelona, asking shyly, "Why these three?"

Ritchie answered for both of them in a deadpan tone, pushing each pin up to its hilt. "Chase Italian girls. Eat French food. Go to a bullfight in Spain."

Adam made a half turn toward her. "See? *Il Postino*, *The Last Metro*, and *Talk to Her*." He hadn't made much eye contact, but Adam had spoken to her in what language still existed between them: film references. It was the first full sentence Adam had directed to her in more than a month.

After the boys left, Lise lingered awhile over the map. Picking up one of the colored pins, she held it for a long time, considering the jagged coast of Ireland.

Later, knowing Ritchie was downstairs at the computer, she rapped on the boys' bedroom door. At Adam's grunt she ventured in to stand at the foot of his bed. His thumb marked the page of the book he'd been reading, a history of French cinema.

"Adam, what would you think if *I* went away for a while?"

He shrugged. "I think you should."

"I may go to Ireland."

"Wherever."

Chapter Thirteen

And here in Ireland, where she has the leisure to think of nothing, driving the coast road or stooping along the beach to collect her stones, memories return. Her father's features knit together when she least expects. His profile will flash briefly in the periphery: a grin in the gorse hedges, a wink from a tidal pool. She has finally reclaimed enough vision to note his vague resemblance to Adam.

Moments of better times from her locked-away childhood revealed themselves – more innocent collusions shared between father and daughter. There'd been the magic tricks and the card tricks he'd taught her, the artifice behind them revealed only after she crossed her heart and swore never to tell. Lise smiled, remembering the hidden shelf above the kneehole of his desk. They sometimes left things for each other to discover there: the empty halves of a hummingbird egg, a folding scissors, foreign coins, a glass poodle chained to a set of poodle puppies, a rose made of licorice, the best agates found along the cobblestone beach at Lake Baptiste.

In the deep cedar forest near the cottage, using her father's old army binoculars and their imaginations, they discovered quite by accident the trick of growing and shrinking like Alice. They would stand in a patch of moss, their own wonderland, and take turns looking at things close-up through the lens before flipping the binoculars to view the forest floor from a great distance, as if they too had grown suddenly, wildly tall.

When such moments come back now, Lise realizes these memories of her father are accompanied by a secure comfort, for there are times she imagines a warm hand on her back, steering her along. Only since leaving her home and coming to Ireland does she understand what her father must have suffered. Torn between family and lover, he too had made a choice. But in choosing, his heart gave way – he'd had no cure to mend himself, no *remedia amoris*. No magic stone to stop the bleeding. Lise now knows she will survive her own decision – that she is where she needs to be.

* * *

She had no idea how long she would be away. Four months, perhaps six. Stephen assumed her haste to leave Canada had to do with Charlie, and she didn't bother setting him straight. When Adam was told she'd be leaving in a week, he nodded stonily, offered no comment and asked no questions.

Leonard was very gracious in spite of the short notice, granting Lise an indefinite leave. On her last day at the Center, he perched on her desk and slid the review from the *Toronto Star* across. "I've kept this for you."

The clipping had a poor photo of a seascape and two paragraphs praising Charlie. It was already yellowed at the edges. "Len, you never mentioned seeing the exhibit."

"Well, I *did*. And lemme tell ya, those were the first female nudes to ever captivate *moi*."

"Len."

"See? You're blushing. Seriously, Lise. Lowan's a very talented man."

She tapped her pencil over the clipping. "And?"

"And nothing. The man loves you."

"I know. I know that now."

"So why Ireland? Why not go right to Germany? Isn't that where he is?"

"Yeah, but I can't see him just yet. He'll know where to find me if he still wants to."

"Ireland." He sighed. "Sounds terribly romantic."

"It rains hammers, the food's dreadful and there's no central heat." Lise stood. "C'mon, are you going to help me with these boxes or stand there swooning?"

She'd already cleaned out her desk, given away odds and ends. She kept her few framed photos, Charlie's painting of the headlands, and the old dictionary that had once belonged to her father. Hoisting its weight into a box, she realized she never had looked up the word *coptic*, still had no idea what the word meant.

Her things from the house were already stored, and her personal belongings had been winnowed down to three suitcases. The crate of paintings would be shipped separately. She packed the old army-issue binoculars she'd rediscovered in the cottage at Lake Baptiste during the frigid days after New Year's. And while she had no photograph of her father to take along, the binoculars had once held his face more clearly than film ever could.

To her list of things to do before she left Canada, Lise added, Find Charlotte. She needed to return what she had taken: his last words, intended for Charlotte. Lise understood the woman might not welcome the intrusion of memories, of grief. Charlotte might even be dead, but if nothing else, Lise could find her grave.

She wrote to her father's law partner, an aging judge, asking what he might remember. But his response was emphatic and curt: *If Hart had a mistress, he kept it quite a secret.*

Her father's only sister, Christine, lived in a nursing home in Peterborough. Lise visited, hoping the old woman might be lucid for long enough to dredge up a reliable memory, but each mention of Charlotte's name elicited different responses.

"Aunt Christine, think, now. *Charlotte*. Does that name mean anything to you?"

"Oh, *her*," the old woman sniffed. "Our governess from Ottawa. She used to spank me for passing gas. A beastly woman."

"No. A different Charlotte, Hart's... *friend*?"

"Speak up, dear, I cannot hear you."

"Hart's mistress?"

"No need to shout. *Mistress?*" After a blank stare, Christine sat up, smiling. "Of course I remember Mistress! She had the silkiest fur, such a good mouser—"

"No, Auntie. Hart's *lover.*"

Christine scowled. "Don't be saucy. Go now and get my tea."

Her father's two oldest friends agreed to meet her for lunch at Walter's Lodge. She drove to Lake Baptiste and waited for them in the pine-paneled lounge, wondering if it would sound silly for her to call them "uncle", as she used to. On the phone she'd discovered that Dennis had sold his fishing resort and had retired alone along the north edge of the lake. Arthur was living with his daughter, city-bound after more than forty years as a bush pilot and guide.

Both were so old, so changed, that it took her a moment to tell one from the other. A sudden, unsettling sadness washed over her: her father would be the same age had he lived. She rushed to help Dennis with his coat.

"Hart's little girl! Why, you're the spit of Annette, rest her soul."

"Christ, Den, she's twice as pretty."

She noted the ravages of time; both were rheumy-eyed and stooped, bundled in layers of vests and acrylic sweaters. As younger men they'd worn the serious outdoor uniform of khaki, wool-flannel, and leather. They'd smelled of paraffin, bug dope, tobacco and wood smoke. But when Dennis kissed her cheek, Lise caught a waft of rot. He was the quiet one, always with a bit of straw clenched in his teeth. There'd always been the bit of straw – she wondered where it had gone, wondered whether such habits were forgotten or forsaken.

Arthur was the talker – the bighearted little man with a wink for everyone, a joke if he liked the look of you. She remembered him being jittery, always in motion, forever rifling through the numerous pockets of his fishing vest, rolling neat cigarettes from the tin of papers and the grimy chamois pouch of tobacco. When he had nothing to smoke or whittle, he'd run his hands through his thicket of russet hair, as if he might find something there to occupy himself.

How perfectly her father had bridged the shoulders of Dennis and Arthur. It seemed he always had an arm draped over one or the other. Lise realized she'd rarely seen these men out of her father's reach.

Over beers they told vaguely familiar stories: how her father, after running over Arthur's foot with his Jeep, had commenced carving a black willow cane for him but took to it with such precision and detail that by the time the cane was finished, Arthur could've won a footrace.

They ate hamburgers, and Arthur reminded Dennis of this time or that. The afternoon they all overfished the limit, and Hart had gotten them out of the scrape by bribing the game warden with an offer of free legal advice. There was the night the three spent huddled in the cab of a ditched truck during a freak May snowstorm, having to spoon for warmth. "You can imagine the jokes we came up with that night."

Arthur tapped a finger on the plate glass, pointing to the frozen lakeshore. "Your dad knew this lake like his hand, but he pretended like he was some city boy, green." He nudged Dennis. "And sometimes he was, weren't he, Den? Christ, you remember when he wanted to get rid of that leaky rowboat? Decided the easiest way would be to sink it?"

Dennis laughed until Arthur had to pound his back. "Your dad rowed hisself out to the middle of the bay with a hatchet. We just sit on the shore watching and scratching our heads, and I bet Denny here ten dollars Hart weren't that dumb. But damned if he didn't do it – hacked a hole in the bottom of the boat. Stood there like, watching his feet disappear. God Almighty, you shoulda seen his face. Give Hart credit though – never called out to be saved, just held that hatchet above his head and went down with the ship, like he deserved. When he walked outta that lake he was dripping like a lab, and laughin' like he meant to do it like that all along."

"Course he meant to, you dope. Hart was too smart to be that stupid. He did it to *entertain* us."

"Maybe. Then he took cold, 'member? Coughing like he'd bring up a lung?"

"That's right, and you bought him that bottle of whiskey with the money you won."

Lise had known the moment these two walked through the door of the lodge that there was no sense in asking them about Charlotte. Her father would never have burdened these two with such heaviness. The space in the booth between Arthur and Dennis was occupied with the grinning ghost of better times. As the afternoon waned, she saw there was no need to make up some excuse for having gathered them together. What was clear but unsaid was that she'd come hungry for the details, and they'd fed her.

She looked up her father's legal secretary, Miss Daniels, and went to her bungalow in Mississauga. She remembered Miss Daniels as being extremely pretty and buxom, but the woman who opened the door was rocking with obesity and leaning on a cane. Still, some loveliness survived on Miss Daniels's face; her eyes were the same intense black and her thick hair still held a wave, though it had turned a floury white.

They drank weak coffee while Miss Daniels listened to her story. Without a word she struggled up from her chair and left the room. When she returned, she had a cumbersome, old-fashioned Rolodex, which she set down in front of Lise.

"This was your dad's. Don't ask why I chose this, instead of one of his gold pens or a paperweight to remember him by, but after he died so... I guess this seemed more intimate, what with his handwriting and all these doodles." She turned the crank so the cards fanned forward. "Most everyone he knew is in here."

As the cards fell, Lise saw that many had a caricature of the person listed, cartoon doodles in black or blue ink, some humorous, and many familiar. "Oh, my God, that's right. He drew, didn't he?" Lise thought of the place cards Adam had made for Christmas dinner.

"He did. And quite well, but none of those cards holds a Charlotte. I'd know. And I cannot tell you a thing about the woman, except that she existed."

Lise looked up from the Rolodex. "You knew? How?"

Miss Daniels blinked. "You wouldn't know it now, but I've turned a few heads in my time."

"I remember."

"Well, your father's head was one I couldn't turn, hard as I tried." She took a heavy breath. "And believe me, I tried. Once, during a Christmas party, I made a real fool of myself, dragging your dad into one of the empty offices on some ruse. I tried to get him to kiss me." She put down her coffee cup. "You know what he did? He held my hand – just like a priest would've – and he told me I was a wonderful girl. He said he was sorry, but he was already in love. I knew he didn't mean Annette, your mum. I knew by the way he said it."

"*You* were in love with him?"

"For years. I'd have lain down on broken glass if he'd asked." She laughed. "But Hart had morals. He never asked me to so much as tell a white lie, you know, like telling a caller he wasn't in when he was. And believe me, that's out of the ordinary in a legal office." She sighed. "Tuesday and Thursday afternoons is when he met her. I knew because he always stood a bit straighter those days and was so careful with his appearance. He had the barber those mornings. Supposedly he went to his club for meetings, but the invoices that came indicated he never ordered anything to eat or drink those two days each week, not so much as a coffee. That's all I know, really. He saw her twice a week for ten years. That's what I know."

"Ten *years*?"

"Your father was a good man and his family meant everything to him. He talked about you and Paul all the time."

"Did he?"

"Of course. I remember him calling you his Mitten and something else, some character from some book?"

"Roo?"

"That's it! Roo, such an odd name."

"It's from *Winnie-the-Pooh*. He'd called me that because I was always hiding somewhere, always popping up."

Miss Daniels walked her to the door, wheezing. "You sure you want to pursue this? Hart went to great pains to protect you all. He must've wanted to protect this lady, too."

"I suppose."

"You think upsetting an old woman is gonna give you some peace?"

"I don't know." Lise took the woman's plump hand. "I really don't…"

Miss Daniels smiled sadly. "Sometimes there's so much hurt tied up with someone's dying that we forget."

"Forget what?"

"To grieve."

She sat in the car a long time before turning the key.

Lise visited the park near the old law offices, where a row of empty benches lined the icy walk. So often, at least in films, park benches seemed the preferred venue for a rendezvous. Perhaps her father had met Charlotte here, in this very square. Quite probably, she decided. But the snow-covered park was too cold to linger in, so Lise took refuge in the cathedral across the way.

Stepping into the vast space of the nave, Lise realized this was the church with the pipe organ she'd once feared as a child. Its murmur and thunder had been the tones she'd recalled when first seeing Charlie's seascapes.

The church was nearly empty, the organist practicing a soft tune that accompanied Lise to a small side chapel. She lit a candle for her father and a second for Charlotte. As she touched the flame of one taper to another, she hoped her father and his lover might have found some peace. Hoping also that whatever they'd had was worth the pain.

Back outside, she encountered a funeral procession. Mourners, most of them elderly, were being guided or helped from cars and limousines at the curb. The lead limousine disgorged an elderly man with a shock of white hair and a cane hooked over his arm. He carried a silver urn in both hands, refusing help from the driver as he climbed the steps. Without taking his eyes from his burden, he held the urn with such care Lise imagined something ticking – a bomb, a human heart.

After crossing the street, Lise turned back to watch the widower's progress up the icy steps. A few mourners, black-coated and black-veiled, were linked, while others climbed singly up an expanse of stairs as wide as the building. Lise was stilled by the familiar graphic of the scene when one black-garbed woman bent over her cane, casting the shadow of a bass clef across the granite. From afar, mourners staggered along the horizontal lines were notes and half notes: measures set to a page of music. A requiem.

As the last mourner was absorbed into the black slice of the cathedral door, the church bell sounded. Its ring caught her off guard and a rush of fear closed Lise's throat as a vast shadow crossed above. A raft of crows streamed from the belfry, the birds forming a black net, lifting and loosening as if shaken by some unseen hand. The flock took flight in all directions, a shredding trailed by fading crowing.

She did not breathe until the last crow had disappeared. Then with one inward gasp of frigid air, the fear passed, and she felt her heart shift slightly in her chest – as if a bit of her own blackness had lifted away.

* * *

Halfway to the car she stopped in her tracks. She might just let Charlotte go, she realized. Hadn't she only despised the woman – and obsessed over finding her – because Charlotte had loved the same man she had?

Miss Daniels had been only half right when suggesting Lise hadn't grieved. The real thing, the important thing Lise had never done was forgive her father – not for Charlotte, but for dying.

If she could forgive that, perhaps one day Adam might forgive her for loving Charlie.

* * *

Across the expanse of an ocean, lying in bed under the cottage eaves, Lise has begun to mourn and remember, if only in dreams.

On her bicycle she pedals toward her father over an impossible distance, putting her muscles into it, as he's urged her. A distant ring of the approaching ice cream truck jangles against his voice as he calls out, *Make it to me, Mitten*, and his bribe, *I'll buy you a Push-Up!* Sun winks at her from between green leaves as her bare feet make furious rotations; her body and the bicycle seem one thing, her heart thrumming the rhythm. Her father's face comes clear, picking up where the home movie left off, the scene that had shown his profile before fluttering to white. But this time he turns his face toward her, and Lise sees him, finally.

The Freezee truck's ring grows louder. Her father's soft brown eyes are clear, so close she can make out the darker flecks of green in the irises. His temples crease as she skids to a stop at his feet. As in any perfect dream, there is liquid ease, each movement a waltz step as he plucks her up and twirls her. The Freezee truck's bell rings and she and her father are face-to-face, grin-to-grin.

The tring of a foreign telephone jolts Lise upright from sleep. She fumbles for the phone, her chest pounding.

Who would call so late? *Adam?* She grabs in the dark, catching the receiver.

"Hello?"

A slight delay, then, "Hello? Hermit, you sleeping?"

"Siobhan?" The alarm clock reads 2 a.m.

"Yeah. Sorry to wake you."

"That's OK. I'm waking up now. You all right?"

There's a pause. "No." Siobhan's voice sounds incredibly young.

"What's wrong?" Lise snaps on the light. "Where are you?"

"Boston. At the airport. I'm boarding in a few minutes. Can you fetch me at Shannon tomorrow?"

"You're coming home?"

"It's a long story." Her voice is muted with tears and static. "Can you?"

"Of course." She rips a page from the paperback for something to write on. "What flight? What time?"

Siobhan is puffy eyed, slouching through the arrivals door under the weight of a large backpack. Pressing through the crowd, Lise is shocked by her pallor: Siobhan's usual paleness has lightened to a chalk-white mask. When they hug, Siobhan sniffles and clings a long moment. "Hey, Hermit. I missed you."

"Same here." Lise takes her shoulders. "But so sentimental! A bit out of character, Ms. Conner. Tears?"

"I know, I know. Can't seem to stop lately, but it's not me, really. Just my eyes, they're like fucking spigots."

They find a clear space in the crowd, and Lise roots in her bag for a tissue. "Did you rest at all on the plane? You look done in."

"I'm knackered. They don't let you in peace long enough to sleep, what with all the announcements and questions. It's like the bloody Inquisition, and those narrow seats aren't room enough for one, let alone two." Siobhan stands back to pat her belly, barely rounded under the loose fabric of her shirt.

Lise stares from belly to face and back again. "Oh, Lord. Siobhan, you're not—"

"Knocked up? That's what the Yanks say. I am."

Lise freezes, her hand still buried in the depths of her bag.

"Cat got your tongue, Hermit? Sorry, but I thought I'd get that bit of news out of the way before breakfast."

"…pregnant?"

"Yup. C'mon, I'll perish if I don't get some food in us."

In the upstairs cafeteria they watch the activity of the car park. Each time a vehicle leaves, a dry shape of pavement is left.

"I actually missed the drizzle, can you believe?" Siobhan yawns, showing white molars, then peers at Lise over a slice of toast. "I missed the *rain*, I said."

"I'm digesting your surprise. How long?"

"How *far gone*, you mean? Three months and five days, to be exact. It happened the night before Colm left here for the States, so I know to the hour." After the scalding tea and rubbery eggs, some color has crept back into Siobhan's face.

"You want to keep the baby, then?"

"Well, if I didn't, I'd hardly be back in Ireland, would I? I'd have got rid of it in Boston." She forks yolk to the side of her plate, pulling a face. "I s'pose somebody has to want it. Colm doesn't, of course. Career and whatnot. He asked me to get an abortion."

"What did you say?"

She curls her voice to a lilt. "Oh, I'd hate to rattle the pope, now, good *Oirish* lass like meself." Her laughter is thin. "Do you ever think things happen for a reason? I mean, I knew before I went over it was hopeless with Colm." She poked her abdomen. "I knew this would happen when it did, and I did nothing to stop it. Am I stupid, or am I just accepting what's gonna be handed me anyway?"

"You mean fate?"

"I'm jet-lagged, I mean fuck-all."

"There, you're more yourself now."

"I hate him." Tears pulsing along her nose are quickly rubbed away with the heel of her hand. Lise sees Siobhan's nails are bitten and dirty. "I love him and wish I didn't. Bastard."

"I'm so sorry."

"So am I. I hope you don't mind my trying this out on you before I have to tell Grump and Gram Maggie?"

She gathers up her purse and pulls the backpack from under the table. "Let's get you home."

Siobhan brightens. "Gram and Remy's house?"

"Oh, no. Your father's first, I'd say. We owe him that."

Siobhan sleeps most of the way. It's afternoon by the time they reach Danny's. She rings the bell while Siobhan props herself against the stucco.

"Sure you don't want me to come in with you?"

"Am."

When she hears movement from inside, Lise hugs the girl quickly and backs away. "You'll be all right."

"I will, sure, Hermit. Hey?"

"Yeah?"

"I never did thank you."

Nearing Rafferty's Road, she slows and turns the car onto a rutted single track. Back in Toronto she'd gazed at Charlie's wild painting of the headlands countless times, and here she can see the actual jut of land in every manner of daylight, from dawn to sunset. Driving from Danny's house, she now sees it from a completely different angle. For as many times as she's imagined standing at its edge, she has never considered venturing to the headlands alone.

She urges the car on as it labors over the rough incline. "C'mon, Morris, you can do it." Catching her eye in the rearview, she says defensively, "Margaret speaks to *cakes*." At the peak she pats the dash.

Wind bends her sideways when she climbs out. Remy has warned her of the strong gusts near the cliffs. "People get lifted off now and then." He'd shrugged. "Tourists mostly."

On the cliff path she crouches, pulling herself along on tags of gorse until she finds a level spot on the farthest point. She lowers to her haunches and scoots closer to the edge, a ball of vertigo slipping under her ribs. Lise dips her hand into a crevice to anchor herself. The wind doesn't sheer eastward over the water, as she's expected, but riffs from all directions. Her jacket billows like a jib, the gullies of her ears are scoured.

Leaning forward, she can see the water below but cannot hear the waves for the wind.

Just before leaving Canada she'd confessed to Leonard her fears of leaving one life to perhaps fail in another. When she told him she might not be brave enough for it, he'd admonished, "The only failure's in *not* trying. Trying's the true bravery."

Siobhan had been unafraid to follow her heart. It had been a risk to go after Colm, but she'd gone and had given her best. What bravery that must have taken.

All is risk, she thinks. *It's a risk to be sitting here.* The next gust of wind – so strong it could easily tip her forward into the sea – presses her back and down to safety. Her hand is rooted. The longer she sits, the less dangerous her perch feels.

Back in the cottage, she goes directly to the dining room and takes the painting from its hook. She tears off the mended brown paper backing to reveal the name of the village curving in Charlie's hand. Underneath, she adds a simple message in her own cursive: *Come here to me*.

It is up to him now.

She packs the painting, addresses the padded box to Charlie's Cardiff studio. If he's not arrived there yet, he will soon enough – his teaching assignment in Germany is nearly over.

At the post office she insures the package for a ridiculous sum, wincing when the postmistress heaves it among parcels in the priority bin. She stands overlong at the counter until the woman grouses, "It'll get where it's going."

"Sure. Sorry."

"It's an important package, then?"

"Quite."

"And aren't they all?"

Since Siobhan's return, Lise has only ventured from the Kleege place a few times. She spends most of the longer spring days working on her stone path or sitting in a sheltered spot between the old sheep barn and an ancient outhouse.

She's hauled out a wicker chair and settled it against the barn where sun washes the wall at her back. Here, in the late afternoons, she reads from her stack of library books or writes letters she cannot mail – on her last visit to the post office, she'd been so rattled with the details of mailing Charlie's painting that she forgot to buy stamps.

Today the sun is shouldered aside early by a fine mist that by afternoon has plumped itself into a downpour. Out the kitchen window, Lise watches rivulets cut tiny canyons into the driveway ruts. She decides to drive to the village before shops close.

Once finished with her errands, she drives down the Conners' lane but only coasts past their house without braking. Since Siobhan's return, she's left them alone to take in the news and have time to let it all settle. But Lise misses them. Movement from the Conners' kitchen blurs through the lace panel over the window, and as she cranes her neck to glimpse Remy, her elbow hits the horn. A second after the sharp blast, a corner of curtain is lifted.

She sinks down in the seat to avoid being seen, then realizes how juvenile her behavior is. Skulking in the streets. After parking in the Conners' drive, she sheepishly lifts the knocker at their door.

Remy answers. He gives her a wide grin and ushers her in. "Ah, we knew she'd be back."

"Siobhan?"

"You! Siobhan makes plenty noise about hating this place, but it's in her like breath. A course she's back. We were just wondering over tea when you'd poke your head in."

"Here I am."

"And looking like you could use a bit of cheer." Remy seems genuinely glad to see her.

"You're not angry?"

"And what've I to be angry over?" He shakes his head. "Siobhan's home safe, now isn't she? And I doubt very much you're responsible for her condition."

When she doesn't laugh, Remy squints at her. "You're rather long in the jaw – have you not heard from your son yet?"

"No... but he's traveling now anyway. On that trip I told you about?"

"Right, well, you know how the phones are in places like Spain... and *Italy*, for God's sake."

"But I've posted so many letters."

"That's the postal service for you. You're not in Canada anymore, Dorothy!"

He's gotten her to smile. "That's *Kansas*, Remy."

"Course it is." He presses her through to the kitchen. "You'll hear from him in time. I know it."

Margaret turns from the sink. "Thought I'd heard the door. There you are like some ghost! Are you well, dear?"

"Well enough."

But when she touches the old woman's arm, Margaret frowns. "Your hands are a sight – like a bricklayer's! What in heavens are you doing out there? Cutting turf?"

"Laying a path to the beach."

"I'm getting some salve for that blister."

Remy rolls his eyes. "Aw, woman, if it were a nurse she'd wanted—"

"Hush." Margaret stares at Remy until he sputters and goes to the sideboard, returning with three glasses and a decanter.

After Margaret tends to her hand, they each accept a glass from Remy, who grins. "A toast's in order, I'd say."

Margaret unties her apron. "What should we drink to?"

Lise lifts her glass. "To Siobhan's health."

"Cheers."

"*Sláinte.*"

After they sit, Margaret offers a second toast, beaming. "To great-grandparenthood!" They tap glasses and pitch the liquid back, Margaret's eyes watering with the burn.

"Right." Remy turns to her. "Siobhan will be moving in here with us for a while, at least till the baby comes."

"I've Danny's old room nearly fitted out for her." Margaret raises a hand to cover a delicate hiccup. They sit in the kitchen's alcove, sinking into the plush chairs.

Remy's brows hitch. "You don't imagine she'll be wanting to *have* it in this house? You know, with all that natural breathing like a cow? Or squeeze it out in some water tank like they do now?"

Margaret tsks. "She'll go up Sligo to a proper hospital where they've all the machines and a special room called a birthing suite. Can you imagine?"

Lise curls her feet under her on the recliner and leans back in the pleasant haze of the kitchen. Remy winks. "And I suppose you'll be there to film the whole affair?"

"All that blood and howling? No, I don't think so."

"But they do that now, don't they?" Margaret puzzles. "Film a birth! Why, I wonder – for posterity's sake?"

"*Posterior's* sake, more like." Remy slaps his knee.

Margaret sighs. "Pity Mr Conner here's not as funny as he looks."

A third glass is raised, this time in Lise's direction, Remy offering, "To friends, then."

"*And* loved ones." Margaret takes her husband's hand.

"Near and far," Lise adds, the catch in her voice barely noticeable.

* * *

At the door, Margaret frowns. "Now there was some bit of news. What was it, Remy?"

He steps into the vestibule. "Right, I'd nearly forgot myself. Did you not hear? Old Mrs Kleege's flat out with pneumonia."

"Oh?"

"Death's door." Margaret shakes her head.

"Circling the drain." Remy spirals the air with a finger.

"Remy!"

He snorts, "Kleeges'll be selling, I have it on good authority. And I've more or less figured what price the land'll bring. The cottage is useless, but still, I may consider buying the place and maybe leasing it to someone reliable?" He's smiling at Lise, the gap in his teeth wide. "Course that's presuming you'd be inclined to stay here. Or, maybe you'd like to buy the place."

"Buy? Oh, Remy, I don't know…"

"Don't answer now. There's plenty time to think."

Chapter Fourteen

Since her return, Siobhan has had daily rows with Danny, who has taken the news of the baby well enough but insists Colm be held responsible for some form of financial support. The girl often escapes the drama by stopping by the cottage.

If Lise is out walking, to the headlands or the cemetery, or away on some errand, Siobhan will let herself in with the key hidden under the bench. Often she'll raid the refrigerator, leaving more of her one-line notes: *I now weigh seven stone. Will sing for food. You're out of cheese.* Depending on her mood, Siobhan might turn the camera on herself. Lise has set it up on a tripod aimed at the leather armchair in the parlor. She has shown Siobhan how to change reels and operate the new remote. Lise never knows what's been committed to film after Siobhan's been by. There are snippets of her adventures in Boston: rank stories from the Shamrock Bar, hilarious imitations of Americans and raw, tearful musings over Colm. More recently, Siobhan's begun vivid dialogues regarding pregnancy, some serious, others not: *"Mothers! You've all banded together like some cult. If any of you told the REAL truth about what this pregnancy bollocks is like – such as having to puke into the pocket of your coat at the movies, or the smell of hair becoming toxic – wouldn't the entire fucking species come to a screeching halt? It would! A bloody, screeching halt."*

Such rantings are usually spun out by the time Lise returns to the cottage, where an uncharacteristically quiet Siobhan will have put the kettle on to boil.

Today, it's Lise who natters away, making small talk, waiting for the girl to join in, but Siobhan's quips and comments are few, as if she's emptied her thoughts into the camera. Perhaps grief over Colm has leveled her. Or the strange imbalance of pregnancy. They take the teapot outside, where Siobhan curls on a blanket to read a glossy magazine while Lise works laying stones. The path is lengthening, is several meters long now.

Sighing over a boring article, Siobhan turns to face the sun and within minutes has dozed off. Lise pauses when she hears the soft snore and glances over to see Siobhan's hand resting protectively, instinctively over her middle. She remembers her own months of pregnancy, the cycles of exhilaration and exhaustion, the shameless pursuit of food, the freakish changes in her body – all accompanied by a strange complacency. And at the lumbering end of it, there'd been the shock no one had prepared her for: that in labor she'd wish for death before it was even half over.

But neither had anyone prepared her for the feelings she would have for Adam. It doesn't really seem so long ago now, yet her own baby has somehow grown into a young man who at this very moment is traveling a few hundred miles away in Europe, off on his first real adventure.

What she'd give for a word, a postcard.

April has brought softer rains and longer, light-filled days. Shopping in Ballina, Lise buys a lightweight jacket, but when the clerk finds out where she's living, he persuades her to buy both the hooded jacket and a waxed Barbour. She chooses a pair of green Wellingtons – the ill-fitting pair of Mrs Kleege's has sprung a leak.

When she coasts down her drive, she's not surprised to see Siobhan's car. Edging into the hall, she sees her standing in the kitchen frying something at the cooker. A young man with his back to the door hunkers at the table. He has longish hair and is drinking one of her beers. Lise pauses in the doorway. Could this be Colm? Has he done the right thing and followed Siobhan home?

She closes the door loudly to warn them, calling out, "Making yourself at home, I hope?"

Siobhan turns, grinning. "Ah, there's our Hermit now." She wipes her hands on the towel tucked over the bump in her jeans. "And look now, while you were out I found this fella roaming the road, asking after you."

"After me?"

The young man turns, wiping foam from his goatee. Lise's new Wellingtons slip to the slates, one rubbery thud, then another.

"Hey, Mom."

Walking the beach, Lise can hardly take her eyes from her son. His face seems leaner, his limbs easier in their joints. She wants to touch his goatee, to wrap him in hugs, but settles for leaning into his shoulder. They find a dry bit of sand where they can look out toward the low islands. When he sits down next to her and wedges his heels into the sand, the sheer physical fact of him jars her.

Adam tells her that after visiting Italy, he and Ritchie parted in Paris when Ritchie decided to return to Rome to pursue a girl he'd met there.

"I've been dumped." Adam shrugs. "And Paris on your own really sucks. So, I decided to come here. See how you are."

"I can't believe it." When she takes his hand, there's no resistance. "You're *actually* here."

"I wasn't going to come. I thought you'd be with that guy, the painter."

"With Charlie? I've been alone this whole time, Adam. You didn't know?"

"I know now."

"You didn't read my letters?"

"I didn't open them when they came. But then – I dunno why – when I was packing I threw them all in my backpack. I read them on the train through France."

"So you know everything."

"Yeah. I s'pose that's why I'm here. I just wanted to say thanks, for all that stuff you wrote, you know, about your dad, and those stories of when you were a kid."

The muscles in Lise's jaw ache from smiling. She cannot think of a thing to say.

After the sun goes, they trudge through the sand and along the shallow gulch to where the path begins. "You're the first to walk on it." She follows him to the front door of the cottage, where he sweeps his arm in a "you first" motion.

When they'd left Siobhan in the kitchen earlier, she'd been eating rashers and sniffling into a fistful of tissues. But the kitchen is empty now, and Lise sees the dishes have been washed and the pan left to drip. Her Wellingtons have been picked up and added to the line of shoes along the hallway. There's a note on the table.

I give him a ten. Sorry, have demolished the jam.
S.

"That girl, is she always so... up and down?"

"Yes." They both laugh.

"So, it's OK if I stay?"

She turns from lighting a lamp to see if he's joking.

"How much time do you have?"

"A week and a day."

Lise closes her eyes. *Eight days.* After months of wishing for an hour, it's more than she would've dared hope.

Keeping Adam to herself in those first days, she lets him drive the Morris over back roads. Once he has the hang of the right-hand drive, they pack up and embark on a meandering road trip. They visit the wild Donegal beaches and the Stone-Age dolmens. They cross the border and drive half a day to Giant's Causeway. Their B & B has a parlor perpetually decorated for Christmas. For two days they drive roads with no numbers or names, eating their meals in the car until greasy chip papers stain the useless maps tossed to the back. Empty soda cans roll under their seats.

Lise poses Adam in front of tourist sites as an excuse to take his picture, and embarrasses him by asking passers-by to snap shots of them together. They have a contest to see who can find the worst souvenir. Adam wins easily – his rosary made of pressed bog muck dangles from the Morris's rearview – and they use hers, a linen tea towel printed with the lyrics to 'Danny Boy', to shine the fenders after washing off gull droppings.

When they return, the Conners make an appropriate fuss over Adam. Remy even closes up shop for a morning to guide them on a short tour through the village. As they pop in and out of shops and public houses, Lise is pleased to realize how many of the villagers she's come to know, at least well enough to introduce to Adam.

Adam claims that after his short time in Italy and France, it's a great relief to be in a place where English is "sort of" spoken, and after meeting and chatting with several of the more colorful locals, he entertains Lise and Margaret with his impressions. He mimics Mertie, from the pub, and Kathleen, the surly postmistress, and does a dead-on imitation of Remy, whistling each s with an airy flourish.

When they meet up with Father McIntyre in front of O'Dare's, the priest asks Adam about his travels. When Adam mentions that he's been to Rome, the priest brightens.

"Did you see Vatican City?"

"Ah, yeah. My cousin wanted to see the buildings, right? And it just happened to be Sunday and there happened to be a million Italians there, for Mass or whatnot, so they trotted the old guy out and somehow got him propped up for the blessing."

"His Holiness? Did he seem poorly?"

"Vegetative, Father. Like a popetato. Can I buy you a pint?"

* * *

After leaving the priest, she and Adam take turns kicking a plastic bottle along the lane.

"It's OK here. And the old guy's a stitch."

"Remy? He likes you, too."

"Yeah." Adam goal-kicks the bottle over a ditch. "Sometimes I think... it would've been nice, you know, to have had a grandfather. You ever miss him? Your dad, I mean?"

"Sure."

"Until you wrote me, you never said much about him."

She took his arm. "Well, I can now."

"Why now?"

"Because I've begun to remember the good."

Along with most everyone in the village, they are invited to Danny's Sunday barbecue, his first party in the new house. The patio spreads under the shadow of the great salmon-colored house. Groupings of plastic chairs surround plastic tables with checkered cloths.

Remy shakes his head. "Will you look at it? It's like bloody America."

Siobhan snorts. "America's worse, if you can believe."

Margaret has taken over cooking and stands at the grill with Adam as her helper. She's fitted him out with an apron identical to her own, down to the ruffles. The old woman and the boy flip burgers and sausages onto plates for the line of guests.

Remy winces as he lowers himself to the bench, joining Lise. "Good-natured lad, letting her truss him up like that."

"I think he's fallen under her spell."

Siobhan laughs, balancing a paper plate mounded with food. "If I was three years younger and not preggers, I'd be on him like that apron."

"Siobhan!"

"Grump!"

A sudden look passes over Siobhan's face and she scowls at her plate. "Ah, not again. Christ on a cracker." She shoves her plate into Remy's hands and trots to the edge of the overlook to retch.

Remy begins to rise, but Lise presses him back. "Let her be. I'll get her a glass of water."

As Lise passes Adam, he points to Siobhan with his spatula. "She OK?"

"She'll be fine."

Margaret sighs. "God help her if she's anything like her mum. Poor Brigid couldn't keep down so much as toast for five months."

Walking through the crowd and toward Danny's outdoor bar, Lise realizes what's missing from the party. Danny is watching, making sure everyone has a drink, but he's standing alone.

"It's all couples here, Danny, none of your..."

"'Fillies', Remy calls them. Nope. Didn't invite any."

"Really? I would've liked to meet one. Or two." She winks.

"Nah, you wouldn't." He shows her where the glasses are and twists open a bottle of water. "Truth is, now that I'm suddenly old enough to become a grandfather, maybe I should think about hauling in the tackle."

It takes her a second to catch his meaning. "Colorful metaphor, Danny."

"Well." He grins.

From where they stand, they can see Remy with his arm around Siobhan, recovered now, and Margaret, who has left the grill to dab at her granddaughter with an apron corner.

Danny sighs. "They're on her like a pair of bookends."

"You're just as bad. I saw you steal the cigarettes from her bag."

"For her own good. She's got a Conner inside her."

"Do I detect pride?"

He shrugs. "And look at your own boy there. He's a straight-on sort, isn't he?"

"He is that."

"Ha. *You're* sounding Irish now."

Danny follows her eye to Remy and Margaret, who've clasped hands behind Siobhan's shoulders. "I see what you mean now – about them being friends. That it's maybe a comfort for them to have each other. You know, to depend on."

"In their decrepitude?"

"Nah, you know what I mean."

"They're more than friends." She looks at him. "They still do it, you know – have sex. Siobhan told me."

"Ah, Jesus! Of all the things I didn't need to know."

She laughs until he stops her with his question, leaning in and serious. "Your Adam, now, does he know about your painter fella?"

Forgetting the water is meant for Siobhan, she takes a long drink. "He does. He has. For a long time."

"And does he know you're waiting on him here?"

"Danny, I never said—"

"The lot of us are waiting. Did you think you were alone?" He doesn't wait for an answer but picks up a wine bottle and moves toward a guest with an empty glass. Lise is left standing amid a swirl of people, a set of faces she's come to know – some familiar and friendly, some dear. She grins, at no one in particular.

Remy trudges up the cemetery path with her, resting every few dozen yards. At the halfway stone, they look over the wide sea while Adam easily climbs ahead, carrying Lise's camera and the food basket. Lise feels nearly athletic next to the old man, but pretends to huff when he does. At the first tier of graves he stoops, hands pressed to knees, and takes several labored breaths.

He's made this pilgrimage to properly introduce the dead. As they approach the row of stones, he takes off his cap, his thin hair immediately lifting into grey wedges. The Conner family headstones form a semicircle. Remy's youngest brother, two infant sisters and his parents – fifty years married – all crowd together in their bed of earth. Remy crosses himself and kneels, using his mother's headstone for leverage.

As he pays his respects, she tugs Adam's jacket sleeve and they discreetly back away to skirt the graveyard. Lise shows her son the unmarked plot she's been tending. The azalea has now budded, and new grass is sprouting in fine tufts. As she tidies up, plucking litter from the ground, Lise tries to explain how she's come to borrow this grave.

Adam shrugs, and Lise sees his incomprehension. She only smiles. "You might understand, one day."

They look over the rugged crest of graves, where Remy is now on his feet, wiping the blade of his penknife after having scraped clean the grooved letters of each Conner name. Limping toward them, he chuckles. "Nothing like a bit of banter with the dead!" He nods back at his family. "We're all caught up now."

When Adam takes the camera from its case, Remy points to it. "You want stories? There's a wealth here." At a white marble slab carved with twining roses, he shuffles to a stop. "Now here's one worth telling." He waits patiently for Adam to load the film and focus.

"In 1916 Mary McDonough was a healthy schoolteacher, aged but twenty-two years. Dropped stone-dead while correcting essays. Died the very instant her twin brother did, on the other side of the country in the post office building in Dublin, during the Insurrection – her of an aneurysm, him a gunshot wound to the head."

"For real?" Adam leans in.

"Real as rain."

They move on to a marker with a later date. "This one I remember very well, Jimmy Nolan, an old farmhand for Hourihan's. Died Christmas morning while milking his favorite cow. He'd wanted to make things cheerful for the herd, see? So he'd decorated the hayloft pulley with mistletoe. But then the pulley come loose from its mooring to crown him, so the undertaker found bone shards and mistletoe in his mouth." Remy nods. "Shame, too, for he might've lived another five or so years, he was that spry at ninety-eight."

At a grave marked *Malley* he lowers his voice. "Bona fide ghost. Nan Malley, our postmistress years back. Grandmother to thirty-seven flame-headed little Malleys." Remy perched on the limestone marker. "Drove her post van over a cliff on the headlands road in a fog. See here, August of 1962. Her ghost, blue as the water she'd drowned in, was spotted every dusk for a fortnight after the accident. There she was, tossing envelopes and parcels to the sand. Letters washed up on the beach for weeks, and according to the story not one bit of post went missing."

"You don't believe that?"

He smiles at Lise. "Sure if one of those letters wasn't my own. And I've kept it. Only my name, half-legible, and inside a page with a grey wash of ink and a spoonful of salt."

As Remy recounts the fates of these characters, Lise wonders how near truth he strays. But when she questions Remy over the more bizarre stories, he holds fast. Like a piper he leads them weaving among the graves, regaling them with the lives and deaths of those who can neither correct nor corroborate. The facts aren't as important as the remembering, she understands. And Remy insists that for as long as these names are said aloud and those few like him bother yet with their stories, the dead aren't forgotten.

When they've circled back to the Conner plot, Adam asks him to tell some story of his own people, nearly underneath his feet.

"Another day." He mock-punches the boy's shoulder. "When you come back here on your next vacation. I've talked too much now. I'll be late getting back to Margaret and my tea."

Lise objects. "But I've brought a picnic."

"More for your lad to eat, then. Margaret's expecting me by now." He winks. "Waiting only sours a woman." Remy takes a few steps nearer his mother's grave, smiling. "And isn't this a great place for a song? You'll know this one." He nods toward his audience of graves. "*They* do." His baritone echoes between the cold walls of the two churches.

> *Of all the comrades e'er I had*
> *They're sorry for my going away,*
> *And all the sweethearts e'er I had*
> *They'd wish me one more day to stay.*
> *But since it fell unto my lot*
> *That I should rise and you should not*
> *I gently rise and softly call*
> *Goodnight, and joy be to ye all...*

Before the song finishes, he's turned to hitch down the hill and out of sight.

Lise shivers to see his footprint clearly pressed into the loam over the bit of Conner plot he's claimed will one day be his own. Edging near Adam, she watches Remy's progress down the steep hill. He's whistling now, notes drifting up along with the soft clatter of rolling pebbles.

Once down, he makes his way to his car, where Lise can see, even from the high plateau, that he's smiling. Always smiling, she realizes, when on his way to Margaret.

Adam is leaving in the morning, and there are subjects she hasn't yet broached. When they sit down near the headstones with their picnic, she faces him. "Adam, do you believe in soul mates?"

He plucks lettuce from his sandwich. "I s'pose."

"You know your father and I weren't that for each other?"

"Well, you weren't together very often, and when you were..." He shrugs and tosses the lettuce to a gull perched on a headstone. "Would you be happy with this painter?"

"I might." On the road below, Remy honks a few short blasts to let them know he's off. From Remy she's learned that explaining facts of the heart is futile, that an analogy or a story is usually better. As she recalls that advice, a bygone image fills the frame of what she's trying to impart.

"Here's the thing. When I was your age, just starting university, I was waiting for a bus one night, and just across the street I could see into this house. There was a woman sitting in the window. She was only about the age I am now, but back then I thought she was old. Her arms were sort of wrapped around her like she was cold, and there was a man sitting near. He was reading a book but kept looking at her. He got up and took his cardigan off and draped it over the woman's shoulders. And I thought, *Well, that's nice.* It was just the sort of thing people do for each other.

"But then the man did something else, something extra: he took her hair and eased it from the cardigan, very gently, and fanned it out over her shoulders. And then he walked away. That was it, really. Just that gesture. But I saw the look on her face – all *lit*. I knew then I wanted to have what she had, someone who might do such things for me." She looked at her son. "I don't know when, but I lost sight of that, of knowing what I wanted."

"Why?"

"I dunno. I just gave up on it. Until…"

Adam nods when she says it.

"…until Charlie."

On their way through the gate, she glances back.

"Adam?"

"Yup."

"Bury me here, OK?"

He grins. "Right now?"

"I'm serious."

"Sure, Mom." He takes a few steps ahead and turns. "Hey, you'll say goodbye for me? To Remy, I mean."

* * *

Adam stows his pack in the back of the Land Rover Danny has given over to Siobhan. She complains out the window, "How I'll ever afford the petrol for this? But Da's got this severe case of grandfatheritis before the sprog's even born – claims this barge is much safer for us than my Honda. He cannot fathom we'd all be much safer if behemoths like this weren't endangering the roads. Sure you don't want to come along, Hermit?" Siobhan climbs out from the high bucket seat, lowering herself out by the steering wheel.

Adam has accepted Siobhan's offer to drop him at the airport in Dublin, where she'll spend the weekend shopping for baby things with Brigid.

"No, thanks, Siobhan, you'll want to spend time alone with your mum. Besides, Adam and I can say goodbye here."

"You're sure?"

"I am. And thanks for taking him."

"It's a favor to me, actually. Adam can help drive when I start bawling, you know, should we drive past any of the things that set me off now, like trees or signposts." Siobhan hops. "I need to use your loo, quick like. No length at all to my pipes anymore – it's food in, food back up, tea goes in and two minutes later—"

"Go."

She backs away. "Adam, you'll open my crisp packets for me and stop this tank when I need to bok them up?" She turns to trot toward the cottage.

"Absolutely," he calls after her. Turning to Lise, he asks, "Mom, does *bok* mean what I think?"

"Uh-huh. There's a roll of paper towels on the backseat in case. You have the phone cards I gave you?"

He pats his jacket pocket. "*And* ticket *and* passport. I'll call when I land."

"And?"

"And *yes*, I will write. Promise."

She smiles. "I'm staying here, Adam. I won't be back to Canada."

He looks over her shoulder at the cottage, and beyond, where the sea is crinkled with sun. "Yeah. I figured. You're OK here, aren't you?"

When Siobhan comes out, she gets a running start toward the vehicle and vaults upward into the seat. "Much better. Can hardly wait for the ninth fucking month of this."

The engine roars and Adam is belted in, the door shut. Lise steps onto the running board and tries to hug him again through the open window.

He reddens. "Hey, there's something…"

"Yes?"

"Well, you know."

She closes her eyes. He needn't say it. The old comfort they'd shared has settled back over them. He's forgiven her, or at least has begun to.

"I know."

She walks behind the Land Rover as it rocks up the drive, the magic of her father's binoculars keeping it close. Distance between her and the vehicle is pulled tight. Even as the vehicle grows small, she doesn't stop walking, does not look away, will not lower the eyepiece until the Land Rover is a mere speck and the thread of dust has settled back to the road.

For half a day she has watched paint dry. In the best light of afternoon the parlor is finally finished. "Golden hour," the painters call it. The walls absorb sunlight, the plaster washed with the palest of the palette Remy has mixed, hardly any pigment at all, just a tint suggesting warmth and coolness at once: the eggshell of a tern, foam edging a tidal pool.

On hand are a hammer and a crowbar from Remy's shop. It takes fifteen minutes to open the crate, and a half hour to unwrap all the paintings. Paying no attention to the order of the canvases, she tosses Bubble Wrap and paper aside to settle each painting against the dried wall.

Wading backward through the drift of packing material, she sees they have been set down out of order, but still her eye goes naturally left to right. They are exactly reversed from how she'd first seen them. In the gallery in Toronto the paintings had been hung depicting the story of a woman in the private act of dressing, slowly covering herself. Here she is not dressing, but disrobing; not covering but *revealing*. A different story altogether.

In this new order the first painting shows her clutching the front of her dress as if ready to pull it over her head, half of her face curtained by hair. She's not shy this time but rather beckons slyly: *Come closer.*

In the second painting she's not looking at the bruise so much as inviting the viewer to touch it; the tilt of her head isn't a bow of shyness but an opening to kiss the nape of her neck. The strap of her dress isn't being pulled up; it's been loosened to let it fall.

Seeing what Charlie has managed, she feels behind her for the sofa, sits blindly. In reverse, the paintings give meaning to the phrase he had once so confounded her with.

They had been making love; she was over him, crouched. Nothing beyond the bed existed, nothing mattered but his solidness slowly sealing and resealing her. Without opening her eyes, she knew he was watching, for he kept reaching up to brush aside the hair falling free.

It became a game – her swaying in the opposite direction so he would have to brush the sweep of hair away once more, then again, and again. Each time he reached to her face, she blindly bit at his fingers, occasionally catching a knuckle or edging his palm with her teeth. When she laughed, he didn't respond. She opened her eyes to see he had grown serious.

"Who am I with now," he asked, "the girl or the woman?"

"Pardon?"

"Who are you now?"

He was inside her. *What was he asking, for God's sake?*

He persevered. "Who is with me now, the woman? Or the girl who wants to be found?"

A slow discomfort spread over her, the same feeling she'd had being called upon in school when she should've known the answer but did not. Her physical need evaporated; her rhythm over him stopped. She sat, filled with him and confused.

Easing herself away, she swung to the edge of the mattress with her back to him. "What's the right response, Charlie? Because I don't understand."

After a pause he edged closer, sighing. "There's a bit of girl deep in you, Elle. A girl who never got let out. She was here a minute ago, teasing, playing." He took her shoulders and turned her to face him. "Don't lose her altogether." Charlie gathered tears on his fingertips and pressed her face to his neck. "It's all right, you know."

"*What* is?"

"Giving in to the girl."

How well he'd known her. And through some magic he had wrought her past and present into the same images. Before she understood what of herself had gone missing, Charlie, without intending to, had made shape of a lost girlhood, had reconstructed who she'd been before the day her father's heart shut down, when that bit of her own had frozen too.

The last painting in the crate, the mysterious eighth canvas, had not been included in the exhibit. It is a straight-on, full-faced portrait, exactly life size, with no embellishments, no setting. In Courbet colors, Charlie has painted her with fine strokes on canvas so smooth no brush marks are visible. It might be a mirror in her hands for how real she looks, as if ready to speak, lips parted, as if she's about to say, *This is me.*

Picking up the hammer and the packet of picture hangers, she decides. The paintings will be hung as they are – eight images of a woman giving in to the girl.

* * *

All the reels have been processed save the one in the camera. An editing suite in Sligo has been booked. Of her footage of the Conners, certain bits are gone. Margaret's secret is already cut out, swept up and tossed. Lise relabels the reel filmed in her first days on the shore – her walk along the beach, the frames of herself moving toward the cottage window. These scenes will make a perfect background for the credits: the filmmaker, revealing herself.

And now, with the new footage since Siobhan's return and the bits Adam has filmed in the cemetery – Remy singing 'The Parting Glass' – she has nearly all she needs.

Nearly.

She positions the chair by a window so that a square of ocean and sky will blur behind her. Checking the mirror, she decides to let her hair be, frizzed from the salt air. The cable in her hand allows her to zoom the new camera and turn the machine on and off from a distance.

Shifting in the chair, she looks straight into the lens. With no hesitation she presses the button and in a clear voice, she begins.

"My name is Liselle Annette Dupre."

Epilogue

Do your roots drag up color
from the sand?
Have they slipped gold under you –
rivets of gold?
Band of iris-flowers
above the waves,
you are painted blue,
painted like a fresh prow
stained among the salt weeds.

H.D.

The coast road has changed little, though traffic increases somewhat with each summer season. Tourists in rental cars often stop Liselle to ask directions, assuming she is a native. She looks the part well enough: wax cap tilted over her brow, loose Aran sweaters and laced walking boots. She only needs a crook and a sheep or two, really. Or so Charlie says.

She can recall the morning he arrived as if it were yesterday – a day very like this one, all azure and white, with gulls hanging aloft. Charlie had hitched a ride from the Arches Hotel, asking the driver to let him out a mile before the headlands. Liselle was laying stones on her path, the day warm enough she wore a T-shirt and chinos rolled halfway up her calves. Something yet nothing made her look up from her task, and she'd shielded her eyes to glean a figure on the road, one so far away it could have been a man or a woman, young or old. She rose without hesitation and calmly clapped the sand from her hands. Ten minutes later she met Charlie rounding the curve of the road where the gorse is thickest. His jacket was over his arm and he held a wilting fistful of bluebells. His eyes were the same: he looked at her the same way.

That afternoon they drove in to fetch his luggage and to ask the postmistress how two foreigners might go about posting their marriage banns.

Today the road is mercifully empty, affording her leisure to remember. Liselle leaves the macadam to climb the footpath, short of breath by the time she reaches the graveyard. She leans against the ancient cross, taking in the view. Between the coast road and the headlands, the cottage is a whitewashed rectangle in a wild square of sea grass, the finished path is a scaly tether connecting the cottage to the ocean.

She turns to walk the haphazard rows, noticing a deep pool of rainwater over one grave. The weight of sodden earth sometimes breaks through caskets to mix with bones, and when this happens, Liselle fetches the spade and fills the wound with earth. Only a few graves here are seen to by relatives; the rest she tends herself. She'll remember to keep her eye on this caved one.

The cemetery's a forgotten place, mostly. As she clips grass or pulls weeds she reads names on each stone aloud, reciting their stories like a rosary – a string of fates now known by heart. She progresses slowly toward the newest headstone, where stalks of lavender tip stiffly from the vase. Plucking them out, she replaces the stems with a spray of white lilies she's grown in her own tiny greenhouse. After raking the plot smooth, she settles on the nearby bench.

Danny had insisted on the massive headstone, so large it couldn't be brought up the hill. It had to be hauled overland by tractor, stone fences taken down and rebuilt after it. The letters are deep, laser-cut script on glossy marble.

Father.

There is promise of a warm day. Liselle has learned the coast's moods now, can make a forecast with a sniff and a glance. It is, as Remy would claim, a good enough morning. After saying his name aloud, she adds lines of his own story, telling it in the manner he would. "Remy Conner was the local hardware man, best remembered for having written fifty thousand lines of a continuous poem to his wife. One morning, after writing what he felt was his best line ever, he shook his aching fingers and claimed to his beloved, 'Margaret, I think that bloody song is finally done.' That said, he died – the cup of tea still warm in his hand."

She sits through a few windswept moments before beginning, as she usually does, by telling Remy's bones things he already knows, that the sky is beautiful here, that the herring are poor this summer. There is gossip about the librarian and the delivery driver from the local brewery. Her stories are told fat with detail, the way Remy has taught her. When she finishes with the local news, she takes a letter from her pocket. It is from Adam, postmarked Los Angeles, where he's a partner in a start-up film production company. The envelope includes a strip of vending-machine portraits, showing Adam and a beautiful Korean girl with hair like a deep yard of silk. Lise glances from the letter to Remy's chiseled name. "Listen to this, now. I asked Adam how he knows she's 'the one', and this is his answer: *Mom, all I can say is this. Su was sitting on my lap and I made her laugh so hard she peed on me. Peed on me. While I was changing my jeans, I decided. I just know. So I've asked her now. Will you come in November?*"

"So you see, maybe it *is* just as you claim, Remy – that love's a thing wiser than ourselves." She glances again to the photo and sees how Adam looks at the girl, as if he'll split with joy. It seems a long time ago now that she'd scoffed at the old psychic in Mexico, at the absurd notion of dark-haired grandchildren. She folds the photo strip into her wallet, next to little Aaron's picture.

Liselle is Aaron's godmother. "Your great-grandson needs a haircut, Remy. You'd spin if you saw him. And what a terror he is in the shop." Even as she complains, there is pride in her voice. "But he's so like you... babbling on with his little stories. Sometimes I think I'm listening to a reincarnated soul. It's all Siobhan can do to run the place and keep the boy occupied. But school starts next month, so we'll all get some relief."

There is movement at the gate as a young hiker hangs her backpack on the post.

"Well, I'm not long to sit here, anyway…" Her words trail off. She'd hate to frighten the young hiker with her muttering.

There's a wedding in Galway she's due at by mid-afternoon. Filming weddings is great fun (she's even admitted this to Leonard) and the work pays well. She'll only film those couples that seek her out, having heard about her anachronistic style. It seems the vintage look is in vogue, as much in demand as Margaret's wedding cakes. Each final edit includes a minute or two of Margaret decorating the cake, her ministrations and little rambling monologues, ever more rambling, these days.

Margaret sometimes spends whole days in Remy's chair, sitting under Charlie's oil portrait of him – tortoise-faced and ginger-colored, the gleaming eyes so true to life. Margaret will endlessly leaf through the book of Remy's poem-songs. Danny and Siobhan edited all the poems and put them in order. They found an old-time printer in Cork who letterset them on thick paper and bound them in leather. When Margaret reads the lines and stanzas – each dated – she is able to place herself in her best history, her life with Remy. And though she can still make the cakes and sing any song, she's often found wandering the village looking for her husband. The doctor says it's the beginning of Alzheimer's, but she and Siobhan have known for years. Danny doesn't like to hear about it but knows his mother will need real care soon enough.

"But you don't want to know all this," Liselle whispers toward Remy's headstone, which spans two plots and has a blank space on the marble for another name. She rests her elbows on her knees and tilts in Remy's direction, sighing. "So there you are."

* * *

Descending the church path, she crosses over the road to a trail that ends at the shore. The route is rough but worth the trouble, for there are long stretches where she can walk clear beaches. Liselle gathers pieces of sand-worn beach glass to add to her collection; she has enough now to finally start making the chandelier she's been planning. She hopes Adam and Su don't think it *too* bizarre a wedding gift.

The sun is high by the time Liselle reaches her own small crescent of beach. The cottage, as plain as when she first saw it, is somewhat better dressed now, with new roof slates and painted trim. Only the sheep barn, converted to a painter's studio, has seen real change: its bank of sloped skylights reflects clouds, and a wand of smoke slants from the chimney. A fire's been lit.

A wave soaks her boot as she bends to pluck a small treasure from the surf.

Something rolls in from the sea each day, it seems. And Liselle dutifully retrieves whatever washes up. Today it is a mariner's compass, useless, its crystal gone. Its arrow is intact, stopped like the hand of an unwound clock to indicate west, over the water, the direction she is facing.

Liselle can see herself as if from above, her form coming into focus from a great height, as though through the magic of a binocular lens, or some benevolent eye. She stands slightly bent, in an *f* shape, examining the object in her hand with awe and some gratitude. Distance blurs the edges of her figure and softens her angles. In one instant her image is caught.

This moment at the edge of the sea is hers. Sun settles a warm patch between her shoulder blades, and Liselle closes her eyes, inhaling salt air and feeling the round shape cool in her palm. Standing so still, she might be a woman in a painting.

Acknowledgments

I'd like to thank all at the Tyrone Guthrie Center in County Monaghan, where this story began amid the rushes and shimmer of Annaghmakerrig. The ghosts-in-residence were particularly helpful.

Time and support was given by Art Omi's Ledig House International Writers Program; the Oberholtzer Foundation; Gibraltar Point Center of Toronto, and the Ragdale Foundation. Thanks to my sisters, Mary, Valerie and Julie, who offered many quiet days at their cabins.

Funding came from the McKnight Foundation and the Loft. Geniuses at ArtSpace Online, So Design and Electronic Media generously donated many in-kind marvels and services.

Special thanks to word-stalker Sarah Venart for her fearless editing and for raising the bar for well-laid lines. Catherine McKee cast a fastidious and gorgeous eye over the Irish details of a rugged draft. Copyeditors Rachel Careau and Peggy Freudenthal made these pages presentable.

The Bonne-Andersons (larger than they appear in the rearview) stuck around through the most difficult chapters. Thanks to the Über Babes and Miss William for their *knockers up* encouragement and faith.

And Sam, always, for everything.